I0760410

THE STORM AND THE DARKNESS

THE HOUSE OF CRIMSON & CLOVER VOLUME I

SARAH M. CRADIT

Cover Design by Sarah M. Cradit
Editing by Shaner Media Creations

Publisher Contact:

sarah@sarahmcradit.com

www.sarahmcradit.com

PRAISE FOR THE HOUSE OF CRIMSON & CLOVER

"Cradit's words flow in prosaic candor like a melody of the ages: pronounced, patient, lingering, and beautiful.

Dionne Charlet, *New Orleans Examiner*

"Her (Cradit's) talent for creating atmosphere rivals Daphne du Maurier. This is modern Gothic with fierce smarts. Can't say it enough. I loved this book."

Christopher Rice, *New York Times* Bestselling Author of *The Heavens Rise*

"It takes a great writer like Cradit to weave the threads of so many characters into an enjoyable story. I have no doubt that the name Cradit will one day be associated with the echelon of gothic fiction writers, namely Radcliffe, Blackwood, and Rice."

Becket, Bestselling Author of *The Blood Vicicanti* and Former Assistant to Anne Rice

"Sarah Cradit's writing is tight and masterful. Her keen sense of how to pace a book and her ability to use just the right language to express the desires, fears and hopes of her characters is flawless."

Ionia Martin, Vine Top 100 Reviewer, Readful Things

"Cradit does an incredible job of building suspense. It's a slow, moody, edge of your seat suspense with a palpable sense of foreboding. This atmosphere kicks the book off and slowly escalates as you sink deeper into it."

Julie Whiteley, Clue Review

"The plot flows so quickly that you reach the end of the story well before you are ready and without realizing how much time has gone by since you were enchanted, committed and flung into the world of the Sullivans, Deschanels and their friends. You become a part of their lives as you are reading the books and think about the characters long after you have finished reading the book."

Stephenee Carsten, Nerd Girl Official

ALSO BY SARAH M. CRADIT

KINGDOM OF THE WHITE SEA

Kingdom of the White Sea Trilogy

The Kingless Crown

The Broken Realm

The Hidden Kingdom

The Book of All Things

The Raven and the Rush

The Sylvan and the Sand

The Altruist and the Assassin

The Melody and the Master

The Claw and the Crowned

THE SAGA OF CRIMSON & CLOVER

The House of Crimson and Clover Series

The Storm and the Darkness

Shattered

The Illusions of Eventide

Bound

Midnight Dynasty

Asunder

Empire of Shadows

Myths of Midwinter

The Hinterland Veil

The Secrets Amongst the Cypress

Within the Garden of Twilight

House of Dusk, House of Dawn

Midnight Dynasty Series

A Tempest of Discovery

A Storm of Revelations

A Torrent of Deceit

The Seven Series

1970

1972

1973

1974

1975

1976

1980

Vampires of the Merovingi Series

The Island

and more

The Dusk Trilogy

St. Charles at Dusk: The Story of Oz and Adrienne

Flourish: The Story of Anne Fontaine

Banshee: The Story of Giselle Deschanel

Crimson & Clover Stories

Surrender: The Story of Oz and Ana

Shame: The Story of Jonathan St. Andrews

Fire & Ice: The Story of Remy & Fleur

Dark Blessing: The Landry Triplets

Pandora's Box: The Story of Jasper & Pandora

The Menagerie: Oriana's Den of Iniquities

A Band of Heather: The Story of Colleen and Noah

The Ephemeral: The Story of Autumn & Gabriel

Bayou's Edge: The Landry Triplets

For more information, and exciting bonus material, visit www. sarahmcradit.com

For James

"I went to the woods because I wished to live deliberately, to front only the essential facts of life, and see if I could not learn what it had to teach, and not, when I came to die, discover that I had not lived."

Henry David Thoreau

THE LOVERS

1
ANA

"All I'm saying is, *Deliverance* was based on a true story."

For the past hour, Nicolas had been trying to talk her into coming home to New Orleans. Ana rifled through the fridge, looking for something easy to make.

"Sure. Right," she said, as she often did when he rambled.

"Anywhere that doesn't have cell service might as well be Iceland," Nicolas added.

Ana laughed. "They have cell phones in Iceland."

He dropped his voice low. "I'm talking about the parts without cell service, Ana. Dark places, where you can't even pronounce the name of the village you're in because it has sixteen consonants and no vowel, and there are more active volcanoes than people."

"The more worked up you get, the less you make sense." Ana sighed. "Anyway, how's everything at home?"

Nicolas gave an exaggerated yawn through the phone. "Your father is fine, your stepmother is fine, Adrienne is fine, blah blah blah. Would you like to hear about the weather? I could give you the score of the Saints game, if you're so inclined."

"You act like those things aren't important."

"They're not," he said. Silence on his end for a moment and then he added, "and if you did care so much about how the family's doing, you wouldn't have abandoned us."

"Stop being an ass," Ana retorted lightly, but knew he could hear the slight reprimand in her voice. Nicolas had a way of finding the line and leaping over it. Normally she enjoyed the parry, but the circumstances were different now.

Of course, Nicolas had no way of knowing that because, for the first time in her life, she'd kept something from him. *Quarter-life crisis*, she told him when she revealed her plans to move to Maine. He'd known better, though, seeing right through her lie, allowing her to maintain the illusion because he loved her. She didn't know what stopped her from telling him.

That's a lie. I know why.

It hurt him that she was lying. It hurt *her* to do it. Nicolas was more than her cousin. He was her closest friend, and only confidante. Telling herself he probably did the same, probably kept things from her, too, didn't make her feel better.

"Have you shown anyone your parlor trick yet?" Nicolas asked.

"Oh, God, no. Everyone on this island already treats me like a pariah. I don't need them knowing I'm a freak of nature."

"Not a freak of nature, darling. Just a Deschanel."

Ana wasn't the only Deschanel with a special talent, but she might be the only one who wished the "Deschanel gift" had passed her over. It was more a curse than a blessing.

"How did your family escape it, then?" she asked. Not only was Nicolas born without special abilities—*benign*, other Deschanels liked to say—his father and four sisters had also

Ice Mer Dominion
Aqualis
Gates of Hell
Angel's Landing
Port City
Northern Capital Province
Desert Were Territory

SUGGESTED READING ORDER

Legends of Love novels are a part of an interconnected stand-alone series. You can read in whatever order you'd like. However, we'd suggest:

A COURT OF FIRE AND FROST

A COURT OF SEAS AND STORMS

A COURT OF WIND AND WINGS

Welcome to Aranthium

We are delighted to share Phaedra's and Aidoneus' story with you!

Before reading, we want to take a moment and acknowledge that this novel is a New Adult fantasy romance novel, and it contains open-door sex scenes. Cursing, violence, death of a family member, parental trauma, brief mentions of male infertility, and substance abuse are present.

Enjoy!

Daniela and Elayna

been passed over in whatever power, genetic or otherwise, was responsible for doling out these gifts.

"Heathens," he said casually.

"There are plenty of powerful heathens in this family," Ana countered. "But you specifically set that bar rather high."

After dinner, runny chili from an only slightly rusted can, she wandered onto her front porch, gazing out into the Atlantic. She shielded her eyes from the vibrant orange hues of the setting sun as she looked out across the sparkling water. From where her house sat, on the eastern shore, she couldn't see the mainland, but could make out traces of smaller, barren islands to the east. Alex told her the view would disappear completely in the winter, leaving the island shrouded in blinding fog. She wondered again if she'd done the right thing in coming there.

What was my father thinking when he bought this place? It had been a gift to her mother, Ekatherina, who died days after Ana was born. *Yet another failure. A healer who killed her own mother.*

Ana caught the view of a fishing trawler in her peripheral, off to the west. Her gaze shifted from the sunset to the man captaining the vessel. He'd come back to shore every day at the same time, all week. Alex told her some of the fishermen told time by the sun. She wondered if Finnegan St. Andrews was one of them.

As Finnegan eased alongside the small pier, a young boy hopped off and started tethering heavy ropes to a series of short, thick poles. Moments later, Finnegan joined him, and helped finish securing the boat. Together, they carried large metal-framed traps from the boat to the storage shed at the dock's upper end.

After placing several of the live lobster into an ice chest for the child, Finnegan watched him scamper up the beach, toward a path leading to the main road.

He stretched his strong shoulders as if shrugging off a tremendous burden. As his arms came down, he perched his hand over his eyes to shield them from the sun. He caught sight of Ana on her porch, and waved. She waved back.

This had become a welcome daily tradition during the seven days she'd been on Summer Island. Finn was the closest thing she had to a friend, next to Alex, though they'd never actually met. She knew it would be simple enough to introduce herself. Especially since she might not even have to say much, as everyone in town already seemed to know everything about her.

She wouldn't, though. Waving was safer.

Ana set a bowl of milk on the porch next to an old comforter. Cocoa wouldn't be back until later in the evening, most likely. She didn't know where the little one went all day, but she always returned at night, hungry and grateful for Ana's comfort. Ana wondered if the cat had been someone's pet once, for she'd immediately warmed to human affection.

Ana never had any pets of her own back home. Growing up, her stepmother, Barbara, had been allergic to almost everything, and then when Ana left home, her focus on education left little room for anything else. After four years of undergraduate studies, she dove back in for another four for her double masters. She would've continued as a student forever, if her favorite professor hadn't offered her a job teaching English at Tulane. It was an unlikely career choice for an introvert, but it made her happy to feel useful.

Then she left. Left the job, her family, her hometown, Nicolas. All of it.

She hadn't known anything about Summer Island, Maine before her arrival a week earlier. She'd never even seen a picture of the old home inherited from her mother. All she knew—and all that mattered—was its distance from New Orleans, both in geography and similarity.

The recorded population of Summer Island was two hundred and fifty, but Alex told her it was actually two hundred and four if you didn't count the families who only had weekend or summer homes. Although it was a diminutive two-point-two square miles in size, the town was relatively self-sufficient, having many of the basics. The key service they seemed to be missing was a medical facility but, surprisingly, there was a veterinary clinic. The vet was one of her neighbors—the young lobster fisherman's brother, in fact—but his standoffish behavior made Ana think twice about striking up a conversation.

Geographically, Summer Island was the furthest human-inhabited island east of the mainland, a sixty-minute ride on the Casco Bay Ferry to Portland. Alex said there were a handful of folks who commuted daily into Portland, but the restaurants, bars, post office, grocery store, and other businesses were all run by islanders.

"It makes it easier in th' winter," he told her. "Otherwise, we'd have people not showing up for work half th' winter."

"What do you mean?"

"The ferries close down for a spell each season, sometimes more'n once."

"So how do you get off the island if there's an emergency?"

He shrugged. "Ya don't."

Alex didn't seem the least bit concerned about that potential, but the thought definitely unsettled her. Ana took living in a big city for granted, being near everything she could possibly need. Every bit of information he eagerly shared left her with a dozen more questions, some she'd ask, and others she never would. She disliked feeling silly, or being perceived as an outsider, and her lack of knowledge elicited both.

As caretaker, Alex Whitman knew the house better than anyone. The conditions of his charge had brought him out once a week for the past twenty years, and he'd done his job unfailingly. By the time Ana arrived, he'd already winterized the house, for the most part. He was excited to show her how he'd covered the exterior faucets, turned off unused valves, and other details Ana had never worried about in a city of banana trees and the Gulf humidity. His eyes widened, hands taking to the air in lively animation as he proudly described the level of care and caution he channeled into his work. He was certainly thorough, and undoubtedly passionate, and it was clear the old four-bedroom Victorian had been in good hands all these years, despite having no permanent mistress.

His enthusiasm was catching, if not strange. He was so excited about his job, Ana wondered what he did for *fun*.

Alex was middle-aged, in his fifties, Ana guessed. There was nothing remarkable about him, from his growing baldness to a nondescript nose, mouth, and chin. She wouldn't have been able to pull him out of a crowd. The only thing that stood out to Ana were his eyes, a radiant blue that flashed with flowing intensity when he talked.

"I have overseer duties for yer father's house and about ten o'er homes on the island. Summer folk. Ya know, they say coastal Maine is the new Cape Cod," he told her, beaming. There was no end to his anecdotes about the island and the homes he looked after, but about his personal life he'd only reveal that he lived alone.

"Actually it's my house," she corrected him. Of course they thought it was her father's. His office paid the bills, and it wasn't as if Ana had ever bothered to visit.

"Well, I reckon I stand corrected," Alex apologized with a blush.

Ana appreciated him, but she didn't realize how much until after she'd been on the island for a week. She'd established a daily routine involving a venture into town to explore, before heading home with groceries. She noticed everyone taking the time to wave at each other, or stopping to chitchat. With dark clouds looming on the horizon, everyone's thoughts turned to the timing of the first big storm. Ana felt as if she was watching one large, ongoing family reunion. Her heart ached for New Orleans, and her own people.

Initially, she tried to embrace her new home with enthusiasm, waving at the same people she saw waving at others. But they didn't wave back, and most of them dropped their eyes, pretending not to see her overtures. No matter where she went, her reception was the same. The lack of returned smiles, the downturned eyes in place of warmth, left her with a sinking feeling that stayed with her, long into each evening. She was unwelcome here.

When she told Alex about her experiences, a blush rose in his cheeks and his normal animation transformed to a nervous fidget. "Miss Deschanel—"

"Alex, you can call me Ana." With a laugh, she added, "You might be my only friend here."

"O'right, Ana then. Forgive me for just coming out and sayin' it, but everyone *knows* who ya are."

"What does that mean?" Her eyes narrowed. It wasn't possible for anyone here to know the real reason she left New Orleans. She'd told no one.

"Your father, Miss," Alex said with a guilty look. "It's just, being locals and all and not having the money that yer family has... it sometimes rubs people the wrong way when outsiders see their town as a vacation home. It isn't to say... I mean...

that, you know, yer family has done nothing *wrong*, exactly... oh geez, listen to me..."

His rambling continued as he stumbled over his own words to correct himself, but Ana understood his meaning well enough. Ana's father was Augustus Deschanel, and there were few who didn't know that name. He was a local legend in New Orleans for having started his media business with money he'd saved from his own work, a remarkable accomplishment coming from a family of billionaires who could've funded it without a second thought. Augustus wanted to do it alone, though, and the business turned into an international empire within a decade. While the people of New Orleans were proud of Augustus for his humble work ethic, the rest of the world saw him as yet another money-hungry businessman. It never occurred to her the islanders might have a derogatory opinion of the distant family who owned the stately house on the bend of Heron Hollow Road.

As Alex showed her how to use the generator—*trust me, you'll use it*, he'd promised—he assured her he would talk to people and that things would get better. "They're good folk," he kept saying. "Truly, they mean no harm."

Ana thought then of Nicolas. Her father. Her students at Tulane. Of late nights in the Quarter, the trilling hum of cicadas, and the sun's fiery orange rise over the banks of the Mississippi. The homesickness caused a sinking flutter in her chest as at all she'd left behind.

How long am I going to do this? How will I even know when it's time to go back?

"As long as it takes," she whispered, and waved at Alex as he drove away.

2
NICOLAS

It was difficult to unnerve Nicolas Deschanel. He'd experienced more craziness in thirty years than many saw in an entire lifetime, and for the most part, remained calm no matter what storm brewed around him.

He lived alone at *Ophélie,* the old family plantation an hour's drive along the Mississippi, west of New Orleans. There wasn't much left of it anymore, aside from the land. He lived in the Big House, a giant Greek Revival monster with Ionic columns running roof to base, and broad galleries spanning all the way around. Beyond the primary residence, most buildings had fallen into disrepair, overlooking the miles of sugarcane and swampland which backed the property. He'd never lived anywhere else, only occasionally disappearing for a sabbatical somewhere far from home. Even his modest apartment on Frenchmen was only used as a convenient place to flop after a night of carousing in the Quarter.

The plantation was old and lonely. Nicolas Deschanel was exactly the opposite of either of those things, a fact he went to great lengths to sustain.

He enjoyed his reputation as the premier playboy of New Orleans, and surrounded himself with those who either contributed to the illusion or didn't disavow him of it, anyway. He loved the Quarter; the debauchery it promised, beckoning, where he could drink as much as someone twice his size, and stay out twice as late as the frat boys. Though handsome, the first thing a stranger noticed about Nicolas Deschanel was not his looks, but his wild and enigmatic charm. The combination of these things brought a variety of women to his door—sexy, smart, adventurous, boring. There always came a point where Nicolas realized the specific charms of the specific girl were no longer specific or charming. He saw no gain in limiting himself.

Even now, at thirty years of age, he was still, always the life of every party.

When Nicolas wasn't out cultivating his reputation, he appreciated the quiet and seclusion of *Ophélie*. Nic's now-deceased father had favored his daughters born with Nicolas' nanny over Nicolas, his first child and natural successor, and, breaking with tradition, had willed the estate to them instead. Years later, his sister Adrienne righted that wrong, content to live with her husband, Oz, in the Garden District and let Nicolas take his rightful seat. She said she didn't want the same upbringing for her own children, but Nicolas didn't see what was so bad about it, really.

Then again, he hadn't experienced the wrath of Cordelia Deschanel day in and day out. Cordelia, who was his mother but *not* the mother of Adrienne and her three older sisters. His mother could be mercilessly cruel to anyone she thought minimized her son's importance in the household. To Nicolas, she'd been loving, but to the girls, a nightmare. The father they all shared more than compensated for the lack of maternal nurturing by having ostracized Nicolas in every meaningful way, while placing his daughters on pedestals.

All but Adrienne were gone now, a part of his past that seemed almost unreal, like a dream of long ago. His mother, father, and three half-sisters perished in a car accident, en route to a family vacation Nicolas hadn't been invited to. Adrienne escaped, but disappeared for several excruciating years.

If Nicolas had to pinpoint it, this was probably where things began to change in his friendship with his best friend since boyhood, Oz. Oz, who'd loved Nicolas first, but loved Adrienne more. Although there was still love between Oz and Nicolas, brothers in all but name, there was also a darkness, the kind that comes with sharing unspeakable tragedy. The kind that never entirely goes away.

There might now be invisible walls in his friendship with Oz, but there was one person with whom Nicolas shared everything. Someone who, no matter what happened, loved him without judgment, without darkness.

Anasofiya.

No one but Ana knew, or understood, what it was to have everything and still be empty inside. Nicolas had never really been a part of his family. He was only a baby when his father forsook his wife, turning instead to the nanny to father his remaining children. Nicolas and his sisters were always divided by the ugliness that festered between Charles and Cordelia, and while he loved them, he didn't know how to be a part of them.

Ana and Nicolas were born only a few months apart. When Ana's mother died shortly after her birth, Nicolas and Ana shared a nursery, and nearly everything else—from their toys to their solitude—from that point forward. They'd even shared their friendship with Oz. As they went from children to teenagers, Ana and Oz grew apart when an attempt at dating soured, and Nicolas grew to love Ana even more when she was solely his. In many ways, Ana was the reason Nicolas never wanted to marry. She was the one person who knew him—truly knew *him*, not the person he projected to the world—and he didn't want there to be anyone else in the world with that depth of insight.

Now she was gone, and he didn't know for how long, or even exactly why. He'd supported her stated reasons for going, only because he understood her perpetual, quiet anguish. He'd felt the build-up coming, and was unsurprised at the subsequent boil-over. They could speak without speaking, so no words were necessary. Nevertheless, he made it known he supported her, as her father had, though they both knew Augustus Deschanel didn't know who Ana was, what burned inside of her, haunting her private thoughts. Nicolas' only regret was his insecurity prevented him from offering to go with her. Ana was the one person he couldn't handle rejection from.

Yet. Something wasn't sitting right with Nicolas. At first, he chalked it up to his sadness at her leaving, but it soon developed into doubt. Maybe *he* was the real reason. He'd never really given thought to what their friendship would mean as they grew older and started settling down into their permanent lives. Was it possible she felt trapped? That his friendship was somehow stifling her, keeping her from growing into the person she wanted to be?

He was a Deschanel, heir to one of the largest, wealthiest, and most powerful families in New Orleans. A family of telepaths, telekinetics, healers, and seers. But Nicolas's power started and ended with his occupation of the family seat, *Ophélie*. He'd never see the future, never read someone's mind. He was benign, and that never bothered him until now, when he wanted nothing more than to see into Ana's thoughts, so he could find his way to her again.

Nicolas shrugged off these worries, as he did whenever

something unpleasant dared to cross his mind, but they didn't entirely disappear. To make matters worse, Oz was acting strange—strange for Oz, anyway—and had blown off every invitation Nicolas extended to grab a beer. He claimed he had "family stuff" going on, but Nicolas was beginning to wonder if he'd done something to piss him off. It wouldn't be the first time. But Nicolas couldn't recall a single obnoxious thing he'd done to Oz, not recently. He thought about simply asking what was wrong, but in Nicolas Deschanel's experience, *what's wrong?* never led anywhere good.

Although he'd never admit it, with the only two people he'd ever cared for acting distant and strange, for the first time in his life, Nicolas was lonely.

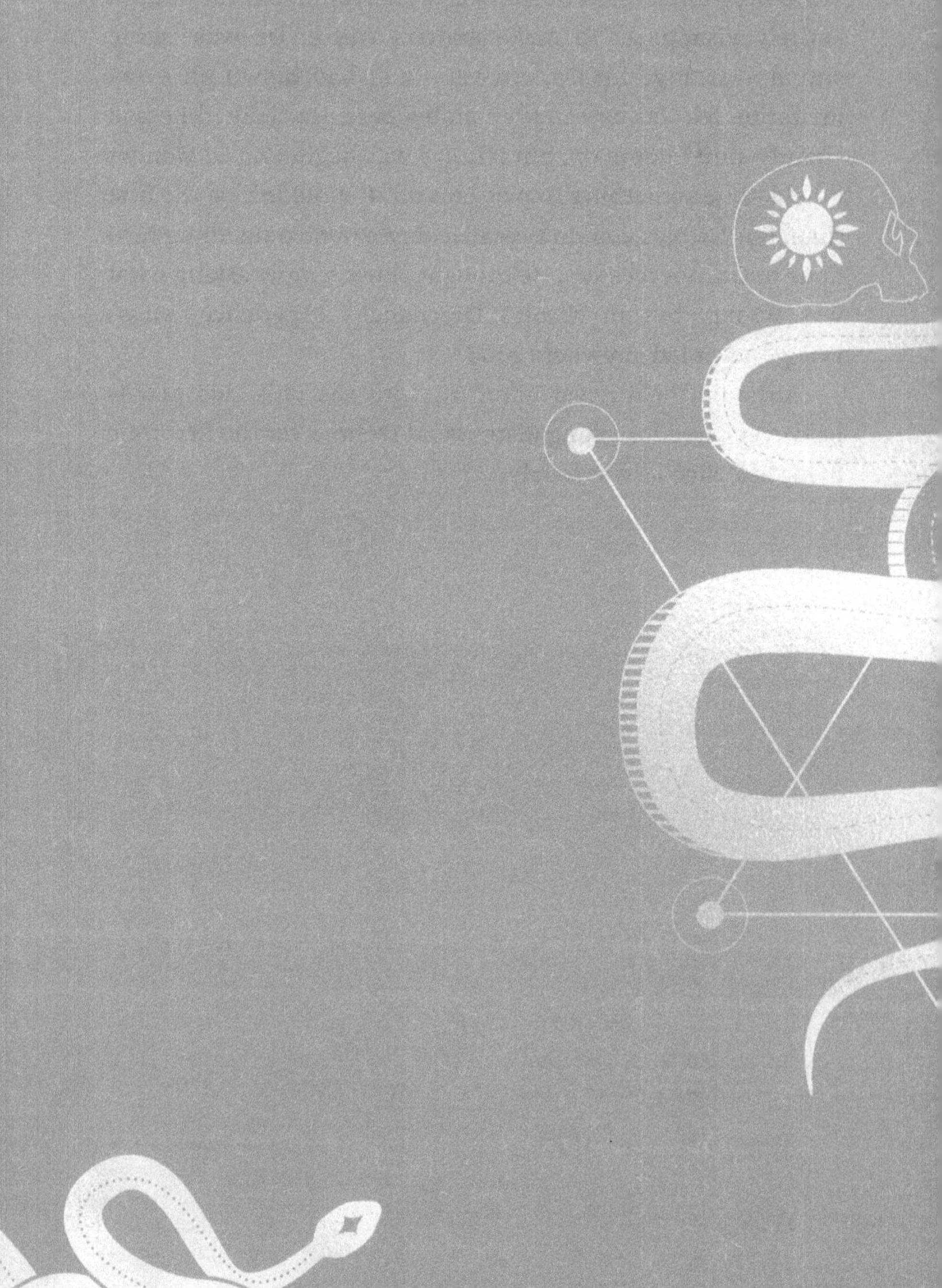

3
ANA

Ana decided to brave the lack of hospitality from the locals and try takeout, having grown tired of boxed and canned food.

Alex recommended Jack's, which he said was the best burger joint in the state of Maine. *And better custard than anything on the mainland, either*. He said that about most things on Summer Island, but it had to be an improvement from what she was eating at home.

Androscoggin Avenue, the island's main street, started at the north end of the island and broke off into two roads about a half-mile from the South Shore: Chickadee Lane to the west, and Heron Hollow Road—where Ana lived—to the east. If the weather was warmer and the skies not so dark, Ana would've enjoyed the walk into town, but instead she fired up her father's old car.

The weathered '76 station was the first indication she'd left the residential area and entered town. Past that was Flanders Grocery, and then further down on the right side was the official city building, with all the municipal departments. The rest of the "town" consisted of two unnecessary stoplights and a series of bars, shops, and empty buildings along the mile-long Androscoggin Avenue. In the center of a roundabout stood a large Civil War-era fort. No one could say what the name had been or what glories it had seen, but the wood was rotted and putting the deterioration on such crude display only called attention to the strange marriage of the town's pride, and its unwillingness to spend on basic maintenance

"Mayor Cairne's been askin' for money from Portland but e'er since we broke free they ain't fixin' to give us a dime," Alex had complained to her. "Anyhow, drive the strip nearly all the way to Edgewaters' at the North Shore, and just 'fore the road turns into a private drive you'll see Jack's. It's small, but the red, white, and blue stripes are hard to miss."

Ana was surprised to see so many people there. Jack's was no bigger than a shack, with two windows—one for ordering, one for pick-up—and as Alex had said, the building was painted in large patriotic stripes. The parking lot was tiny, and half the spots had erupted cement running through them, rendering them useless for all but trucks. With the crowd gathered, she had to park down the road.

Walking up to the window, Ana counted ten people in front of her. She slid in line behind a tall, dark-haired gentleman.

He turned around and she recognized him immediately. It was Jonathan St. Andrews. *Doctor* St. Andrews, as the islanders called him, otherwise known as the town veterinarian, and the unpleasant neighbor she'd been avoiding.

He looked at Ana, his expression blank, giving no indication of his thoughts, for what was an awkward ten seconds or so. Then, he turned back around without a word. She blinked and stared at his back, trying to process whatever had just happened.

Ana avoided awkwardness at all costs, and she didn't want

it here. But she was also raised to be kind to others, and the two weeks she'd been on Summer Island had been an example of the opposite. Jon's childish behavior was at the pinnacle of this inexcusable rudeness, a treatment she'd done nothing to deserve.

Emboldened, she tapped him on the shoulder.

"Hi," she said. "I believe we're neighbors."

With a response that sounded more like a grunt than actual words, he continued facing forward.

The blood rushed to her face, and her toes curled in silent anger. Not even in New Orleans had she met someone who was so openly ill-mannered without cause.

Ana took a deep breath and stepped in front of him. He couldn't hide his shock at her boldness, but he quickly recovered himself, and tried to push past her again. "Ana Deschanel," she said. She thrust her hand forward.

His eyes darted to the left and right. Realizing there was no avoiding the exchange, he reluctantly took her hand and mumbled, "Jon St. Andrews," before dropping it just as quickly. As though she carried the plague.

This was the first time Ana had seen his face in clear view, and she was surprised to learn he wasn't much older than she was. He didn't look anything like his younger brother, or at least what she'd seen of Finnegan from a distance. Finnegan was stockier of build with a raw, rugged earthy strength. In contrast, Jonathan was tall, much taller than she'd realized before he turned to face her, with hair the color of midnight that looked as if it would be overly soft to touch. He had the unmarred softness of a man who'd never seen hard days, but his eyes betrayed a much different truth; the color of emeralds, but the depth of an entire forest. If not for the unbridled animosity on his face, he might even be handsome.

Handsome, though, was the last description she had on her

mind now that she was face-to-face with the reclusive island vet.

"So you're a veterinarian?" Ana probed. She almost enjoyed his disquiet, after his rude introduction.

"Yes," Jon confirmed, shifting from one foot to the other and back. He continued to look past her as if waiting for someone, but no one came. His face lit up with relief each time the line moved forward.

"What do you do all day?"

"Excuse me?"

"Even if everyone on the island had pets, I can't imagine there'd always be a need to help them," Ana clarified. "How do you stay busy?"

Jon stared at her, blinking with a slow deliberateness, as if trying to decide whether he should be bothered to respond at all. "I stay busy," he finally replied. He once again looked past her, at the line, willing it to move faster.

"Aye! Ana!" a voice called out behind her, and she turned to see Alex waving enthusiastically, heading her way.

"I see you've met our beloved veterinarian," Alex said as he joined them in line, clapping Jonathan on the back. Jonathan flinched and grunted in clear annoyance, but Alex didn't seem to notice.

"Ya know, he's the first veterinarian this island has had in over two hundred years?" She gave a polite acknowledgement and, encouraged, he added, "aye, and his father was our only physician as'well. Family of medical geniuses, the St. Andrews men are!"

Jon's lips twitched again at the mention of his father. "'Course," Alex continued, "e'ryone was hoping Jon would be a doctor as'well. Ya know, Andrew St. Andrews was the best doctor in the whole state of Maine, you best believe, and he did a lot o'things he weren't supposed to, like surgeries and whatnot, and right out of his own house! He did it out of love, ya know, love for this island and the people, and oh, Jon, you were his assistant back in those days, ya?" The question seemed rhetorical as Alex continued to go on and on about Andrew St. Andrews and his wonderful, but unorthodox, medical practice.

Ana watched Jon as Alex talked. His eyes took on a darker pall the more his father was mentioned. Irrationally, Ana found herself feeling sorry for the unpleasant man, as she watched his expression evolve from annoyance to pain.

"Alex, I've been meaning to ask you, should I be keeping the cupboard doors under the sink open at all times, or only at night?" She was bailing Jon out, even though he'd given her no reason to. Jon's lips twitched into what might have been a smile, as he turned back to face the line.

Alex was also dining alone, and offered to join her. She wasn't opposed to some lighter company after the unpleasant interaction with her neighbor, so she accepted and they took the burgers back to her place.

Ana didn't know if they were the best burgers in Maine or not, but they were better than anything she'd eaten since she arrived.

After Alex left, Ana spent the afternoon returning emails from friends and family, including a handful from some of her students. Seeing their names in her inbox caused a sharp pang of regret.

Her father had been holding out hope she would join Deschanel Media Group, but she didn't have the heart for business. She was sorry he hadn't had sons, or even a more willing daughter. It was looking more and more like he was either going to groom one of the cousins to eventually take over, or go public and take a backseat, though Ana couldn't see her father taking a backseat to anyone.

When Professor Jones asked Ana to step in as a Professor of English, it was supposed to be temporary until he found someone else. Later, she'd remember the glint in his eye when she accepted, and wondered if he knew then how much she'd love the purpose that came from mentoring others.

She missed her students, her classes, and the feeling of belonging that only really came to her when she stood in front of a class, speaking about those things she knew best. Ana related to people most easily when she was helping them, offering a bit of herself.

Ana's thoughts darkened as her mind wandered back to all the nights in the Quarter. The routine was always the same. First, pick him out from a crowd. This was easy; "he" was the one scanning the bar, looking for the same thing. She'd make eye contact, let him, whoever he was—and he was always different—buy her drinks, then back to his place. Sometimes she learned "his" name, sometimes she didn't.

When she realized this was more than an occasional thing, she moved to bars in Treme, where there'd be less chance of being recognized. It wasn't the embarrassment she might bring to her family weighing on her, but the shame she felt in herself. For being incapable of connecting with another human being in any meaningful way. For allowing herself to seek companionship in ways that were dangerous and completely unlike anything else she had ever done or wanted to do. She was fortunate to have never run into anyone who might have recognized her.

At least, until that last night.

Was this what was meant by the Deschanel Curse? Many Deschanels believed the family had a centuries-old curse brought upon them by a greedy ancestor who sided with the wrong faction during the Civil War. Ana thought it was ridiculous, but sometimes, when she'd wake up next to an unfamiliar face with an all-too-familiar headache, she wondered if there wasn't some truth to the claim.

Then there was this ridiculous "gift" she'd been granted, simply by being born a Deschanel. *Healers are rare*, her Aunt Colleen liked to tell her. Aunt Colleen was a healer too, but her ability actually worked. When Ana laid her hands on another person and imagined their wounds healing and their body mending, nothing happened. She could only heal her own cuts and scrapes. *You're not focusing enough*, Colleen would say. But if Ana focused any harder, she thought her brain might explode.

If only it worked on my mind, and not just my body. What I wouldn't give to fix that.

Cocoa jumped into her lap and rubbed her face against Ana's, creating a welcome distraction. Ana didn't come here to dwell on what had happened. She came to distance herself from the whole sordid affair, to figure out what was wrong with her. To understand why she'd done what she did that last night in Treme, and if there was any way of repairing the damage.

Later, when Finnegan offered her his daily wave and smile, she was reminded once again about the type of men she'd taken to bed—firemen, policemen, laborers... all strong, rugged, masculine—and she realized why she hadn't introduced herself to Finnegan St. Andrews.

He reminded her of everything she'd thought she needed back home. Everything she didn't want for herself anymore.

4
FINNEGAN

The first storms were going to come early this year, although if asked to say exactly how he knew, Finn didn't have a rational explanation. He'd spent all of his twenty-seven years on this small island, most of them watching the tides, winds, and behaviors of the seasons. His mother taught him how to observe using more than his eyes, and so he could smell, hear, and even feel the subtle changes brought on by a coming storm. He didn't even check the Beaufort Scale anymore, nor did he listen to the weathermen. He trusted his own senses more.

Easing alongside the dock, Jeremiah nimbly leapt to the wooden pier and tied down the ropes. *Forbia* was the love of Finn's life, an old, formidable forty-foot fiberglass trawler built for the sturdiness of large hauls and not much else. She'd helped him pull in lobster since he was a teenager, and he rarely lost a trap, even with his bold eight and nine trap trawls boldly marked with blended colors of the Irish and Scottish flags. Other fisherman marveled at how little equipment he'd lost over the years. *And I couldn't explain it to you if I tried, just like I can't describe how I know the weather before anyone else does.*

Their catch had been average, but he'd been hoping for more, predicting barely two weeks before the storm season hit. Finn was one of the few fishermen still out on the sea this time of year, and most thought him reckless. He'd be less concerned if he'd been able to stock his reserves better this season, but business was booming, so more catch had gone to consumers and less to the household.

The St. Andrews boys inherited a nice sum of money when their father died three years back, but they left the resources untouched. Their father always taught them reward came with hard work, and they'd never lived with excess.

Finn had learned more than sensibility from his father. Andrew St. Andrews, to the casual eye, had been an average, unremarkable man, but to the people of Summer Island he was a local legend. He brought his wife, Claire, to the island before their sons were born, with their few belongings, paying for the old white and grey Colonial on the eastern shore with cash. Nothing was known about the doctor and his wife except that he was Scottish, she Irish, and they'd come from the Highlands of Scotland to open the island's first medical practice.

The ferry service back then was even more limited, so having access to medical care seemed to drown out all the unanswered questions about the St. Andrews' family origins. Everyone soon learned Dr. St. Andrews was no ordinary physician. In fact, he was something of a rogue, practicing not only routine family care from his household, but also emergency procedures, often using very unorthodox methods. If he ran out of vital equipment, he'd sanitize ordinary household goods as makeshift substitutes. Most of what Andrew St. Andrews did in his home office would've caused him to lose his medical license had there ever been an earnest investigation.

At first, the community didn't know what to make of this, but when Dr. St. Andrews saved Mayor Cairne's life, performing an emergency appendectomy, the St. Andrews clan became honored members of the community overnight. The residents of Summer Island worked as a collective, and the secrets of the St. Andrews' renegade medical practice would go with them to the grave.

It was Jon who took after their father, having inherited that same gift of healing hands and finesse under pressure. From the time Jon was seven or eight, he'd assisted their father in the evenings, and as a teenager there were certain procedures he was allowed to do by himself. Andrew observed his son's work with beaming pride, which always left Finn feeling a hollow emptiness. He didn't begrudge his brother, as he loved Jon, and he'd known, even as a child, his older brother was... different. But there had been times Finn wished he'd inherited their father's gift, too.

Then, Jon had thrown it all away. Two years of medical school wasted, when Jon shocked everyone and dropped out, enrolling instead in veterinary school. That marked the end of Jon's sacred relationship with their father, who'd never forgiven his eldest son. He could never understand or accept Jon's choice, and he carried the unyielding burden of disapproval to his death. It was a fractured relationship Finn knew Jon regretted deeply, even if he never said so. Finn understood Jon's reasons, but he was the only person who had ever understood Jon.

Few things bothered Finn the way they did Jon. While Finn was quick to temper, he was also quick to cool, never holding a grudge. His father had abandoned any hopes of mentoring of him when he was young, when it was clear he was made more for physical labors than mental ones. However, his mother cherished him in a way she'd never been able to nurture Jon.

A petite Irish redhead with round cheeks and big blue eyes, Claire St. Andrews was the picture of love to Finn. She spoiled and coddled him, kissed his bruises, and told him colorful stories about growing up in County Clare, Ireland. She read to him, fed his interests, and indulged in silly imaginative games. This, she did away from the disapproving eye of her husband, who didn't believe there was enough time in the day for fun and play. After his father dismissed Finn as unfit for the family business, Claire had taken the time to help him discover what he *was* good at. As a schoolteacher, helping Finn find and explore his potential was second nature. And while Finn didn't have the gift of science, he did have a sense of the world around him, which she encouraged him to embrace.

She shared with him her love of books, and he devoured material faster than she could add to their modest library. His father watched with a skeptical eye when his youngest son pursued a Liberal Arts degree at Bates College in Lewiston. *I don't know what's worse, Claire... a son who wants to fish for a living, or this. I should have taken more care with him, and not let you feed his whims...*

But the sea's call was stronger. His mother remained his biggest supporter when he returned to the island with a new goal. Finn picked up on the lobster trade well and quickly, with many third and fourth generation fishermen coming to him for advice on the best areas and techniques. Business was always good, even for a small-time, old-fashioned seaman with a clunky boat and dated equipment.

After hauling the traps to the storage house, Finn and Jeremiah slowly removed the lobster, separating the hens from the cocks. Finn had dozens of large water tanks lining the large space. He frowned as he looked at all the empty chambers. *Hopefully I'm wrong. Maybe there's more time.*

Jeremiah eagerly took his two lobster as payment, and

headed home to his mother. Finn only received Jeremiah's help on school breaks and weekends, but his assistance was invaluable. Finn refused to hire a deck-hand full time, although he could never say exactly why except that he preferred his own way of doing things. "There's a reason you named that damned boat *Forbia*. You really are 'headstrong!'" Jon ranted whenever the subject came up.

Finn took a deep breath, closing his eyes as he inhaled the crisp, salty air. There was no love of Finn's, past or present, that could ever rival the love he had for the sea.

He removed his hip-waders and extra layers of clothing, hanging them to dry. Through the salt-encrusted shed window, he saw Ana Deschanel reading, though not very successfully, as the wind blew her book and hair into a tangled mess around her face. He chuckled to himself.

Finn stepped out of the storage shed with that evening's dinner and waved at her. She returned it with a smile. He hadn't introduced himself yet, because he sensed she wanted to keep to herself. Jon speculated she must have gotten into some kind of trouble, to be sent to Maine on the cusp of the long winter, but Finn thought Jon was being overly critical. He also had a strong sense that Jon was wrong about her.

Even at a distance, she'd become a part of Finn's daily ritual. Wake, dress, and go out on the water. Return, dock, handle the catch, and wave to her as he made his way back up to the house. On the odd day she wasn't sitting on her porch, or on the bench at the edge of her property, something felt off. He couldn't say he liked her, exactly, because he didn't even know her, but their brief exchanges were as much a part of his routine now as waking, dressing, and going out on the water. He'd readjust when she returned home, of course, but for now her presence was a welcome addition.

From what he could see, she was pretty. Dark red hair with

pale freckled skin that always appeared flushed from the wind and weather that must be so new to her. She wore a wool sweater and jeans, both very natural on her, as if she was born for this setting and not the heat and lighter clothing of the South, where she was from. He'd only been up close to her once, in town, and he couldn't recall the color of her eyes, but he did remember they were intense, like Jon's.

Finn thought again of the coming storm, and hoped Alex had sufficiently prepared her. For locals, the inevitable island shutdowns were standard fare, but if Ana wasn't ready, it would be a long winter for her. He resolved that, whether she wanted her privacy or not, he couldn't in all good conscience let her go into the worst part of the season without knowing she was adequately equipped, and decided to go see her before the storm rolled in.

5
ANA

Ana started up the gravel path leading to the Casco Bay Lighthouse. Every afternoon, during her walk, she'd reach the narrow hill leading up toward the lighthouse and keep walking, ending up instead near Edgewater's, and then back through downtown toward home. Today, something compelled her to climb the hill and investigate.

The old, crumbling structure piqued her interest. Despite its necessity, it seemed so out of place, jutting awkwardly from the raised earth. Moreover, it didn't look anything like she expected. Disparate from the tall, graceful white structures on scenic postcards, the Casco Bay Lighthouse was a shorter, squatter building painted with loud, peeling stripes of red and white. It reminded her of a clownish barber pole, forgotten and left to rot.

The dilapidated structure sat atop the highest spot on the island, Edgewater Point, and the only hill on Summer Island. A man-made rock base raised the diminutive monolith even higher. *It has to be high enough for mariners to see the light*, Alex informed her. Ana wondered if the forlorn cylinder looked less pitiful from the sea.

Even from the bottom of the long, gravel hill, the curled paint and broken railings were clearly visible. This sent unexpected chills down her spine. They dangled by what seemed little more than a thread and didn't have look to have been broken gently.

The cool breeze lapped at her face as she climbed higher. The path took her far above the shoreline, offering a clear view of the Atlantic with her many ships. Undoubtedly, one belonged to Finnegan St. Andrews.

When Ana reached the top, the wind slowly died, and the base of the lighthouse came into full view. Up close, it looked even more derelict than it had from afar, the white stripes having faded to a dull gray. The red, in contrast, was bright as fresh blood. Around the base someone had installed a sloppy cyclone fence with barbed wire at the top, and signs stating: KEEP OUT and PRIVATE PROPERTY. The weeds and vines, twisting up and around the bottom few feet of the lighthouse base, left the impression the building was not only private, but abandoned.

Graffiti, angled along the graying stripes, shouted: DESTROY HERON HALLOWS and JESUS LOVES CARLA. Neither of those messages meant anything to Ana, but she made a mental note to ask Alex later. He seemed to know everything else about this island.

Ana caught a glimpse in her peripheral of what looked like grave markers. Upon closer inspection, they were the simple white crosses common along highways to mark traffic fatalities. Yet, there were four of them, like a small, private cemetery. She knelt down in the gravel and read their names: *Carla Edgewater. Lionel Shepherd. Sandra Finnerty. Emily Caldwell.*

"What on earth?" she whispered. *Did they all die here?*

Ana stepped back, and her foot slipped in the gravel, nearly sending her over the sea cliff. Heart racing, she righted herself, wondering how she'd missed her proximity to the edge. There were jagged cuts into the rock, indicating there had once been more land between the lighthouse and the serrated merger of water and land below. Looking down over the outcropping of rocks amongst the waves, she realized for the first time how high she'd climbed.

Ana watched the ocean as she backed away, noticing the ships all making their way back toward their respective ports. Goose bumps rose on her arms as the wind picked back up. Moments later, the rain started, increasing in intensity before she had a chance to even search for cover. Within minutes, she was drenched.

Ana pulled her heavy coat tight around her. She turned to make her way home when she backed into something firm, startling her as she stumbled. Strong arms quickly righted.

"Jus' me," Alex's comforting voice sang behind her. "Poor dear, let's get ya out of this rain!" Before she could say anything, he motioned for her to follow as he lit off toward the rear of the lighthouse.

When he entered through a hole in the fence, Ana wondered if he was seriously planning to take her inside. Ana, soaked to the bone and shivering, could do nothing but follow.

Alex flipped a large switch on the wall and the room erupted up in a dull light courtesy of an oversized bulb swinging from a dingy white wire. The lighthouse was much smaller inside than out, and the only sign of ongoing activity was the plain wooden desk in the corner strewn with paperwork. Next to that was a wooden chair and a space heater, sitting on the exposed cement floor. Aside from that, the circular room was completely bare.

As Alex turned on the heater, Ana rushed over and knelt before it, soaking up the heat.

"There ya go," Alex said, soothingly, patting her on the head. "You'll be right as rain in no time." He chuckled at his joke.

"What are you doing up here?" Ana asked, through clattering teeth. "I'm sorry, that sounded ungrateful. Thank you for the rescue. I didn't see anyone else when I came up." She was shocked at how quickly the cold set in here, and how long it took to restore warmth. She was a long way from home.

"Why, I work here," Alex replied, with a note of pride in his voice. "Did I not tell ya?"

Ana shook her head.

"Took over the care on this place about, oh, two years ago now. 'Fore that, it was closed fer about ten." Ana noted he made no move toward the heater. His jacket was only damp compared to hers, which looked like it had taken a dip in the Atlantic. She realized there must be another road leading up the hill, one obscured by the path she'd taken.

"Does it work?" Ana asked. "I mean, is it still in operation?"

"Most certainly," Alex said. "It never stopped workin'."

"Then why was it closed?"

"I don't s'pose ya noticed the crosses out front?" he asked, gazing out the sole round window toward the angry sea.

"Sort of hard to miss four of them. Did they die here? At the lighthouse?"

Alex walked over and pulled the chair out, settling it in front of the heater. He motioned for Ana to sit down. His sad look of resignation signaled a story was coming. She'd come to enjoy, and even welcome, Alex's stories, though this one was unlikely to have a happy ending.

"Tis a sad tale," Alex started, dropping his voice. He continued looking out the window, arms crossed. "This place used to belong to the Edgewaters. Ya know, the family that owned Edgewaters, that fancy dinin' on the northern coast? You might've seen their names elsewhere, too, being as they once owned half the island." When she nodded, he went on. "T'was a sad thing, what happened to them. Good people, ya know. Anderson Edgewater was a right honest businessman, and his wife, Camille, a real lady. The kind of folks who would stop to help ya load your groceries even if they were in a hurry."

He went on, "They had this lovely daughter, Carla. She was eighteen, and had the most beautiful hair ya ever saw. Smart, too. Kind, like her parents. A girl any parent would be proud of."

Alex paced from the window to the door, deep in thought. Ana watched him, shivering but attentive.

"Course, even good girls meet bad guys." Alex shook his head, sadly. "Lionel Shepherd." Ana recognized another name from the crosses. "No'ne really knows what happened 'tween the two of 'em, I s'pose. Lionel ran with the fast and loose crowd, and e'eryone worried he would take Carla down the same road. We all knew about the downright awful fights she had with her folks nearly e'ery night. Breaks my heart even to think about it."

Alex shifted his attention to Ana, and suddenly, his eyes widened. As if realizing something important had been forgotten, he excused himself and ran out the door. He returned moments later with an old-fashioned metal thermos. Removing the lid, he poured a hot dark liquid that smelled delicious to Ana in her chilled state. Her eyes widened with gratitude as he handed over the modest cup.

"Sorry to have forgotten my manners like that!" he declared, with an embarrassed flush in his cheeks. Ana savored the warm cocoa, cupping the lid with both hands.

"Please don't apologize," Ana said, smiling gratefully. When he gave her a dismissive wave, she continued, "No, really. You've been a godsend to me since the day I arrived. I don't know what I'd do without you."

"Aw, it's nothin'," Alex replied, blushing deeper now. "'*Let your light shine before others, so that they may see your good works and give glory to your Father who is in heaven.*' Matthew 5:16. You a churchgoer, Ana?"

Ana was raised Catholic, her father had never taken them to church. She'd been a few times with Nana Colleen, but even her grandmother stopped attending when her illness took over.

Amidst Alex's warmth and kindness, for the first time in her life Ana felt ashamed to say, "No, I'm not."

Instead of disapproval, Alex smiled at her. "No, I don't s'pose as many of you youngins are nowadays. And that was the case with Miss Carla, too. Though it was more than just a lack of faith wha' ruined that girl."

"So, what happened to her?" Ana pressed, leaning forward with her hot cocoa cupped protectively.

"Well, ya know that wild rides always come to an end, one way or 'nother," Alex said with another sad head shake. Outside, the rain pummeled the earth in relentless sheets. She could hardly hear Alex over the din, but she didn't miss the sparkle of tears playing at the corners of his eyes.

"One night, the two had an awful spat," he continued. His voice cracked slightly. "No one knows fer sure what it was about, but there were rumors Lionel was running around on her.

"Carla pushed him from the top of the lighthouse, and then jumped after him. They both died near immediately, the police said, though the coroner told me in confidence she hit the rocks on her way down, snapping her poor legs and arms like twigs.

"'Twas her father tha' found them, and he closed the lighthouse right quick; just boarded it up and left it to rot, though the town council snapped it back up for a short while. He died the followin' year, and Camille the year after. God rest their poor souls."

"That's terrible," Ana said. She couldn't help wondering what led to their tragic end. "How did they know she was the one who pushed him? Not the other way around?"

"I 'spose no one knows fer sure," Alex conceded, "but days leading up to their deaths, Carla went around tellin' folks she was gonna end Lionel for what he done to her. Folks assumed she meant that Cartwright girl he was s'posedly runnin' with. 'Course, no one expected they should take the words of an angry young girl so literal."

"That's why the railing is broken?"

"Nah," Alex replied. "That was later." Without asking, he poured more cocoa in her empty cup. She smiled in gratitude.

"And the others?"

"Well, there was Sandra Finnerty. An island girl who moved to Portland hopin' to do big things with her life." Alex paced again, and his eyes had a dreamy quality. "When her parents' money ran out, she resorted to... well, less than savory activities." With that last, he twisted his mouth. She smiled inwardly at his properness. "She came up to Edgewater Point to end her life. After that was the sweet Ms. Emily Caldwell, a young woman who'd lost her husband in a boating accident. Th' poor dear walked around the island like a ghost long 'fore she made herself one.

"That's when the town council finally put them signs up, and closed this cursed place down. 'Course, people were calling for the lighthouse closure the very morning after Carla and Lionel died, but back then Summer Island was still on the shipping routes and we couldn't just close the lighthouse, ya understand. But after the last two women died here, the council put their foot down and told the city of Portland that they had better take a look at adjusting the shipping routes, because the Casco Bay Lighthouse was retired. Heron Hallows, e'eryone called it from then on. Still do."

"How did you get involved?" Ana asked. The rain started to die down.

"Well, I s'pose I got tired of looking at the place. Ignoring history don't make it go away," Alex replied. "So I went to the council with a plan to get the lights turned back on, and offered to take the site on as part of my caretaker duties."

She smiled sheepishly. "Don't take this the wrong way, but—"

Alex interrupted her with a chuckle. 'You noticed it ain't the most pretty?" He shook his head, smiling. "No offense taken. I'd like to get her all gussied up, but the council flat refused to fund any restoration, and they made me keep those awful signs up."

Ana was reminded of the Preservation Project, a venture her father started at Deschanel Media Group that targeted old, historical fixtures and funded their restoration. It wouldn't take much to get her father to sponsor a project, if she asked. She especially wanted to do this for Alex, for it was clear how much the lighthouse meant to him.

"Folks like to claim they see Miss Carla and Ms. Emily roaming around up here. The ghosts of Heron Hallows," Alex went on. When Ana raised a brow, he clarified, "No one really believes in ghost stories, of course."

She grinned. "Of course."

Ana glanced up the winding, spiral staircase leading to the top, where the light was. She read somewhere that most lighthouses were now electric, and computer-driven automation meant someone didn't have to man them constantly. Still, she pictured Alex sitting up there, all day and night, staring out to sea, alone. The thought filled her with sadness. He deserved happiness, and companionship, with all he did for others.

"I should get home," Ana said, standing.

Alex's face fell for a brief moment, and then he brightened up again. "All that talk of ghost stories soured ya, I 'spose," he said with a chuckle.

"I'm from New Orleans. We're always good for a ghost story," she reassured with a smile. "But I do need to get into some warm clothes."

"Better do that 'fore the chill sets in," he agreed. "I'll see ya safely home."

Ana followed him to his truck. It sat at the end of a paved road that was obviously the main route up to the lighthouse. As she climbed in, she looked out the window toward the direction of the four white crosses that stood defiantly against the dark, ominous sky.

I could believe there are ghosts here, Ana thought, as Alex turned the truck around and started toward her house.

6

ALEX

The next day, Alex spotted her immediately, edging his way through the crowd of people in the True Value line. The lone hardware store on the island was always busy this time of year, with people vying for last minute supplies. She hadn't been difficult to find, as she was only one of about four redheads on the whole island, but he'd gone through Flanders Grocery, Wells Fargo, the library, the Clam Shack, and even Jack's before finding her.

"Oh, hey, Ana!" he called out, waving as he moved toward where she knelt inspecting several brands of rock salt. "Fancy seeing you here!"

Her blue eyes widened in surprise when she looked up. Alex thought he detected happiness as well. He stood straighter.

"Well, Alex, your timing could not have been better." Ana was eyeing the selection in front of her in befuddlement. "I suppose I can't go wrong with any of these?"

Alex puffed his chest out and tilted his head, speaking with confidence. "Ayuh, they'll all work, but for yer money you really can't go wrong with this," he recommended as he pointed toward a blue bag that was almost sold out. "I reckon you'd be buying twice s'much with the others, and you'd be back here before ya could say 'snow.'"

She smiled gratefully. "It's settled then. And you've saved me once again, Alex."

His heart swelled at her words. "Aw, s'nothing really, but if I can save ya some time and money, ya betcha I will."

She thanked him again and he studied her as she maneuvered through the crowds to the register. She was so unsure of herself. *A small fish in a cruel sea*, he thought. It was a good thing she had him or she might be even more helpless and lost.

He'd been keeping a vigilant watch over her since she arrived. The Deschanel house had been his charge for twenty years, and now she was a part of that responsibility. This meant she had a guardian angel, even if she wasn't wholly aware of the extent of his oversight.

"Ya have a kind heart, Alex," his mother used to say to him. "You'll make someone a fine husband someday." At almost fifty, Alex had yet to fulfill her prophecy. But then, she was a silly woman who'd married a man who didn't love her and treated her worse than the dirt under his feet. Alex gave up on the idea of a wife and children years ago. Ana wasn't the first woman he'd helped along the way. Helping others in their time of need gave him a sense of purpose like nothing else ever had. He was certain it was more fulfilling than any family he could've had. Marriage only made his parents miserable.

He had so much to teach Ana. She was like a lost lamb when she came to Maine, helpless as a child. She watched with appreciative eyes as he showed her all the things she'd need to know in preparation for a long winter on the island; how to run the generator, how to care properly for her pipes. And so what if he'd left a valve loose so that she had to call him back to fix it? Alex Whitman knew from experience that women loved a man coming to her rescue. And, of course, when he'd return to the house to fix a problem, she'd have ten more questions for him.

Alex left the store without buying anything and watched Ana as she walked down to the alley where her car was parked. At the same time, Jon St. Andrews was locking up his vet office, two doors down from the hardware store. When Jon turned around, he ran right into Ana, and she dropped her bag of rock salt. Instead of apologizing, or offering to help, Jon promptly spun around in the other direction and left her in shock, mouth hanging open.

Alex's eyes narrowed. If there was one thing he could not tolerate, it was unchivalrous behavior. He rushed over to Ana and knelt to pick up the bag, apologizing for Jon's rudeness as so many others on the island had done over the years.

"What's his story, anyway?" Ana asked as Alex loaded the bag into her trunk. He could kick himself for not offering to help her carry the heavy bag when she was still in the store. It was a failure he'd be sure not to repeat.

Alex hesitated. What could he say about Jonathan St. Andrews that wouldn't be unkind? Alex supposed Jon was a decent enough vet, although he couldn't say firsthand as Alex had no time for pets. But Jon had always been odd. Most people on the island learned to just leave him alone. Surprisingly, some even felt protectiveness for him. Alex was disappointed that a son of the venerable Andrew St. Andrews could be such a disappointment to his father's honor. Finn wasn't much better, dishonoring his father's memory by becoming a *fisherman*, when he could've been something great. But then, their mother, although a very good schoolteacher, *had* been Irish...

"Alex?"

"Sorry, um, yes, well..." he searched for words. "He's always been a 'lil diff'rnt, even as a boy. My ma babysat the boys a few times and said he would just sit 'n stare out the window sayin' nuthin' fer hours until Claire picked 'em up." He realized that sounded like gossip, and added, "He's never caused anyone trouble here, and the family still donates generously to th' schools, just like their pa always did."

She frowned, her eyebrows knitting. "I mean... *why* is he so unpleasant?"

Alex shrugged. "No one knows *why*, I reckon. His father was quiet, but always social and involved in things in the town, and his mother was the sweetest 'lil thing..." he cleared his throat. "Is there anything else ya need? Are ya good fer dinner tonight?"

"What about his brother? Is he like that, too?" Ana probed. Alex wasn't the least bit interested in discussing the St. Andrews brothers, but she was obviously determined.

"Finn? Nah, Finn's a good boy. He won't cause ya any trouble. Always quick to help, although he does have a temper, from that Irish mother of his I 'spect. Used to get in fights at school defending his older brother..." No use telling her about all his girlfriends. That *was* just gossip.

Ana processed all of this, and he worried she was going to keep drilling him so was relieved when she smiled and said her goodbyes.

"I'm just a phone call away, remember," Alex told her as she waved from the driver's seat. As he watched her drive away, he was disappointed to realize that would be the last time he saw her that evening. He pulled out his small, tattered notepad and wrote down: *Picked up rock salt from True Value*, and then scratched *Rock Salt* off another page entitled *Needs.*

As he headed toward his truck, Sheriff Horn started toward him. Alex thought about ducking into the alley, but it was too late, as the sheriff was tipping his hat at him. Alex grudgingly nodded back.

The sheriff was a burly man in his sixties, who liked to wear uniforms a size or two smaller than he needed. Alex thought he did so because it made him look tougher, as if he was ready to burst out of his clothes at any moment from sheer might. But Sheriff Horn had lost his youthful physique years ago, and was now simply fat.

"Getting ready for the storm season, Whitman?" the sheriff asked, with a nod toward True Value.

"All set myself, just helping out the Deschanel girl." Alex always dreaded conversations with the sheriff, who had never liked him. He felt the sheriff suspected him of anything bad that happened in town, for no reason other than he'd hated Alex's father, Bill, when they were growing up.

"Are ya now?" The sheriff's tone suggested he didn't think much of whatever help Alex was offering. "I was getting ready to check in on her, introduce myself. Make sure she has everything she needs and whatnot."

Alex bristled. "I'm taking good care of her. Ya needn't worry yerself."

The sheriff laughed, his belly trembling. "Oh, I don't doubt that ya are, Alex, but I'll be stoppin' in just the same. G'day." He tipped his hat again and trudged back down the street.

Alex's fists balled at his side; his face was on fire. There was nothing he detested more than being made to feel like he wasn't useful. He dreamed of a day when the sheriff would need him and Alex could spit in his face. Alex erupted in a slow grin at the thought.

Unfortunately, there were more people on the island who thought like Sheriff Horn than those who didn't, and so Alex was used to people who didn't appreciate or value his helpfulness. But there were a few that did... and for every hundred

Sheriff Horns there was at least one Ana, who needed him. Who wanted his help. Alex Whitman could handle, and would even permit, the snide comments from the sheriff and other townies, because he felt sorry for them and their meaningless lives.

They were entitled to their opinions, but Alex drew the line at interference.

He wouldn't tolerate anyone coming between him and his purpose.

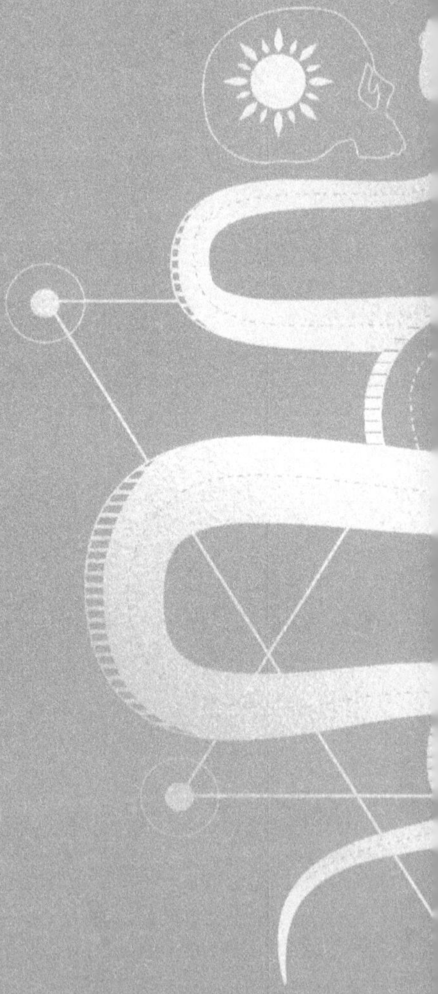

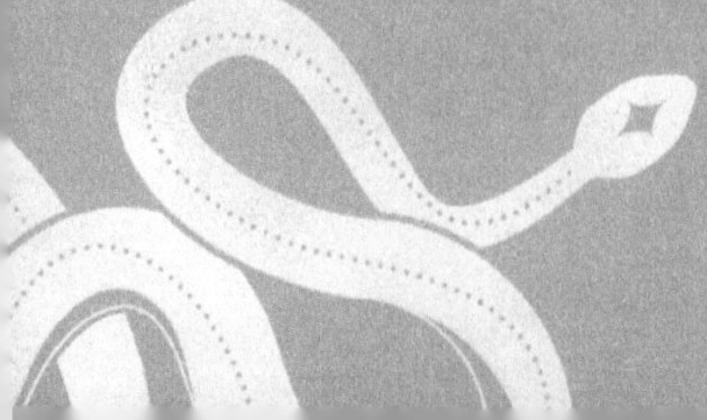

7
JONATHAN

Jonathan St. Andrews awoke at 6:50 in the morning, the moment his alarm sounded. He hit snooze once, and promptly got out of bed without complaint at seven.

He slipped his legs off the right side of his bed, feet finding the slippers he'd methodically laid out the night before. Slippers on, he turned and made the bed, making extra sure the pillowcases were turned so the open end faced inward and the sheets were even on both sides. He smoothed out any wrinkles on the bedspread.

Jon went to his dresser, opening the second drawer, where two neat rows of white t-shirts and black shorts awaited. He selected one of each, careful not to disturb the folds of the others, and went downstairs, to the small room near the back porch where his treadmill was. He set the timer for thirty minutes, at a pace of eight miles per hour, and turned on his music while the treadmill slowly ramped up. He never started his music before the treadmill began, and he always stopped it a minute before the timer ran out.

After a quick shower, where he first washed his hair, then

his body, always in that order, Jon returned downstairs to have coffee and breakfast, but not before a quick scan around the room to ensure nothing was out of place, and all doors were closed.

The coffee was already made, as Finn had been up and gone about an hour before. Although still warm, Jon microwaved his cup for thirty-seconds before adding two precise teaspoons of milk. He heated up a muffin—forty seconds—and placed it on the table first, before the coffee, but didn't sit down until he pushed in another chair that sat halfway out. "Finn," he muttered.

It wasn't important what day this was, because this was the same routine Jon performed every day, even on weekends. But, in the past three weeks, Jon had added one more item to his daily ritual: checking to see if the lights were on at the neighbor's house. He harbored an irrational fear of the unexpected knock on the door, and while it might be unavoidable, he didn't welcome being caught unaware.

At eight, Jon unlocked the doors to his small office in town, flanked by city hall on one side, and an empty building on the other. His office didn't open until nine, but Jon liked to spend the first hour checking in on any overnight patients and reading up on his files.

You could've been a fine doctor. His father's words, once so hurtful, now rang hollow. He knew what he'd given up, because doing so had been his choice. One he never regretted.

Sometimes he still opened the door to his father's old office; that large, dark room which started as a converted den. Later, Jon had helped expand it by tearing down the walls into the family room. The equipment—both that which his father was approved to use in his home and that which he was most certainly not—remained untouched, buried under sheets and dusty plastic. In his father's final years, patients arrived from beyond the island, including some of the surrounding communities and even the mainland. Dr. St. Andrews not only performed the procedures willingly, but was able to do them at a fraction of the cost of the larger hospitals. He never turned away a patient unable to pay.

Jon sometimes wondered how his father had been allowed to get away with it for so long: the intravenous equipment, the gurneys, the scalpels, and operating instruments. Jon's hands burned hotly as he recalled the first time his father handed him a scalpel.

"You want me to hold it?" Jon had asked.

"I want you to cut." His father's face had been so even, impossible to read as ever.

Jon was surprised, but also ready. He'd watched his father doing this for years and, at sixteen, had seen the procedure many times. Removing a gall bladder was something he could've described with his eyes closed. His father always taught him by asking questions—*Why am I doing this, Jon?*—rather than simply telling Jon what to do. *Why am I holding the clamp here, instead of further up? Why is this area more prone to bleeding? Why do we use less sedative with this procedure?*

Jon always knew the answers, and like his father, was exceptionally calm under pressure. Jon hadn't hesitated when his father handed him that scalpel. Drawing in a deep breath, he steadied his hand, and made the cut.

But never had he been tested more than when it was Finn on their table, bleeding and near death.

Jon was eighteen. Finn had just turned thirteen.

Several years before, their father began teaching Finn how to navigate the old fishing skiff, a project boat that was never quite finished. This act of mentoring was a begrudging one, as Dr. St. Andrews was still deeply disappointed by Finn's lack of potential, but he saw it as the one way he might forge a connection with his younger son. By the time Finn was twelve, he was already captaining the boat, though their father never let him go out alone.

"Never trust the ocean," he'd say. "The day you think you have her figured out is the day she'll have you."

But Finn was young, and adventurous, and made up his mind to captain the boat by himself on his thirteenth birthday. Jon was unable to stop him.

"You're either coming or you're staying, but this ship is going out to sea today," Finn had said, chest puffed, hand on the mast, proud. Jon feared a bad ending, but he couldn't let Finn go alone.

They were a half-mile out to sea when the propeller became entangled in an abandoned trawl. Finn panicked and leaned over the side of the boat when a fin broke off and sliced across his chest, knocking him unconscious. The fin ricocheted and gashed Jon in the chest. It was a blow that should have knocked him out as well, but as the adrenaline coursed through his veins. Jon radioed his father, who calmly walked him through how to get them home. With his brother dying in his arms, the ride was perilously long and Jon trembled so hard he couldn't hold on to the radio.

His father waited on the dock, lifting Finn as if he weighed nothing at all. He sprinted back to the house with Jon in tow.

"What does your brother need, Jon?" his father asked as he cut away what was left of Finn's shirt.

"You're asking me that now? *Now*?"

"Calm down and tell me what your brother needs," his father said evenly. His palms spread across Finn's chest, the towel blossoming, erasing any trace of the white.

Jon's breaths came short and forced. His whole body was aflame, and his pulse throbbed so hard he thought his heart might burst right through his chest. This was *Finn* on the table, not merely some patient. His little brother. His only brother.

Jon gripped the table and forced himself to breathe in, slowly, out, slowly. "We need to close his wound and dress it. He needs something to stave off infection, and... he needs something for the pain."

"What else does Finn need?" Andrew St. Andrews asked as he replaced the towel with another, never letting the pressure off.

"He needs blood," Jon said finally. "He's lost too much."

His father looked at him squarely, and then Jon understood. They would stabilize Finn together, and then Jon would need to give his own blood to save his brother.

The next couple of hours moved forward in endless agony, and, despite his father's cool demeanor, Jon saw the wideness of his father's pupils and the sweat beading around his face and neck. He was scared, too.

Jon had lain on the gurney next to his brother, and let his father take his own crucial life force for transfer to his brother. Jon succumbed to the exhaustion of the day, but before he nodded off, he felt his father pull away the gauze of his own wound. In all the commotion, Jon only vaguely recalled him putting the gauze on to begin with.

"Superficial, but you'll have a scar to remember," was the last thing Jon heard before he drifted off to sleep. Years later, a thin white line, from chest to navel, was the least of Jon's reminders of the incident.

He never understood how Finn could return so easily after that. He couldn't wait to go back out and was on the sea a week later, to their mother's dismay and their father's annoyance. "He's on his own," his father had said with a dismissive wave as he turned back toward the house. But Jon never relaxed when his brother was out to sea, even if *Forbia* was twice the boat that old skiff had ever been. Even now, Jon's fear was still very real.

As the day wore on, the rain turned to hail and the sky took on a dark, ominous hue. Thunder crackled, and the air was still and electric. Jon hoped Finn had the good sense to end early, as more storm clouds rolled in on the horizon. Finn had been predicting the first big storm arriving a couple of weeks before the weathermen forecasted. Jon, though a man of science, trusted his brother more.

It had been slow day at the office, but that was to be expected. As that Deschanel girl had rudely pointed out at the burger shack, business wasn't exactly booming on an island so small. But Jon had earned the respect of veterinarians on the mainland during his residency. Several of them made sincere, ongoing attempts to entice him to practice in a larger office with better equipment, though Jon wouldn't be swayed into leaving Summer Island. They settled for his consultation services, and this was what he did on days when there was little else to do. He liked knowing what was on his schedule. His worst days where the ones where he went in without knowing.

But his need for ritual was only a distraction, a blanket of protection offering consistency and quiet. Seclusion. The avoidance of the inevitable awkwardness of small talk, getting to know someone. Uncomfortable silences.

When Jonathan met someone new, he couldn't find within himself the desire to forge a deeper connection. Because once he did, he couldn't let go, move on, and forget. He never forgot. Was it any surprise, really, that he'd become a veterinarian instead of a doctor? He was a man more comfortable bonding with animals than people. Had his father really not seen it?

Jon relied on the comfort of how consistent their neighbors were. He'd known them all his life, and most accepted Jon the way he was.

Except the house that had stood empty on the property to their east threatened to ruin everything. Every season, his anxiety built as he waited to see if the Deschanel family would fill it for the summer, and bring unwelcome expectations upon him, as their neighbor. But thirty years passed since it was purchased, and no Deschanel had visited the home since the early days. The only movement in the house came from the weekly visit of the overseer, Alex Whitman.

He should've known, when the house never went on the market, that someone would eventually show up.

Jon was in his back office reading about treatment options for a Yorkshire terrier with a pancreatic tumor when the familiar jingling of the bell sounded above the main door, startling him out of his concentration. He set his pen down to the left of the folder, and walked down the short hallway to reception.

Ana Deschanel was standing in front of him, drenched and shivering. Water pooled near the entrance and several rogue balls of hail rolled around near her feet. Jon's eyes moved from the floor, to Ana, and back, and then rested on what she held her in arms.

The limp, bleeding body of a brown cat.

As Jon moved toward her, Ana's eyes widened with a mingle of horror and relief. He moved to take the injured, possibly dying, cat from her arms. Ana was crying, and when they passed the cat between them, he felt she was trembling as well.

"I... I tried... I couldn't fix her... I tried," she sobbed. *Of course you couldn't fix her, you ridiculous girl. That's my job.*

Jon gently lifted the cat into his own arms, and, without a word, he turned and walked back to his procedure room.

As the swinging door closed behind him, he heard the soft, muffled sobs from the front. He ignored them and went to work.

A WEEK PASSED AND JON WAS STILL SHAKEN. HE WAS THANKFUL TO have had other patients to occupy his mind, like Mr. Jenkins.

The old dog lay on the table, still sleeping after a successful surgery. His owner, Jessica McElroy, went to get something to eat. She offered to bring dinner for Jon as well, but he politely refused. He was hungry, but felt uncomfortable saying yes, so he had silent starvation to look forward to unless Finn saved some leftovers.

Mr. Jenkins' chest rose and fell as his body filled with each breath. Jon ran his hands across the dog's face, and Mr. Jenkins responded with a low, happy sigh. Jon hadn't thought the dog was going to make it, but everything went better than expected. It looked as if he would survive the night too, and maybe live to see his tenth year. Jon smiled in the darkness; a rare thing, and something almost always reserved for moments like these, and the hairy beasts on his table.

Jessica returned an hour later. She'd brought extra for Jon anyway, and left it in front of him even after his polite refusal. He ate in spite of himself.

She enjoyed her own meal in silence and he was grateful for it. He wasn't sure why human interaction was so painful for him. He had friends growing up, and in college. In medical school, even, though he didn't like to think about that time of his life. It might've been around then he started to change and grow into himself more.

"I'll be right back. I need to call my husband," Jessica

announced, before heading toward reception. Everyone was so comfortable with each other on the island that no one bothered asking whether it was okay to use someone's phone. He both loved and loathed that fact. Loved the easiness, loathed the familiarity.

No, that wasn't entirely true. There was comfort in familiarity. When you were familiar enough with someone, you understood them in ways others did not. People on the island understood Jon was a good and reliable man, but also knew he wanted to be left alone. They didn't question why he didn't come to town events, or celebrations, or that he wasn't yet married—or even in a relationship—at the age of thirty-three. They didn't exactly understand his choices, but they accepted them. They protected their own.

Jon remembered the exact day Ana showed up because that's when the panic attacks started again. The day she arrived next door with her five suitcases—yes, he'd counted—and her intense look. In the evenings, sometimes, he'd sit in his study, which faced east and her house. His heart leapt anytime she stepped into her foyer, or approached a door; a door she might think to come out of. He wanted her to stay on her side, much like he wanted the people on the mainland to stay on theirs.

A week ago, she stood holding the dying cat, soaked from the rain, looking helpless. Had she shown up instead at the door to his home with a basket of baked goods, he might have hidden quietly until she went away. But Ana had come to *his* territory, with a wounded animal.

He'd taken the small cat into the back, but nearly jumped when, moments later, she pushed through the door. She was rambling before he could even say a word.

"Someone hit her with their truck. I watched them. I... I watched them, and watched them look back... and drive away." Her eyes were still teary, but she'd taken great pains to steady herself.

"Did you see the driver?" Jon had asked, without looking up.

"A man. Forties, maybe, big. He was driving an old red Ford pickup, and he had this bumper sticker that said—"

"*My wife said I had to choose between her and fishing. I'm sure gonna miss her*," he finished.

"You know him?"

Unfortunately, they all knew Jim Sharp. With so few residents on the island, a drunken slob who went out of his way to cause problems for anyone smaller than him didn't exactly blend into a crowd.

Jon worked in silence on the cat, as she paced the room, arms crossed. A few times Ana tried to say something but stopped, and he was grateful for her control. The cat's wounds were mostly superficial and looked worse than they actually were, so after he stitched her up, he told Ana he'd take the cat home with him to keep an eye on her.

"You do that?" Ana asked. "What happens to her after?"

"I'm not sure," he hedged, though he knew exactly what would happen to little Cocoa. It wouldn't be the first stray he'd brought home to keep an eye on and ended up adopting. Finn's dog, Angus, was once a patient. "But if she lives, it'll be because of you."

"Not me," she countered, meeting his gaze for the first time.

He shrugged, but it mattered to him when he saved a life, and when others could witness his gift.

"After this, maybe you'll let me properly introduce myself," she said after a pause, extending her hand. "Anasofiya Deschanel."

Jon nodded and turned away, his heart racing, hating these

moments where he knew he was supposed to do something, anything, and instead failed. Why was he like this? The air grew cold between them. Of course it seemed rude, but was he really capable of, or willing to, explain the details of his psychological make up to her, simply because he couldn't return a handshake and an introduction?

"All right, well I already know who you are," Ana relented, some of the warmth gone from her voice. "How much do I owe you?"

He felt bad. But not bad enough to apologize. "Nothing," he said, his back to her still. "You did the cat a favor."

Jon felt her stiffen behind him. "I thank you again, Dr. St. Andrews. I'm sorry for the inconvenience. You know where I live, if Cocoa needs anything else."

She lingered for a moment. When he said nothing, she left.

"Sheriff Horn said you helped Ana today," Finn had said, later that night. Finn had been drinking at the Thirsty Wench, and was home even later than Jon.

"Ana? Oh, you mean the new girl." Jon had pretended not to know who she was.

Finn gave him a side-eye glance. "Uh-huh. The new girl. The one who has you all agitated. The one who you watch at night, horrified she might come and, God forbid, introduce herself. The one I've seen you watching me wave to in the evenings. The one people say you were actually rude to in public. The one with the pretty red hair. *That* new girl."

Finn was the only person allowed to tease him, but that didn't mean Jon liked being ridiculed. "She won't be here long enough for us to care one way or the other," he grumbled.

"She seems nice. I didn't notice any horns. Alex didn't mention a forked tongue or fangs. She keeps to herself... like *you.*"

Jon had sensed that about her, but it didn't change the fact she'd interrupted his careful balance. He didn't really want Finn talking to her either, because if they hit it off, then he might have to see more of her. Jon was used to Finn's girls, but only because he'd known them his whole life. It wasn't as if they ever lasted long, anyway.

"You know the cat is hers," Finn said.

Jon looked up, surprised. "Hers?"

"Well, a stray hanging around her house, anyway. She's been feeding it and made a bed on her porch. She even gave the cat a name. Cocoa, I think. Alex was talking about it tonight. I swear that codger is in love with her, the way he goes on and on… course that would be a first for him… Pa always said he was a eunuch…"

Jon barely heard the last of his brother's ramblings, but the first part of what he'd said took him off-guard. Feeding a stray was something *he* would have done. But Jon's feelings were not logical, and so instead of praising her, he was annoyed she'd done something worthy of his praise. He now also had to worry about her wanting to come visit Cocoa once she figured out Jon had brought her home to convalesce.

No good deed ever went unpunished.

JON WAS STILL LOST IN HIS THOUGHTS OF THE PRIOR WEEK'S EVENTS, when Jessica returned from calling her husband. "Jackson said the storm's coming. Soon."

Yes, he knew that, thanks to his brother. Finn had always had the gift of sense.

"You go home. I'll keep an eye on Mr. Jenkins a while longer and he can spend the night at our house."

"Thanks Jon," she said, already pulling on her coat. Islanders might be used to storms, but there was no amount of pride bigger than their good sense. "If the roads are open, I'll come by tomorrow to get him."

"Either way."

After Jessica left, he surprised himself by wondering how Ana was getting on with storm preparation. Annoyed with his sentimental lapse, he returned to stroking the soft fur of the sleeping Mr. Jenkins.

8

ANA

The town's reception of Ana grew less chilly as time passed, but she was still completely taken aback by the rudeness of Jon St. Andrews. She understood it wasn't always easy to meet others. Was she not, also, a perfect example of a societal defect? But she'd never—*never*—treated anyone the way Jonathan St. Andrews had treated her.

Was he one of the narrow-minded gossips who thought she was some spoiled rich girl here on her daddy's money? Was that it?

It wasn't true, anyway. She'd inherited her mother's share of Deschanel Media, but hadn't touched any of it. She lived simply back home, maintaining a small Chartres Street flat in the French Quarter, but the rest of her money went into savings or investments.

She started to question whether she was really getting anything from the change of scenery, or if she'd simply traded one problem for another. New Orleans wasn't so different from this small island. The people who'd put down their roots all knew each other; their histories, their secrets. Different accents, same problems.

As a Deschanel, she was different from most people, but it went beyond her family. She knew—had always known—she was unlike the girls she went to Sacred Heart with. There was something quiet, and dark, and... *craving* about her. She hadn't come to Maine to find herself. She *knew* who she was. She'd come to squash it, privately, away from the eyes of people who thought they knew her. She was thirty, and the thoughts screamed at her to fix it *now*, before it was too late.

She'd lost count of her transgressions after the first month, and then one month stretched into almost a year. The men she chose didn't require conversation or understanding. They didn't need to know who she was, why she was in a seedy bar in the Faubourg Treme; why she couldn't connect in a normal way with anyone.

Nicolas had known about the behavior, of course, but Nicolas didn't judge. It was only the last thing, the catalyst for her departure, that Nicolas would never know about. Not from her, and likely not from the other party involved. The latter had too much to lose, and it was really to protect *him* that she'd left town.

Being in Maine hadn't helped her to forget, nor had it given her any deeper understanding of how to forge a healthier path. She felt like an outsider, an interloper, and this only magnified her existing feelings of isolation and despair.

And now, a storm was coming.

"Come home, Muffins. You can be a whore there or you can be a whore here, but *here* is so much more fun," Nicolas said that night on the phone.

"Pot. Kettle. Black," she joked back. She flopped back in the tall, velvet armchair in her sitting room.

"Come home, Ana."

"Not yet."

"There's *nothing* wrong with you. There are plenty of self-important assholes out there who will tell you otherwise, but a healthy sexual appetite is nothing to be ashamed of."

That's not what I'm ashamed of. I'm ashamed I brought someone else down into this mess with me, someone I care about, and I can't take it back.

To make matters worse, she was still completely shaken by what happened with Cocoa. She'd watched the little cat saunter down the long driveway and step into Heron Hollow Road, only to observe helplessly as a truck swerved out of its way to hit her. The truck squealed off, leaving Cocoa hurt and broken on the road.

Ana had closed her eyes and placed her hands over the tiny body. *Heal! Come on, dammit!* She'd focused so hard, imagining positive energies around Cocoa, seeing the little cells come together in harmony So hard that the blood rushed to her head and she fell back into a puddle. *Please, Cocoa. I'm so sorry.*

When she failed to heal her, she didn't even think twice about taking her to see Dr. St. Andrews; didn't worry about his rudeness, or the possibility he might even turn her away. She'd simply rushed to save the little cat that had become an important part of her life in Maine.

In the end, Jon *had* saved her—*because I couldn't; because when it came down to it I couldn't even save a cat*—but Ana wasn't sure if she would ever see the little kitty again.

Then today, she accidentally broke the power cord to the fridge and spoiled nearly everything inside. For the first time, Alex didn't answer her phone call when she reached out for help and advice.

If she was looking for signs telling her to go home, they were all around her. Frustrated and hopeless, she grabbed the book she was reading and went out to the porch to try and clear her mind.

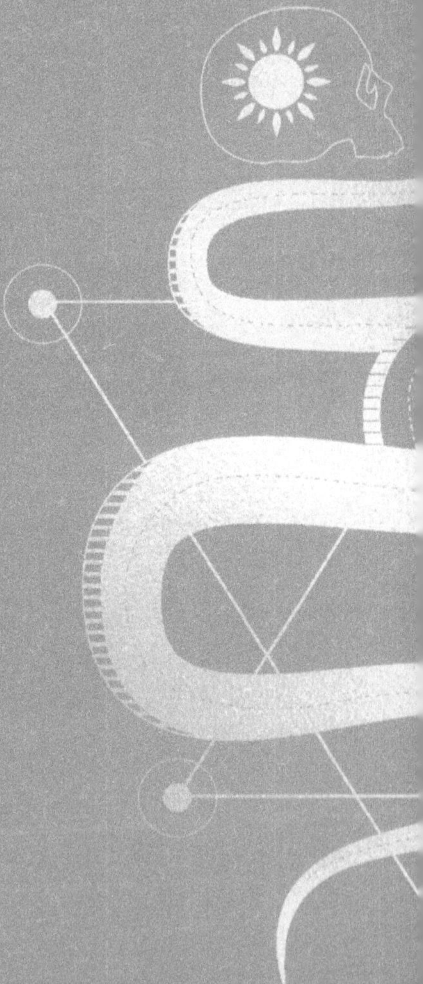

9
FINNEGAN

Finn was tempting fate with his continued jaunts to sea. The experienced fishermen had given up back in October. But Finn watched as their food storage dwindled. There were days where all of it went to sale. He started to question the business arrangement he had made with Anders Cartwright, the Portland business mogul who had been the first to get Finn St. Andrews to sign on the dotted line, but he knew his father would've been proud that Finn managed to turn a less than academic endeavor into a successful business.

He locked up the storage house. Instinctively, he looked east toward the Deschanel house and, as usual, Ana was there. He smiled and waved, and she returned the gesture.

Today, he thought. *I'll do it today. After I shower.* Every time Finn had resolved to visit the pretty neighbor, his nerves had gotten the best of him. But time was running out. He didn't know why he was avoiding the task. *I'm acting like Jon for god's sake.*

Finn started back toward the house, when he noticed she'd started to jog toward him, tripping slightly over slime-covered rocks on her way. He thought to go help her, but both his hands were full, and before he knew it she was standing right in front of him.

Blue, he thought. *Her eyes are blue*.

Ana was even lovelier than she appeared from afar. Her red hair sparkled and cracked in the setting sunlight, and she brushed it from her pale face as the wind of the coming storm fought with her. She had a splash of freckles over her tiny nose, and her lips were full and pale, not much darker than her skin. Her cardigan sweater was pulled tightly over her thin frame, and he couldn't help but notice how the hem of her sweater flared around the hips, and her arms, folded against the cold, did nothing to hide the fullness higher up.

"I'm sorry, I was wondering if you knew when the last ferry to town leaves?" Ana asked. She had her book in her arms, crossed tightly over her chest. He wondered if she even owned a winter coat.

"Six, so you just missed it," Finn said. "And unfortunately, there might not be another one for a while, depending on how bad this storm is."

"How bad do you think it'll be?"

"If you ask the weatherman, he'll say a few inches, and then clear in a couple days."

"I'm asking you." She watched him closely.

Finn laughed. "Well," he said, "I think we might be here for a few weeks before things clear up and get back to normal. But I'm no meteorologist."

"Even in New Orleans, they're no better than I am at predicting anything," she teased lightly, but her smile immediately faded. "And the stores close so early on the island..." She sighed. "Well, I suppose canned food is still food, although there's not much left of *that,* either."

When he gave her a strange look, she added, "I did something kind of stupid." Ana squeezed the book tighter, but didn't look uncomfortable so much as cold. He sensed a change in the air between them. "Alex gave me a list of things to do to finish winter-proofing the house. The power cord for the refrigerator was already on its last leg and I accidentally *broke* it. The food all spoiled before Alex could get here to help me."

She looked nervous as she awaited his reaction. Finn guessed it took a lot for her to come over and talk to him. He could see she felt silly. "Don't feel too bad," he reassured her, "the house is very old, and those wires were probably original. It was bound to happen, it's only an unfortunate coincidence it happened to you."

"Terrible timing, though," Ana said. He knew what she meant. With the ferries closed, the grocery store wouldn't be getting any new meat or vegetables in from the mainland. Most islanders stocked a couple month's worth of meat in their freezers for this very reason, and hers was now lost. Thinking of his own empty freezer and sparse tanks, Finn regretted he wouldn't be much help.

"Alex called a bit ago and said the Farnsworths on the other side of the island have some extra food and he's going to see if he can buy some from them," she added with a sigh.

"You wouldn't be the first person who had to dip into the town food storage."

"Oh! Here I am asking you questions and I haven't even introduced myself. I'm Anasofiya, but Ana is fine." With one hand still holding the book to her chest, she thrust the other toward him.

Finn laughed and shook her hand. "I know who you are," he said. "No offense, but everyone does. I'm—"

"Finnegan, yes, I know, too."

"Just Finn is fine."

He looked down at the lobster in his hands. The bug's claws had been moving the whole time, and he noticed she kept adjusting to avoid being snipped. He remembered Jon was working late that evening, to watch over the McElroy dog.

"Wanna come over for dinner?" Finn asked her, with a touch of hesitation. He wasn't sure how she'd take an invitation like that.

Ana blushed but quickly recovered. "I'd love to, but I have the fridge airing and the freezer defrosting." She laughed. "You know, real riveting stuff."

"We can eat at your house, then."

"I've never prepared a lobster before, and the house is... a bit of a mess."

Finn laughed. He'd been observing her the entire conversation. How she looked, acted. She wasn't flirting, and she wasn't nervous. Uncertain, perhaps. "Ana, I couldn't care less how the house looks, and I'd never let anyone cook my lobster, anyway. Not if I intended to eat it."

Ana laughed and accidentally dropped her book. He reached down and picked it up for her, and as she took it she said, "All right, then, Finnegan."

He smiled. "Just Finn." *She's very pretty*, he thought again. And he supposed he was good looking, too, because everyone always told him so. But there was something very different about Ana Deschanel, something that kept him from viewing her through the ardent lens in which he viewed most women. He didn't know what to expect from the evening, but he was looking forward to it. He forgot about his shower, and Jon, and the problem of their winter food storage.

Ana took the lobster from him—maybe she wasn't afraid of the claws after all—and they walked back to her house in comfortable silence.

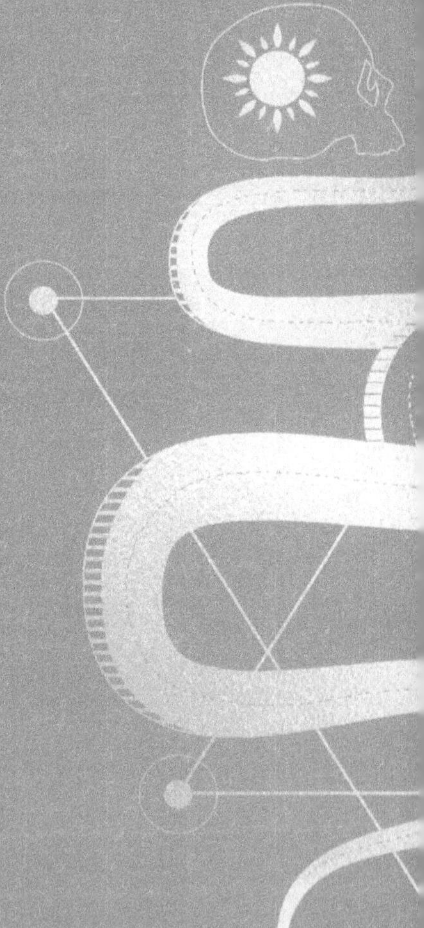

10
ALEX

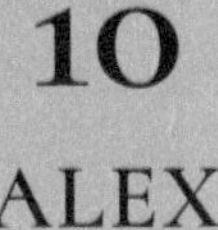

Alex could kick himself for missing Ana's call. Coincidentally, he was doing something for her at the time she tried, and failed, to reach him. The central heating in the upstairs of her house was faulty, and Alex had been looking into a portable heater she could use in her bedroom. His cracked lips spread into a wide, beaming smile as he envisioned her face when she realized what he'd done to ensure her comfort. He might even be the last person she thought of each night before drifting off into a warm, comfortable rest.

Unfortunately, True Value didn't have any left in stock, and he wouldn't make it in time to catch the last ferry to Portland. He had it in his mind to ask the Farnsworths if they had any extras lying around—they were known for being packrats and if they didn't have something, no one would—but something told him to go home first. When he checked his messages, he heard Ana's panicked voice describing the incident with the fridge.

Alex smacked his palm to his forehead. He was forgetting

things again! He'd known the cord was rotting, and that, at some point, during the cord wrapping exercise he'd set her on, she'd discover it and call him. But he was having trouble keeping track of these things, and his headaches had come back.

He called her back before the message finished playing, and his heart leapt at the lovely sound of Ana's relieved voice flooding his ears. He quickly and boldly told her he was going to arrange getting some of the Farnsworths' reserves and would bring them by later that evening, or early the next morning.

After he hung up the phone, an amazing thought occurred to him. As all of Ana's food had spoiled, she'd have nothing to eat... and she could hardly cook even when she *had* food. He reckoned she'd not had a hearty, home-cooked meal since she arrived.

An idea took form in Alex's head. A brilliant, wonderful idea.

He'd bought some fresh cod the day before that would bake up nicely. He went to work quickly in the kitchen, humming to himself as he prepared the fish with garlic and basil, potatoes, and fresh steamed broccoli.

She's going to love this, Alex thought to himself as he worked in happy silence. He recalled the light in her eyes whenever she asked for help, or the darkness when talking about how others had received her. He couldn't do much about how the island's residents treated Ana, but he could be there when she needed him. Tonight, he would save the day and she wouldn't even be expecting it.

He carefully wrapped the prepared meal in foil, placing it in a box, then delicately topped it with towels, hoping that would preserve the heat long enough. He raced out the door, and then stopped abruptly.

Wine! he thought. *What a lovely surprise that will be!*

Alex was not much of a wine drinker, but the Aldridge's had a small, backyard vineyard and always gave him a bottle of wine when he came out to fix something around the house for them. He had nine of them sitting in the pantry, untouched. Studying them, he realized he didn't know the differences, but guessed a red would do, and ran out the door.

Alex thought his heart was going to beat clear out of his chest. He didn't know what to make of his excitement, but this felt somehow... *different* than any of the other times. All of the other women he'd tried to help in the past had become distant, and ungrateful, eventually beginning to resent Alex's aid. In contrast, Ana never failed to thank him or appreciate him. He pictured her beautiful, relieved smile when he found her, drenched and helpless at the lighthouse. Part of him enjoyed how the rest of the town ignored her and, in the case of folks like Jon, were outright rude to her. It meant that he could be there for her, to make it better, and show her what it was like to have someone who truly cared. Who'd never treat her in such a way.

As he pulled into her driveway, he stopped and backed the car up, parking on the shoulder of Heron Hollow Road. It would be better to surprise her. One surprise after another. She was going to be beside herself!

He carried the box down the driveway with a skip in his step, his heart beating faster as he drew closer. When he approached the large colonial, he saw her in the window and the blood rushed to his head so fast he almost dropped the meal.

A smile slowly began to spread across his face, but then died on his lips as he noted she wasn't alone.

Finn St. Andrews.

Alex's eyes narrowed into even slits. His grip on the box

tightened. He heard the foil crunch inside and that destruction of his hard work angered him further. His temples erupted in heavy, deep throbs, one of his headaches imminent. He set the box down on the side of the driveway, dinner forgotten.

He should leave, but he had to know what was going on. It was possible Finn was just being neighborly. She couldn't be spending any regular time with Finn, or she wouldn't have asked about him. But then, maybe that was *why* she had asked... because she wanted to know if Finn was okay for dating? No, no... Alex shook his head furiously. No... it was probably just that she'd called Finn when she couldn't reach Alex earlier about the fridge.

But that didn't make sense either, as he'd talked to her not so long ago and she knew he was coming over later.

The sharp ricochet of questions darted furiously around his mind. He put both his hands against the side of his head, trying to crush the pain from the ache growing by the second. He had to think... *think*!

The sound of Ana laughing carried outside. It was so beautiful it would've stopped his heart under other circumstances, but this time, he wasn't the cause. From where he stood, he saw Ana and Finn head toward the living room. Alex crept around the side on tiptoes. As he approached the front, the sounds of their voices stopped him from going further. They were on the porch, no more than a few feet from him.

"So? What's the verdict?" Finn asked her with a note of playfulness.

"Nope. Sorry. After the way you talk about your own cooking, I'm not feeding that ego."

"Aw, come on. Do you know how long it's been since I've cooked for a girl? How am I supposed to know how to cook for the next one?"

"The next one?" Ana pretended to be offended. "I must

have quite the effect if you're already thinking about the next girl."

The pain in Alex's head pulsed with such force he considered bashing his forehead into a rock to silence it. Finn had *cooked* for her. And they were flirting. *Flirting.*

He couldn't hear what they said next, but they both erupted in more playful laughter, then Ana said, "Meh, it was all right, I guess. I wouldn't kick it out of bed." Even more laughter.

"I could bring more over if you want," Finn offered. "You're going to need food after your kitchen disaster."

Alex could almost hear her smile. "That's really kind, but I think Alex is going to bring some by later."

Finn laughed. "Alex is a special guy."

"He's been a huge help to me since I got here," Ana said generously. "I wouldn't have known half of what I needed to do if it weren't for him." At this, the throbbing in Alex's head ebbed some.

"I think he likes you," Finn teased.

Ana chuckled. "No, I highly doubt that." Alex narrowed his eyes. The giggling, the flirting, this wasn't Ana, not at all. She was quiet, and thoughtful, and kind. Not one of *those* girls.

"You've made quite an impression on him. He talks about you all the time."

"Alex is a nice guy," she said, hesitantly. "A little odd, I suppose, but what's the harm in that? He' been a godsend to me. He's my only friend here."

A little odd? What the hell was that supposed to mean?

Finn smiled. "I'm glad to know you haven't been out here alone."

"I'm sure that's why it took you a month to introduce yourself," Ana scolded.

"I was trying to respect your privacy."

"Someone in a small town trying to respect the privacy of the new girl?" She laughed shortly. "Forgive me for being skeptical."

Finn moved toward Ana. They were now face to face. "I sensed you wanted your space."

The silence on the porch was so thick that Alex was afraid to even breathe for fear of giving himself away. He had a horrible, sinking feeling they were kissing, or about to. His stomach dropped, but then, to his relief, Ana turned away.

"It's getting cold," she said.

Finn lifted a sweater from a nearby chair and draped it over her shoulders. "Storm is coming," he observed, standing behind her. "Let's go in."

The sound of the screen door clanking against the wooden frame reverberated through Alex's skull, in tortured repetition. The pain was so intense it was now also a sound, a high-pitched screech so deafening that Alex worried surely others had to be hearing it too. He gripped the sides of his head and stumbled back toward the driveway, kicking the box of food over as he did, hobbling down the long stretch toward his truck.

Alex threw himself across the bucket seat, nearly tearing the glove box open. He rifled around for the pills and his hand grasped a bottle, finally. He ripped the childproof lid clear off and swallowed twice the recommended dose. The rest dropped to the floor. Alex flopped back on the seat, desperate for breath.

Finnegan St. Andrews was young, and handsome, and seemed to have almost no care in the world. Alex knew his history. Knew about all of the girls Finn had dated on the island, and how none of them had lasted. Ana didn't deserve that! She deserved better. She deserved to be cared for, and respected. Finn would see her as nothing more than something new to play with.

Alex closed his eyes and waited for the pain to pass so he could drive home. When he finally started the engine, the throbbing was a dim memory and his mind was again clear.

"My job is to take care of you Ana. I've always done my job, and this time, I won't fail."

11
FINNEGAN

Finn wasn't sure what it was about Ana that interested him. He barely even knew her, and she was entirely different from the kind of women he normally dated, with big personalities and small tendencies for commitment. His lifestyle was simple, and he expected women who were in it for more would realize this at some point and the relationship would go no further. He dated accordingly.

He wasn't nervous around Ana. Didn't feel the need to put on an act, or be tough. She was down-to-earth, and instantly put him at ease. Even when she caught him watching her, he wasn't embarrassed. He wasn't coveting her so much as studying her, eager to understand the enigmatic woman who lived next door to him.

Over dinner, she commented that it must be painful for a lobster to be boiled alive, and he told her that the lobster had no pain sensors. She seemed amazed he would know that. "If only we could be as fortunate as lobster," she remarked.

"Fortunate enough to be boiled alive and eaten?"

"No, to be able to go through the worst things imaginable, and feel nothing."

She was joking, but Finn saw something in Ana's eyes that made him want to hug her.

Later, when he'd cut his finger with the kitchen knife, she'd confused him even further. She immediately ran to his side and took his hand in hers, and, eyes closed, drew in a hard breath. He started to tell her it was fine, to lie that it didn't hurt, but then, suddenly... it *didn't* hurt. The bleeding stopped. She looked as surprised as he did, but not nearly surprised enough, and when he asked her what that was about, she mumbled something about how squeezing a wound just right dulled the pain.

Finn grinned at her with growing suspicion. "My father was a doctor, and I don't remember that technique."

After dinner, he asked her why she'd come to Maine.

"I don't know, exactly. I guess I wanted something different." She paused, cautiously, as if she expected him to call her on the lie. When he didn't, she relaxed and added, "I'm not living off my family's money. I know that's what people think. I've made my own money, doing my own things."

"I didn't think that, and I wouldn't know what others say," Finn told her. "But I understand about getting away."

"You seem happy here."

"I am happy. But sometimes, I think it might be nice to try something else."

Ana nodded, a dark, faraway look in her eyes. There was more to her story. Finn sensed she even wanted to share it with someone, but she seemed to have a fortress built around her truth.

They talked for hours. She told him about growing up in New Orleans, as an only child, mentioning only in passing the money her family came from. Though he was curious, she didn't linger on the topic, and he didn't push when he noted her embarrassment.

Finn told her about growing up on the island. About his father's visionary medical practice. He talked about his choice to both go to college and subsequently abandon the endeavor. He also told her about Jon, and how he'd quit suddenly to attend veterinary school.

She raised an eyebrow at that, but said nothing. Finn appreciated her restraint, for he'd spent most of his life defending Jon and didn't want to sour the connection growing between them by having to do it with her, too.

As they talked, he realized there was another reason he went after a certain type of woman. The smarter ones made him feel inadequate. It wasn't enough that he went to the same college, and read the same books. That he understood the things they talked about, but excluded him from. He would always be Finnegan St. Andrews to them; the fisherman. Those worlds didn't blend.

But around Ana, who was clearly well-educated, he felt like he was in equal company.

"How long are you staying?" Finn hoped she heard nothing more than a simple question in his voice.

"I don't know. It seems changing locations didn't change anything. Maybe there's something fundamentally wrong with me." Ana laughed, but he didn't think she was joking.

"There's something fundamentally wrong with *all* of us."

She dropped her eyes to the table. "It's more than that, with me."

He had that sense again, that she had stories to tell and needed to get them off her chest. "No pressure, but I'm a good listener."

Ana shifted her gaze toward the window, still avoiding his eyes. "I had a nice time tonight."

"I don't judge people, Ana," Finn said. "I've had enough cast my way to know it hurts more than helps. Whatever you say, I'll still go home tonight thinking about what a nice time I had, with the nice girl next door."

"Sounds like a challenge." She tried to laugh, but the sound died on her lips.

Finn didn't say anything. He feared she'd stop talking and withdraw altogether if he tried to argue with her, and he wanted to hear what she had to say.

"I don't know how to talk to people. I don't know how to talk about my feelings, and I don't know how to help others with theirs."

He couldn't help himself from saying, "You're doing it right now."

Ana gave that same short laugh, as she tucked her hair behind her ears. "Because I hardly know you, and I know that once you realized I'm incapable of knowing you better, I'm not going to know you for much longer."

"We've all got our things, Ana. But go on. I'd like to prove you wrong. Maybe you're not used to that."

Her eyes glistened, but no tears spilled. Her breaths came rapidly, bringing a rosy flush to her cheeks. "I don't have any friends except my cousin, and he's as messed-up as I am. I haven't had a boyfriend who lasted longer than three months, and every relationship I've ever had ended because of me. Because I'm too emotionally detached."

Finn realized this was probably how Jon felt.

"It isn't that I don't feel things," Ana continued. She looked down at her water, swirling it around in the glass. "I don't know how to explain to people what it's like to be a prisoner of your own thoughts. Of a darkness you were born with and can't shake."

"Why do you have to explain it to anybody?"

"Life isn't so neat as that. You don't get to enjoy a bond with someone who only knows part of you."

Finn shook his head. "That's not what I mean. You don't owe anyone an explanation of who you are. Those who care about you already know you. They get it."

"As I said, I've driven away everyone except my cousin."

"I'm still here," Finn said. "You haven't scared me off yet."

Ana stared out the window, at the ocean. "I don't really remember how it started. I have needs, too, I suppose, and a one-night stand isn't a crime. When it was over, I felt no guilt, just relief. Happy, honestly. I don't even remember learning his name, only how freeing it was not to have to explain myself."

Finn couldn't help himself from laughing. "So you discovered you like sex. Congratulations, Ana, you're human!"

"Maybe if I'd stopped there. But it went from once a month to once a week, to several nights in a row, different men every time. I didn't know any of them. Didn't want to. I went through so many I had to change neighborhoods." She looked up at him. "At some point I lost count."

Finn hadn't been expecting this admission, but he wasn't put off. "Would you feel better if I told you I lost count at some point too?"

"You think I'm making this up."

"I know you're not," he said. "And I don't care. Do you see me running out the door in horror? I don't do relationships, either. Never have." That wasn't entirely true. He had before, but he was older now, and knew he had nothing to offer a woman.

Ana stared at length, studying him. "I don't want to be like this," she said finally.

Finn wasn't sure the best way to respond. She was obviously in angst over this side of herself, and he couldn't relate to feeling that way. He knew who he was, knew his limitations, and had accepted them long ago.

"Do you know why I never came by to introduce myself?" she asked, eyes fixed on his. "You remind me of exactly the kind of man I'm trying to stay away from."

Finn didn't know what to make of that, either. He wanted to insist he wasn't like the nameless men she took home with her, but how could he, without trivializing how she felt? "Maybe I'm a good influence. I mean, you're here, talking about your feelings, something you claim to be incapable of doing. We could have had sex three times by now."

She laughed, caught off guard. "This has been the strangest conversation of my life. Maybe the longest, too."

"I could say the same," he agreed with a soft laugh. "But, for what it's worth, I don't think there's anything wrong with you." He lowered his voice. "You wanna know why I do it?"

Ana hesitated, then nodded.

Finn pointed at the ocean. "Every day, I get up, get dressed, and go out on the sea. I come home every night and have dinner with my brother. Sometimes I go into town, go drinking, and go… well, you know… but that's it. I don't want anything else, and, like you said, I am who I am. There's no woman out there who's going to want that for the rest of her life." He stopped and put his hand over hers. "We all have our reasons."

After the words were out of his mouth, a very unexpected feeling took over him. As he watched her sad face, the sea, his rituals, became distant and unimportant, and he could see himself wanting more. He felt a flush rise to his face and he took a deep breath, trying to slow his growing pulse.

Ana opened her mouth, but stopped short of saying anything. Finn witnessed a thousand thoughts swimming behind her bright blue eyes. An entire conversation passed between them, wordless.

He was afraid to consider the implications. He wanted to kiss her, but after everything she'd just told him, it would only push her away. *You remind me exactly of the kind of man I'm trying to stay away from.*

Ana looked past him then and pointed out the window. "Wow! Would you look at that?"

Finn turned. The snow had started, and was already coming down with a furious energy. At a glance, he noted there was already a couple of inches on the ground, and that would grow considerably before morning. He guessed about two feet, if not more, before it paused to draw breath.

"Ana, are you going to be okay here by yourself?"

"It's just snow, right?" The corner of her mouth twitched in an uneasy smile.

"I really don't want to, but I need to get back to the house. My brother will be home soon, if he isn't already. We need to move the lobster tanks up to the house or we won't be able to get to them if the snow lasts." Finn took both of her hands in his, suddenly emboldened. "Come with me. You can even stay a few days if you want, and I'll show you how to navigate this strange island when it shuts down." With a cough, he added, "We have a guest room."

"I don't think your brother likes me very much," she said. "And besides, I can't rely on the kindness of strangers for everything. I did take your lobster, after all."

"My brother doesn't like anyone," Finn countered. "And I hardly think we're strangers anymore."

"Me vomiting my problems into your lap is a bit one-sided, don't you think?"

"Fine," he said, focusing an intent look on her. "I'm going

to tell you something I've never told anyone before. Not even Jon."

She smiled slowly. "I'm intrigued."

He cleared his throat. "I'm afraid of the ocean."

Ana laughed so hard she choked on her water. "All right, goodnight Finn."

He put his hand on the table and leaned toward her. "Serious. I almost drowned when I was thirteen and I've been terrified ever since." His hand moved instinctively to his chest, as it often did when recalling that harrowing day.

"Then why are you a lobsterman?"

"Because it's who I am," Finn said simply.

"I see," Ana said. "You better get home to your brother. Maybe I'll drop by tomorrow."

A nice brush-off, but a brush-off nonetheless. Or was it? Hard to tell with her.

She walked him to the door and when she opened it, the wind and snow blew in with such force they had to shield themselves. Finn wrapped her in his arms when she gasped at the shock of cold. Boldness overtook him, and this time he did kiss her. She stiffened at first, and then her hand slid up and gently caressed the back of his head as she returned the kiss. Unexpected warmth coursed through him, and he wished more than anything that he'd taken care of the lobster before coming over, so he could stay with her.

"Be safe," she cautioned and put her hand on his chest. The heat of her palm cut through the harsh cold. He slipped his hands over hers. "And maybe I'll see you tomorrow."

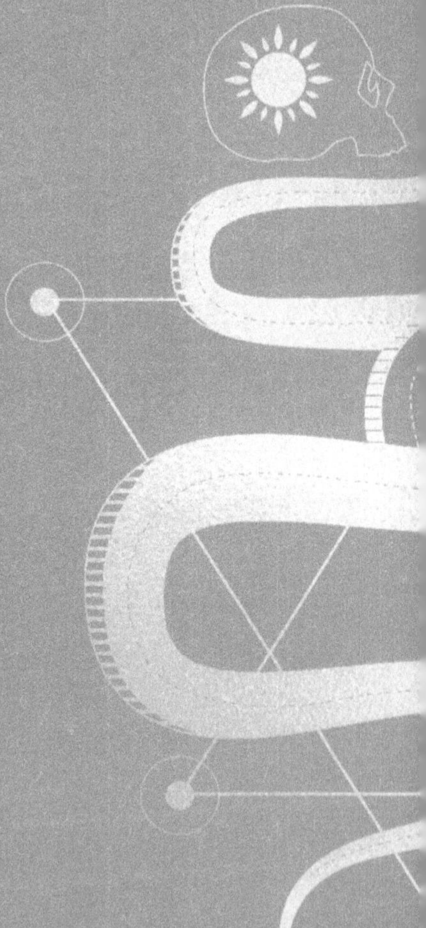

12
ANA

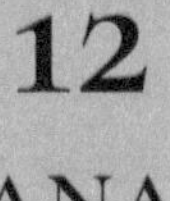

For the first time in years, Ana was exhilarated.

Finn.

She was used to the waves, the shared smiles. The building anticipation as she awaited both.

She wasn't used to conversations like the one they shared over dinner. The confessions. The mutual understanding of a series of choices and a life others didn't accept.

And that kiss.

She could very clearly picture his sandy, wind-tousled hair. The small scar above his lip. His brilliant blue eyes. The cut of his muscle under the dark brown sweater. That smile... it was as if he knew something he shouldn't. Here was someone whose life was so simple, no frills, and yet he seemed sincerely *happy*. He didn't even flinch when she shared her darkest secret with him. He understood.

Ana still felt his hands on hers, roughened but at the same time soft, like rocks smoothed by the tide. Finn was made for the labor of the sea, but that was not all he was made for.

She recalled how his face fell when she turned down his

invitation to come over, but Ana had spent the evening explaining herself so surely he understood?

Much as Ana tried to apply caution, she couldn't convince herself that what had happened tonight was wrong. It didn't feel anything like all those other times, even though Finn fit the profile. Instead of shame, she was renewed by a fresh, and unusual energy.

And then she'd healed him.

It had *never* worked with anyone except herself. The doctors viewed Ana as a medical marvel, healing from wounds in a fraction of the time and never needing ongoing care for breaks and sprains. She'd been hit by a car as a child, and the injury resulted in dozens of broken bones. She nearly died. Then, she'd closed her eyes and slept for seven days, letting her "gift" work its magic. When she awoke, her bones were healed and she was like new again, as if the accident had never happened. Her father finally had to stop returning the doctor's calls, because he was practically begging to run tests to figure out how she had come by her miraculous recovery. It had taken a generous donation to the research labs to finally get them off his back. Though she could help no one else, she'd always been able to help herself.

Except... she *had* helped someone tonight. This unpredictable ability of Ana's had worked with Finn, and she had no idea why.

Ana caught herself cleaning the same dish for a full minute, taking long pauses in the middle of drying, as she recalled how his lips felt on hers. How he smiled at her all evening, and how she felt more comfortable being open around him than people she'd known her whole life. The more she talked, the less encumbered her words became. How was it that Finn had opened a window to a part of herself she didn't even know was there?

She wasn't sure why she'd told him such personal things. Maybe she'd hoped to jump ahead to the part where he fled in horror. It would certainly solve the future problem of any awkwardness when he found out who she really was.

Or maybe she told him because she'd hoped he might react exactly the way he did.

I healed you. I helped you and I don't know how I did it. I don't know why it worked.

As the snow continued in relentless waves, Ana started to wish she'd taken Finn up on his offer.

ANA PICKED UP THE PHONE TO CALL NICOLAS, BUT STOPPED SHORT OF dialing. For some reason, she didn't want to tell him about tonight. She didn't want to hear his jokes, or his smart-ass analysis. She didn't want to ruin the way she was feeling, because she had no idea how long it would last.

The one person Ana did want to speak to was someone whom she'd never really met and never would. Her mother.

Her mother's story was not a happy one, but so much of it remained unknown to Ana. She knew her mother, Ekatherina, had fled the USSR when she was nineteen, leaving her family behind in the hopes she could make enough money as an *au pair* to send for them. It became immediately clear she wasn't qualified for that job, but the family she worked for recognized she did have a head for business, and enrolled her in accounting school, at their own cost.

She joined Deschanel Media Group as a junior accountant, insisting that, instead of Ekatherina, they call her by the anglicized version, Catherine. By that time, the magazine had started to grow in popularity. Within a year of her hiring, the magazine expanded well beyond anything they'd ever imagined. Ana's father, Augustus, was twenty-three.

The story of their courtship had never been shared with Ana. She didn't even know how it started. Pictures from their brief marriage showed her father happier than she ever saw him in later years. His body language suggested he liked to keep his wife close, and Ana saw a warmth in him that was unfamiliar to her. Ana had asked a lot about her mother, but there were only a few things he would say to her. Only that Ekatherina was extremely intelligent, and had looked forward to being a mother more than anything in the world.

Shortly before Ekatherina became pregnant, her young sister, Anasofiya, died in Russia from a prolonged illness at the age of fourteen. Ekatherina was heartbroken, and felt she'd failed her family. Ana's name on her birth certificate was Anasofiya Aleksandrovna Vasilyeva Deschanel, named after the aunt she'd never met.

Ana's stepmother, Barbara, had tried to keep the connection to the Russian side of the family alive for Ana, but the relationship existed superficially through cards and letters.

Ana loved her stepmother, but Barbara's love for her was best expressed through her care, through cooking and tending after Ana in practical ways. They'd never had the kind of relationship that encouraged confiding about anything important. Ana liked to imagine that if her mother had lived, they'd have been close, the best of friends, and maybe, just maybe, Ana might have turned out differently.

But if Ana was anything, she was a realist. Her mother wasn't here, and Ana was who she was. She didn't know if tonight should give her hope, or serve as another reminder of what life could have been like if she was someone else.

• • •

ANA FINISHED WITH THE KITCHEN. AS SHE STARTED TO TURN OFF THE lights and head upstairs for the night, she noticed something shiny on the edge of the counter.

Keys. Not hers.

She examined them. There was an old, battered anchor, and several keys of varying sizes. It was obvious they were Finn's. For all Ana knew, they could be keys to his storehouse, which he'd insisted was his reason for needing to be home. He was probably searching his pockets right now.

Ana decided to give him a call, and then realized that she didn't have his phone number. She searched desks and cupboards for a phone book, but there didn't appear to be one in the house. She flipped open her laptop to search online, but the small light on her wireless data card was red, and with a glance outside, she deduced why. Remembering Alex, she called him next, hoping he'd have the number, but he wasn't picking up.

She stood in the middle of her kitchen, at a loss. *This is so silly. I'm going through all this to figure out how to get ahold of my* next door neighbor.

Ana glanced over the sink, through the window, at the relentless attack of snow, resolving it would be easier to go over now than later. Finn had shown her a kindness tonight and this was the least she could do to repay it.

She pulled her sweater over her head and slipped into the heavy winter coat purchased for her time in Maine. Glancing back, she switched off the lights, unsure of how long she'd be gone. When Ana opened the door, the wind gusted into the room so hard it nearly blew her backward.

Although Finn lived next door, there was no easy way to get over to his property. Going down the driveway was far longer because the roads didn't intersect for almost a quarter-mile, and then she'd have to double back. But going across the properties from the waterside was hilly and rocky. It wouldn't be easy with several inches of snow already covering the ground, and more incoming.

Ana reminded herself there was nothing extraordinary about snow in Maine, and started toward the St. Andrews property.

Every step from her warm home brought the chill deeper within her. Ana had traveled all over the world, but snow was still foreign to her. Trudging through close to four inches of it felt very *real.* Even the locals didn't spend time outdoors in this weather, Finn had told her.

About a hundred feet from home, she considered that maybe if the keys were important to him, he'd come back over and get them. *But what if he doesn't realize until morning, when we're all snowed in?*

Ana reached the edge of her own property, and could *feel* the ocean as it responded to the thrust of the winds and snow. It seemed to her that the gods themselves were crying out. Was this really what they were used to here? And was she really going to have to deal with this repeatedly over the long winter ahead? *Stop being such a wuss,* she told herself. *I'm only going next door.*

Ana approached the rocks separating their properties, before sloping down into the small outcropping of shore. She'd need to go slow here, and tread carefully, or she could very easily slip and hurt herself, the rocks already covered in a white blanket. She crouched down, thinking how silly she'd look if anyone was watching, and used both hands and feet to pull herself across the rocks.

She wished she'd had the sense to buy gloves. Her feet struggled to find bearing as she moved across each rock, slowly, cursing herself for not waiting until the storm had subsided. The snow fell so densely, she couldn't see more than a foot in front of her, and after a few minutes of this she was no longer sure which direction was the right one. Not even the lighthouse was visible.

Well this is a fine mess, girl, was Ana's last real thought before things went bad. Her foot gained, then lost, traction on the rocks, her hand instinctively reaching for anything solid to regain her balance. Finding nothing but snow, her hands flailed, and her other foot lost traction.

At once, Ana was sliding, falling, and everything went black.

13
JONATHAN

Jon watched his brother come in, late, smiling. A girl, most likely, though Finn picked a poor night to be out playing around.

"You're home just in time," Jon said, as he placed Mr. Jenkins in front of the fireplace. The dog heaved one shuddering sigh and then settled back into his normal, sleepy breathing. "Some of the roads are already closed."

"I wasn't on the roads," Finn responded, flinging the snow off. "But I could've told you they'd be closing them soon. My guess is they'll be closed for a while."

Jon remembered he'd seen Finn's truck in the driveway when he pulled in earlier, and started to piece things together.

Finn sat down next to his brother, taking in the full heat of the fire. Their father installed central heating years ago in the old house, but both boys always loved the natural warmth of a nice, crackling fire.

"You were next door," Jon said. It sounded more like an accusation than he intended.

"Don't worry, your sanctuary is safe. I invited her, but she turned me down." Finn added, as if purely to gauge a reaction, "she said you don't like her."

Jon grunted. "Don't like her? I don't know her."

"Don't want to, is more like it."

Finn took off his wet socks and tossed them in Jon's direction. Jon smacked them away in annoyance. "You're right, why would I want to, when she's just a part-timer?"

Finn looked around the room, then stated sarcastically, "I don't see anyone else here, Jon. Just you and me. No need for pretense."

Jon made a sound under his breath, then stood, heading toward the kitchen for a glass of water. "When is she leaving, anyway?"

"She didn't say. Maybe never."

"Or until her daddy decides to pull back the funds."

"You can be a hermit all you want Jon, but you don't have to be an asshole." Finn's smile disappeared. He shoved his cold feet dangerously close to the fire. "She owns that house herself, and she's here for her own reasons. She doesn't owe us explanations."

Jon finished drinking and, feeling unusually reckless, dropped his glass into the sink. The loud clink echoed. "Defending her now?" he taunted. "Must be serious."

"You really need to blow off some steam," Finn said in disgust and left the room, leaving Jon feeling like he'd gone too far. Teasing was easier than being reminded of who he was. He was being unfair to his little brother. Finn might poke fun at Jon, but he also protected him. Finn was the one who'd make an excuse for Jon when he was feeling unsocial before an event. The one who bought the groceries, made the phone calls that needed to be made, and bailed Jon out of awkward conversations. People always called Jon the smart one, but Finn was smart too, usually in ways that mattered more.

Jon found Finn near the back door, slipping into a dry coat. He was starting on the boots and snowshoes, when he looked up and saw Jon. "I could use some help with the tanks," Finn said, as a peace offering. "If we shovel the dock and ramp, we should be able to get them up here safely." Jon knew Finn was disappointed in himself, and he heard what Finn didn't say. He should've done this earlier, instead of spending an evening with Ana. He should've kept Jeremiah longer and moved the goods before the snow hit. Jon saw no point in hammering his guilt.

Jon laced up his own boots, and bundled into his thick jacket, scarf, gloves, and finally his fur hat. Finn was already out the door with the snow shovel by the time he finished, and so, without needing conversation, Jon went around the side of the shed to get the snow thrower. This was work they'd been doing together for years, and even with experience it was long and arduous. It could be midnight before they finished plowing and moving everything. But the town would be shut down tomorrow, so the brothers would have all day to rest and recover, maybe longer. This might be the storm that would shut the island down for weeks.

They shoveled in companionable silence. The snow muffled the sound, making talking pointless. Jon glanced to the east, toward Ana's house. He wondered what happened that evening between her and Finn. Finn was smiling when he came home, yet she hadn't agreed to join him.

Not because of him, you ass. Because of you. Jon felt badly about that, but overpowering his guilt was relief she'd stayed in her own home. She might have been stuck with them for days. Maybe that's what Finn wanted.

He wondered sometimes if he was the reason Finn stayed on the island. Finn talked a lot about how he loved the sea, and his routine, and the simplicity of his life, but Finn had a spark in him, too. Despite his efforts to convince himself, and the island, otherwise, Finn was more than a fisherman. There was a burst of life in Finn, as there was a darkness in Jon. He felt a twinge of remorse, recognizing his role in Finn's decision to never cultivate that part of himself. *Finn is a man grown and old enough to decide his own future*, he told himself, unconvincingly. *If he wants to leave, he can leave.*

Still, he wondered, if Finn was content with this life then why had he bothered going to college? There had to be at least a part of his brother that thought about a life away from the island, and the sea. But Finn never talked about it, shutting down whenever Jon tried to approach the subject.

The only sign Finn still held on to another dream was the piles of books arriving with Finn's monthly shipment from the bookstore. His room was filled with heaps of them, some stacks running floor to ceiling. Jon thought about converting their parents' old room into a library for Finn, but a part of him intuitively held back from acting on the idea. Private himself, Jon understood there were reasons Finn confined his interests, and the resulting columns of knowledge, to his room.

We all have ways of torturing ourselves I guess. Thinking about these things only made the work seem harder, so Jon emptied his mind and focused on the task at hand.

It was about an hour later when he heard Finn scream: "*Jonnnnnnnnnn*!"

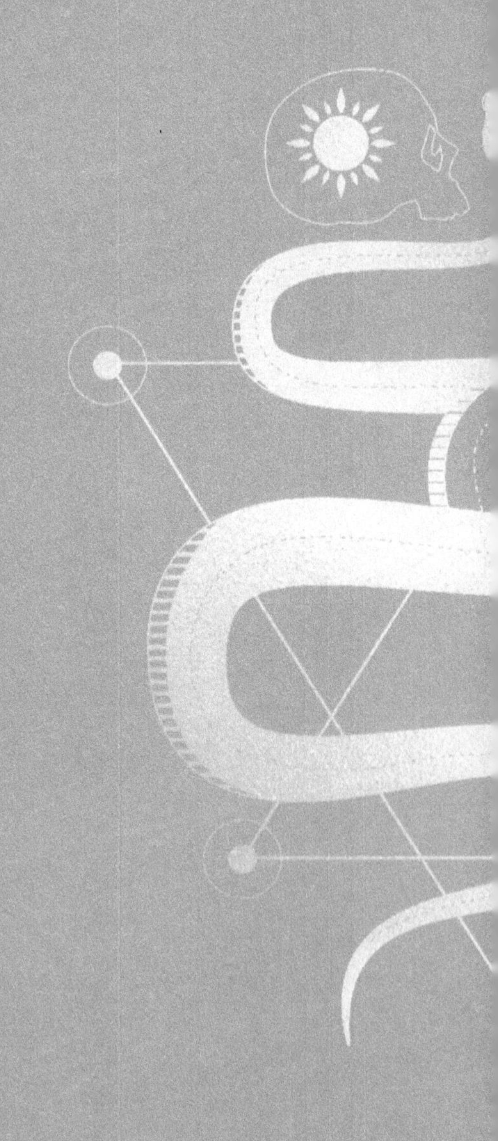

14
ALEX

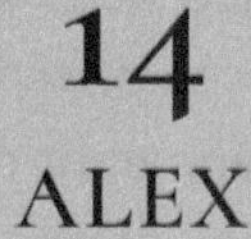

Despite the worsening storm in his head, along with the one now coming to life outside, Alex had managed to remain calm long enough to drive home. He'd survived enough winters on Summer Island to know the snowfall tonight was nothing to take lightly. But even the medication couldn't keep his anxiousness at bay once he was safely within the walls of his own home.

A little odd. He couldn't believe she hadn't done more to defend him. Him! Her biggest advocate and only ally on the island since she came here. He, who had rushed to her side at the drop of the hat.

It felt like he was burning from the inside out. Stumbling to the kitchen, he clumsily poured himself a glass of water, savoring the cool sharpness as it went down. His hand swiped for a chair and he slumped down in it, drinking his water in measured sips, trying to catch his breath again.

It was Finn; it had to be. She'd said those things to impress him. There'd been no mistaking the meaning in Finn's words. Like others on the island, Finn didn't appreciate all Alex did to help people. Well, Alex didn't much respect Finn's motives, either.

Andrew St. Andrews had been a good man; unorthodox, but good. Those qualities seemed to have skipped his sons. Jon was rude to people for no apparent reason. And Finn? Well, he was a skirt chaser. There was no way around it. Alex didn't like gossip, but he knew Finn had charmed half the women on this island, and not settled down with a single one of them. He was going to do the same thing to Ana. Alex was certain.

He was so angry at himself for leaving like that, when what he should've done was put an end to the nonsense before it went anywhere! And now, the storm was coming in heavy. He couldn't just drive back over there now, could he? Worse, he thought, the snow would act as a reason for Finn to stay with her, or for her to go over to Finn's, to ride it out.

With a furious curse, Alex kicked the chair across from him and it landed with a clunk on the hard linoleum. He could not —would not—fail her the way he had failed those other women! In each case, there'd been that one moment of perfect clarity where he knew he would either save them or he wouldn't. He was fast approaching that moment for Ana.

His mother's voice came back to him. "'Lotta women will tell you their man beats 'em because it helps 'em, keeps 'em in line, but it ain't true," she'd said to him, usually after a particularly rough row with his father. "The men do it 'cause they're *weak*... and *powerless*... and this is the only power they know. The only power they'll ever know is the one they feel standing over a helpless woman who *cain't fight back*."

Alex couldn't remember a time when his father hadn't sought to subdue his mother with his fists. And if not fists, sex. Many nights Alex had been subjected to the sounds from their bedroom. His father's disgusting grunts, mingled with his mother's terrified screams.

While his father said nothing, his eyes would meet Alex's as if daring him to say something, to challenge him.

"I hated you both," Alex whispered. He went to put his glass in the sink but he missed, shattering it all over the dirty, peeling linoleum. Ignoring the mess, he opened a wooden drawer near the fridge and pulled out a set of keys. He barreled down the hall toward a very special room seldom used anymore, but containing things more important to him than anything else in the house. *There's more meaning in this room than there is on this whole godforsaken island,.*

He fumbled with the keys, dropping them twice before successfully unlocking the door. In his agitation, the door swung open too quickly, tumbling several items from his old wooden desk to the floor.

The room was nearly bare of furnishings. There was the old wooden desk, chipped and listing to one side. A dirty cloth chair went with it, and the dented file cabinet so overflowing with paperwork the doors no longer closed. But it wasn't the few pieces of tired, cheap heirlooms that made this room special to Alex, but what he'd done with the walls.

They were painted light blue, but anyone coming into the room would never know that because there was not even an inch of bare wall to be found. It was covered in pictures and newspaper clippings, wall to wall, ceiling to floor; even the ceiling itself. There were several old poster and cork boards holding some of the cutouts, but many of them were taped or tacked to bare walls. In one corner, the clippings had been put up using drywall screws, when Alex had run out of traditional adhesives. Light shining through one section of newsprint served as the only sign a window existed. It highlighted the perpetual swirl of dust in the air.

Alex dropped silently into his creaky chair, and a sense of peace stole over him. One he only found when surrounded by these memories. His sense of purpose—of knowing what he was born for, what he was meant for—was back, unmarred by all the earlier, distracting emotions.

Looking from face to face, from one smile to the next, Alex was back in the driver's seat.

As his eyes scanned the room, he habitually started with the ones who meant the most. There was an entire wall dedicated just to these three:

Carla Edgewater, 18, and Lionel Shepherd, 18, fell to their deaths from Casco Bay Lighthouse in bizarre murder-suicide. Next to the clipping, Alex had taken a color picture of Carla, a candid, with her beaming cheerleader smile and flowing mahogany hair.

Sandra Finnerty of Portland, 23, found at the base of Casco Bay Lighthouse following apparent suicide. Alex's picture of Sandra was taken at the Thirsty Wench on Androscoggin. She was holding up a beer in a toast, but wasn't looking at the camera. Her mouth opened in a cheer; her short blonde hair was in a ponytail.

Emily Caldwell, beloved member of the Summer Island community and recent widow, was found this weekend after an apparent suicide. Caldwell, 26, is survived by her parents, Richard and Susan Jarvis, of Bangor. In this picture, Emily was getting into a car outside the Lutheran church. The photo was taken at her husband's funeral, so she'd been crying. Her eyes had caught the camera momentarily and there were two hollow orbs staring back, buried behind long, dark hair.

There were multiple articles and clippings about each of these women, alongside more of Alex's private photos.

The other three walls and ceiling were covered in similar articles and black and white news pictures. Women from Oregon to Hawaii to Georgia.

The one thing all of these women had in common was

simple: someone had failed them. Specifically, someone had failed to *save* them.

Not all women wanted to be saved. Not all women were grateful toward those who tried. His mother was one of those women.

"Why are you angry with me, Ma? He'll never, ever hurt you again," Alex had pleaded, while still holding the bloody axe. It was so heavy and yet impossible to let go of. A thousand thoughts and motivations drove him, but at the forefront had been the smile he'd imagined on his mother's face when he released her from her prison.

Instead, her eyes had been hard as steel, filled with tears, but not of joy. "You killed the only thing I eva loved," she said. There were never words, not then or ever after, that cut Alex as deeply.

When a woman was that detached from reality, there was only one way to handle it. He'd always prayed it wouldn't come to that.

These were Alex's reminders of why he was here, and why, no matter what stood in his way, he couldn't afford to fail.

For Ana, there was still hope. He just needed to get her away from Finn long enough to show her.

15
FINNEGAN

This wasn't happening. It couldn't be. Finn seldom prayed, he did it now, followed by pleading, and then bargaining.

It seemed an eternity before Jon reached him, but when he did, Finn felt his brother's shock before he was close enough to see it.

"Christ," Jon whispered.

Jon's hands were on his jacket, pushing him away, but Finn couldn't move. The blood was frozen to her head. *So* much blood. She didn't move at all, and with the snow blowing around her, he couldn't detect the rise and fall of the telltale breaths.

Jon pushed him again, and this time Finn stepped away, his gaze still fixated on her, unbelieving, terrified.

Jon lifted Ana, sliding his arms under her knees, rocking her back against his shoulders. As he moved her higher into his arms, her coat shifted and something dropped from the side pocket, landing in the snow.

Keys. Finn's keys. *Oh my God. She was coming to our house, for me, to give these to me.* Tears burned in his eyes, but there wasn't time for that. When he snapped himself out of it, Jon was already heading back to the house, moving as quickly as he could manage through the deep snow.

Finn pulled himself up out of the icy drift and ran back to the house, though he couldn't see more than a foot in front of him. His internal sense of direction carried him true, as it must have done for Jon, because when he reached the back door, it was still wide open and neither Jon, nor Ana, were anywhere to be seen.

He caught his breath. Jon's shoes were at the bottom of the stairs. Finn flew up the steps in pursuit.

Jon had laid her out on their parents' bed, and was taking off his own jacket, gloves, scarf, and hat. Jon's face betrayed no emotion other than determination. He looked up at Finn and instructed calmly, "Help me get her clothes off."

"*What*?" Finn stood with hands on his head, panting. "She's nearly frozen to death and you want her clothes off?"

"Finn. Calm down," Jon ordered. "Help me get her clothes off, so we can get her warmed up."

"We're gonna kill her," Finn choked. He paced, restless, searching for an anchor.

Jon slapped Finn across the face. The sound bounced off the walls, the sting intentionally startling. "She *is* going to die if we don't get her out of the *wet* clothes. Do you understand now?"

"Right," Finn said, dazed. "Right."

Jon already had her jacket and shirt off, when Finn started on her shoes. They weren't even snow boots, just sneakers. *Oh, Ana.* By the time his shaking hands unlaced them, Jon sighed impatiently, tugging at her pants. "Go draw a warm bath. Quickly. Not too hot," he barked at Finn.

Finn fumbled with the knobs on the old porcelain tub,

trying not to think about what she looked like lying in the snow, or what could happen if they couldn't help her. He focused on one step at a time: right knob hot water, left knob cold water. *Plug the drain, test the water. More hot water. Test the water.*

Jon stood in the doorway with Ana in his arms. She was naked and dead to the world. Finn experienced a sharp moment of clarity when he saw his brother's arms come around her sides, fingers brushing the underside of her naked breast, other hand resting under her pale bottom.

But Jon's face was all business.

He nudged Finn out of the way, and nestled her into the bath as Finn stood motionless. "Go get Dad's medical bag," Jon commanded. "Make sure the stitch kit is in there. If not, find it." When Finn didn't move, Jon said, with more force. "*Finnegan. Please.*"

It took a moment for Finn to register the request. He'd almost forgotten Jon had been trained by their father. It was easy to forget, when Jon himself refused to acknowledge his abilities. But Jon *was* trained, and Jon had a gift. If anyone could fix her, it would be him.

Finn returned with the bag to find Jon kneeling next to the tub, gently cleaning Ana's bloody face with a washcloth. She was still unconscious, but the ashen grey in her cheeks pushed back with hints of healthy pink. She no longer bore the colorless pall of the dead.

"She has a pretty serious head wound. I don't know how long she was outside in the cold and what problems that might've caused." Jon turned to look at his brother. "Tell me truthfully, how long are we going to be stuck here with this storm?"

"I... I don't know." Finn was pacing again, his voice cracking.

"Finn, calm down and talk to me. *Finn.*" He felt Jon's hand on his leg. "I need you to help me. I need you right now."

Jon had never said he needed him before. It had the calming effect that Jon had evidently been hoping for. Finn took a deep breath and predicted, "It might be a while. Days, maybe weeks."

Jon lowered his head and sighed. "I can stitch up her head wound. We can feed her, and keep her warm. But I don't know when she'll wake up. Hell, I don't even know what equipment still works..." Jon's voice trailed off and Finn knew he was thinking of all the things in the medical office Jon had studiously avoided for years. "I have no idea how serious the trauma is. What she really needs is an MRI..."

Finn nodded. He understood what Jon was saying, even if he didn't like it. "You can fix her now, but it might not be enough. You can do your best, but it still might not be enough..."

"Let's get her dried off and into something warm," Jon decided, once again lifting her limp body into his strong arms. This time Finn didn't hesitate when he stepped toward them to wrap a towel around her.

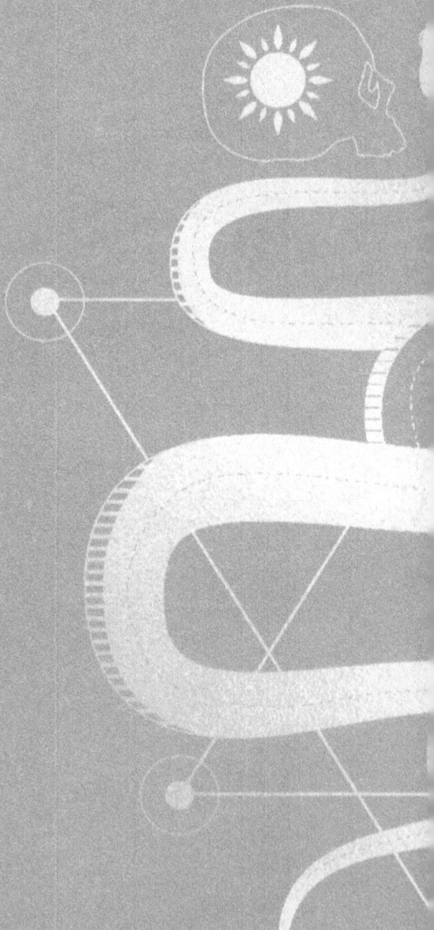

16
JONATHAN

Jon sipped his coffee, watching for hints of sun over the horizon. The snow continued, lasting longer even than Finn had expected. Through the dense white flakes, Jon could just make out the edge of the sunrise.

The adrenaline from the night had worn off, leaving Jon overcome with exhaustion. Once he got Ana cleaned up, he had a clear view of the gash in her head. The cut was deep. It was hard to tell for sure, but she seemed to have lost a lot of blood. She'd need a transfusion. The equipment was there, and two healthy and willing donors in the house, but he couldn't guess at her blood type. The wrong choice would kill her.

That he'd even entertained attempting a blood transfusion told him how tired he was. He'd been awake for almost twenty-four hours now. The early morning tempted him with a nap, but he was afraid to sleep. Every hour he went upstairs to check on Ana, afraid if he didn't see her chest rise and fall it would be because he had failed.

They'd dressed Ana in their mother's old flannel pajamas. Finn insisted they put more than one pair on her, but Jon explained they didn't want her to overheat, either. She was likely to develop a fever once her body started to stabilize, and she was already at risk of infection. Jon relented at his request to put thicker socks on her.

Finn was upstairs in the bed with her, but he wasn't sleeping any more than Jon was. If Jon was anxious, Finn was something else entirely. He watched her breathe with intense vigilance, worried she might have a deadly concussion they couldn't diagnose in their home; that she might have a brain bleed, or a hemorrhage. Jon wanted to reassure him, but he had the same worries.

Finn had calmed down long enough to get Ana cleaned up, dressed, and settled in bed before he lost it again. He rambled on about keys, how the whole thing was his fault. Jon insisted he take a valium, and Finn reluctantly complied.

"I don't know what I would've done if you hadn't been here. God... if you'd stayed later with the McElroy dog, or if we'd waited until morning to start the shoveling. Jesus Jon, did this really happen?" The medicine had calmed him, slowing his emotions to a steady stream of guilt and fear.

"You can't think of the 'what ifs,'" Jon answered. What else could he say? Finn was right, but these things happened every day. Paramedics arriving late to a crash scene, a pedestrian unknowingly walking past someone who can't cry out for help. This is why he went into medicine. To be the one who could make the difference. To make the seconds that counted, count for something. When he was tending to Ana, his anxiousness around her vanished. He was a doctor, at his father's side, his only concern keeping her safe.

As stressful as the night had been, it was the first time in a long time Jon felt alive.

Once Ana was stable, Finn buried his face in his hands and cried. Not tears of the moment, of fear, or of anxiousness, but real tears. Jon felt his heart lurch for the only person he really loved.

He put his hand on Finn's shoulder. "Why don't you go lay down with her? It might help you relax, and I'm sure she'll want a familiar face when she wakes."

When Finn looked up, he was a young boy again. The thirteen-year-old who wanted to be a sailor. "Will she? Wake up?"

"Of course," Jon lied. He honestly couldn't promise anything with certainty. The brain was a mysterious organ and everyone responded differently to trauma. As much as he wanted to comfort Finn, he really needed to be alone. He put his hand on his brother's shoulder and squeezed. "Go on."

Finn nodded without another word and went upstairs. When Jon checked on them throughout the night and morning, Finn watched her, one arm propping himself up, the other wrapped protectively around her. Her face was still and unmoving, but her breathing was steady now. By some miracle she hadn't suffered any frostbite.

In a couple of hours, Jon would need to insert a catheter and start her on fluids. If she was still asleep by the evening, he'd add a feeding tube to filter her nutrients. These were all things he remembered how to do. Had done them many times at his father's side. He presumed all of the requisite supplies would be easy to find in his father's office, but he wasn't ready to go in there. He wanted to enjoy what was left of his quiet morning.

As the sun continued to rise, now a hazy orange glow pushing through the blizzard, he thought again of his father. Andrew St. Andrews would've been both proud and ashamed of him last night. Proud of how well he'd acted under pressure, for saving that girl. Ashamed afresh that Jon gave up his career in medicine.

He never understood. No one did, but especially not him. Jon didn't need understanding, though. Mostly, he needed to be left alone.

I'm not you, he'd said to his father, when he delivered the news he'd left medicine behind.

No, you're sure not.

Jon finished the rest of his coffee and gave another glance outside. When Finn was more alert, he'd have to ask him what he thought about the weather. If things were going to get worse.

As he stood at the sink, fading fast, Jon knew he needed to sleep. Who knew how many days or weeks they'd be snowed in? The snow level was around fourteen inches now, and it wasn't letting up. They had a patient upstairs who was going to need help under difficult circumstances, made even more complicated if he wasn't alert and able to function properly. *Two hours*, he told himself. *Then I'll go in and get the equipment.*

He climbed the stairs, stopping at the door of his parents' old bedroom. Finn lay wrapped around Ana, but his eyes were closed now, and he snored softly. Jon added a thin blanket on top of him, checked her breathing and vitals once more, then let them sleep. Finn would want Jon to wake him up, but he needed rest, too.

Jon closed all the doors, and placed his slippers at the side of his bed. Before succumbing to his exhaustion, he reflected on how much life was about to change for all of them.

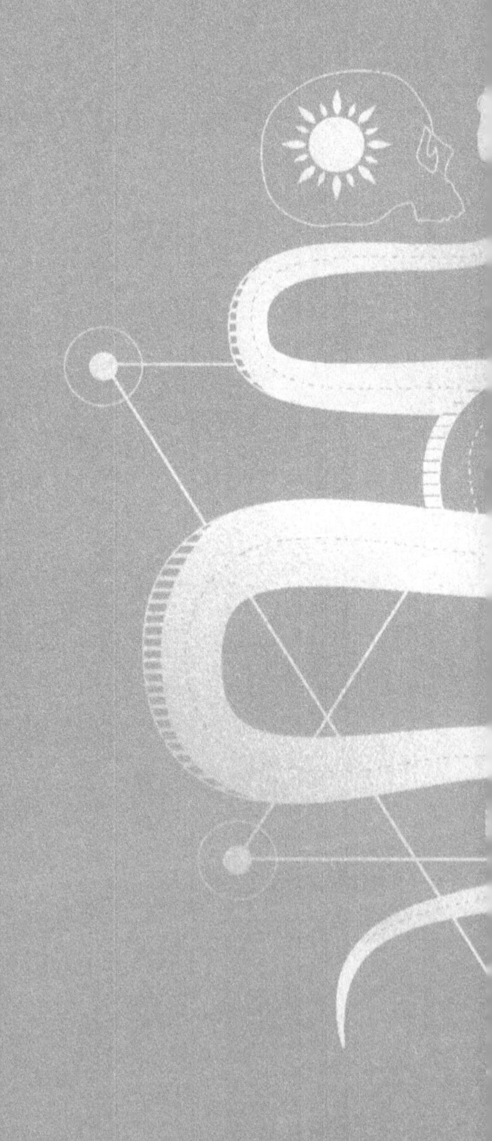
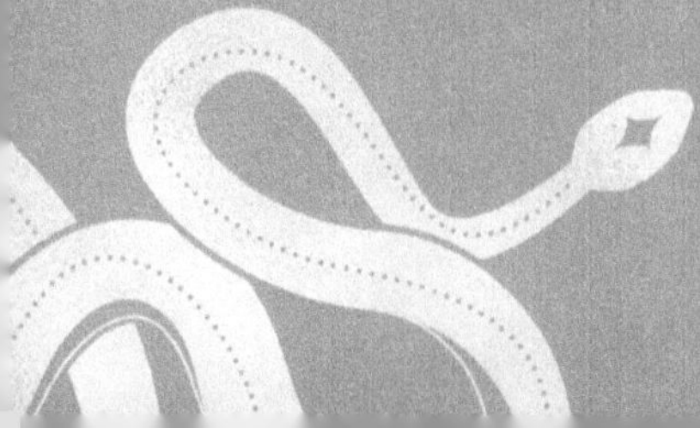

17
NICOLAS

Ana had called every night. Even if the conversation was limited to a quick goodnight, she still called. One evening she had lost track of time and called him at past one, but she he'd still called.

Not one, but several days had passed since Nicolas had heard from her.

Something was wrong.

On the fourth day, Oz stopped by unexpectedly.

Oz was by himself, which was odd enough, given how rarely he left Adrienne alone these days. Oz lived in perpetual terror of Adrienne having a breakdown of some kind, the kind that might result in her bolting again. Adrienne hadn't been the same since losing her memory years ago, and Nicolas didn't think she ever would be. But while Nicolas accepted the change, he wondered what Oz would've done differently if there weren't two children in the equation. P*robably nothing. Old boy loves to feed his tireless hero complex.*

Nicolas loved his half-sister, but he respected Oz for having the patience and love to deal with her utterly broken spirit, because he could not.

"And to what do we owe this extraordinary pleasure?" Nicolas asked with an exaggerated bow.

"Do I need a reason to stop by?" Oz ignored him, brushing past with a distracted look.

"You usually have plenty of reasons to stay away."

Oz turned back toward him. The sight of him sent a shock through Nicolas, and he was reminded how long it had been since they'd seen one another. His friend's shiny black hair was somehow duller. His brilliant green eyes looked more like the fading shade of dried moss. Oz's skin was drained of color and life, as if he hadn't eaten or slept in some time. Nicolas opened his mouth to say something, then decided not to.

"What do you have for liquor around here?" Nicolas heard Oz flipping through the cupboards in the kitchen.

"You know that's not where I keep it. I mean, it's not like we've been sneaking liquor since we were thirteen or anything," he chided, and led him to the parlor. Nicolas opened the sliding doors to a large oak bar built into the wall. "Where's your brain, Ozzy? Did you leave it at home with your balls?"

But Oz didn't react to the teasing as he normally would. He took the drink Nicolas held out to him, quaffed it down, then handed it back for a refill. Nicolas stared at him in astonishment, then made him a second.

"How's Ana?" Oz asked.

Nicolas cocked his head. "Are we making small talk? How's your mother, then?"

"Quite well," Oz responded, clearly missing Nicolas' sarcasm. "So Ana's faring well in Maine?"

"'Faring better than you I hope." Nicolas continued to watch his friend closely. The odd, wild look in his eyes, the complete disengagement from his words, the way he kept flinching and brushing his hair from his eyes, hair that wasn't even *in* his eyes.

"I'm fine. Thought we could have some guy time."

"'Guy time?' Really, Oz?" Nicolas wasn't interested in deciphering the complexities of Oz Sullivan's mind, but he was utterly bewildered at his bizarre behavior. "I doubt we'll be doing anything, with you on the verge of a complete nervous breakdown."

But Oz was hardly listening, instead stirring his drink with a finger, seemingly fascinated with the swirling ice cubes.

Nicolas, never fond of mystery, wasn't sure what to make of any of this.

He leaned over toward Oz and waved his hands in his face. Oz looked up and met his eyes with the same glazed look he had since he arrived. "Sorry, what?"

"You know, it would've been quicker to drink at home, instead of driving almost an hour out here, right?"

Oz set his glass down. When he looked at Nicolas this time, Oz appeared slightly less dazed, though it seemed to take great effort. "I'm sorry. I just... things have been kinda stressful at home lately. I needed to get away."

"Stressful," Nicolas repeated. He expected him to do something desperate, like jump out the window. "Well, marriage and brats would be the end of any man, but how is this different from normal?"

"It isn't... I mean... it's... I don't know..." Oz stood suddenly, bumping the table so hard his drink sloshed over the sides of the glass. "I should go."

Nicolas shook his head in disbelief. "You just got here! Ozzy, are you on *drugs*?"

But Oz was already on his way to the door, and if Nicolas knew anything about his brooding friend, it was the impossibility of getting him to speak when he was in one his darker moods.

"Sorry again," Oz called, pulling the door behind him. He paused briefly, and then said, "Tell Ana..."

"Tell her *what*?" Nicolas snapped.

"Nothing," Oz changed his mind. "Nothing. We will... I promise we'll get together soon. You and me, I mean. Sorry for dropping in on you like this."

"Don't mention it." Nicolas waved distractedly, feeling like he'd been hit by a small hurricane.

NICOLAS WAS GENUINELY PERPLEXED. HE'D OFTEN ACCUSED OZ OF being as moody as a woman, but he couldn't remember ever seeing him act like this.

It had been so unexpected and bizarre that it was enough to distract him from his thoughts about Ana. He decided if Oz wanted to talk, he would. Figuring out how to contact Ana was a more pressing concern.

He didn't want to call her father. Augustus was a busy man, and if Nicolas bothered him with this, and then nothing was amiss, Augustus wouldn't be happy. On the other hand, if something was wrong, and it was something Ana didn't want her father involved in, then Nicolas would feel *her* wrath.

They didn't know anyone else on the island, but there was that overseer. Whitman. He only knew the name because it was written on a piece of paper, folded inside his family Bible —a book he really should give to Adrienne, the more he thought of it, since she was the only Deschanel bothering to further the family line—listed as *Emergency Contact for Ana*, in her handwriting. She felt safer if Nicolas had the information, she'd said. *Just in case.* Under the number, she'd written: *Peace out, sucka!*

He set down his cognac, and picked up the phone in the study. Cradling the receiver again, he walked over and closed the double doors as an afterthought. He lived alone if you didn't count the four people on staff, and he preferred this conversation be private.

Nicolas lifted the receiver and dialed.

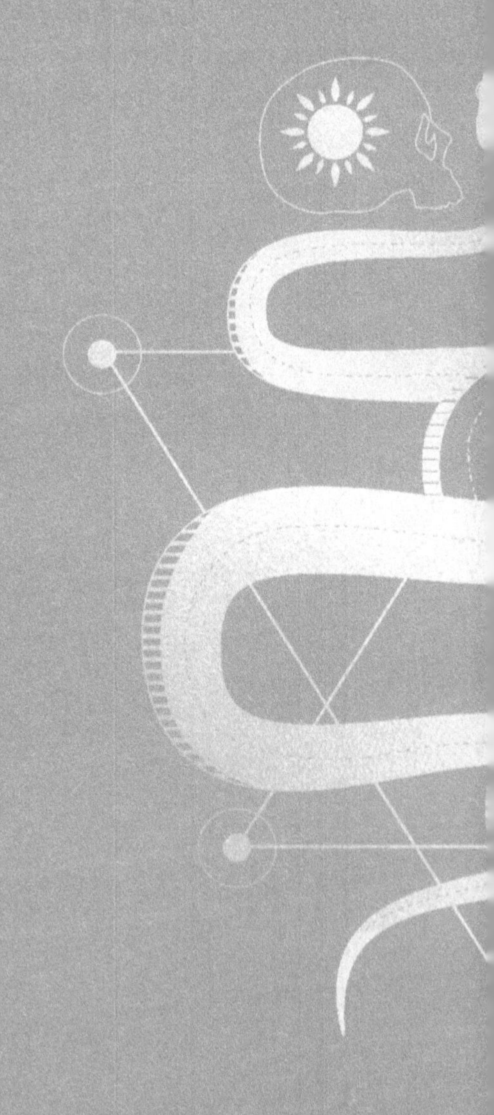

18

AUGUSTUS

Incompetence. Why did it feel as if Augustus Deschanel was constantly surrounded by it? People who didn't understand the value of quality, taking the requisite time to ensure delivery was in-line with expectations. *His* expectations. An old boss, in another life, told him once the only way to ever be really successful was to hire five hundred versions of yourself. But then, you would never change, never innovate.

It wasn't like this in the early days, but it wasn't only Deschanel Media Group who had changed.

Years before Ana was born, when the business was a single magazine, Augustus had visions of grandeur. He envisioned a conglomeration of magazines, an empire founded on the highest quality publications, built leveraging the creative acumen of the best and brightest minds. Proudly, he'd imagined Ana at his side for all of it. At first, teaching her about the business, then slowly folding her in, with an internship in high school, and a job after college. She'd work her way up until she knew the ins and outs as he did.

But that wasn't what she wanted.

Ekatherina had died and Augustus' second wife, Barbara, couldn't have children. His dream stopped with Ana, and while he'd never, in those early years, imagined being a father at all, now, in his middle age, he was facing the idea of naming a professional heir not his own.

Ana did have skills that suited the family business, but they were on the other end of the spectrum. While she understood business, she had an artist's heart. So had he, once upon a time, but it was that love of the craft which made him want this career to begin with. He hoped she might see the connection and embrace it the way he had, but so far her involvement felt more obligatory than passionate. He'd never force her. Augustus' ability as a Deschanel was the power of persuasion, and he'd used it on others when it suited him. But he had never, and would never, use it on his daughter.

He didn't really understand Ana. It was a terrible thing for a father to admit. She had a brilliant mind. She'd won awards and national recognition for her writing and school projects, and, later, a full scholarship to Tulane.

But she also had the dark mind of an artist. He should know, having seen plenty of them come through the doors looking for freelance work over the years. Her mind was never at rest.

Augustus thought it might be genetic, if that was a trait which could even be passed genetically. Ekatherina's darkness had consumed her, but it wasn't only Ana's mother who had this in her. Augustus' sister Evangeline was the same. The entire family was talented, but there were the few dark horses as well, like Ana and Evangeline, who operated on a completely different plane, and also suffered for it. Augustus could only theorize about it, because he couldn't understand them.

Ana used to say it felt like there was more than one of her, and that the two parts were always in conflict. Augustus had sent her to counseling. The first one diagnosed her with Asperger's, and the second said she most certainly did not have anything actually *wrong* with her, per se, but that children with higher IQ's frequently had more challenges adapting to social situations. Neither diagnosis was useful in the end. She'd never had problems making friends, having been involved in sports and clubs, and even a sorority in college. Her trouble was taking those friendships deeper. Her trouble was with herself.

It was his idea to send her to Maine, when she said she needed to leave for a while. While Ana was generally restless, before she decided to leave she'd grown exceedingly agitated and even more withdrawn than usual. When he broached the idea, she simply smiled and said thanks. What she would get out of the experience, he could hardly guess. He'd come to a point where he stopped hoping for her to be something that matched his own expectations of success, and instead wished for her personal happiness.

Their conversations hadn't changed much over thirty years.

"How are you doing, sweetheart?"

"Good."

"Anything new going on?"

"Not really."

He made her call him every week from Maine. He would've preferred more often, but she hated small talk, and he was consumed by things at the office anyway. Even as a child, she'd only engaged in conversation when there was a point. She could never understand the value in "bullshitting about the weather." Another sign business management wasn't in her future.

Augustus checked the clock. Ten minutes to ten. Barbara was only patient until ten or so and then the calls would start. He couldn't fault her. He did work incredibly long hours, seeming to disregard her needs. That she'd adjusted her life around his idiosyncrasies was a sign of her commitment to his happiness, and it reminded him of how little he'd done over the years for hers.

Ana hadn't called yet, and probably wouldn't at this hour. She was supposed to call several days ago. Presuming she'd lost track of time, he called her instead, but she didn't pick up.

Even knowing his daughter's disinclination for phone time, Augustus was disappointed. He'd hoped that she would put her misgivings aside for their weekly ritual because she loved him. Sometimes he considered her difficulties a misunderstanding, and then, moments like these, he had trouble excusing her thoughtlessness. Moments like these, Ana reminded him of her mother.

The clock chimed ten. Barbara called. His secretaries went home hours ago, so he answered it himself. "Turkey sounds lovely," he said, shutting down his computer as his wife told him with hopeful excitement about how she'd first brined, and then injected sauces into the bird, continuing to describe the rest of her evening with the same detail. She made dinner much later now, since the last time he'd come home before eight was when Ana was still living at home.

"On my way now, dear," Augustus said, as he slipped his arms through his trench coat. He'd just have to try Ana again tomorrow.

19
NICOLAS

Worthless overseer. What do we even pay him for?

"The roads are closed," Whitman said, when he answered Nicolas' call. "And most of the phone lines have been unreliable."

"Don't y'all have snowplows?" Nicolas was incredulous. Shouldn't they be used to this stuff? Plan for it?

Heavy sigh from the other end. *Clearly thinks I'm a complete idiot.* "Aye, Mr. Deschanel. We have snowplows, but ya have to understand that when God decides he's goin' to play his games, man's machines can only do s'much."

"I fail to understand how your island can completely shut down in a storm, when storms are pretty much the only thing you have up there, no?"

Another sigh, possibly annoyance this time. "No'sir, ya forgot moose, and Stephen King."

Nicolas smiled. *Oh, he has jokes now.* "Look. Maybe you think I'm being difficult but I haven't spoken with my cousin in a week. It's unlike her. She isn't answering her phone when I call, and—"

"Her phone is prolly down," Alex interjected.

"*Or,* she isn't answering because something is wrong." When Alex didn't respond, he added, "Isn't there someone who can check on her? Coast Guard, or whatever? Surely you have emergency vehicles?"

"We do, but only fer emergencies."

Nicolas tried to keep his voice level, despite his growing anger. As unhelpful as he was, Alex was also the only person Nicolas had contact with on the island, and who might be able to help him figure this out. "Would a missing person in a storm not be an emergency, Mr. Whitman?"

"We dunno know that she's missing. It's not uncommon a'tall for people to go dark when the big storms hit. We only have s'much equipment to clear the roads, and the island doesn't have the power and phone resources that the cities do. We can sometimes be without power, or phones, for weeks. Heck, we even had a winter where we were dark almost the entire season. People here are used to this, and they have expensive generators, and solid planning, and we get through it."

"But Ana is *not* used to this. This is her first Maine winter... well, hell, it's her first winter at all, really. All we ever get is a drop in humidity here. She has no idea what she's doing," Nicolas reminded him.

"I went over and helped her winter-proof the house. I showed her how t'use the generator, and where the food storage went. With all due respect, I went out of m'way to make sure she *did* know what she was doing 'fore the storm hit." Alex sounded more proud than defensive.

When Nicolas said nothing, Alex offered, "Maybe I could try to call the neighbors. There's only a couple'a houses out on the bend where she lives. The St. Andrews boys are good folks, so if they're not snowed in I could ask them t'check on her."

Nicolas brightened a bit. Now they were getting somewhere. "Perfect. But if her phone lines are down, won't theirs be, too? And for that matter, shouldn't yours be?"

"I live on the other side of the island. They usually go down in sections. But yea, if hers are down, theirs will be too. Though, if they answer—"

"Then we know it's not her phone line," Nicolas finished, realizing the implications of Alex making this phone call. What would he do if something *was* wrong? Hopefully one of the brothers could go check on her, but what if they couldn't?

Nicolas was getting ahead of himself, and was never at his best when his mind spun this way. He felt that same helplessness when his sister went missing.

Stop over-thinking this, you idiot. You're acting like Oz.

"Can you call now?" Nicolas pressed.

"Absolutely. And I will call ya right back."

"Please do."

20
ALEX

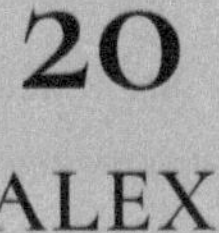

Alex cradled the phone and exhaled. He didn't like liars, but lying was exactly what he was going to need to do. And do it well. He was taught never to tell untruths, but even his mother recognized there were times when a lie was not only better, but safer. She'd died believing it.

Though several days had passed, his nerves hadn't recovered from overhearing Ana and Finn's conversation. While his mind searched for the right thing to do next, as the storm worsened, his options dwindled. He was far from giving up, however. The call from Ana's cousin only quickened his desire for resolution. If Ana wasn't communicating with her family, either, then Alex knew he had no time to waste. He only hoped he wasn't too late.

Alex took another deep breath. Steady. With one hand he squeezed the back of the chair, and with the other he slowly dialed the phone. Nicolas Deschanel answered on the first ring.

"Good news! Ana is just fine. She was a little shaken up

from the storm, so she's been staying with the boys. They're taking good care of her, ya know, so alls' well." Alex hoped he sounded convincing.

Silence and then finally an exhale. "Thank... *god.* I know it probably seemed like I was overreacting, but I was worried, with it being her first winter and all..." he rambled on some more, but Alex only heard bits and pieces because the realization Nicolas believed his lie filled him with nervous excitement.

"Aw, don't fret. It's natural to worry about yer loved ones and she's lucky to have someone care so much. I'm sure once she's back home, she'll give ya a call and tell ya all about it. Heck, I'm sure she'd call from their house, but long distance is so expensive these days..." As soon as it was out of his mouth, Alex regretted it. *Long distance is free you idgit!*

A long pause from Nicolas Deschanel's end. "Sure, sure, well I appreciate your help Mr. Whitman, and if you happen to talk to them again, tell her she can call collect." *Well, at least he didn't call me out for lying.* "Okay?"

"Of course, I sure will, Mr. Deschanel. Now take care."

"Thanks. And you."

"Do be sure to call if I can be of anymore assistance." *Please stop talking, you old fool.*

"On second thought, why don't you just give me the number for where she's staying?"

Alex dropped the phone in the cradle, pretending not to hear the last request. No, he couldn't give Nicolas Deschanel that phone number. That wouldn't do at all.

His phone rang again. Alex knew who it was, and what he wanted. He stared at it, waiting for the call to go to voicemail, but once his voice sang to the caller to leave a message, the caller dropped.

Alex sunk into the sofa and closed his eyes. He hadn't lied about calling the boys. He started calling them the morning after the storm started, long before Nicolas Deschanel had reached out asking him for help. Unlike Nicolas, Alex realized that even a day without communication with Ana was worrisome. He didn't need nearly a week to trigger a call to action. She needed him.

When the brothers didn't answer his calls, Alex thought, *Well let's try the Auslanders,* who lived on the other side of Ana, further around the bend. Much to his surprise, they did answer.

"Oh, Mrs. Auslander, so sorry to bother ya," he said. "Yer phone lines are fine then, yea?"

"Oh yea, they haven't gone down at all. Lucky year, Mr. Whitman. It's only the roads right now," she said. "And the power, from time to time."

Phones were fine there, which meant they should be fine at Ana's and at the St. Andrews place. Yet, neither were answering. "Say, Gertrude, ya haven't heard or seen anything from the new girl have ya? I was just wantin' to check in with her and make sure she's faring okay."

When Gertrude responded, she lowered her voice, and it sounded like she was covering the phone with her hand. "See, I was hoping she had come to stay with you. The lights in her house have been off for days, and no one has turned them on at all. I know, I've been watchin'."

Ana Deschanel was not the first person to struggle in a Maine storm, nor would she be the last. But getting her family involved would only worry them unnecessarily. The island was closed, and until it was open, there'd be nothing they could do for Ana.

But now that Alex knew for sure she was missing, his mind

resumed churning. If he waited for the roads to clear, he could be waiting a while.

Enough thinking. Inaction is doin' nothin' for that girl, and it may already be too late.

It was time for Alex to get involved.

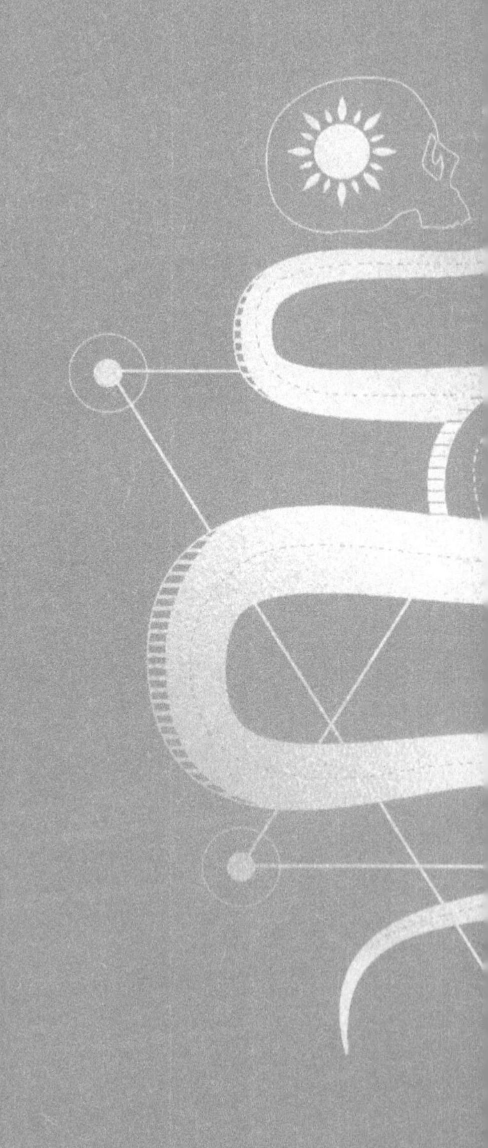

21

NICOLAS

Nicolas smelled the bullshit, but he didn't understand *why* the old overseer would lie to him.

Ana had mentioned these boys before. The younger brother she hadn't met yet. But Jonathan St. Andrews... Nicolas knew she didn't like him. Their interactions were unpleasant enough that she'd taken the time to talk about the man's rudeness at length.

So now he was supposed to accept she was hanging out, drinking hot cider, and playing Yahtzee with them? Something about that didn't sit right. Then there'd been a marked changed in Alex's tone between the two calls. On the first, he couldn't hide his annoyance, and then, on the second, he was almost *too* eager to help. Nicolas felt pretty certain Alex wasn't being forthcoming, but what he couldn't understand, no matter how much he racked his brain, was *why*.

And now, the crazy ass wasn't answering *his* phone, either.

Nicolas considered a *Deliverance*-style situation. Obviously they had to eat during the winter. Then, he imagined a sex-slave ring where Ana was sold to Ukrainians. She was thirty, but still had her looks, and could still pass for twenty-two in the right light. It wasn't *that* far-fetched.

Even at his most imaginative, though, Nicolas had a hard time believing they were keeping her as a food source or a means of income. But if not, then what?

Nicolas made some phone calls. First he checked into flights, and although some were cancelled, they expected to have more operational the following week into Portland, and sooner into Boston. He then checked the Coast Guard, and they recommended he call the Casco Bay Ferry service. The man there told him even if he could get a flight into the area, getting to the island was a no-go for a while. Sometimes, he said, when the winters were *wicked harsh*, the ferries might not run at all. He told Nicolas there were some private services, but they were even less likely to run in bad weather.

Nicolas was stuck with information he was fairly certain to be inaccurate, and no means of going there to check for himself.

He had only two options, he figured. Sit back and let the helplessness consume him, or find a way to get to Summer Island, and Ana.

22
JONATHAN

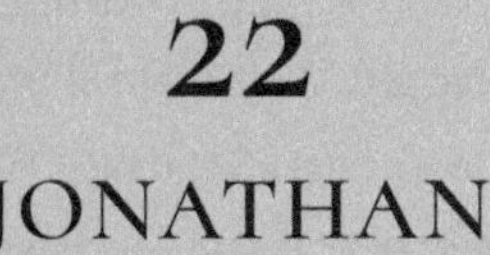

Ana was still unconscious a week after they found her. Jon didn't have the experience to know when she might wake up, or what kept her from doing so. All he could do was continue to ensure she had fluids, nutrients, and regular monitoring.

Although Jon had seen patients at his father's practice independently, usually when Andrew was out of town or tending an emergency, this was by far the most complex and serious case he had managed himself. If it weren't for his father's training, Ana might have died. Equally, if his father hadn't been a medical cowboy, with all his contraband equipment, Jon wouldn't have had the needed resources.

Finn kept a vigilant watch. He still slept by her side, and spent most of the day there. He had an old copy of *Walden Pond* he read to her off and on.

Jonathan knew there was no real medical evidence that talking or reading to an unconscious patient helped in any significant way. It was usually prescribed for the families, not the patients. But when Jon suggested it, Finn leapt at the idea. He was hungry for anything that might make him feel useful.

The storm had worsened, continuing a few days after they found her. Finn predicted it would last a night, but it had lasted three, with no wane in intensity. They were now buried in two feet of snow, with the roads closed for the foreseeable future. Summer Island was virtually shut down… and shut off from the rest of the world.

When Jon saw the number of the overseer come up on his phone display, a sinking feeling emerged deep within him. He knew why Alex Whitman was calling, and he also knew Alex didn't like him one bit. Alex was one of the few people on the island who didn't accept Jon for who he was, and anytime they passed in town, he could see Alex taking his measure. He was pretty certain Alex figured him for a closet serial killer or some other sort of psychopath, and Jon didn't possess the skills, or the desire, to set the record straight.

The funny thing was, Jon thought the same thing about Alex. While Finn laughed it off, claiming Alex was simply strange, Jon could never shake the suspicion that Alex knew more about his parents' murders than he let on. Most of the islanders felt sympathy for the man who had, as a boy, watched both his mother and father slaughtered, miraculously escaping the same fate. To Jon, Alex bore the shifty, dishonest look of someone hiding something significant.

But while Jon had never gossiped about Alex, Alex hadn't done him the same courtesy. There were others on the island who would take their animals to Jon's office and keep an eye on him the entire time, their faces betraying their real feelings. What did they think, that he had become a vet for some sick and twisted purpose?

People fear what they don't understand, Finn had said once. *You're not an open book, so they can't read you. And if they can't read you, they fill in the blanks with their own ideas. Human nature is distrustful.*

It's really none of their business who I am.

Since when have people on this island cared what is, and is not, their business?

So yes, there were a handful of people on the island who assumed the worst about Jon. If there were more, they were better about hiding their feelings. The overly suspicious handful included Jon's neighbors two houses down: Gertrude and Hans Auslander.

The Auslanders were second generation Germans, both born on the island. The rumor around town was that they were also cousins. First cousins. They had no children, and were both nearing seventy. Nosy, assumptive, they were extremely prolific within the gossip circles. Many of the island's rumors started with one or both of them. In the case of Jon, he was almost positive Gertrude was responsible for ninety percent or more of the slander about him. While she was quite pleasant to his face, Jon knew what a malicious piece of work she was.

When Alex Whitman called the first time, Jon didn't answer because he was indisposed. Then, Gertrude the Gossip called less than an hour later, and he knew something was up. When Alex called a second time, Jon's avoidance of the call was deliberate, and that was when the sinking feeling started to set in.

It was pointless to tell Finn. He'd laugh and tell Jon he was being paranoid. His brother, who in one breath could be understanding about the distrustful nature of people, in another would tell Jon off for being too distrustful himself. *Not distrustful. Realistic.*

Then, the phone lines *did* finally go down. Jon didn't feel nearly as relieved as he might've expected. Although he wouldn't have to agonize over the calls from Alex and the Auslanders, Jon and Finn's only tie to the outside world had been abruptly severed. By the end of the week, with Ana still unconscious, Jon found himself wishing he'd reached out for help when he had the chance, even if any assistance from the mainland was on the short end of a long shot.

There was also the matter of Ana's head injury. It was not only healing well, it was almost completely *gone*. Jon's first reaction was to look at the other side of her head, to see if he was mistaken on the wound location. But no, it was there, in the correct place. But... healed. It had the pinkish look of a forming scar.

He asked Finn for a second opinion.

"Look at the cut on her head. Tell me what you see." Jon had nodded toward her, arms crossed.

"What am I looking for, exactly?" Finn squinted.

"Her wound! Describe it."

Finn flashed him an odd look, and Jon could almost read his little brother's thoughts. *He thinks I've gone off the deep end. That I haven't had enough sleep.*

"Ooookay," Finn said and leaned over her. "Am I supposed to tell you the colors... or compare it to a shape... or?"

"Just tell me how it looks compared to when we brought her here!" Jon snapped.

"Oh! It looks great," Finn praised and smiled at him. "You did good Jon, it's almost like the gash was never there."

"Thanks," Jon replied, and dismissed him. *Almost like the gash was never there.* Yes, that was the problem. Lacerations didn't heal that fast. With a cut that deep, they should be changing the bandages for a few more weeks. Even in ideal conditions, the healing she'd experienced in a week would take months. Maybe years.

He had no medical explanation, and no one to call, or ask. When he checked the old medical books in the library, there were examples of people healing quickly, but not at freakish rates like this. If she was miraculously regenerating this fast, why was she not awake?

Jon often found himself wandering to the study, where Mr. Jenkins and Cocoa were convalescing. Both had healed well, but with the roads closed, they remained under Jon's care. Angus, their old Saint Bernard, was Finn's dog, but these two furry patients—much like any of the animals Jon brought home to watch over—felt like an extension of Jon himself. He curled up on the carpet next to Mr. Jenkins and let his head come to a light rest on the dog's chest, listening for the soothing sounds of a regular heartbeat. The dog gave a light, relaxed shudder, as all animals did when they detected Jon's comforting presence.

The easy part for Jon came in saving their lives. The challenge was in returning them to their owners, and saying goodbye.

Except, Cocoa's owner was here, Jon realized. Surprised he hadn't thought of it sooner, he lifted the brown tabby and carried her gently into the room where Ana was resting. As soon as Jon set her down on the bed, Cocoa instantly nuzzled under Ana's hand, purring, looking for affection.

Finn looked at him with an expression Jon read as shock mixed with happiness.

Later that evening, Finn came to him and said he needed to try and recover some of the catch he'd stored.

"Impossible," Jon countered. "There's two feet of snow outside. Our snow thrower can't handle that. Hell, neither could our small plow. We're going to have to wait."

"No," Finn responded. "Difficult is all. We are going to need the lobster because we won't have enough food for two of us, let alone three."

"All right," Jon conceded, heading for his jacket. "You're the expert."

"No. Only one of us can work on it. Someone needs to stay with Ana."

Great, Jon thought. "Where's the key to the plow then?"

Finn shook his head as he maneuvered into his winter gear. "It's quicker if I do it, because I know exactly where to plow, and what to do. Your delicate lady fingers won't last as long," he quipped.

"Then who's going to stay with Ana?" Jon asked, ignoring the jab.

"You, obviously," Finn said, and then was out the door, the screen banging behind him, before Jon could say anything else.

23
ANA

Cold snow... warm hands... ice against her face, warmth consuming her... throbbing in her temple, the amplification of her heartbeat with every breath... pulsing... as if her head was literally going to explode...

"... I went to the woods because I wished to live deliberately..."

... not her thoughts, or her words... someone else's...

"... to front only the essential facts of life, and see if I could not learn what it had to teach, and not, when I came to die, discover that I had not lived. I did not wish to live what was not life, living is so dear; nor did I wish to practice resignation, unless it was quite necessary..."

"Does it help her?"

"Yes, it helps her." Lying.

Later. "The storm is over."

Later still. "A week. It's been a week."

"I can't..."

Black and grey cells, blooming into pink and white, healing, multiplying. *Yes, sleep Ana. Heal.*

Soft fur against her arm… a gentle purr. Warm cotton… hot breath against her neck… hand twined in hand. Familiarity. Warmth. Confusion. Safety.

Deeper, deeper. Sleep. Heal.

24
FINNEGAN

When was the last time Finn used the word love?

He loved conquering the sea. He loved the little island where he'd been born and raised. He loved the taste of coffee from Tim Horton's. He loved a lobster roll—when he was the one making it. He loved his brother Jon. Had loved both of their parents. When had he last said it, though?

Yesterday. To her. Sort of. To her sleeping body, he'd said something close enough, with no response other than the same light breathing he'd heard for a week. He hadn't exactly said *I love you,* either, but *I could love you.* Was he a fool? He had feelings for a girl who wasn't even *awake.*

Being in love was unappealing to Finn, on many levels. He had his life all figured out. His days were his own. He chose his commitments. He didn't have to compromise. He never had to think about whether or not his decisions affected others, or make promises to change, promises he couldn't keep. Jon had no expectations of him whatsoever. His dog, Angus, only required Finn to feed him twice a day, and give him the occasional dose of affection. Finn had a low-maintenance lifestyle, filled with the few things he cared about, and that was how he liked it.

That night at Ana's house had changed him. He didn't understand just how, or how much, but he wasn't the same man. Even if she didn't know it, he'd grown closer to her these past days as he unloaded the contents of his thoughts and memories in a way he'd never done with anyone, just as she'd done with him.

Angus warming up to Ana had been another defining moment. Angus was the nicest dog in the world... to Finn and Jon. To everyone else, he was Cujo's bigger, uglier cousin. He'd bark at everyone when taken for walks, pee on someone's foot if they lingered too long, and growl like a wild predator if someone came to the door. In reality, Angus was the gentlest dog on the whole island, and everyone knew it, except Angus.

After the first night, Finn went down to get something to eat and when he came back, Angus had wiggled his oversized body under the covers, cuddling with Ana. Cuddling! His head rested on her chest, eyes daring Finn to move him.

Angus ultimately relented in giving Finn his spot back, opting to curl up at the foot of the bed, on the floor, guarding. Each time Ana stirred, his ears perked hopefully.

Finn had talked to her, read to her, and told her stories. Lots of stories. Mostly embarrassing tales from his youth. He talked about Jon, his father's practice, his mother's patient instruction, the people they grew up around. He talked about his books.

Sometimes, forgetting that their conversations weren't interactive, he'd laugh at parts of the story where she should be laughing, or pause for reactions. When he realized a response wasn't coming, he'd chuckle and keep going.

He even told her about his "first," Andrea McElroy, sister to

Jackson McElroy, father of Mr. Jenkins downstairs. After that rolled off the tongue with relative ease, he actually told her about Tara, his college girlfriend. Tara was the only girl that Finn had ever used the word "love" with, but she was also the one who'd opened his eyes to what his future love life would be: a series of casual encounters. What was it she'd said when they broke up? That Finn going to college for a degree in literature was like putting a pig in a tuxedo. Tara thought he was trying to be something he wasn't. He never understood this point of view. His mother had taught him he could be anything he wanted.

Finn talked a lot about what they'd do when she woke up. He would to take her out on his boat and show her the sea; how to set the traps, buoy the trawl. He wanted to take her all over the island and show her the hidden spots visitors normally missed. To the old mill and the granary, the forgotten lake. Up to the old, haunted lighthouse.

Finn continued to plow the path. Scoop, lift, backup, dump, down again, scoop, lift, repeat. Even through his protective winter gear, he was chilled to the bone, shivering. Finn knew he would have to do this job in shifts or risk getting sick. The storm was over, and the air was still, but a biting cold pierced the air. The freezing rain at the tail end of the storm left a thin, but dangerous, layer of ice atop the snow.

He wondered if Ana had family they should call. He'd mentioned it to Jon, but his brother had rejected the idea, reminding him that until Ana woke up, they would have no way of getting contact information.

Jon had been very attentive to her medical needs, and was diligent about keeping her fed, hydrated, her wound dressed, even if he was unnecessarily methodical and cold about it. Finn laughed to himself, imagining his brother, upstairs, awkwardly staring at the wall while sitting by her side.

Off to the east, past Ana's house, Finn could see the Auslander home, and what looked like Hans standing on the porch, looking his way. Although the house was a good half-mile away, the view was clear, and Finn waved. Hans didn't wave back, continuing his stare in Finn's general direction.

He didn't think about it for long. His mind kept wandering back to Ana.

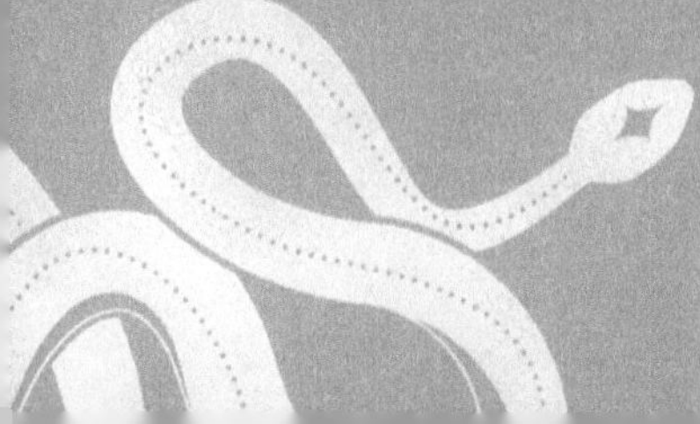

25
JONATHAN

Day eight of Ana's long rest came and went without ceremony, but the elapsed time wasn't lost on Jon. The longer the girl remained in her deep sleep, the more potential for things to go wrong.

Though the phone lines had been down for days, it wouldn't be long before Whitman could get his truck across the island. He'd have plenty to say about Jon and his methods, never mind that Ana was alive because of his quick thinking and experience.

The only reason Jon thought the Auslanders hadn't found a way over was their lack of mobility. Alex had been taking care of their errands for several years now, and they hardly ever left the house, except for town events. Gertrude only allowed Alex to help with certain things, anyway. Trips into town were a chance to chat with the other busybodies about the latest town gossip.

Jon wondered how much her desire to be nosy and "help-ful," could or would overcome her better sense. Finn seemed to think there was another storm coming, and for the first time in his life, Jon welcomed it.

He was in a constant state of anxiousness, between Ana's continued sleep, her miraculous and medically impossible healing, and the growing concerns regarding fellow residents. Constantly restless and feeling helpless, not knowing when she'd wake up and if she did, if she'd be all right.

He couldn't resist the urge to continue studying her wound. The pink scar tissue was fading, and if he could believe what he was seeing, she might not even *have* a scar in a few days. *I'm losing my mind. There's no other explanation.*

FINN SPENT THE ENTIRE DAY PRIOR PLOWING. UNFORTUNATELY, HIS efforts proved to be for nothing, as he discovered the storm had blown the doors down, and spilled the tanks. Most of the lobster had perished, rendering them inedible.

"Weeks of fishing, gone." Finn was angry, and in one of his rare melancholy moods.

Jon had no words of comfort for him, but he silently mourned Finn's wasted efforts. "How many days of food do we have left?"

Finn ran his hands through his hair, blowing out a deep breath. "A week, maybe? More? The roads might open up in a few days, but I think the next storm coming in is going to close them back down again."

"But we have the canned food, right?" Jon pressed.

"I took most of it over to Gertrude and Hans two weeks ago, remember?" Jon did remember. Finn had done it out of kindness, when Alex had been remiss in his grocery duties.

"Yes, but you were supposed to replace it."

Finn sighed, shifting in shame at his obvious and unforgivable miss. "I meant to, but time got away from me."

"Seriously, Finn?" Jon stopped. He forced himself not to chastise him any further. Recent days had been taxing on them both. "So what are our options?" he asked, realizing he already knew.

"Get across town somehow to the food storage..."

On the other side of the island. "Christ."

"Well, there's Dad's old snowcat..."

Jon laughed. "That old beast has been sitting out in the driveway for a decade. Dad never even bothered to cover it."

"I know, and I have no idea how to use it. I mean, the damned thing is for *commercial use* for god's sake. Dad said people go through training to operate this kind of equipment..." Finn's voice trailed off. "But it can't be that hard, right? And it's unlikely there will be anyone else on the roads."

Jon paused, honestly speechless. When had this situation gotten to the point where he'd allow his little brother to risk his neck going across town in an oversized vehicle that no one knew how to drive, and hadn't been started in over a decade? Why hadn't he used the phone to call for help, when it was still an option? How had they let it get this far?

He could see Finn sharing the same thought process. Before Finn could speak, Jon said, "I'll go."

Finn laughed. "No way. You might break a nail."

"Hilarious. I won't have you risking your neck."

"You won't even get on the quads in the summer."

"That's different. It's because I don't actually enjoy riding them," Jon protested, only half-lying.

"And you're scared as shit to crash in one. You've never manned *Forbia*. You don't run the plow..."

"You're no more qualified than I am to drive it," was the best Jon could come up with.

"And you're no more qualified to fly a plane than I am, but

who would you rather trust your life to if the pilot suddenly died?"

"If Ana wakes up, she's going to want you there."

"You can be there, right? You did it before with no problem," Finn teased, both of them remembering Jon's discomfort. He'd sat there, hands in his lap, shifting his focus between various things in the room off and on for hours. He'd get up for a drink, come back, fidget some more. Jon supposed talking to her would have been a better way to pass the time, but he could think of absolutely nothing to say. His awkwardness apparently extended even to unconscious women.

Before he could say anything, Finn was already out the door, apparently off to see if he could get the snowcat fueled and fired up.

26

ANA

College graduation. Everyone was there. Her family, fellow students from the past four years, good and bad; her friends and sorority sisters. Everyone who was anyone in her life was packed into the crowded stadium.

Ana sat clutching her degree amidst the laughter, applause, anecdotes, and nervous speeches. She could've been giving the valedictorian speech. No one but Nicolas knew she'd intentionally dropped her grade point average to avoid standing in front of thousands of people. Her comfort meant more than a silly title.

She fidgeted, as the familiar wave of panic rushed over her. The sounds around her were hardly loud, but in her heart and chest they were deafening. Her head pulsed with every new round of applause; every name called. She was grateful for her chair because the dizziness rolled in and out, like the flow of an ocean tide.

"Just keep your eyes on me, Muffins," Nicolas had said before the ceremony, using his private nickname for her. She hadn't asked him for help, hadn't said how nervous she was. He'd known. If they didn't have two very different sets of parents, she would have sworn they were twins.

She tried to do exactly as he suggested, but she kept losing him in the sea of faces. He'd deliberately worn a bright pink shirt to make this easier for her, but the crowd seemed endless and not even that stood out.

Ana squeezed her toes tightly into her shoes, one of a half-dozen private ways she controlled her stress. When that didn't bring relief, she nestled her tongue firmly against the roof of her mouth, inhaling, exhaling. The few times she was called to accept something at the podium were the easiest because it kept her mind focused on controlling each step, one foot in front of the other. When she was idle, it was much harder.

After the ceremony, her family crowded around her with words of encouragement and pride, but it wasn't until she felt her cousin's hand slip into hers that her heartbeat slowed some and the normalcy returned. She accepted hugs and returned kisses in a blur of familial comfort, while holding tightly to his hand.

"You are *normal," Nicolas said to her once. "And if you're not, then we're all seriously fucked because if everyone else is normal and* that's *the standard, we might as well start preparing for the zombie apocalypse."*

"Well, start preparing fucker, because it's coming," she'd said.

Oftentimes, she had no idea what point he was trying to get across with the things he said. But it didn't matter, because she laughed. Reassuring her was Nicolas' real intention.

Ana was never one to label herself. It was the years of therapy, and her father's failed but earnest attempts to understand, that had done that. Complicated was not a word she used to flatter herself, and it had little do with the family she came from. She would have always preferred to be simpler, even if Nicolas assured her people like that *were harbingers of doom.*

The graduation party was next. Ana mentally steeled herself to exercise yet another social skill she lacked: small talk.

Nicolas gifted her a few moments of sanity by telling the family he'd drive her over. In the car, he didn't bother telling her how nice she looked, how proud he was. He knew she didn't need to hear that from him. He said only, "I'm bouncing tonight if the beer sucks."

He'd never failed her. Never let her down, never abandoned her; had always been there in the moments she was most afraid.

So why, why was he not there now, when she was in the darkest place she had ever known. Why?

ANA OPENED HER EYES.

27
NICOLAS

Adrienne called him a couple times to see if he knew anything of Ana's whereabouts, but Nicolas told her he wasn't worried. Ana and Adrienne were very similar creatures, except that Ana had never been through anything as traumatic as the few lost years Adrienne endured. Adrienne was healing, but would always be broken. Nicolas and Oz had an unspoken, shared fear that certain stressors would break her again, and this time she'd run off for good. He wouldn't trouble her with his concerns, especially considering they were of the potential missing person variety. Too close to home.

Nicolas met Oz for drinks several days after Oz's peculiar visit. It was Oz's idea, and despite how things had gone the last time they hung out, Nicolas was relieved both when Oz suggested it, and also when he acted as though nothing at all had happened. This was preferable for Nicolas, who had bigger things on his mind than his friend's mood swings.

It didn't take long before Oz, in his usual quiet, diplomatic way, confronted *him* and asked if something was wrong with Ana.

"I think something has happened, yes," Nicolas said cautiously.

Oz eyed him. "Something has happened?" he echoed.

"Ah, fuck, I don't fucking know," Nicolas said, dropping his guard. "It's been eight days. We haven't gone that long without talking in years, and she's called me *every goddamn day* from Maine. That dumb-fuck overseer told me she was fine, and over at the neighbor's house or some shit, but his story was really fucking weird, Ozzy, like he was hiding something. Now, he won't even answer my calls."

Oz leaned over his beer. Nicolas couldn't see his expression. Nicolas half-expected Oz to offer a reasonable explanation, but he seemed to understand that wasn't what Nicolas was after. "What are you going to do?"

"I've been asking myself the same question every day for a week, Ozzy. So far none of the answers are working out for me."

"Have you thought of going up there?" Oz's eyes were wild again suddenly, the way they'd been the last time they met.

Nicolas snorted. "Fuck yes, I have. You know I have. I can get a flight into Boston or Portland, but the island is shut down. None of the ferries are running, and I can't find someone who will charter me over."

"Well, that has to change soon, right? People can't be stuck on an island forever without someone helping out," Oz said confidently. When Nicolas looked up at him, Oz dropped his eyes again, looking back down at his drink.

"You'd think Ozzy, but you'd be wrong. One of the guys I talked to said there are winters where the ferries don't run at all after the first storm hits. They *prepare* for this shit," he ranted, knocking his fist on the bar. "You know, it's times like this that make me consider investing in a private plane."

Oz gave him a half-hearted smile. "Right, because if you had one, you'd know exactly what to do with it."

"That's what a fucking *pilot* is for, Ozzy."

Nicolas felt better after talking to Oz, even though he was no closer to figuring out what he wanted to do. Subsequent calls to Alex Whitman remained unreturned. He knew he should go up there anyway, try and throw his weight around. Even if he didn't find a way to Summer Island, he'd at least feel less useless than he felt sitting around New Orleans.

As if reading his mind, Oz ventured, with a touch of nervousness in his voice, "If you want, we could go up there. You and me, I mean."

"What about Adrienne?" He left the rest of the question unspoken.

"She'll be fine for a few days," Oz said, sounding more as if he was trying to convince himself.

"Hey, you need a few days off. I'm not judging," Nicolas threw his hands up with a laugh.

Oz rolled his eyes, but said nothing. Nicolas had touched a nerve, but this time he didn't think troubles with Adrienne were what was on his friend's mind. Oz had been acting weird for a while. Despite his overriding concern for Ana, Nicolas couldn't deny his interest in figuring out what was going on with Oz. Especially now when, of all things, Oz had offered to join him.

"If I can help out at all, even if only by being your incredibly handsome and charming wingman, then that's more useful than I've felt at home lately," Oz answered, still inspecting his beer.

"Let me think about it," Nicolas said, but he had already thought about it and decided. Though he was still concerned for Ana's safety, a small part of him began to wonder if her elusiveness wasn't personal after all. If she wasn't trying to send him a message, of sorts. If that were to happen—if he were to show up, only to find she had been intentionally avoiding him—then, selfishly, he wanted Oz there to soften the blow.

You know Ana. She's always preferred to be alone, Adrienne had said to Nicolas, when he was the one supposed to be reassuring her.

Yes, but she's always made an exception for me, Nicolas thought, but didn't say, to his sister. He and Ana had faced everything together, hand in hand, presenting a united front against the world. They'd never needed anything but each other, and she'd never once shown any indication this bothered her.

No, Nicolas concluded, *something is definitely wrong. She would never shut me out.*

Nicolas decided they'd leave right away. He'd have his assistant make the arrangements.

In the meantime, there was someone he needed to visit first.

28
ALEX

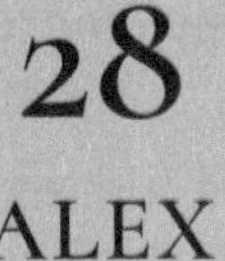

Alex could make excuses all day about the weather outside, but as long as he was in his house doing nothing, he was as guilty as the St. Andrews boys. *Who knows what they've done to her due to my inaction.*

"We're gonna see dat boy on the news one day," Alex's mother had said about Jon, years ago. She shook her head, as if there were some things in life that couldn't be helped. "Poor Claire. One child is hell's spawn, the other a future serial killer." Angela Whitman was wrong about a lot of things, but Alex had never forgotten those words. And neither brother had ever done a single thing that would change his opinion for the better. True, Jon was kind to animals, and Finn was always the first to help Mrs. Auslander plow her driveway, but Alex knew even bad people were not *all* bad. Everyone had something nice you could say about them. His mother had taught him that, too. It was why she never left Alex's father, Bill, even when he beat her so badly she could no longer stand upright.

The calls with Nicolas Deschanel were eating at him. There

was a change in the man's voice at the end of their last call, one that made Alex wonder if his lie was really so convincing after all. *No matter. He can't do anything for her. No one is getting on or off this island for a long time.*

The Auslanders radioed him earlier that afternoon, telling him Finn had fired up Andrew's old snowcat and headed north. *Where that boy is goin' is anyone's guess*, Gertrude said, but Alex was sure he knew. The only thing that would get people risking their neck on the roads was a lack of resources. The town food storage coincidentally backed Alex's own property. He estimated Finn would make it there by late nightfall, and returning at that time would be hazardous.

It was a given Alex would watch for him. The bigger question looming in his mind was whether or not he'd offer Finn his hospitality, or something else.

Alex fidgeted in his study. The window fogged from his hot tea and it made him sleepy. Alex would need to have a plan before Finn arrived. And what if Finn wouldn't make eye contact when he asked if he had seen the girl? Or if Alex shuffled his feet and lost his words? What would Alex do then? Hold Finn against his will? Call the sheriff? Go out to the house himself, where the crazier brother was still holding poor Ana hostage? What then?

And what if Alex did go with Finn back to the St. Andrews home, attempt to rescue Ana, and she refused his help? She wouldn't be the first. Alex's mother had done exactly that, and learned her lesson the hard way. All those other women. He could have helped them, he knew he could have. He would've done anything to save them. But how do you save someone from themselves?

Ana was different. He knew she was. She had to be. There was no doubt in his mind. But then, why was he covered in sweat, pacing endlessly? If it were true, why hadn't he gone over there immediately, and demanded answers? Why had he waited *over a week*?

No, he told himself. *She's the one. She has to be.*

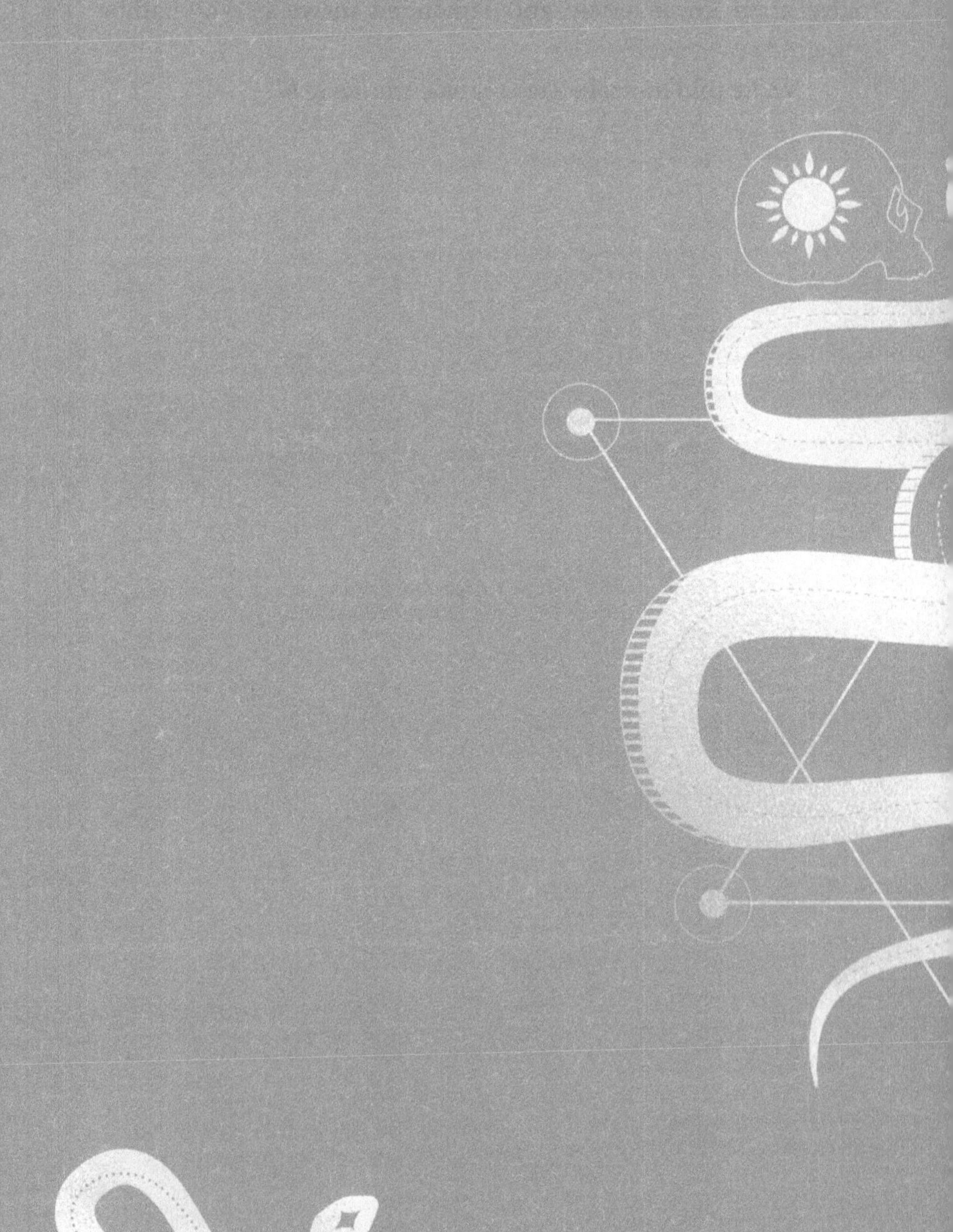

29
AUGUSTUS

Augustus couldn't decide which emotion was most overwhelming at the moment: anger or worry. Anger was easier. He experienced both on a daily basis. When he was angry, he was, if nothing else, in control. He could decide when he was ready for the anger to subside, and move on. There was no confusion or hesitation, just a realization, followed by action.

Worry, on the other hand... worry was full of holes; full of unknowns and things Augustus had absolutely no control over. His thoughts would take over, spiraling in dangerous directions, and then the anger would return, because nothing angered him more than being out of control.

A week was a long time not to hear from his daughter. She could be peculiar at times, but she was always good to her family. This was the girl who'd technically lived on campus but stayed at home most nights. The child who used to fall asleep in his study because she'd rather be close to him, even if he was working. The young lady who'd called him when her boyfriend had become too friendly. She didn't call Nicolas, she called

Daddy. She was introspective, and maybe even challenging at times, but they were deeply connected in their own ways.

She was either being uncharacteristically selfish or something was wrong. Believing she was being selfish was easier. Anger was controllable, and temporary. If something *was* wrong, then sitting in an empty skyscraper in the Central Business District of New Orleans made him about as useful as that intern he fired today.

"If you're fine and just being a brat, God help us both," he muttered as he picked up the phone once again. He sighed as he set it down, the results no different.

"I thought you might still be here, Uncle Augustus," came a startling voice from the doorway. It was past eight, and the rest of the office had left hours ago. He was used to being the last one to leave. "Am I interrupting?"

"No, Nicolas, it's fine," he said, scattering papers around his desk, embarrassed to be caught lost in his thoughts. "Did you need something?"

Nicolas sat down without being invited, but this didn't surprise Augustus. He was just like his father, Charles, who did as he pleased, and dared the world to adjust and follow suit.

"I'm going to Maine,." He came right to the point. "I can't say for certain, but something feels wrong and I can't sit back here like a fucking lame duck anymore." He winced. "Pardon my language."

Augustus set his mouth in a tight line. This changed things, but he had a responsibility to stay composed, for both their sakes. "So you haven't heard from her, either." He didn't know why he hadn't called Nicolas sooner. There was a small, insecure part of him that believed maybe she was calling everyone *but* him.

"Neither has Adrienne. I've booked my flight, and I'm leaving in a few hours. Oz is coming. The hard part is getting to the island. It's closed and they have no estimate on when the ferries will run again. I am planning to go anyway, wave around the family credit card, and see how far it gets me."

Augustus nodded, though he was already aware of the island situation. He had his secretary make some phone calls. *Thinking about surprising my daughter*, he'd said. Purely informational calls. No reason to get worked up over nothing, and he was still convinced there was an explanation for her silence.

"Perhaps the phone lines are down," Augustus said in a controlled voice. "If the island is shut down, it would be surprising if the phones were working fine."

Nicolas shook his head, sinking back in his chair like a wayward teenager. "No. I talked to the overseer. He said the phone lines were fine, as of a few days ago. Even if they're down now, it doesn't explain the first few days."

"What else did he say?" Augustus bristled.

"That she was fine, and hanging out at her neighbor's house. I asked why she hadn't called if she was fine, and he gave me some bullshit excuse about long distance calls being expensive. Even he realized it was bullshit. So I asked him to talk to her and tell her that if the neighbors were so cheap then she can call collect. When I tried to ask for their number so I could call directly he hung up on me." Nicolas sat up. "But that was almost a week ago, and do you think she's called?" He went on. "So, I looked up the neighbors' number, and tried to call myself. There's been no answer for days."

Augustus felt better already. *If the overseer said she was fine...* "She'll call when things clear up." *Control. Resolution. Back in the comfort zone.*

Nicolas laughed. His face flushed crimson, eyes narrowing. "No, she's *not* fine, Uncle, and I knew it before I even talked to that idiot. I don't trust him."

"What reason would he have for lying, Nicolas?"

"Who the fuck knows? I don't need to waste time wondering, because I know Ana. I know she would've called. She would've known that I'd be pulling my hair out with worry, and so would you, and Adrienne. The only thing Ana hates more than her own pain is being the cause of others'."

"Ana went to Maine to be alone. Has it occurred to you she might want space?"

"She doesn't," Nicolas stated confidently.

Augustus shifted in his leather chair. Nicolas was making it harder to put the worry to bed and he felt that cold, unwanted feeling coming back; the control receding. "I know," he started, slowly, methodically, "how close you two are. I know—"

"With all due respect sir, no. You don't." Level, intense gaze.

"—and I know your imagination is getting the better of you." *I have to believe that, because the alternative...* "And Nicolas, I *do* know. When my brother lost his mind, and Ekatherina died, it was me who ensured you and Ana had each other. Me who had you brought to Magnolia Grace to be raised with Ana, and when Charles decided it wasn't a good look for his son to live with his brother, I sent Ana to your place, as much as I could. I know how close you are because I laid the groundwork."

The look his nephew gave him suggested he'd never known this. Ana hadn't either. Augustus saw no point in pressing upon sore subjects with her.

Nicolas stood. He carelessly wiped his hands down his wrinkled shirt. "I wasn't looking for permission. I thought you might like to know."

Leave it alone, Nicolas. Ana, please call.

"I think if we give it some time..."

Nicolas gripped his spiky dark hair in frustration, as if ready to rip it out. "Time? Uncle Augustus, it's been over a week since *anyone* in the family has heard from your daughter. We have a man saying she's fine and having the time of her life, but he doesn't know that we *know* Ana, who she is and how she acts. She's quiet, but she is *ours*, and she would never, ever, *ever* let us suffer like this needlessly. She isn't cruel." He moved to the door. "I know you don't want to face this. Do you think I do? Without her..." Nicolas' voice trailed off, and he took a deep breath. "I can feel it in my bones. She *needs* me."

Yes. Augustus had felt it too, but ignored the nagging sense. Addressing it meant admitting he may have sent his daughter into danger and he could not—would not—believe something could ever happen to her.

Defeated, he reached into his desk and pulled out a credit card. He handed it to Nicolas. "Take this, then."

Nicolas waved it away. "Thank you, though."

Augustus stood up and opened Nic's hand, placed the card inside, and closed it again. "I'm not asking."

Nicolas nodded, looking at the card, or his feet, Augustus couldn't tell. "I'll call when I get there."

"Yes. And as soon as you know anything." He lowered his head so he could meet his nephew's eyes. "Anything, Nicolas. No matter what."

"I will," he said and left.

Augustus stood in the center of his office, feeling the blood drain from his face. He was now acutely aware of which emotion had won the battle.

30
JONATHAN

Nightfall was drawing near, and Finn wasn't back. Jon hadn't expected him this early, but it was no less disconcerting being unable to reach him, or know how he was faring with that damned snow contraption.

Jon remembered when his father had brought it home. It was the day Finn got suspended from high school for getting into a fight, defending Jon.

Their father had been so excited over the blasted thing. The model was built in the seventies, for military search and rescue operations, over six tons of heavy steel and rubber. Dan Gundersson had traded it as payment for his long-running medical tab, and Jon's father didn't care that he'd never use it, that it was ridiculous and impractical. "Dad, the island is only two miles long," Jon had said.

Andrew St. Andrews had given him the eyebrow raise. Not the quick rise and fall of amusement, but the other one. The disapproving one. "Your brother will understand."

Of course Finn would understand. Finn was good with his hands, was more masculine. What was masculinity, really though? A way to measure a set of interests and abilities? Jon had always felt masculinity was less about ability and more about confidence, but saying so would probably result in his father calling him soft. He could handle people calling him different, odd, but his father's thundering voice, the word *soft*... nothing else hurt him like that.

But then their father had received that call from the school. Andrew St. Andrews had spent more time than he would've liked there, usually meeting with Finn's teachers about his failing grades. Their father had chalked it up to Finn's lack of focus, but Jon knew it was quite the opposite. No teacher had bothered to challenge Finn enough to keep his grades up, or focused on his studies. On the mainland, Finn might have been put in advanced placement classes, but the small school on the island had nothing like that. Finn had been forced into special classes when his poor grades were mistaken for a learning disorder. Jon was furious at their neglect, but Finn only shrugged and said it didn't matter anyway. But it *did* matter, and even Jon could see that.

If it wasn't Finn's grades, it was his temper. Such was the case the day the snowcat joined the family. "I see. I'm coming," Andrew had said to the caller, leaving the house without another word, the snowcat forgotten. It stayed there until Finn dusted it off to find food.

"Stop fighting my battles, I don't need you to," Jon had said that night as Finn stood at the edge of the porch, eyes burning. Finn wouldn't be able to sit that night, and maybe the next day.

Finn laughed, snuffling through his bruised nose. "I'm not doing it for you," he said proudly. "If I walk away from a fight, I'll never hear the end of it."

"And if you don't walk away, one day you might get seriously hurt," Jon pointed out. Finn had been getting in fights since he was old enough to put his fists up. This wasn't the first time he'd done it to defend Jon. "What happens when you're older, and you're in a bar, and this time there's no principal to jump in and suspend you both?"

"My ass hurts enough already. I don't need two dads," Finn spat.

When their father died years later, Jon assumed their father's role as Finn's protector and teacher, even though by that point Finn had been on his own long enough to graduate college and start his fishing business.

Except this time he hadn't protected him. He'd allowed him to take that thing across town after one of the worst storms Jon had ever seen. Finn always did whatever he pleased, but there was usually a way to stop him, and Jon had only tried half-heartedly this time. He could have tried harder, but he was so scared they'd run out of food. He sometimes hated himself for his fears.

He used his finger to mark his place in his book, and studied Ana. Without the pressure of conversation, or Finn lingering, he could finally take her measure. She was unusual looking, but pretty—at least, he could see what Finn saw in her. Her red hair was long, and a deep auburn mixed with flecks of fire. Her medium cheekbones gave her face a softness, with an angel's kiss just like his mother's, deep, turning her mouth into a pout. Her lips arched up to meet it, soft and inviting.

Jon understood what Finn saw in her physically, but he was unable to grasp the connection otherwise. He noticed from the moment she walked into his office that she was different. Different like *he* was different. People looking in might have felt their hearts warmed at the thought of two lost souls finding each other, but it didn't work that way. They were the way they were with everyone, no matter how much that other person might understand.

He wondered if she was pretending to be someone else for Finn. Jon had tried it before, too, thinking maybe if he tried hard enough it would become true. He remembered Shannon, how he'd done it for her, how she'd seen right through his attempts. She loved him anyway, she'd said, a concept that had baffled Jon, but as it turned out, she'd believed she could change him for the better. Shannon believed Jon would outgrow his idiosyncrasies, and that, through her acceptance of him, he'd grow and blossom, becoming whole. But Shannon had been wrong, and the last thing she ever said to him was an accusation for being exactly the person he had always been.

"I am as whole as I'll ever be," he said to her.

"You're a shell of the man you *could* be, and you're dead inside," she spat.

He didn't blame Shannon for the inevitable end of their relationship. He knew it was his fault. The year they dated, he'd been so enamored of her that he'd thrown all caution aside. In the end, he'd shrugged her off, in the same way he'd shrugged off medical school. They were both gone, but would always serve as reminders of why it was better to see the world through realistic eyes than hopeful ones.

That was the last time he tried to connect with someone. It was lonelier this way, but it was so exhausting seeking acceptance, and the reward too small to matter.

Where was Ana in her acceptance of herself? Still holding on to hope that maybe she'd grow out of it?

His hand brushed hers, letting it come to a temporary rest. They could never be friends, never seek to understand each other. Things would go back to the way they were if and when she ever woke up. But for now, in this moment, he could console her with a touch that said: *I understand. Me too.*

But then Ana Deschanel opened her damn eyes.

For several, awful moments, they stared at each other. Her eyes, wide with panic, seemed to almost tremble in their sockets. There were no sounds in the house. He could no longer hear the soft hum of the heater, or even his own heartbeat, which he could definitely *feel.* He sensed her own fear and confusion coming at him in intense waves. Which one of them dared break the silence?

"You," she said finally, her voice unsteady and strained.

31
FINNEGAN

Finn shivered violently, the cold penetrating straight to his core. His longing for the crackling heat of the fireplace had never been so acute.

He knew cold. He'd been raised in it. Learned all the tricks for staying warm. How to be aware of his pulse at all times. Methods to protect his body from frostbite. To wear layers, but careful to never sweat inside the warm clothes. Ways to insulate his extremities. He *knew* all of these skills, but being a cautious islander, in a town that was often cut off from the world during storms, he'd mostly avoided situations where he'd need to put them to use. He logically knew how to build a house, but if someone put a hammer in his hand and wood at his feet, he couldn't be confident there'd be anything useful at the end.

Taking the snowcat out was foolish, but it was also their only viable choice if they intended to avoid going hungry. Even if the island's roads opened, the lone grocery store would stay closed, with no way to replenish their stock. It was a near certainty that the ferries wouldn't resume with another storm imminent. Mayor Cairne had been trying to get the city of Portland to be more flexible for years, but he'd never been able to get beyond initial discussions. With a population of hardly more than two hundred, Summer Island was no one's priority.

Asking others for help was out of the question, too. Other than the Auslanders, there weren't any neighbors nearby, and the Auslanders wouldn't have any to spare anyway. The first storm had been stronger than anyone predicted, and this was why they'd created the town food storage building in the first place.

Jon thought Finn was an idiot, or at least blind. His quick jump to silence the phone hadn't gone unnoticed. Had Finn not been the one who worked for years to protect Jon from his own, unfair reputation? He hoped Jon had a plan. For now, all Finn could do was make this beast of a machine run long enough to get to the food storage and back. It had taken him over an hour to get it running and stocked with supplies. As a result, Finn started his trek much later than he wanted. Darkness would be descending soon.

The snowcat didn't move very fast. Compounding the lack of speed was the necessity of restarting each time it died, his heart racing, fearing it had finally given up the ghost for good. There were so many instruments and gadgets Finn was unfamiliar with, and half of the instructions were in some Eastern European language.

He'd need to find a warm place to rest before dawn broke. Jon's office was only two blocks away from the food storage, and Finn knew he kept a rollout bed in the back, for long nights. *Or, there's always Alex Whitman, next door,* he thought, and laughed.

The slow drive was agonizing. He passed familiar landmarks at a crawl, acknowledging he could potentially *walk* there faster if he didn't need a place to put food for the return trip. He first saw the '76 station; the orange ball towering in the air with snow draped over the top, making the number look more like 16. Slowly, the Flanders Grocery parking lot came into view. Eventually, he could make out the Civil War fort. It appeared even more neglected now, as if the snow's harsh brightness highlighted every broken and rotting beam of wood.

Finn focused his mind on what he knew was coming next so he could fool himself into feeling as if he were making progress. *City Hall, Maritime Museum, Jon's office. I only need to get past Jon's office, and then make a right turn and I'm almost there.*

But as daylight waned, and the town streetlights flickered to life, Finn increasingly missed the warmth of his home.

And he missed Ana. He thought of her waving, their familiar ritual, then imagined her doing it from *his* porch. Maybe that was jumping too far ahead. They'd done little more than have dinner together and kiss... but he'd never kissed anyone like that before. Never talked to anyone like that. Never confessed his fear of the sea.

Finn realized, even if she didn't, that she was so much like Jon. How could he not recognize the same darkness he'd grown up alongside? It wasn't a challenge to him. It was a part of her, like it was a part of Jon. There was so much he wanted to say to her. That he knew, and *understood*, and it didn't bother him. He'd give her anything, any comfort, acceptance, whatever she needed.

It was a wonder to him Jon didn't like her more, but there were facets of Jon's mind that would always remain a mystery to Finn.

Finn wished his mother was still living. She'd see everything he saw in Ana, and appreciate the qualities he was growing to love. *You never fear, my son. God has much in store for my Mighty Poseidon.* That was her private nickname for Finn, when everyone else derisively called him Ahab after his horrible boating accident. He hated being called Ahab, and she knew that, so she gave him a nickname he could love. *Poseidon, the great god of the sea.*

One day you'll have a family of your own.

I don't need a family. I have you, Mama.

There will come a day when you'll have me only in your heart. When that day comes, God willing, you will have another's arms to fall into.

I just want to be on the sea.

And you will, Finnegan, but there's more to life. Your heart is big enough for the entire sea and then some.

He reached past his jacket, to his shirt pocket, his thick glove ungainly but still finding what he was looking for: Ana's necklace. A small cross with emeralds in the center. She said it had been her mother's. His hand went to his own neck, and the cross he wore always... *his* mother's. They'd both held tight to a piece of the women who'd given them life, only to leave them too soon.

Jon said Ana shouldn't be wearing jewelry while she was asleep, in case she hurt herself. Finn absentmindedly slipped it into his pocket, only remembering its presence now.

Remember how I said one day I'll live only in your heart, Poseidon? His mother lay dying before him, fading from cancer.

I'm not ready. You have to fight back, there has to be something...

No, sweetheart. Her thin, shaking hand had found his and dropped something into his palm. Her cross. *This is yours now, Finnegan James. You wear this and I'll always be with you. Someday, you'll give this to your child and they'll know the beauty of love and life and family, as we have.*

Finn left his hand over his mother's cross, remembering her final words to him. "Ana," he whispered, his breath fogging the thick window in front of him. He smiled, and warmth rushed through him for the first time in hours. The trip suddenly didn't seem so bad. "Ana."

32
OZ

Oz zipped his small suitcase, only giving a passing, distracted thought as to whether or not he'd packed appropriately. It was past eleven at night. Nicolas would be by soon to pick him up, and then they'd be off to Maine.

Oz felt so guilty when Ana left, but after a while the guilt had dissipated, replaced by overwhelming relief. Unfortunately, relief was supplanted once again by guilt, and the subsequent heaviness on his heart. It came and went this way, in cycles.

He was so close to telling Nicolas the truth that day he showed up at *Ophélie*. Nicolas had no idea what to do with Oz's erratic behavior, and so had predictably ignored it. But later in the bar, he'd given Oz an especially meaningful look. There was no way Nicolas knew, because if he'd known then they wouldn't be having casual beers together.

I'm not sure he would've been angry so much as jealous.

Adrienne and the children had already left for Oz's parents' house, where they'd be staying while Oz was gone. Oz was still, after all these years, afraid to leave Adrienne alone. It was just as well they were already gone, because he was consumed with the weight of his thoughts.

What if something did happen to Ana? It's possible Nicolas isn't overreacting. He's right that Ana wouldn't be this inconsiderate... so what if she's hurt? Missing? Dead? It would be my fault...

Of course it was his fault. He could've stopped her from leaving town. *Should* have stopped her. She left not only because of Oz but *for* him, and he hadn't even thanked her for this act of selflessness. *Because all I could think about was what Adrienne would do if she found out. What it would do to her, and to me, and our family.*

As a teenager, Oz had loved Anasofiya Deschanel, but it was a love never meant to be. His love grew for her over the course of their childhood, culminating in two completely chaotic, passionate, crazy months, starting the night of their junior prom. But where Oz was bursting to show that love, Ana's aloofness, nothing new to him, but somehow harder to accept as her boyfriend, eventually drove him to leave her. And then, when that snap decision led to regret, she'd moved on with his cousin Clancy, a perceived betrayal too close to him for his ego to move past.

Oz never considered there might be unresolved feelings or things left unsaid over the years. After the breakup, things had been awkward at first, but then she had, frustratingly, pretended like nothing ever happened so he did the same. The close friendship they cherished before their relationship never fully recovered, but they could hang out comfortably again. Things didn't exactly go back to normal, but they went back to something close enough.

Until that night two months ago at Full Moon Bay, in Treme. There had been a hazy thickness in the air between them that had nothing to do with the shock of seeing each other in a seedier area of town, so far from their normal hang-outs. The fear and intensity in her eyes that night, when their gazes locked as he walked through the door, was the most acute emotion Oz could ever recall seeing from her. The look on own his face wasn't much different.

"I always knew you were a stalker," she said coolly as he slid back the old wooden chair and sat down across from her. She'd recovered so quickly from her shock at seeing him that he wondered if he's imagined it. The music was the usual muffled, static-filled jazz on cheap speakers. The bar was full, so no one took any notice of Oz when he came in. This was how he liked it. One look at Ana confirmed she came here for the same anonymous experience.

"Waiting for someone?"

Her eyes were still wide as she followed his movement, but she managed to hide most of the emotion that had initially betrayed her. "In a manner of speaking."

"Which means?"

Ana didn't answer him. "It's a bit past your bedtime, no?" She raised an eyebrow.

He decided not to answer her question, either. "How about I buy the first round?"

She shrugged, acting indifferent. "If you want."

He bought more than the first round. They traded off for the next couple of hours, until he lost count of how many they'd consumed, and whether or not they were even on paying the tabs. He didn't care, either, because he was so caught up in their conversation he didn't notice the time slowly slipping away. Ana was relaxed and carefree, and he started to see the side of her that, years ago, he'd accused her of not having. When she laughed, she threw her head back, her whole body shaking. And in perfect harmony, he'd laughed with her so hard his sides hurt.

Oz saw her once again through the eyes of his sixteen year-old self, and all the past fourteen years disappeared.

At some point, Ana watched a man walk through the door, and despite Oz's attempts to keep her engaged in a charming story, the conversation took a more serious turn. She wasn't laughing anymore, her eyes fixed on the man as he walked to the bar and ordered a drink.

"I've slept with him," she said, voice hollow, all traces of laughter gone. She looked around the room and nodded at another man saying, "Him too."

Oz didn't know how he was supposed to react to that. He didn't know whether she was bragging, stating plain facts, both, or neither. He could never tell with Anasofiya what her intentions were. Only that the relaxed, playful Ana from earlier in the night was gone. Moments before, Oz had been almost dizzy with drink, but now felt painfully sober.

"I don't know their names," she continued. She scrunched her mouth up and said, "Well, I do know his." She nodded at one of the three men. "Josh."

"I don't understand," Oz said. "Why are you telling me this?"

Her face was impassive, her eyes heavy and dark. "You asked me if I was meeting someone here. I was. I was waiting for another one of them," she nodded again toward the different men she had slept with, "to show up. A new one. A different one."

He still didn't grasp her meaning, but he knew she was crossing that invisible boundary, the one that ordinarily kept her from opening up to others. He didn't want to do anything to upset this stream of consciousness. He wanted to understand.

"That's why I come here," she said. "Or Carl's, or Voodoo Lounge, or wherever else I end up. To find someone I can take home and never speak to again." She looked around, her gaze even and steady. "There's too many familiar faces here now. I think I've overstayed my welcome."

Oz reached across the table and grabbed her hand. She didn't seem to notice, occupied with signaling the waitress her intention to close out the tab. Oz wasn't ready to leave. He wasn't ready to go home. He felt something he hadn't felt in so long. Exhilaration? Hope? He knew the night would have to end eventually, but he wanted to delay it as long as possible.

Oz didn't know why they'd happened upon each other in that dive bar, and he didn't care. He didn't care about the silly hurts of their past or whatever her demons were. He wanted to be in the presence of someone who took his mind off Adrienne. Someone he'd known his whole life, and once loved. He loved his wife so very much, but it was a love slowly killing him. Sometimes he thought he might claw his own eyes out in frustration at how hopeless his situation was. While he couldn't stand living with the constant anxiety of waiting for her to run, or leave, he couldn't live without her, either.

But this night, Oz wasn't thinking of any of that.

He watched Ana as she paid her tab, signing her name in one messy line. She closed the small black book and stood up in one move, gliding toward the door without looking at anyone. He followed her out, and when she turned to say her goodbyes, he put his hands on either side of her soft, pale face and kissed her.

"Adri—" she tried, breathless, but he pressed his lips against hers to stop the words. He backed her into the wooden building, feeling her at first reluctant, then willing, slipping her arms around his shoulders.

Oz didn't remember her flagging the cab, nor any of the details of the drive to her apartment. Oz only faintly recalled the sound of the car driving off as he stumbled with Ana onto the sidewalk, twisted in a sweaty embrace.

"I want you," he panted, slipping these words into any momentary pauses as they fumbled up the stairs and into her apartment. "I want you..."

She might have asked him a few times in the cab if he was sure? If this was what he wanted? But by the time they were in her home, and her bed, there were no further objections from Ana. Her experiences with strange men had left her far more commanding and skilled than he recalled from the night of their prom, the night he took her virginity. Back then, she'd looked at him with wide, frightened eyes, but now they were forceful, hungry. Not even with Adrienne had he experienced such intensity. He realized, as night turned to morning, that his longing for her was so great that it would never be satisfied. He didn't know this Ana. Whoever she was, he couldn't get enough.

But when, late the following morning, he awoke next to her, the humid breeze sweeping through her open windows across his face, the only thing he felt was horror and regret. His heart leapt into his chest. His palms were covered in sweat, both fresh and dried. She was already awake, leaning over her dresser with both hands.

Oz was too consumed by his own feelings to think of hers. His mind reeled with the events of the previous night—*that amazing night, that horrible night*—and he was rambling. "Oh god, what did we do? Oh god, oh god..." Ana tried to help him find his clothes but she was too slow for him, so he snatched them from her hands. She tried to reach for him but he pushed her away, accidentally knocking her to the floor. "I... I'm sorry," he mumbled but was looking for his wallet, his keys, his phone.

He'd twelve missed calls, all from Adrienne. Of course she'd called. Oz had never stayed out all night. He'd never *not* come home.

"Colin!" Ana screamed, using Oz's given name, bringing him temporarily to his senses. "No one has to know," she asserted, when she knew she had his attention. "That will never happen again."

"Are you mad? Look at me?" He lifted his shirt to reveal the marks from her lips, hands, fingernails. "It's all over me! It's all over my face! It's all over *your*—well no, nothing is on your face because, as usual, you're a frigid bitch!"

She slapped him and the sharp sound reverberated through the quiet room. "I didn't hear you complain last night," Ana said with an eerie calm, as if he hadn't yelled at her, as if she hadn't slapped him so hard his face was fire. "I'm sorry it happened, Oz, but your life doesn't have to end because of a mistake."

She slowly dressed in front of him, her face only slightly betraying her own inner turmoil. "Tell her you got beat up," she suggested. "Robbed, left for dead in an alley. She'll believe you. She'd never suspect you, of all people, of doing something like this."

He couldn't believe how calm Ana was, and it only made him angrier. "She's your *cousin*, Ana! How are *you* going to face her? How are you going to face *Nicolas*? How can we possibly keep this a secret?"

She laughed, and he had the urge to return the slap from earlier. "You know how I'll keep it from Adrienne? And Nicolas? Same way you will. Because I love them, and I'd rather see them happy than unburden my guilty conscience, causing them pain and possibly destroying their lives."

"You don't sound very guilty," he accused.

When Ana looked at him then, he saw the tears in her eyes. He saw the dark circles; the lines. He saw her toes curling around each other, something he'd seen her do years before. "We can't take it back, Oz," she said softly. "I wish we could, but we can't. So what option do we have, other than to do our best to forget it happened?"

Oz softened. Ana wasn't a bad person. She'd been his friend for many years, his first love, and in thinking back on her actions after their breakup years ago, she'd actually done him a favor pretending nothing had happened. It saved his friendship with Nicolas, and meant his life could go back to normal.

It could've been worse. She could've been sick with remorse, insisting they go straight to Adrienne. She could've been crying in a corner, asking why he did this to her. She could've responded in a lot of damaging ways, but instead she'd approached the situation logically, as he should. They made a terrible error in judgment, but they didn't have to ruin everyone's happiness over it. Could she be right?

The tears flowed down her face now, and she looked away in shame. She'd never liked anyone seeing her cry. He went to her, remorseful at his earlier behavior, and laid his hand on her shoulder. She still carried the perfumed scents from the night before, but there was also that light, fresh smell he knew as hers. Of clean laundry and a windy day at the beach.

She slipped into his arms, and as he held her, he was overcome with the extent of his feelings for her. She'd been in his life as long as Nicolas. The first girl he'd ever loved. The one he might've ended up with had she been able to let him in.

Right then, though, the only woman who mattered was Adrienne, and getting home to her as quickly as possible. He couldn't tell her. Ana was right, that would be selfish. He could make it up to her by trying to understand her better, and being more empathetic of her situation; less resentful.

Oz walked away from Ana's apartment that day feeling an unexpected hopefulness he knew was strange given the circumstances. On the way home, he was filled with memories of Adrienne, when he'd loved her deeply, and his worries were nonexistent. Oz would do anything to recapture that magic. His complete betrayal of Adrienne had opened his eyes, bringing him out of his numb existence to the realization of how much he still loved her.

Adrienne bought his story, as Ana said she would, but that only brought Oz's guilt back to the forefront, dwarfing his newfound happiness and energy. The more time went on, the more the guilt crept forward, pushing his hopefulness to the recesses of his troubled mind. He didn't know how to recover that feeling of empowered euphoria he had after leaving Ana's apartment.

He hadn't wanted to, but he found himself calling her. Each time they spoke, he could sense Ana growing progressively worried for him. "I can't do this," he'd tell her. "It's eating away at me, like a cancer." He couldn't stop reliving the night with Ana, but lately the memories filled him with longing, not shame. He wanted to see her again. Wanted to remember her again, as the love of his youth. When he suggested it once—"Just to talk, you're the only one I can talk to about this,"—she gently refused.

Oz should've known Ana would leave. He was ashamed of all the cruel things he'd said to her. For all her aloofness, her heart was a mile wide. She'd given him an out. Ana had given him a way to save his marriage.

Now there was only guilt, guilt, and more guilt. Oz wouldn't let her suffer any longer for a mistake they'd shared together.

33
ANA

Ana was speechless. She willed her body to move, but it paid no need. Her head throbbed with such intensity that her vision pulsed, making the room flow in and out of focus. She stared at Jon in very real terror, a prisoner in her own body. She wanted to scream, talk, anything, and in the end the only word that croaked out was, "You."

Both of them realized where his hand was, at the same time. *What the hell is going on*? She tried to sit up, but her vision ebbed into blackness and she quickly found the pillow again. Jon rushed to tend to her and, her mouth still uncooperative, spoke with her eyes. *Back off.*

"You… you're awake." He seemed nearly as flustered as she was. She needed to know what was going on, whose bed she was in, how she'd gotten there. Questions… she had so many questions, so many that her head couldn't wrap around all of them so they spun there, unasked, making her head ache all the more.

Ana looked at the IV in her arm, and her hand felt for the tube in her throat. She pawed at it like a wounded animal and

Jon rushed back to her side. He pleaded with her to calm down so he could remove it. She nearly threw up as the tube brushed the back of her throat.

"I'm sorry if that hurt..."

Ana opened her mouth to respond but no sound came out, only dry, heaving gasps. Her throat was full of cotton. Jon seemed to realize that, at least, and he made a clumsy move to grab what looked to be his water, bringing it to her. She wanted to snatch it from him and help herself, but her body was stiff, the tingling telling her it was still trying to wake up. Warily, she let him put his hand behind her head, and tilt the glass toward her dry lips.

"Thank you," she said, surprising herself at the sound of her voice. Sound, feeling, sensation. How long had she been here?

When he put the water down, she closed her eyes to get control of herself. She did this when the world spun out of control around her, but it wasn't helping this time. Her toes tried to curl, but her muscles rebelled. What was the last thing she remembered... dinner with Finn? No, it was after that, but her head hurt so bad...

"Easy," Jon encouraged tentatively, as if he was a visible witness to her internal struggle. "You've been asleep for over a week, you need to take it slowly."

Ana watched him, unable to do anything else. He looked horrified. *What does he have to be so worked up about?* she wondered. It couldn't be that he was frightened of her, could it? She couldn't even prop herself up in a civilized manner.

The familiar ache in her chest started, spreading throughout her body. Her dead limbs came to life at this new sensation, but the ache was overwhelming. *Nicolas, where's Nicolas*? He'd always been there when she needed him. Where was he?

New Orleans. And I'm in Maine. And I've been asleep for—what did he say?—over a week?

Ana wanted her own bed, her own surroundings. She needed to feel in control even to breathe, and hadn't gained any of her beloved sense of control.

She remembered that accident from her youth, that horrible accident. *I don't understand how your daughter can sleep for a week and wake up perfectly fine,* the doctor kept saying.

Do you remember sleeping for a week, Ana? her father had asked, when they were home again.

No, Daddy. The doctor's questions had terrified her.

Don't be scared, darling. It's how your body protects itself against bad things. You go to sleep, and when you wake up, you're all better. That's not so scary, is it?

No, I guess not...

Jon was still staring at her, but when the breaths she pulled grew ragged and hard, he moved to sit on the edge of the bed to examine her. He had his hand on her forehead, the other pulling a stethoscope from the drawer. His close proximity worsened her physical reaction. *Go away, go away, go away.* "Go away!"

He sat back, blinking. "I have medical training," he explained, his eyes pleading for understanding. "I've been taking care of you while you were asleep."

"You're a *vet,*" Ana panted through her panic attack. Her toes curled harder and her tongue was fixed to the roof of her mouth. *Breathe.*

"I know people medicine too," Jon insisted. "I trained for years with my father. It's a long story." He sat back further, allowing her space. "We didn't know when you were going to wake up. He would've been here, but he went to get food. I'm sure if he'd known you were going to wake up he would've waited—"

She cut off his rambling. "He?"

"Finn. My brother." He looked concerned, as if he might need to ask if she knew her name and who was currently president.

"Oh." Of course. Finn. Things were still fuzzy, but the connections were coming back. "I was coming here to return his keys..."

"When you fell?"

Ana looked at the bed. "I guess that's what I did."

"You don't remember?"

"It happened so fast." The rocks were slippery, the snow whipping around her so furiously she couldn't see her hands in front of her anymore. Her breathing escalated to wheezing, and this time Jon didn't ask for permission. He propped her head back up, offering her more water, then coaxed her, "You have to breathe."

No shit.

Ana curled her toes tighter and slowed her breathing, forcing herself to calm down. She didn't want to pass out again in this house. Not here.

"I should go," she said, pushing herself up.

Jon laughed. It sounded unnatural coming from him.

"Is that funny?"

"No, it's... here, let me show you something." He came to help her out of bed. She wanted to refuse, but was still shaky and didn't want to humiliate herself by falling on her face in front of him. He walked her to the window and her breath caught in her throat as she looked outside.

"Holy... mother of..." She started to fall, and Jon's arms quickly righted her again.

"Yeah," Jon said. "Over two feet deep. Roads are closed, the ferries are shut down, and we ran out of food because the storage tanks spilled." He helped her back to the bed. She hated feeling weak, but appreciated the strong arm. "That's why Finn went to get food."

"How is he out getting food if the roads are closed?" Ana asked, as he helped lower her back onto the bed. For as much as she'd wanted out of the bed, she felt relieved to be back in it now. Then Cocoa jumped on the blanket, startling her. She gasped as she saw, with relief, how nimble and healthy she looked. The cat rubbed up against her and purred loudly. Ana ran her hands over her soft fur, feeling a lump rise in her throat. *He did this, and he's been caring for her ever since.*

"He took the snowcat." Jon frowned, and Ana could see this disconcerted him. "If he doesn't make it back tonight, we can expect him tomorrow."

She didn't say anything. These guys knew storms. Certainly more than she had when she'd foolishly risked her neck to deliver some keys, of all things.

Jon pulled out a leather doctor bag. She tried to sit still while Jon checked her pulse, her eyesight, her reflexes, and what seemed like a hundred other things. He asked her a series of questions to test her memory.

"You seem to be okay," he said, perplexed, as if he was expecting her to have no heartbeat, or be speaking in monosyllables. "I'll have to monitor you, of course, but..." He touched the side of her head again, checking her neck, the base of her scalp. She wondered if maybe he *wanted* something to be wrong.

She noticed the large medical books lying open on the desk across the room. *Or maybe he's realized that I'm doing a heck of a lot better than I should be.* Whether he had or not, Ana had no intention of explaining it. He'd never believe her anyway.

"I appreciate what you guys did," she said.

Jon shrugged, and put his instruments back in the bag. "Are you hungry?"

"Not really," she said. "And I thought I had to use the bathroom, but apparently I already did," she indicated the catheter bag dangling off to the side, attached to her waist by a belt. She cringed to think of him inserting it. *I know people medicine too.*

His face flushed crimson. "It was either that or let you soil yourself. Sorry." They shared another awkward moment as he leaned in and lifted the sheet to remove it. Turning his head to the side, he reached his hand toward the connected tube and pulled quickly. She gasped in surprise at the stinging pain.

"Sorry again," he said, already placing the catheter into a sand-colored plastic bowl.

"I owe you. I probably would've died out there." Cocoa purred in agreement.

Jon shrugged. He didn't take compliments any better than Ana did, which didn't surprise her. "I'll be back in a bit," he said awkwardly, and was off before she could say anything else.

She was surprised to realize she wanted him to come back. Ana didn't want to be alone, even if it meant the company of someone as sour as Jon St. Andrews.

34
AUGUSTUS

Augustus still remembered the day Ekatherina Vasilyeva showed up at the Deschanel Media Group. They were preparing to sign a deal expanding the magazine beyond New Orleans. It was 1972, and everything had been much simpler.

Colin Sullivan, of Sullivan and Associates, had sent her over. An attorney friend, Joseph Connelly, came to Colin asking for help in placing her. Colin arranged the meeting between Joseph and Augustus.

"She came to us as an *au pair*, but she's awful with children," Joseph had said. "With people in general, actually. I think she signed up for this because it's what all her friends were doing, but it's really not her thing."

"Why should I take her?" Augustus had laughed. How did he get talked into relieving another man's burden?

"Because she *is* good at something. Math. Accounting, specifically. I put her through business school."

"You paid for this Soviet immigrant to go to business school?" Augustus was incredulous.

"Well, yes," Joseph had said, nonplussed. "It seemed like the right thing to do for a girl with her talent. Colin says you're hiring for a junior accountant. I realize you have your reservations, but I can't recommend her enough, Augustus. I don't think you'll be disappointed."

Augustus didn't simply take Connelly's word for it. He called the business school and asked for her records. Back then, no one questioned a request like that. *Our very best student,* they'd said. *Very quiet girl. Never any trouble. We hope she can find a company to sponsor her. Would be such a shame if she was sent back to the USSR.*

Augustus was twenty-two at the time and it was this youth that Joseph's words appealed to. He knew what it was like to have obstacles to overcome on the way to the realization of a dream.

She was hired without an interview. When she showed up for her first day, he mistook her for a lost child. She was a tiny thing, with pale blonde hair and big blue eyes. A year older than he was, according to the paperwork, she didn't look a day over fifteen.

"Pleasure to meet you, Ekatherina," he said, taking her hand.

"Please, call me Catherine," she replied in a tiny voice. Her accent was strong, but her English was crisp. *She's been preparing for this for years,* Joseph had said.

He sent her off to work with the accounting department, and mentally moved on to more pressing matters. It was a pleasant surprise when, relatively soon into her employment, he caught wind of the uproar she was causing. To the angst of his tenured accountants, she was making suggestions. Proposals that saved the company money, but also ideas on how to wisely expand, and where to invest.

The CFO came to Augustus, complaining, "She's impossible to work with! She has an idea, and expects us all to listen, but if someone else wants to present, she zones out. You need to talk to her!"

But Augustus challenged, "You need to find a way to work with her, Stephen. Her ideas are better than yours."

Catherine was the hardest worker in the office, leaving as late as Augustus most nights. He grew used to seeing her in the evenings, and often escorted her out well past dark. She didn't want to talk about her family, or her life back in the USSR.

But Augustus didn't get that far by letting things go, so he did his own research.

Catherine had been born Ekatherina Aleksandrovna Vasilyeva, in the USSR. She applied to be an *au pair* on the pretense of creating a better life for herself, but her real goal was much larger: to make enough money to send for her family: her mother, Elena, father, Aleksandr, and her two younger siblings, Aleksei Aleksandrovich and Anasofiya.

Augustus was fascinated by this small, quiet girl who'd bravely ventured across the sea, on her own accord, to start a new life. He appreciated and identified with her ambition, but couldn't penetrate beneath Catherine's façade sufficiently to relate on a personal level. She was well-guarded, living in fear of being sent back; of being a failure.

I know that feeling as well. Everyone expected me to fail. But I didn't. You won't either. He wanted to reassure her, but every time he worked up the courage, there were others around. He respected she wouldn't want everyone to know her business, and might even resent him.

One evening, after everyone else had left, he found her in the office she shared with the other junior accountants, alone and crying. She wiped her face when she saw Augustus standing in the door, but he'd already seen her pain and was determined to fix whatever was amiss.

"What's wrong?" he asked her, several times, before she would answer.

She held up a tiny gold cross, broken into two pieces. "It was a gift from my *mammochka*. It's all I have."

He took it from her and studied it. The gold was of inferior quality, and the chain flimsy. He wasn't surprised it broke, only that it hadn't sooner.

"I can fix it," he said, and slipped the keepsake into his pocket. Her large blue eyes blinked in surprise at his kindness.

Several days later, he returned the cross to her. Her eyes marveled, a hint of moisture giving them a nearly luminescent quality. Augustus hadn't simply repaired the heirloom, he'd improved it. In addition to augmenting with extra gold, in the center now sat several brilliant emeralds.

"Your birthstone," he explained.

"This is too much," she half-heartedly protested. Tears forged a wet path, over her porcelain cheeks to her brilliant smile. She clutched the cross in her hand, the way a child would hold a beloved toy.

"I want to help you send for your family, Catherine."

Her smile faded and her eyes narrowed. "I'm saving my money. I can do it."

"But I can do it faster." He didn't know anything about romance. Nothing about sensitivity, nor the subtle language of love. He only knew he was drawn to her. "Marry me, and I'll do anything for you."

It took months to convince her, but the following year she accepted his proposal. They were married in a small ceremony at *Ophélie*. He gave her a third of the company, and made her the CFO, despite objections from his peers in the business community that she was too inexperienced, and he was thinking with his heart.

Unfortunately, getting Catherine's family to the States was

harder than Augustus imagined. A year into their marriage he'd made little progress, and tragedy struck. Catherine's young sister, Anasofiya, died at the age of fourteen. Catherine was heartbroken, feeling that she'd abandoned her family, while she enjoyed her new, opulent life.

Soon after, Catherine became pregnant, but it was too late. Her spirit was broken. She was ashamed of her decision to come to the United States, and blamed herself for Anasofiya's death. She stopped taking care of herself, and was ordered to bed rest. She refused.

"If you won't do it for yourself, do it for our daughter!" He was angry, not understanding how she could completely shut down... how she could shut *him* out.

"I don't want my child born into this world!" She'd wander the house in her nightgown, wailing, crying, cursing the gods. Her blonde hair was a rat's nest, as she refused bathing or brushing of any kind. "Rather she be with God than live like this!"

Augustus' younger sisters, Evangeline and Colleen, answered his call for help. Both had been born with special abilities, like most Deschanels. Both were healers.

"This isn't a medical issue," Colleen tried to explain. The women did their utmost to comfort him, but the situation was beyond hope. "We can't fix this."

"Maybe seeing her daughter will snap her out of it," Evangeline offered, but behind her words was unmasked skepticism.

"How can you not fix this?" he demanded. "You're supposed to be healers! You're Deschanels!"

Colleen shook her head sadly. "It doesn't work that way. We can't cure afflictions of the mind and the heart. That's not magic; that's a miracle."

And though Augustus had a skill of his own—the skill of

persuasion—he couldn't pull his wife back to the living, either. He endured slowly watching her lose her mind, spiraling further into the hopeless recesses of melancholia.

Catherine died a few days after Ana was born. She suffered in silence, said nothing, and died alone. *She didn't want me to call my sisters. She didn't want to be fixed. She was punishing herself.*

Augustus planned Ana's sixteenth birthday for weeks. He knew what he wanted to give her, but was nervous about presenting a gift that once held such significance. It represented the chance he once took, and the dreadful results.

But that chance also gave him his only joy in life. His daughter.

He wondered if Catherine would've wanted him to pass it on to their daughter. Whenever Ana asked about her mother, Augustus said Catherine was so excited about becoming a mother... that she'd sing to Ana in her womb, and make plans for their life once she was born. But none of this was true.

Catherine had cursed her daughter's existence and threatened to throw herself down the stairs, to end it all. She once tried to stab her belly with a steak knife, and another time he caught her reading the warnings on a bottle of drain cleaner. How much of it had been the melancholy, and how much the real Ekatherina, he'd never know. The truth was that he'd never known his wife at all. In retrospect, it felt more like a business transaction.

That decision affected Ana even today. Ana was smart and focused like her mother, but had also inherited the same darkness that swallowed Catherine whole.

When she was little, Augustus cast himself as the overprotective father, never letting her out of his sight. But as she grew older, he found himself actually encouraging her to go out with friends, including boys. He often found her in her room, writing. *Why aren't you out with your friends?* he would ask. She'd only shrug, and go back to composing her thoughts.

He wanted to plan something large and exciting for her sixteenth birthday, but she flatly refused to take part. "Dinner, just the two of us would be nice," was her emphatic request. His guilt for spending so much time at work overpowered his desire to force her into something more social. And dinner would be the perfect chance to give her this gift he had agonized over.

"I want to give you something," he began that evening, once food had been served. She looked at him with her mother's big blue eyes. He could see both sides of Catherine reflected there: both the light and the darkness. "It was your mother's."

An unusual smile spread across Ana's face as she awaited the gift. He pulled it from his pocket, remembering both the sad look on Catherine's face when she handed the necklace to him, broken, and the light in her eyes when he brought it back, better than before.

Ana walked around to his side of the table and lifted her hair so he could help her with the clasp. He fastened the sturdy lobster-claw, then kissed the top of her head. She surprised him by turning, wrapping her arms around his neck, and squeezing tightly. It was sweetly reminiscent of when she'd been very little.

"This is the best gift anyone has ever given me," she whispered. He could feel the hot tears on the side of his neck. His eyes welled up, too.

"She would have wanted you to have it, my dear. She loved you so much. Happy birthday, Anasofiya."

He would give her another gift, though it was one she'd

never know about. The gift of believing her mother had loved her with her whole heart. And in giving her this false memory, he'd be doing himself a kindness as well.

I'll share Catherine as I wanted her to be, not the way she was. We can both remember her thus.

He couldn't allow himself to dwell on how the melancholia devoured his wife's soul; her very will to live. Nor would he compare the circumstances, because then he might find that Ana's trip to Maine was another version of Catherine's wandering the halls in her nightgown.

35
OZ

"Fuck me sideways, it's cold here!" Nicolas exclaimed. On the pier, several heads turned, but he was oblivious, as always. He'd been griping ever since they stepped off the plane.

"What were you expecting?" Oz asked, his hands deep in the pockets of his new coat. It most certainly *was* cold, and entirely unlike anything they'd ever experienced in New Orleans. They were still wearing shorts this time of year. Prior to this, he'd never owned anything heavier than a windbreaker. Their first stop had been to a sports equipment store near the airport, to purchase the proper outerwear.

"Do you even know where we're going?" Oz inquired.

"Ozzy, when I need you to know, I'll tell you," Nicolas retorted.

"So, you're saying you have no idea."

Nicolas scoffed from his peripheral, trying not to move too much in the cold. "Of course I have an idea. I just don't know exactly how the idea is going to play out. Humans are a fascinating species," he said with sarcasm.

"Right. Well, should we get something for breakfast then, while the forces of the universes align, or whatever it is that we're waiting for while standing here freezing our asses off?"

They ducked inside the lounge of a hotel near the waterfront and both of their moods improved instantly with the rush of warmth.

On the plane ride to Portland, Nicolas hadn't said a word. He fidgeted in his seat the whole way. First, chewing his nails, then the sides of his mouth, then the obnoxious clucking sound effects started, prompting the guy in front of them to ask Nicolas to shut up. *Your mom likes it when I do that*, Nicolas said, but the man in front already had his headset back on, and Nicolas returned to fidgeting with his pen. His focus was all over the place.

On the drive into town, he started going on about the price of gas. Oz let him ramble, nodding occasionally.

This was a good thing for Oz, whose thoughts were also all over the place. Having Nicolas distracted meant he could disappear into his own head without drawing attention to his mental absence.

Some said Ana and Adrienne were similar creatures, but with Adrienne, you almost always knew where you stood, and more importantly, where *she* stood. Only in her most desperate moments did his wife retreat inside herself and shut the world out. Ana had spent her life cultivating the fortress around her.

Nicolas said it was the other way around, that Adrienne was the one you couldn't ever read, and with Ana, you got exactly what you got. Oz couldn't see it, and Nicolas said that was because Oz refused to see Adrienne without taking off the rose-colored glasses first. Oz told him to look in a mirror. Nicolas insisted he was well aware of Ana's flaws and loved her *for* those, not in spite of them.

"I don't ignore Adrienne's issues, if that's what you mean," Oz had said defensively.

"Ignore, overlook, pretend they don't exist. Semantics, Ozzy. When you see Adrienne, you see her potential, and that makes her beautiful to you. You see who she could be. When I see Ana, I see that who she is now is who she'll always be, and *that* is what makes her beautiful to me."

Nicolas was wrong. He did love Adrienne for her faults. They didn't suddenly spring up overnight. He'd loved her for over ten years now, knowing her since the day she was born. She was the same person now as then, and if he hadn't loved her for who she was, then he would've walked away a long time ago.

"Love," he reaffirmed.

"Addiction," was Nicolas' answering retort.

Oz realized there was a young woman sitting at the table with them, in the restaurant they'd ducked into. Blonde, plain, wearing a nice grey wool sweater, jeans, and riding boots. He had no idea how or when she'd joined them, but Nicolas had her engaged in conversation.

"I don't see limitations," Nicolas was saying, leaning over the table in her direction. *Oh,* this *act.* "Only opportunities."

"That's a great philosophy to live by," she was saying. Oz thought her head might fall off from all the nodding. She was trying to be coy, but was clearly already hooked. *Why does this always work?* "But Mother Nature is one hell of a force to reckon with."

Nicolas sat back in his chair, unperturbed. His hair hung down into his eyes in messy waves. "People are cautious. They should be. Life is precious."

Oz bit his lip, studiously focused on the bread and butter.

"But," he continued, leaning forward again, "nobody ever got rich practicing caution." She was hanging on every word.

"Rules are there for a reason, but every rule has an exception. I know someone will be willing to take me to Summer Island. Cash is a hell of a motivator."

She frowned. "How much cash?"

Nicolas leaned back. His bored expression implied he was done with the conversation, but Oz knew better. "If you haven't figured out by now that money isn't an issue for me, then I doubt you can be of much help."

She looked around, then lowered her voice, closing the gap between them. "I need to know some figures. I can't exactly go to my father and ask him to turn the ferry lines back on." *Ah, so Nicolas did have a plan.* "But I do know some fishing boat captains, and a couple of them might be interested if the price outweighed the risk."

Nicolas and the young woman transitioned to full whispers after that and Oz only picked up bits and pieces. No matter. Nicolas would fill him in soon enough. She left, returning ten minutes later, and they resumed their whispering.

Oz looked out the window at the grey, hazy skies. He couldn't see anything beyond the docks, but he'd be seeing whatever was beyond soon enough.

He wondered again where Ana was, what she was doing. If she was okay. There was a sinking shame anytime he thought about her leaving her home and friends so she could put his filthy mind at ease; how he'd let her. He could've called, or written, asking her to come back... he could've done many things that he didn't do. *It's why I'm here now. It matters. It has to matter.*

"We're in business," Nicolas said after the girl left. "We leave at dawn."

36
ALEX

Alex heard Finn before he saw him. The snowcat rumbled from a distance before the headlights flooded Alex's back room. He worried for a while that Finn might have gotten lost, or broken down somewhere, so he was relieved, in a sense, when he finally arrived.

He'd had time to think, and had decided what he wanted to do.

Although the phones were down, Alex's radio still worked. Contacting the sheriff was out of the question. Sheriff Horn had been a good friend of Andrew St. Andrews. The man was blindly protective of both boys, and was certainly not fond of Alex. He had no close or trusted friends on the island. He could signal the Coast Guard, but their first call would be to Horn, and then Alex would get an earful, or three. Horn would want proof, and Alex had none, other than his gut feeling.

And 'sides, Lexie Lou, this is yer moment to shiiine. Cain't be letting others steal your thunder, right? They were his father's words, but he no longer heard the whiny intonation of his father's voice. He'd hated him so much when he was alive, and hated him still. Now when Alex heard his father speak he heard his own voice, mature and in control. *Are you gonna be yer mother's little sniveling Lexie Wexie Woo, or are you going to be a maaan, Alex?*

Don't call me that...

But it's your naaaaaame, isn't it, widdew wexie wooooooo...

Swing, crack, spurt; the shock frozen on his father's face. All the taunting in his expression seized in time. His father's eyes remained wide with horror even as the axe carved a dent in his skull, the blood pooling so fast Alex nearly slipped in it.

Alex's mother—his weak mother, who was really no better than her husband at all, when it came right down to it, that weak-minded, pitiful slut—was huddled in the corner, crying. *Alex nooooooo... whyyyyy... I looooovvveeeed himmm...*

It's no wonder he loved to smash your face in, you stupid, pitiful bitch, Alex had said, swinging the axe at her this time. He missed, and half her face lay flapping as she screamed and screamed, arms flailing, slipping in both her and her husband's blood. The next swing had done the trick. And when Alex was sure they were both, finally, gone, he went into his room and closed the door and the blinds, welcoming the silence with all his heart.

But his father *was* right. If he wanted to help that sweet girl, he'd have to take control of the situation, just as he had before. Alex slipped into his winter gear, checked his shotgun shells once more, then slung the gun over his shoulder and headed to the food storage.

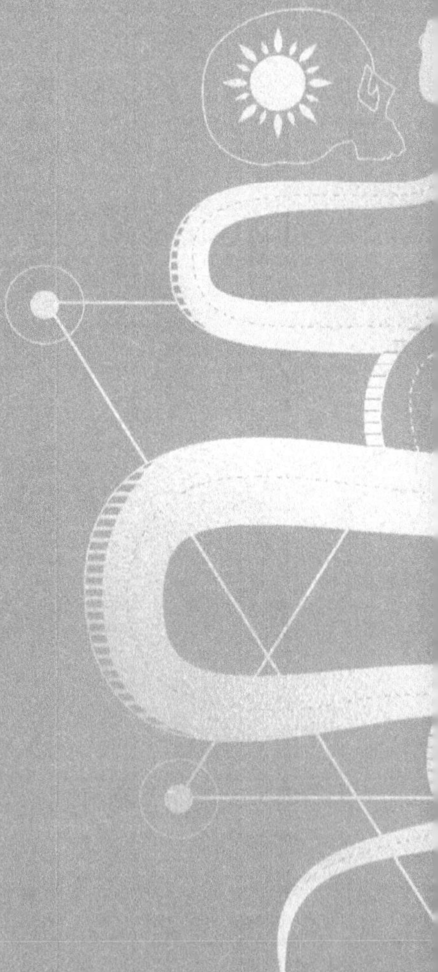

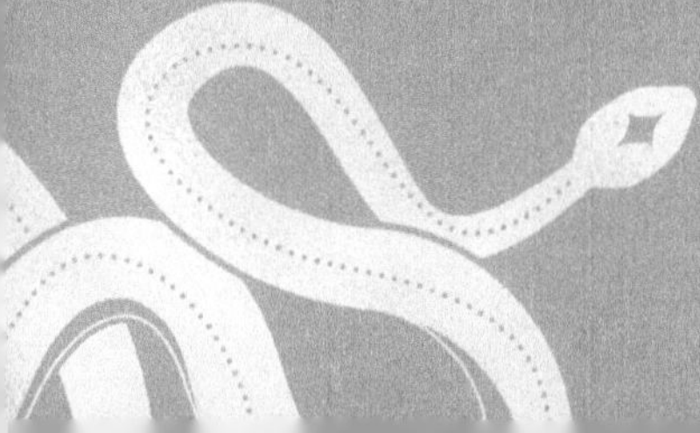

37
FINNEGAN

The snowcat came to a shuddering halt. As the engine sputtered and faded away, Finn was enveloped in silence.

He couldn't get the cat any closer to the small cement building that held the town food storage. It was possible to drive right up to the big steel door if you were in a car or small truck, but the trees on either side of the driveway blocked Finn's wide approach by a hundred feet. Hauling the food back to his vehicle in two feet of snow would take some work.

Darkness accompanied the stillness in the air. *Why didn't the Farnsworths leave the light on?* Finn searched through the cab to find the flashlight he packed for the trip. The light flickered momentarily, and then died. *Shit. I should've checked for extra batteries.*

Finn peered out the front window again. He couldn't see the building, but the moonlight cast a shadow on the trees, and he hoped that would be enough.

Finn had memorized the access code to the building, but in the excitement, had subsequently forgotten it. Reaching into his inner pocket, Finn's gloved hand fumbled for the old slip of folded paper he'd brought along with him, just in case. He pulled it out. *77877*. All residents of Summer Island had this somewhere safe. Finn had never been so glad for Jon's neurotic organizational habits. He'd found it in the Rolodex, taped to a card labeled: *Code, Food Storage.*

Finn removed his gloves and slipped his hand into his pocket again, finding Ana's cross. He threaded the delicate chain around his neck, under his jacket, and latched it. The tiny crossed clinked together.

Pulling his gloves back on, Finn took one last, long deep breath and then opened the cab door. The cold air rushed at his face, stealing the breath from him, as he sunk into snow that came to his knees. The door seemed miles away.

He dropped his face and started the slow hike to the building.

The icy stillness in the air made Finn painfully aware of how alone he was. The lack of children's laughter, or cars moving through the downtown strip was notably absent. The silence was louder than any sound.

He forged on. His steps were heavy and the snow's resistance complicated matters, but he knew each trip back to the snowcat would get easier as the path was flattened.

Finn heard a crunch of snow ahead of him, and stopped. Pulling his hood back to widen his vision, he peered into the darkness ahead. Nothing. *Probably an animal.*

The snow started to soak through his thick layers of clothing and gear. He'd have to move faster. The drive home was long and the heater wasn't working in the cab—another thing his father had left to rot.

The crunching sound echoed again from ahead. This time, Finn narrowed his eyes and tried to focus harder, but the illumination of snow against night cast so many shadows he could make out nothing distinct. "Hello?" he called out, with no response. *Of course not. It's probably a deer.*

Finn continued toward the building, but his heartbeat gained momentum. The crunching sound appeared again, but this time it came from his left.

That doesn't sound like a deer... or a fox... he thought, as he listened carefully to the heavy crunches the footfalls made. They were coming closer, the pace quicker. Then, suddenly, they were right beside him, and the shadow grew into the large, tall shape of a man.

He spun around with his hands out in front of him, and a sharp pain shot through his head as cold steel connected. There was only a flash of light and then Finn was falling, sinking, into the white, icy darkness.

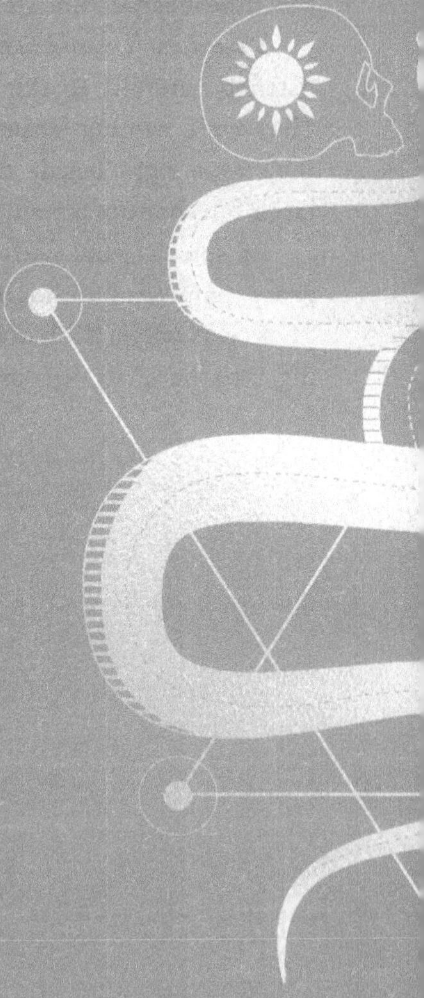

38
ANA

In her dream, Ana was drowning.

She'd been running, cold sweat peppering her forehead, the force of wind beating on her. Running away from something... what, she didn't know... running, running, running.

Shockingly, suddenly, the ice water sprayed up on to her, all around her, the stunning cold piercing her body as she continued to run... through it... into it... submerging.

The release... the sweet surrender.

Then... darkness.

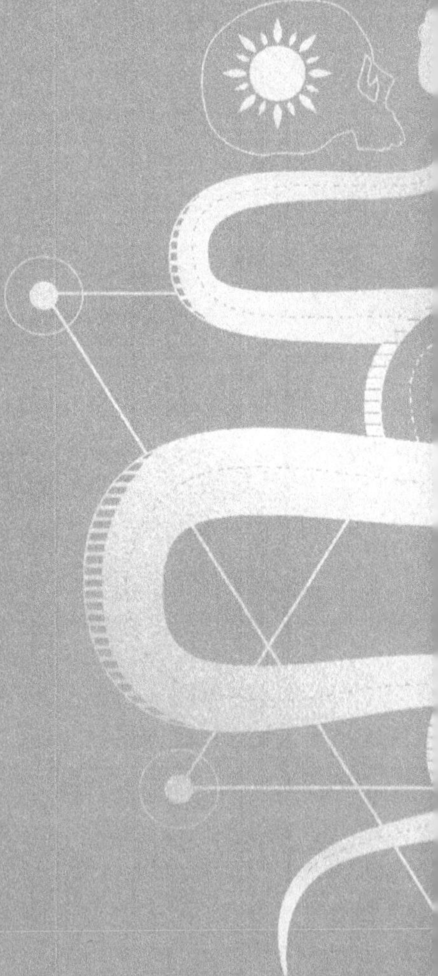

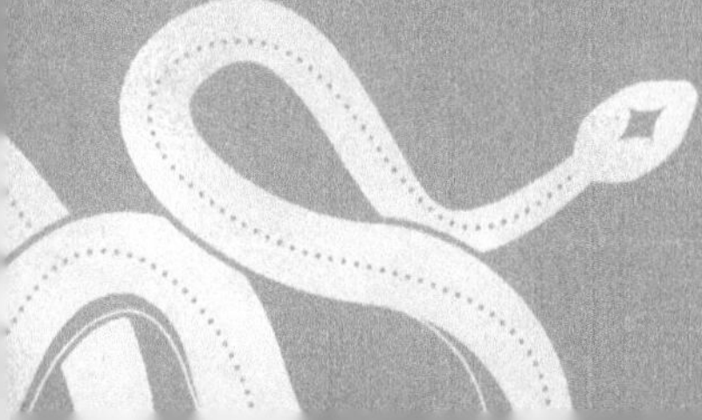

39
JONATHAN

Jon was avoiding the upstairs. He hadn't expected Ana to wake, at least, not then, not with Finn gone. They'd connected for one moment, and then that moment ended, and they were both left with their fear of one another.

He occupied himself by checking on Mr. Jenkins, who no longer needed Jon's attentive care. *This doesn't make up for the way I'm treating her,* Jon thought, but the presence of the dog soothed him, like returning home after a long trip. Angus was Finn's, and Cocoa was Ana's. But for a little while longer, this sweet boy was Jon's, and there was no one he'd rather be around.

Jon should go upstairs and make sure Ana was okay. She was clearly unsettled, and he'd abandoned her when things got weird. Instead, he stayed put, running his hands through Mr. Jenkins' soft fur.

An hour after he left her upstairs, he'd slipped back into the kitchen, putting the kettle on the stove for some tea. *Perhaps she'll want some too*, he thought, but summarily dismissed the idea. When the tea finished, he sat in his usual seat at the kitchen table, staring off into nothing, considering his next move, while searching for any rationale to justify inaction.

What he wanted to do was ask her more about her accident. He wanted to understand her freakish healing. Was this normal for her? Would she be surprised, when he asked? Jon started to wonder if perhaps he'd *imagined* how bad her wound was, because that made a hell of a lot more sense than what he'd witnessed after. Maybe all the blood had overwhelmed him, making it seem worse than it was.

No... I stitched her up. I saw it with my own eyes. It was there, it was terrible, and now the gouge is nearly gone with no rational explanation.

Jon jumped at the sound of thudding on the stairs. "Angus, easy!" he yelled. When the door opened, and the screen door slammed shut, he cussed under his breath. Finn must've left the door cracked and now the stupid dog had gotten outside.

Moments later, Angus came padding into the kitchen and Jon gave him a dirty look. Then he froze. Angus hadn't come from upstairs. Mr. Jenkins was still in the study.

Ana.

Jon leapt from his seat, dashing through the house and out the front door, not bothering with his shoes or coat. He didn't think, didn't hear the screen door slap shut behind him, didn't feel the icicles of cold piercing him as he smashed into the snow.

His body felt like a thousand pounds as he thrashed, his hands shoving snow aside in frustration. Jon could see the path her body had made, but couldn't see *her*.

He followed her trail, pushing the snow with wild swings. He was numb and losing feeling in his limbs when he finally found Ana, half-asleep, crying, and shivering. He scooped her in his arms and retraced his haphazard path.

When the door closed behind them, Ana's blue lips whispered something, but he couldn't hear anything. They were both at risk of hypothermia, both needing warmth immediately. This time he didn't have Finn to assist, but he had no time to lament this as he carried her up the stairs, the heat from the fireplace tickling his ice-cold back.

Both their pajamas were soaked through. Jon moved quickly, shedding first his own clothes, and then helping Ana with hers. She started to come to her senses, but she wasn't moving near as fast as she must have been when she sleepwalked out the door and into the snow. He rushed to start the shower, quickly returning to her side, keeping her close as he helped her toward the tub stall. Jon stepped in, and then pulled her into the shower with him, yanking the curtain closed behind them as the hot water coursed over their freezing bodies.

Ana pressed her cold body up against his, trembling wildly, her discomfort and pride forgotten entirely. Jon wrapped his arms around her, running them up and down her back, her body, all over her, to spread the warmth of the water, to fold her into it.

She lifted her head to face him as the water rushed over her face, between her parted lips. Jon's heart was a mess as he stared back into her wide, blue eyes. Shoving his resistance aside, he pressed his lips against hers in a firm, rough kiss.

"Ohh," Ana whispered, as if for the first time realizing they were both naked, their bodies already wrapped around each other for comfort. Jon forgot his own unease and lifted her into his arms, nestling her body against the shower wall, moving his kisses down her neck, her chest, everywhere.

I know you, Ana Deschanel. And you know me.

Jon wound his hands through Ana's wet hair, afraid if he stopped to think she'd disappear entirely and so would he.

Ana wrapped her muscled legs around his waist. Jon felt her hips rise, and his own movements matched hers as he entered her, the shock of the action forcing him further into the moment, and away from reality. They both gasped, soaked, consumed with the moment, relinquishing to each other the control they'd both held so dearly in the past. He thrust into her, against her, kissing her, devouring her. He was not Jon anymore. Not the same. He was *alive*.

Jon shuddered against her, and moments later felt Ana experience the same release.

He gently eased her down, and they stood, watching each other, panting and speechless. Ana's chest rose and fell in rapid succession. Her eyes were wide with shock.

Her wet hair framed her pale, pretty face, and Jon reached out with one hand to touch it. She closed her eyes and let her cheek fall to a rest in his hand, and with his other he pulled her close against him. They remained that way as the water rained down on them and their silent, private thoughts.

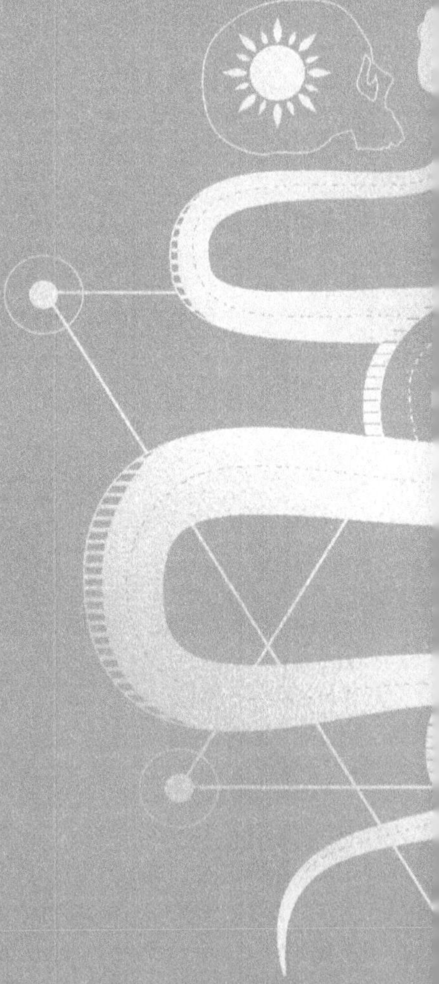

40
ANA

W*hat in the hell just happened?* She released a deep sigh. Jon. *Wrong brother, Ana.*

Jon gingerly helped her into the bed, glancing back at her with an unreadable look as he moved toward the door. He said nothing, but his gaze stayed on her until he switched off the light. When the door clicked shut, she could breathe again.

The night she brought in an injured Cocoa, he'd been repulsed by her. When she woke and he was sitting by her bedside, he'd been terrified of her. Even Finn hadn't disagreed when she pointed out that Jon didn't like her. Well, she didn't like him either.

She curled into a fetal position under the blankets. Her body was sore from sleeping, and now there was another familiar soreness, between her legs. She couldn't believe she'd sleepwalked. How many years had it been since she last terrified her father with nocturnal wanderings? She thought she was past it. Hers was the variety that often got her in trouble, and even put her life at risk. Her neighbor once found her jogging around the block in her bra and panties at two in the morning. But that was years ago.

Each episode had been unique, though this was the first time one ended with rescue sex. *Wrong brother, Ana.*

Wrong brother, indeed. She should go downstairs and talk to Jon about what happened, sort it out, put a label on the unplanned encounter and then swiftly, an end. But she didn't, because she knew how she'd react if Jon came back upstairs and did the same. *And we're alike, he and I.*

That realization made Ana dislike him even more. She was guarded, but never cruel. She never hurt people because of who she was. *But that's not entirely true, is it? How many times have my words or actions mistakenly hurt my father, or even Nicolas? What about the reason I'm here in Maine?*

Ana missed Nicolas so much the ache of it burned deep in her chest. She wanted to call him, but the phones were down. *It's probably for the best. He'd listen to my fuzzy, convoluted story filled with holes and fly his ass out here to rescue me.*

Eventually Ana would have to tell him about Oz. Only now did she realize Oz would eventually have a meltdown, spilling the truth in all directions. Her leaving New Orleans didn't change who he was.

Jon was the more pressing matter. She didn't welcome this conversation any more than he would, but even less so did she want to deal with the ensuing awkwardness.

She made her way downstairs carefully, using the bannister for support. Jon heard her coming, and rushed to offer assistance, but she shook him off.

"Coffee?" he offered. He stayed one step behind, but, thankfully, didn't try again to touch her.

Ana nodded. "Jon?"

"Yes?" She almost laughed when she saw his face. *Bless his heart.*

"That shouldn't have happened." She took the coffee from his hands, their eyes meeting briefly in the exchange. "I like your brother. I don't even know what... what *that* was, but it won't be happening again."

"For sure," he said with a hollow chuckle, and she thought again how unnatural, but nice, it was to hear him laugh. Even better to hear the relief in his voice. "This never happened."

"What never happened?" she teased back.

The atmosphere in the room lightened after that. They both relaxed as they sat in rockers in the family room, looking out the large bay window toward the cold sea. She recalled the afternoons that she'd sit out and wait for Finn, for that brief exchange of waves. *Like a silly girl.* But no one had ever accused Anasofiya Deschanel of being a silly girl.

She could only imagine what Finn thought after everything she'd revealed to him, but it hadn't been enough to chase him away. He even went so far as to invite her to come home with him. She wondered how he felt now that they'd shared this unlikely trauma together.

He's so not your type, Muffins, she could hear Nicolas saying.

Maybe that's why I like him.

"I hope he returns soon," Ana said and meant it. At first she thought he reminded her of the darkness she wanted to leave behind, but instead he was a signal that not everything was always as it seemed. He gave her a startling hope that life could be different, if she allowed it.

Even in her healing sleep, she'd sensed his comforting presence. Finn didn't need to stay at her side, but he did. He wouldn't have known she could sense his presence.

And then Jon happened.

Ana wanted to blame the sleepwalking, but she'd been awake; disoriented, for sure, but a part of her must have welcomed the pleasant assault in the shower, or she'd have stopped it.

Right?

"If there's a classification somewhere between mortal and invincible, that's Finn. He's fearless, but not reckless. He'll be home as soon as he can," Jon reassured her.

Did I really have sex with him? Why? Am I so broken inside that I can't resist, still, the wrong man?

If not for the emptiness following that hollow thought, Ana thought she might start crying and never stop.

Ana sipped her coffee. The bittersweet remembrance of her childhood romance with Oz came over her in waves.

Dating Oz had never occurred to Ana as they moved from childhood to adolescence, despite how very much alike they were. Both preferred the comfort of a book to people, because books provided an innocuous, protective blanket, buffering them from reality. Ana felt safe with Oz, in a way she didn't appreciate until the constancy of his presence was no longer a part of her life. Oz understood her, and accepted the unusual abilities scattered about the Deschanel bloodlines. Some called them a gift, others a curse. To Ana, it was a practical excuse for keeping her distance from others.

Oz intuitively discerned her hesitancy. "Even if you showed them all who you were, they'd never understand," he said one day, as they studied beneath a tree in his parents' backyard in the Garden District. Ana still remembered the way the sun shone crudely through the fall storm, how the leaves from the banana tree served as shelter from the incessant rain.

"But you do," she'd replied, nose down in a book.

He'd responded by smiling from behind his own book, resting his hand on her leg before resuming reading.

But while he offered Ana acceptance, he reflected his own personal challenges through a heavy resignation, moving from one vapid debutante to another, while Ana chose a full retreat from dating to protect her heart.

It was strangely fitting they finally came together on the night of their junior prom, an event which signified to her all the terrors of her teenage life, culminated in one evening.

They'd both come with inappropriate dates: Oz with his latest experiment in normalcy; Ana with a boy she had no interest in, but accepted his invitation anyway at the urging of her stepmother.

When her date inevitably abandoned her, it was Oz who offered her a lifeline to safety.

It started with a dance.

Ana had never been in the arms of a boy before; not like that. The warmth she felt when Oz put his arms around her waist made her realize how real he was, and the weight of that realization overwhelmed her. His breath was hot near her ear; she detected his heartbeat through their joined hands. She would never forget that feeling, the subtle pulsing transferring warmth through to her in soft vibrations. She wondered if everyone noticed things like this. Or if Oz had always felt so good, and she'd simply missed it.

Nothing had ever felt so wonderful, or so terrifying.

The dance led to an escape to a party upstairs, where Ana finally let go of the fears binding her. All the while, Oz was there, holding her up, physically and emotionally, until she could no longer remember why she'd fought so hard against this comfort.

In her intoxication, she'd made a move on him. *Not like this,* he'd said, and then gently held her as she got sick, paying the price for her earlier over-indulgence. She later fell asleep beside him, as he watched over her, and woke up the next morning still wrapped in the security of his arms.

Not like this, he'd said the night before, but things were different in the morning light.

Colin, I've never done this before.

Started your morning next to a hot man in a strange hotel room?

She laughed. *You know what I mean.*

Me either, Ana. But I want to. With you. I've always wanted to.

He protected her once again, by showing her the full extent of his care for her, and how safe she was in returning it. Nothing had ever been more real to her than the sensation of her dear friend bringing her over the precipice of girlhood. She completely surrendered to him, without fear. Understanding then, for the first time, intimacy could be so much more than a burden or something to fear. That her desire to be with Oz could be beautiful, not terrible.

Like everything else in her life, Ana ruined that relationship by slowly forgetting that comfort and rebuilding the wall of solitude. She'd annihilated it completely by sleeping with him years later, potentially destroying his marriage and family in the process.

And now, with Finn, she was repeating the same mistake, and for what?

I can't do this to myself anymore. I can't do this to the people I care about anymore.

And if this is who I'm destined to be?

Ana didn't have an answer.

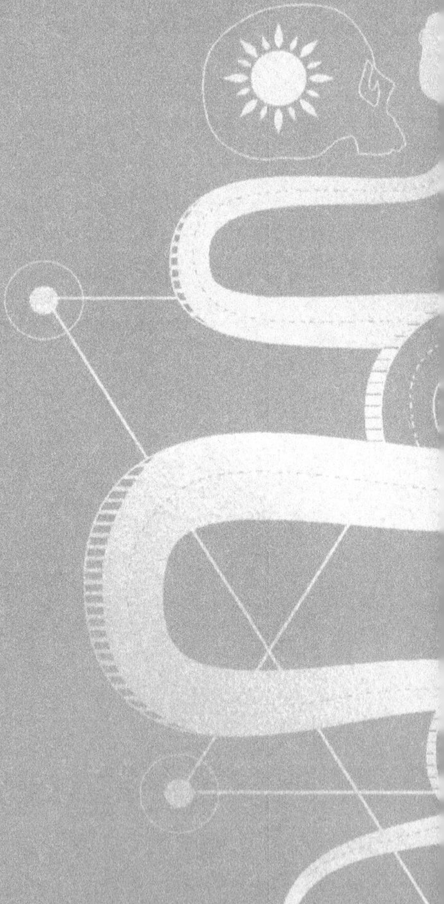

41
FINNEGAN

Finn was still trying to get his bearings. He tried to focus, but he couldn't get his mind off the cold barrel of the shotgun pressed to his temple, and how badly Alex's hand trembled.

"Alex, come on," Finn coaxed, carefully. He was afraid to move his head even a fraction. He knew how a shotgun worked, and didn't want one unloaded in his skull. The old fool might shoot him by accident, his hands were so unsteady.

"Did ya get all the food ya need?" Alex stuttered. He shifted from one foot to the other, back and forth, and Finn felt the barrel of the shotgun correspondingly move left and right with each adjustment. His head ached from where Alex had smashed his skull. He probably had a concussion, but right now that was the least of his worries.

"Yeah. I got enough."

"Then let's go."

"Go where?"

"I'm going back to yer house with ya."

Finn started to ask the obvious questions but Alex interrupted him with a rough nudge of the gun.

He couldn't begin to grasp what the hell was going on. Having known Alex all his life, nothing about this situation made any sense. Jon had always believed Alex had a dark side, but Finn didn't see it. Alex was an interesting cat, but harmless. He'd have thought he was dreaming if not for how real the steel of the old shotgun barrel felt pressed against his bloody, achy skull.

Finn wasn't confident about driving back in the dark. He hadn't planned to, either, but Alex indicated that's exactly what he intended him to do. The streetlights on Androscoggin were on, but only some, illuminating sporadic sections of the road. Compounding the darkness, all the shop lights that would've helped were off. He hardly knew how to drive the temperamental beast, let alone blindly.

As if that weren't enough, while he'd been making a path to the food storage, the new storm had started.

Once they were settled into the cab, Finn said, without turning his head, "Alex. Can you please take the gun off me? I'm not going anywhere."

"Nah, I'm sorry, but I can't trust ya, I can't." Alex was stammering again.

What in the hell happened to him?

"Alex." He tried his father's calm, reasonable voice. "I couldn't outrun you in this if I tried. Not driving, not running. You know that. But if you don't take this goddamn gun off my head, you may as well shoot me, and then yourself, because I'm not driving this gigantic metal monster with a steel bomb about to go off. We can sit here and freeze to death."

Alex thought about it a moment and then lowered the gun, slowly. He was shivering so badly that the barrel made a clickity-clack noise as it bumped up against the buttons on his coat.

"I'll take it away from yer head, but I ain't putting it down," he said, sounding more like a stubborn child than a middle-aged man.

"Fine, just don't point it at me," Finn compromised, starting up the snowcat. Alex jumped next to him as it roared to life. Finn pictured the news after they found the two of them in pieces all over the cab from a rogue shotgun pellet. "Relax, gunslinger."

"There's only one criminal in this rig, and it ain't me." Alex's eyes burned holes in him as he maneuvered in reverse.

He glanced to his right and wondered what he might need to do to keep Jon and Ana safe from this trembling madman.

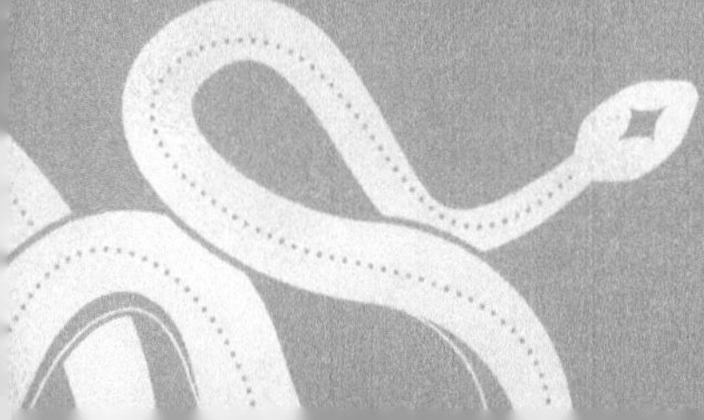

42
NICOLAS

Nicolas never had any doubts that Jennifer would come through, but the longer they waited, the more he worried. He'd been waiting with Oz on the pier for over an hour, in the freezing blackness of the middle of the night.

At first, she told them they'd leave at first light. She called back later and said the fishing boat captain was too nervous about the prospect of being caught and thought night would be better. That, and a new, fresh storm brewed, one that might be worse than the last.

"Isn't that less safe than the already unsafe daytime trip we were planning?" Nicolas asked.

She sighed. "Those are his terms. I even offered him more of your money, and he wouldn't budge."

So be it.

Nicolas asked Oz if he was sure he wanted to come. *You can stay here in the hotel Ozzy. I won't think less of you*, he'd said, and meant it. If captains raised in this weather wouldn't run, then the risks were real. He felt bad enough dragging Oz to Maine with him, away from Adrienne and the kids.

Oz snickered at that. *Our hotel doesn't even have* cable.

Nicolas and Oz exchanged no words standing on the pier, but they both had enough thoughts to keep themselves occupied. Nicolas watched his friend and thought, *Well now we really have been through everything.*

On the flight over, a specific memory continued dancing around the tip of his thoughts, and now, as they waited in the cold darkness, he finally allowed himself to explore it.

It was Ana's senior year of undergraduate studies at Tulane. Nicolas had discovered a letter, peeking out from under her textbooks. *We're pleased to extend an invitation to the English program at Oxford University.*

"What's this?" Nicolas had asked, waving the letter. It was the first time she'd hidden anything from him.

"It's nothing." Dropped gaze, lowered voice.

"Um, the fuck it's nothing, Ana! You were accepted to motherfucking *Oxford*, and you say that it's *nothing*?"

"It's nothing because I'm making it nothing." Her eyes were distant; he hardly recognized her in that moment. *She's forced herself to come to this decision. She wants to go, but she's not going to.* "I've already declined the offer. I'm staying at Tulane."

Nicolas gaped at her in frustrated amazement. "But... *why*?"

Ana sighed, still unwilling to meet his eyes, and Nicolas wanted to take her face in both hands. "I don't... want to leave you," is what she said. But what Nicolas heard beneath her words was: *I don't want to leave you alone.*

"That is the most ridiculous fucking thing I've ever heard you say, Anasofiya Aleksandrovna. And you've said a lot of ridiculous shit." Perhaps if he belittled her feelings, she'd reconsider.

"Seriously, Ana. All fuckery aside. You need to do this." *You need to do this, but a part of me is overflowing with gladness and relief that you aren't. And I hate myself for it.*

But she'd simply shrugged. "I've made my decision. Can we talk about something else?"

Nicolas had dropped the issue, and it never came up again. But that didn't mean he forgot about it. Nor did he forget *why* she'd done it, or the knowledge that his indignant persuasion was weak at best. *I had the power to make her go, and I chose to pretend she couldn't be swayed.*

He rarely allowed his conclusions to travel down a philosophical path, but part of him wondered now if somehow all of these decisions had brought them to where they were now. How every one they made affected every subsequent one. How one choice could start a spiral of events that determined the course of your entire life.

Please be okay, Ana. I know I'm a selfish fuck, but goddamnit, I need you. You're the only one who has ever loved me. Protecting and loving you has been the only thing that's given my sorry ass a purpose.

Nicolas forced himself to keep his mind away from thoughts of what they might find when they reached Summer Island. Since the moment he'd decided to come, he'd only allowed his thoughts of Ana to play on the surface, where it was safe. Whatever they faced, there'd be no formal preparation for Nicolas. He would simply face it, with Oz by his side.

We're coming, Muffins.

"PEACOCK," THEY HEARD A LOW VOICE SAY FROM BEHIND. OZ sniggered.

"Brown booby," Nicolas replied with a sigh, and this time Oz outright laughed. "Yes, we're both twelve, now where do we go?"

The captain led them to a small cabin cruiser at the end of one of the dock arms. The boat was smaller than Nicolas expected, and his stomach dropped. Based on Oz's expression, he had the same thoughts.

"He might not be all here," Oz said quietly. Nicolas set his mouth in a tight line, wanting to disagree but not sure he had grounds to.

The ship was shrouded in darkness. The closest lighting was about fifty feet away, and penetrated little more than twenty feet effectively. Between the insufficient illumination, and the increasing snowfall, they could see only a vague outline of their transportation.

Oz grabbed onto the rope and pulled himself up first, Nicolas hoisting himself after. The captain said they should both go down into the cabin and relax, because the ride would be slow going, if they wanted to avoid detection. Nicolas asked how long the crossing would take, but apparently his generous payment didn't include having his questions answered. There was a low rumble, followed by harsh vibrations that rattled the entire cabin. Then, a sudden jerk, which caused Oz to nearly lose his footing, and they were off. Nicolas peered hopefully out the tiny, murky window into the darkness, but was unable to see anything at all.

"Ana once told me it's about an hour from the island to the mainland, and since this is the *Super Secret Spy Ferry,* I'd guess we can expect it to be longer than that," Nicolas speculated. Oz gripped the small rusted pole near the bench he sat on, face touching his knees.

"Goody," Oz grimaced.

Nicolas rolled onto the bench across from Oz. The hard metal poked his back in cruel synchrony with the strong vibrations of the ship. All internal power was off, so not only were there no lights, but also no heat. Oz was curled in a ball, shivering dramatically. Nicolas rolled his eyes, then rummaged through a nearby drawer, looking for matches, or anything that might give them some light. Finding nothing, he gave up after a few moments.

He heard Oz mutter something like: *Not so prepared after all.*

Nicolas didn't share his agitation. In the grand scheme of things, paying for a small fishing boat to cross the stormy Casco Bay was pretty low on the scale of scandalous things he'd been involved in over the years. Had the reason not been serious, he would've been up on the deck enjoying the thrill!

But the reason *was* serious, and as Nicolas was no good at dealing with serious things, he decided to lighten the mood.

"Ozzy?" he asked, as they both lay on the flat, uncomfortable benches.

"Yes?" Oz didn't try to hide the annoyance in his voice.

"Hypothetically speaking, if Captain Jack up there came down and said to brace ourselves for imminent death, would your first instinct be to have sex with me, just once, before we died?"

The pillow whistled across the room and smacked him in the face. Nicolas smiled, satisfied.

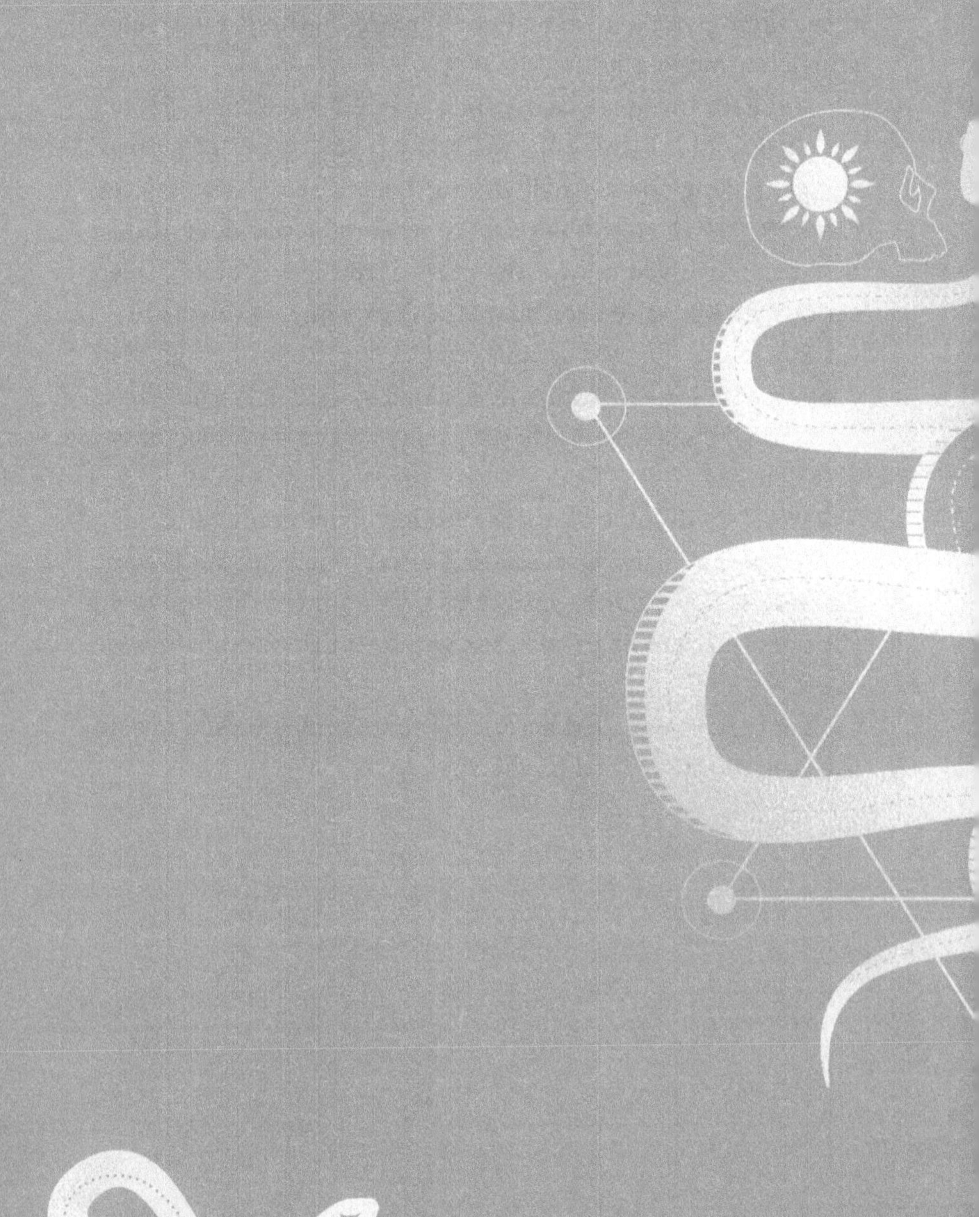

43
ALEX

They were officially headed to the St. Andrews house, and Alex still had no plan.

It'd been easy enough to pull out the gun. Granted, one he barely knew how to use, but that was beside the point. It was obvious he needed to go to the house with Finn and get to the bottom of what was going on. But what would he do once he got there?

Are you really going to shoot someone? What if you get there and everything is fine? Or, what if you get there and everything is not *fine, and you have to take action? Are you going to take them both down? What precisely are you going to do now that you've gone rogue? You put these plans in motion, and now there's no going back. As soon as you put the gun to the head of Finn St. Andrews, a man you've known twenty-seven years, there was no pretending this didn't happen. The wheels are moving forward, whether you're ready or not.*

His internal dialogue was obnoxious. On a positive note, at least it wasn't in his father's voice. He tried responding, ignoring, thinking about something else. Nothing helped. His mind continued to throw questions at him... challenging him, making him doubt his decision to get involved. *Too late now. Time to man-up*. But what did that mean?

Finn wasn't talking, but he wasn't trying to run or get in the way either. At first Alex was afraid he might, but when he saw Finn's face as the young man started to wake up—first the shock, the anger, shock again and finally, worst of all, the betrayal—he knew Finn wouldn't be a danger to him, for now. It would be a different story once they arrived at the St. Andrews house. *If* they made it, Alex thought, considering the intensity of the new, growing storm.

When they did, they'd catch Jon by surprise. Even if Finn managed to signal him, by the time he did it would be too late. There was no cell service and the land-lines were down. Alex vaguely recalled Finn mentioning their house radio stopped working last year, and knowing how flaky the boy could be, he doubted if Finn had bothered to get it fixed.

You better hope he hasn't.

The silence in the cab was almost worse than the debates raging untamed in his head. He'd killed any chance of conversation by putting a gun to his neighbor's head. Even if he came out and asked Finn if they were keeping Ana Deschanel as a sex slave, torturing her and making her bend to their every whim, would he admit it? Alex chuckled at the thought of how that conversation might go.

"Nothing funny about this shit, Alex," Finn observed beside him.

"Was just thinking about something else," he said, apologetically. He mentally kicked himself. *Don't be weak Wexie Woo, he's the psycho here!* His father's voice was back.

"Well, better start thinking about what you're gonna do

when I get this thing home," Finn warned. "You don't pull a gun on a man unless you intend to use it."

"Oh, you'll know my intentions soon," Alex promised. *Try to sound scarier, and confident*, he told himself. "You and Jon both."

Finn laughed.

Christ almighty. He can see right through me. I hate him. "Laugh now, while you can," Alex threatened.

Finn kept laughing, shaking his head. "I wish you could see yourself, Alex. I really do."

Alex's face was scalding. He wanted to hit Finn again with the butt of the gun, but didn't want to wreck and be stuck. "Like I said..." he started, and left the rest to interpretation. Finn would regret not taking him seriously, if not now, then later. *I have a gun, for the love of God!*

Yes, you do have a gun. Once you know Finn isn't going to kill you both in a freak accident, you can use it to your advantage. And you have the element of surprise. Jon doesn't know you're coming, and walking in with a gun to his brother's head won't leave him with a lot of options. Let Finn laugh now, because the satisfaction when he sees what a tough guy you are will be that much greater.

"Can this thing go any faster?" Alex asked.

"Depends on if you want to get there in one piece or not." Finn strained to see. He pressed his gloved hand to the windshield to try and clear the steam. "We might need to stop somewhere until this storm passes."

"We'll stop if I say we stop," Alex commanded, though Finn was likely right. They'd need to seek refuge soon if they didn't want to end up stranded inside the snowcat, freezing to death.

You shouldn't be in a hurry, anyway. You need a plan. And it better be good, because it isn't just the girl you should be concerned about. You could be in a serious pickle if this backfires.

Aye, his father's voice responded, *you best remember you ain't cut out for what waits for you in the pokey, though come to think of it, it might make a right man out of ya, fer once...*

Alex shivered, shaking off the disdainful voice. Hateful or not, his father was right again.

If I sense things are going south, I ain't going down alone.

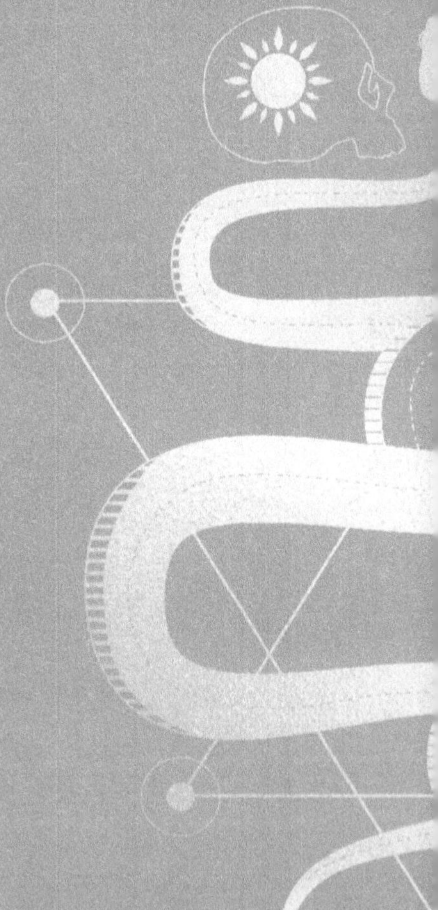

44
OZ

"Do you even know where we're going once we reach the island?"

Nicolas looked up from his cell phone. He'd been trying to get a reception, but as Ana's hadn't worked a day since she got to the island, Oz thought it was a futile effort. Nicolas, stubborn, insisted he only needed to find the "sweet spot."

"I have the address, if that's what you mean."

"And how is that going to be helpful, exactly? Do you have a map? GPS? The roads are closed and the island is covered in snow."

Nicolas continued fiddling with his phone, waving it around, squinting. "We'll figure it out, don't worry!"

Oz had always been exasperated by Nicolas' *laissez faire* approach to life. *We'll get there when we get there. We don't need a plan. Oh, let's see where this road goes.*

"Nic," he said evenly, "please, tell me you have a better plan than that."

"No, not really Ozzy," he replied casually, moving around

the small cabin, arm outstretched. "But the island is small, so how hard can it be?"

Oz laughed, followed by a weary sigh. "We're screwed."

He was tired and cold. On top of that was guilt, and no small measure of fear. Nicolas was free to label what they were doing an adventure, but by all sane measures, this was very high-risk behavior. Nicolas' whole life had been one "adventure" after another. Oz had hoped this time he might have a different approach, given what was at stake.

Nicolas watched Oz from his peripheral. "I'll ask Captain Jack up there. Maybe he can help. I know that she has a dock outside the property, so maybe he can drop us off at her front door."

Oz laughed again. "Oh right, ferry valet. Make sure you have an appropriate tip ready."

"Ah, fuck off, we paid him well enough. Why wouldn't he?"

"Because he doesn't have to? Because Ana's 'dock' is likely for small, personal use? Because this is already dangerous enough without adding more levels of difficulty? Because he's a jerk? Because the sky is blue? Because—"

"I get it. I get it." Nicolas put the phone away and Oz felt immediately better. At least he was paying attention.

"What do you suggest then, Ozzy?" He hunkered on the bench, elbows on his knees.

"Well, I would've come prepared. I would've known what side of the island we were going to dock on, and had a map with Ana's house on it so we could at least make our way there if we have to walk through a bunch of snow."

"Thank you, Captain Hindsight. That's really helpful for the next time. But since I didn't do any of that, what do you suggest now?"

Oz didn't have a clue. People always looked to him for ideas, but he hated making decisions. He wanted Nicolas to be better prepared, not to have to figure it out himself. Adrienne always looked at him like he should know the answer, too. "I don't know," he admitted. "But I think you better start sweet talking our friend up top."

Nicolas sighed. "Fine." He motioned Oz toward the stairs. "Ladies first."

The captain was having a cigarette. Oz got his first good look at "Peacock." He was in his fifties, rotund, with terrible, weatherworn skin. His pockmarked face blurred his features, except for a scar that ran from his middle forehead to the tip of his nose. His skin sagged around his mouth in a way that would disguise a smile, had he bothered to try one on.

"Almost there," he said gruffly, without turning.

"Awesome. So where are we going to be putting down anchor?" Nicolas asked him. He positioned himself in front of Peacock, against the railing.

"Where the ferries dock," he said, still looking out to sea.

"And where would that be?" Nicolas prodded.

"Where they dock," he repeated in the same even tone.

Oz stepped up, sensing Nicolas' growing agitation. "Sir. We need to get to the Deschanel property." No response. "The property that's normally overseen by Alex Whitman. It's on the southeastern corner of the island. Can you at least give us some general direction?"

Peacock took a long, deep puff on his smoke, then flicked the butt out to sea. It disappeared into the fog. Oz had no idea which way was north, let alone where they were in proximity to anything.

"I can't drop you off there, if that's what you're askin'," he answered finally. He coughed and spat off the side of the railing

"That's fine," Oz said, trying to sound amenable. "We just need to know which way to go."

Peacock grunted and walked away.

Nicolas kicked the railing. Oz ignored him and followed the man, into the tiny, glassed-in, captain's room. The equipment was rusted in varying stages of disrepair. Oz tried not to think about what that might mean for their safety.

Peacock bent over a small table, drawing on a map. He traced a circle, a crazy line, and another circle. He handed the map to Oz. "Here," he pointed at the first circle, "is where I am droppin' ya off. Here," he pointed at the next circle, "is where ya wanna go."

It didn't look far on the map, but Oz couldn't see a marker for distance. "About how far is that?" he asked.

"A mile, er so, by roads, but ya know they're closed. Less as the crow flies, but you won't be moving so fast with two feet of snow under ya."

Oz folded the map and thanked him. "We appreciate this."

"My family appreciates the extra year's salary," he said with a nod, then sat down and said no more.

"What a cock," Nicolas said, when Oz returned. Nicolas jogged in place to stay warm.

Oz pulled the map out of his pocket and unfolded it, smashing the wrinkled paper into Nicolas' face. "Who's the cock now?"

Nicolas' face erupted in a big, contagious smile that Oz couldn't help but return. "Ozzy, you are such a bitch, but goddamnit, I love you!"

45
FINNEGAN

Finn unlocked the door to Jon's office. Alex had stopped shaking, at least. Finn suspected he had no idea how to use the gun, and that worried him more than if he had. There were few things more dangerous than putting a loaded shotgun in the hands of an inexperienced man.

"No funny business," Alex said from behind him.

The tiny bell jingled as the door swung inward. The air that greeted them was only slightly warmer than what they'd faced outside, as Jon had forgotten to leave the heat on.

"And we're only staying 'til the snow dies down. I mean it!"

"Trust me, I don't want to be here with you any longer than I have to." Finn walked ahead of Alex with his hands showing, lest the man accidentally mistake his actions for rebelliousness and shoot him.

Finn's eyes scanned the room, taking measure.

"Hmph," Alex replied. "You're awful cocky fer a man who ain't got the upper hand."

Finn faced away from Alex, smiling into the darkness.

"You're right, Alex. I'll remind myself to be sufficiently respectful of your position going forward."

Alex missed the sarcasm. "That's a good boy. It ain't gonna save ya, but it may convince me to have some mercy, when the time fer reckonin' is upon ya."

"All right, Alex," Finn muttered low, under his breath. If Alex didn't want to explain himself, fine. Finn didn't require an explanation. He'd come to Jon's office not for shelter, but to end this ridiculous game.

Finn found the wall thermostat and switched on the heater. The relief would be slow in coming, but perhaps it would at least take the edge off the deep chill in his bones.

Alex followed him into the back room, past the examination tables and into Jon's office. Finn charged ahead, leaving Alex struggling to keep up. "Stop!" Alex exclaimed, as Finn reached for the office door. "*Stop now*!"

Finn raised his hands again. He couldn't hide the edge in his voice. "Alex, do you want food and blankets, or not?"

The gun still resting on his shoulder, Alex looked down at his soaked gear, and then back up at Finn. "Slowly."

Finn didn't need to be told to go slowly. He was pretty certain any surprise would be excuse enough for Alex to send a spray of pellets straight through him, and he wasn't ready to die. Especially not at the hands of this ridiculous old man who'd decided that the middle of a storm was a great time to play cowboy.

Finn didn't care what Alex's motivations were. He only needed to buy time. Food and blankets were the furthest things from Finn's mind, despite the chill in him that wouldn't die. He needed Alex to be thinking about the incoming warmth, to stay focused on it.

"I don't see no blankets," Alex accused, as they entered Jon's tiny office. *Damn you for being so neat*, Finn thought, as he glanced around at the bare room. There was only Jon's organized desk, a cupboard, a small fridge, and a bookshelf.

"They're in the cupboard," Finn lied. He fingered through Jon's keychain, searching for something to unlock it. *Please have blankets in here. And something else.*

"Check the fridge for food," Finn ordered, as he fumbled with the cupboard lock. Alex gasped in indignation from behind him. *Good, let him be annoyed. He can't possibly be half as pissed off with me as I am with him.*

"You can check it yer own dang self," Alex said. Finn imagined that if Alex did not have a gun in his hands, he'd have his arms crossed, pouting. *I'm ticking him off more, by funning with him. He knows I'm not taking him seriously, and it's possible this is going to backfire.*

Eyeing the fridge, Finn suddenly recalled that was where Jon kept most of his animal medicine. Including pre-filled syringes.

I know for sure he keeps tranquilizers here.

Finn abandoned the cupboard, kneeling down in front of the fridge. Alex rambled on behind him, but Finn was single-mindedly focused on trying to locate the medicine before Alex caught on to the diversion.

"Well, is there food in there or not?" Alex demanded. Finn blocked Alex's view, his heart racing as he read through the labels in a rush. *Atenolol. Enalapril. Ketamine. Ketoprofen.* None of these names meant a damn thing to Finn, and he wished, for once, that he'd occasionally paid attention when Jon talked about his job. *One of these has to be a tranquilizer. Jon uses those a lot, and I swear it started with a K...*

When Finn felt Alex kneeling down for a better view, he quickly grabbed the syringe marked *Ketoprofen*. Sliding it under his sleeve, Finn stood in a rush, revealing the lack of food.

"Guess I was wrong," Finn said, as Alex leaned in for a closer look.

Finn found his moment. While Alex examined the fridge, Finn sprung to life, pulling the syringe out and stabbing it into the side of Alex's neck in one fluid motion. In Alex's shock, the gun fell to a startling clank on the linoleum, and Alex went flying into the cupboard. The vase on top wobbled, then fell to the floor, shattering

Alex stared at him in shock, hands pressed against in neck. His shock quickly switched to rage, as he realized what Finn had done. "You little son of a whore! I was gonna go easy on ya, but now I'm gonna *wring your neck*!"

Finn didn't wait for Alex's retaliation. He flew into him, shoving him so hard against the cabinet that it trembled. Alex cursed at him, winded, and Finn threw a punch at his face, wincing as his hand connected and blood flew from Alex's nose in a long, arcing spray. Finn punched him again, and when Alex sprung back, Finn grabbed Alex by the shoulders and threw him across the room, sending him sailing into the wall with a thud. Alex gripped the bookshelf, wobbling.

"We're done with this bullshit, Alex," Finn panted. *Why is he still awake?*

"Yer gonna rot in hell," Alex seethed through bloody teeth, and charged Finn. The move was so unexpected Finn didn't react in time. The push into the cupboard knocked the wind out of him. *No. Oh, no. Ketamine is the tranquilizer, not Ketoprofen. Ketamine. Oh, God.*

"I'm not fucking around with you anymore, you crazy old man!" Finn raged, and barreled into Alex. They both fell to the floor in a mess of jumbled arms and legs, with Finn quickly gaining the upper hand. He had his forearm pressed against Alex's neck. "Alex, calm *down*."

To his surprise, Alex went still beneath him. The man's

wild eyes regarded Finn, darting around in their sockets. As they considered each other, their heated, panting breaths the only sounds between them, Alex's eyes brimmed with tears. Unexpectedly, Finn no longer saw a crazed gunman, but simply the sad, old man that Alex was: age spots, thinning hair, and a lifetime of loneliness.

Finn relaxed his hold, and some of the color returned to Alex's face. "If I let go, are you gonna chill out?"

Alex nodded ever so slightly. His eyes were large, and remorseful. *I almost feel sorry for him.* "Okay. I'm letting go..."

Finn's head filled with stars, and his stomach turned inside out as Alex threw a powerful knee to his groin. He rolled over in pain, struggling to breathe and right himself, but he once again felt the cold steel of the shotgun against the back of his head.

Finn slowly looked up at Alex. The man no longer looked nervous. He no longer seemed the sad, old man with age spots and thinning hair. A wide, blood-filled, clownish smile, spread slowly across his face, and he was every bit the crazed gunman. *He played me like a fiddle. Jon was right about him. Holy shit, he was right all along. Oh, God.*

"*Now*, do you take me seriously?" Alex demanded. Finn nodded, realizing, finally, that to do otherwise might be an authorization of his own death warrant.

"Good," Alex continued. "Because you're going to die tonight, Finnegan St. Andrews. Whether you die here, or at home, is up to you."

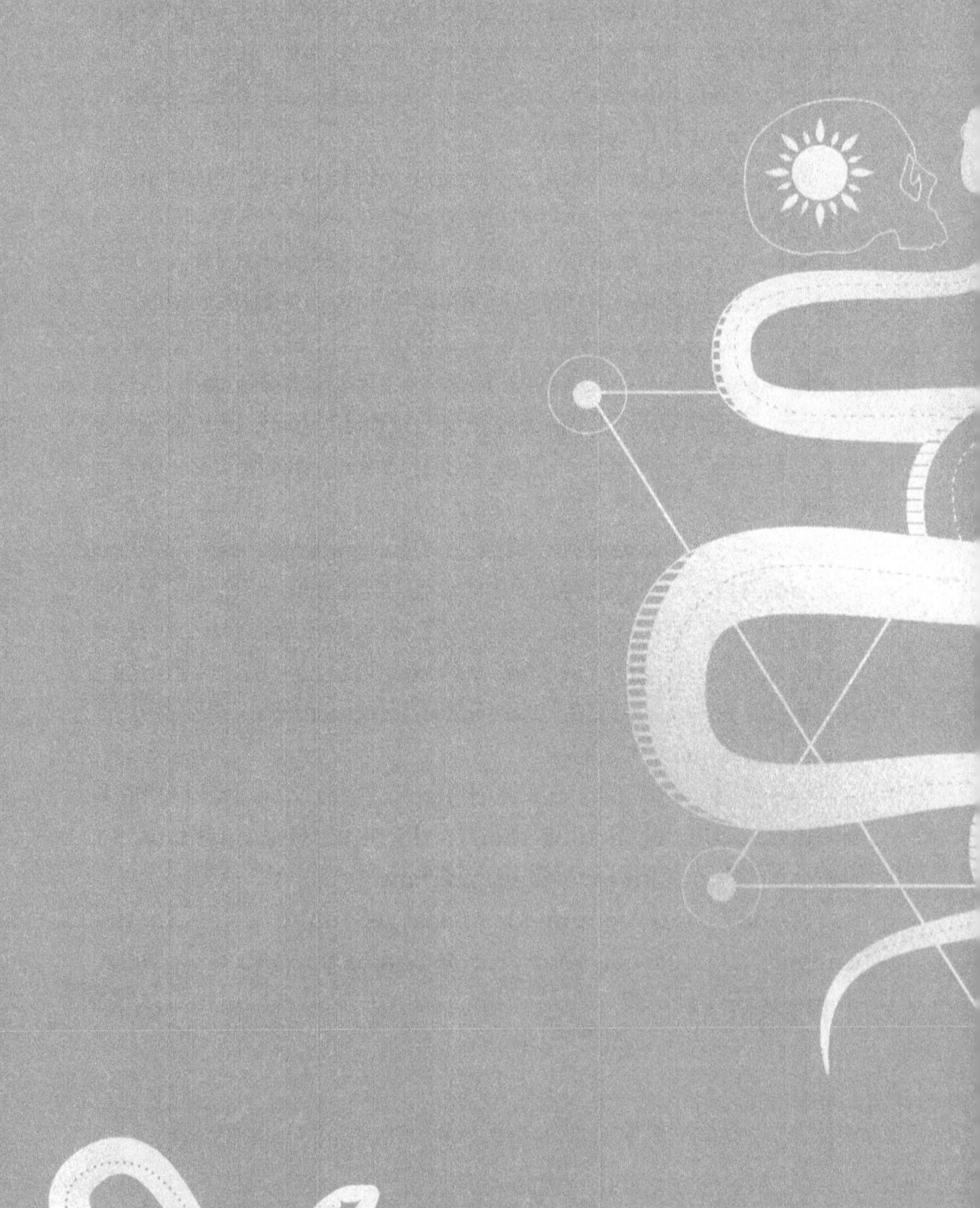

46
NICOLAS

Nicolas wasn't sure what he'd been expecting, but it wasn't this. He could see nothing but snow, forest, and a mass of land. Houses were scattered sparsely along the tiny coastline, a few tiny lights dotting the landscape. He could barely make out the dark outlines of the town itself. Above town, a lighthouse beacon seemed to float and twinkle as it turned slowly. The red and white stripes along the tower's exterior contrasted against the whitewash of the snow, reminding him of a Christmas candy cane.

"How many people live here?" he asked the captain.

"A couple hundred," the captain responded as he squared them up to the port. "Most o' the folks live near the center of the island. That's where the town's at."

"But that's not where we're going," Nicolas mumbled. Oz had studied the map and tried to roughly sketch their plan. The Deschanel home was on the eastern shore, and they were docking on the western. Between the two points was a large wildlife preserve they'd need to cross. There was over two feet of snow on the ground, and the snowshoes they'd bought only seemed like one more hurdle to overcome.

The captain lowered the clunky ladder onto the old pier. It was unsteady, but he insisted on avoiding the main dock. Finding a relatively empty area, he maneuvered in the cruiser.

Their descent was done under the captain's impatient direction. "Go on, I need to get back," the captain urged.

"Could be nicer, for the money I paid you," Nicolas chided, but started the climb down. His feet met the icy dock with a quick slide, but he righted himself as he backed away.

"Won't mean nothin' to me if I die out here," he said, pulling the ladder back as soon as Oz's second foot hit the deck. Oz stumbled into Nicolas, who shoved him straight into the snow.

"Ass," Oz complained, as Nicolas helped him to his feet. The boat was already departing for the mainland. Oz scrambled, shouting and waving, slipping across the deck as he vied for the captain's attention.

"Change of heart?"

Oz stopped yelling long enough to say, "No, dumbass! We need a way to get *back* to the mainland once we find Ana. A smaller detail that, you know, we might want to work out!"

Nicolas exhaled and stared blankly ahead. It was true, he was never much of a planner. He took vacations on a whim, partied whenever the mood hit, and never remembered important dates. "Oz, stop," he said finally, when the boat continued on its course. "He won't help us even if we double the pay. You know that."

Oz sank back against the wooden rail of the dock, deflated. Nicolas thought maybe he was experiencing his first wave of regret at offering to come along. Coming out for a couple days to find Ana was one thing, but knowing they could be there for a while seemed to hit them both at once. Nicolas felt guilty anew for bringing Oz along.

"Look, we can try the Coast Guard again. They'll come if it's an emergency, and I can always knock you out or something," he consoled Oz. Nicolas was always hopeful. Things had a way of working out.

Oz nodded but said nothing. Nicolas didn't press it. Oz had a way of shutting down, and only time helped open him back up.

He pulled the map out of Oz's pocket and spun around to get his bearings. "We need to go east... which is... that way," he said, pointing to his right, and the opposite direction of the lighthouse.

Oz shoved his hands in his pockets and started walking. Nicolas followed.

47
JONATHAN

There were so many unknowns.

Maybe Finn found a way to stay the night, or might even be on his way back. Maybe he'd gotten lost in the storm, or had vehicle troubles. The food storage had a code they all knew in case of emergencies, but what if Finn had forgotten it? All the possible ways thing could go wrong were eating Jon up, but he couldn't pry his mind from the worry.

He abandoned his rocker and window view, and went to clean the kitchen, but it was already clean. He tried busying himself around the house in other ways, checking on his furry patients, but they were fine, and his mind wandered anyway.

Having Ana around made it worse, although he appreciated her outlook on the strange event from earlier.

Jon had expected her to insist on talking about it, dissecting it, making sense of it and what it meant for the future. He anxiously awaited the sound of her footsteps on the stairway.

But then she'd surprised him. She didn't want to talk about it, beyond confirming it was a one time deal, never to repeat. *Oh, and by the way, I'm into your brother.*

Jon was relieved at how easy that went, but later he wondered, was it really that easy to forget?

Jon couldn't help his bruised ego. He wanted to rewind time and be the one to tell *her* it wasn't a big deal.

In retrospect, it wasn't a surprise to him that Ana let him off the hook. She evidently *did* like Finn, enough to panic at the thought of losing him.

What did surprise Jon was his jealousy. His better sense betrayed him, recalling the feeling of her wet, soft bottom in his hands; the way her cheeks filled his palms; how, when he squeezed her hips, they responded by arcing higher, her long arms winding around his neck and down his back.

Jonathan shivered. *Stop. It's just been a while. And she's not hard on the eyes.*

Resigned that any distraction he tried to concoct was not going to be sufficient, he headed back to his rocker. Ana was sitting in it now, gazing out the bay window into the glowing darkness of snow and sea.

He wanted to ask her to move. To tell her that was *his* rocker, he always sat there. He needed to sit there. But talking was harder than adjusting, so he gritted his teeth and pulled up another.

Ana didn't say anything when he sat down. She was lost in her own thoughts. He relaxed a bit. Not even Finn was capable of sharing this kind of easy solitude with him. Only Ana would understand the way for people like them to experience true closeness and comfort was to do exactly what they were doing... losing themselves, together, in the place they each felt safest.

This disturbed Jon, but it also aroused another sensation within him that he hadn't felt in many years.

Rather than dwell in that dangerous territory, he focused on the more pressing concern.

Finn, where are you?

48
NICOLAS

Nicolas wasn't the outdoors type. He was fine at a party, or on a yacht, or doing something wild and interesting. He didn't mind the heat, if he was on a beach in France. He didn't mind the cold, if he was skiing in the Swiss Alps. No one had to tell Nicolas how lucky he was. But while it was no surprise to him he didn't enjoy their trek through the snowy island, it caught him off-guard how badly out of shape he was.

Oz was still grumpy, but cruising right along. He was a distance runner, so his heart and lungs were well equipped for the grueling slog through knee-deep snow that threatened to bring Nicolas to a grinding halt. Every few feet, Nicolas had to stop, leaning up against a tree, and catch his breath. Oz, several paces ahead, would patiently stop as well, doing so without turning around or saying a word. *He's mad at me. He's mostly mad at himself, but he's disappointed in me for being such a slack-ass about planning.* The best way Nicolas knew to make it up to him was to ensure they accomplished their goal, found Ana, and brought her home. When it was all over, and they told the story to the family back home, he would even highlight Oz's quick thinking and military-like prowess in unfamiliar territory. He chuckled to himself.

"I'm glad you find your thirty-year-old ass panting and clutching a tree funny," Oz said, up ahead. They were his first words since the realization they had no way back.

"What else could it be?" Nicolas panted.

"Embarrassing?"

"Sexy?"

"False."

They continued on. Occasionally, they'd see lights from houses, but they were further inland, and the house they wanted was on the shore. They trudged forth, every step a new effort, every breath wreaking fresh havoc on their lungs. Even with the expensive winter gear they'd bought in Portland, Nicolas felt completely exposed.

Eventually, they came to an outcropping, where three houses sat. The space between them was enough for a football field each, but if the captain's crude map was right, they'd arrived at their destination.

"Ana's house is the middle one, according to this map," Oz noted. The house on the left, closest to them, had several lights on. The one on the far right had only a small porch light lit. The Deschanel home was dark as night.

Nicolas' heart was thrumming even faster now. He worried about the lights being off, but it *was* the middle of the night...

The cliffs were treacherous. Snow obscured any hint of where the road might be, so the men took the only route available: an arduous climb down to the shore. They passed the first house, where the ocean had cleared a graveled path. This course forced them back up the craggy demarcation in several places due to the natural jetties of rocks. Oz kept looking back to make sure Nicolas was keeping up. Nicolas would've felt like an idiot if he fell to his death because he couldn't handle a basic, albeit slippery, climb.

Oz urged them toward the house. "If nothing else, it's warmth until we can figure things out," Oz said. Nicolas realized Oz didn't expect to find her there. *Neither do I.*

The door was unlocked, so they let themselves in. The house was nearly as cold inside as the outside had been. Nicolas' breath appeared in front of him. There was a sour smell, like something old and forgotten. "She's not here," he declared, knowing in his heart that a search of the house would prove exactly that.

"Hasn't been for a long time," Oz concurred. He held out a glass of curdled milk. "Found the smell."

Where did you go Ana? Her light blue cardigan was draped over a chair at the kitchen table and he held it, smelling her. If something had happened to her, he'd know it. He'd feel it. *But I do feel it, that's why I'm here.*

"I think we should try the neighbors," Oz suggested finally. He eyed Nicolas clutching the sweater, and Nicolas put it down.

"Which ones?"

"The ones whose property we already passed through," Oz said. "There were lights on all over the house. We could try the other neighbors, but they only had their porch light lit. I say we start with the ones who seem to be awake."

"Three in the morning," Nicolas said. "What do you think is going on next door at this hour? Key party?"

"That would be the lamest key party ever. No one can drive."

Thank god he's joking back. I didn't realize until now that I can't do this without him. "The house is big enough. Maybe they can pretend," he quipped. "All right. Let's do this."

"Wait. Before we go over there, there's something I need to tell you," Oz said.

Nicolas already had his hand on the door. "Seriously? Now?"

But Oz's face wasn't playful. His eyes had the same wild, faraway look they had when he'd come over for that weird visit, and the color built up from their snowy exercise had completely drained away. "Yes, now. I should've told you this before we came to Maine, but I didn't know how and, well, I don't know what's going to happen next door, and what this night has in store for us. I can't hang on to this anymore. It's eating me up, and I have to get it off my chest."

Nicolas didn't like the sound of Oz's words, or the look on his face. The last time Oz had looked so pained was when Adrienne went missing, all those years ago. "Say it, then."

Oz motioned for him to sit, but Nicolas shook his head. "Just say it, so we can go."

Oz took a breath and started talking. He'd always rambled when he was nervous, and he did so now, fumbling through the first part of his story and losing Nicolas entirely. It wasn't until Ana's name came up that Nicolas perked up.

"What does Ana have to do with anything?"

"I know why she came to Maine."

"We all do. Can we go now?"

Oz chewed his lower lip, looking toward the spoiled milk glass on the counter. "She came to Maine because... we had a thing."

Nicolas didn't catch what Oz said at first because he was waiting for another long, meandering story.

We had a thing.

"What the fuck does that mean? You had a thing?" Nicolas demanded.

"We slept together. Had sex," Oz attempted to clarify. "It

was only one time—"

"You had *sex* with Ana? Recently?" Nicolas repeated. There was no way he heard that correctly. Ana would never do that. Not to Adrienne... not to *him.*

"Yes," Oz confirmed, barely above a whisper. "Not long before she left."

"You're fucking with me."

But Oz didn't have to say a word. The truth was written all over his face. *I need to get away,* Ana had said, quickly. Too quickly.

Nicolas' body pulsed with rage. He paced behind Oz, processing, thinking. *Oz and Ana... no, it couldn't be. She would never do that. She would never sleep with my best friend; my married best friend. Her cousin's husband. My heart.*

Nicolas knew this was different than those men in the Quarter. *She told me about those. She was ashamed of them, but not so ashamed that she'd keep it from me.* All this time, she'd said nothing, betraying not even a glimpse of her real reason for going away, leaving him wondering if *he* was the problem. *I am such a fool.*

Oz stood and tried to put a hand on his shoulder, but Nicolas shoved him into the counter. "Stay the *fuck* away from me."

"You have no idea how hard this has been—" Oz was saying, and those words put Nicolas over the edge. His hand was already in a fist, and, he swung it, as hard as he could. It connected with Oz's face so hard he thought he might have broken his hand. Oz flew back into the counter again, then crumpled to the kitchen floor.

Oz clutched his bloody face in the corner, and Nicolas felt a small, cold satisfaction in seeing his pain. Oz was always the good guy; the martyr. He was the self-sacrificing masochist who everyone felt so bad for. *This* put Oz in a new light. Oz could use any excuse in the world for his behavior, but it was unforgivable to Nicolas, and he no longer felt that old, aching sympathy for his best friend. *Anyone but Ana, Oz.*

"I don't know what I was thinking," Oz pleaded for understanding. "The whole night was a blur. I felt horrible afterward. I feel horrible now."

"Oh, my heart fucking cries out for you, Oz! Life has been so *unfair* to you, gifting you with a beautiful wife and two awesome kids!"

Oz shook his head, still clutching his nose. He'd pulled a towel off the counter to try and stop the bleeding. "You're my best friend Nic. I didn't do it to hurt you, or her, or Adrienne, or anyone—"

"That is such *bullshit.* You knew how this would make me feel."

"You mean Adrienne, right Nic? You mean, how it would make Adrienne feel?" Oz's words, though timid and searching, were an accusation.

"Don't you dare judge me, you stupid, selfish prick."

"I wish I could take it back. I can't."

"You made this choice, Colin. *You.* You're not the victim," Nicolas said, as calmly as he could manage. He reached his hand out to Oz, who looked up in surprise. "I'm not going to throw you across the room, though you deserve it."

Oz warily took his hand, and Nicolas yanked him to his feet. Oz looked pathetic. The blood dripping down his broken nose only made Nicolas want to hit him again.

"I'm sorry—" Oz started to say, but Nicolas raised his fist, warning him to stop.

"When this is all over, you can go fuck yourself," Nicolas said. "But, right now, we need to help Ana. We owe it to her. *You* really owe it to her. So, we're both going to suck it up and finish this."

49
ANA

Ana was the first to see headlights wash over the front window and light the living room.

Jonathan was reading a medical journal. He'd shown Ana Finn's book piles and invited her to pick out whatever she wanted. She chose *Anna Karenina*, but she'd read the book before, so her mind wandered before she made it through a paragraph. Her thoughts were on Finn. Worried for the trouble he might be in. Anxious for the moment of his inevitable arrival.

She'd never be able to say what she was feeling, she only knew she wanted to see him. Her betrayal with Jon still burned, but Jon wanted to forget it even more than she did. The secret would die with both of them if they chose. And even so, it was hardly a betrayal when she and Finn weren't even in a relationship.

Except, a label didn't change how she felt. How Finn felt. How they might feel when they both addressed those strange, sudden feelings, together. And if there was a future in the cards for them, she couldn't start it with a lie.

She knew she'd need to tell Finn about Jon, but there'd be a powerful ripple from such a confession, and now wasn't the time to consider it.

Ana's regrets were piling up. Her mind was heavy with images of random moments. Finn's surprised smile after she healed him. Jon's wide-eyed panic when she awoke in his house. Oz's face when he realized what a horrible mistake they'd made. *And then there's Nicolas. What face will he make when he learns what I've hidden from him?*

Her thoughts were interrupted when the snowcat eased down the drive.

"Jon," she whispered. She didn't have to point. The headlamps were so bright that by the time the vehicle turned to face the house, the entire room was glowing like daylight.

Ana set her book aside and jumped out of her seat, but Jon's hand clamped down firm on her arm before she could go any further.

"Something's wrong," Jon said.

She wrenched her arm free, but stayed by his side. "What do you mean? He's home."

Jon shook his head, and slowly rose, never taking his eyes off the window. "Look inside the cabin. There are two heads, not one."

Ana squinted and finally saw what he was looking at. She swallowed. "Maybe he found someone from town, stranded."

His silence told her that he didn't believe whoever was in Finn's passenger seat was some poor stranded local. She couldn't wrap her mind around what kind of danger he could possibly bring back, on an island full of people Finn had known his whole life.

They stood together, unmoving, watching in slow motion as the vehicle inched closer to the house.

"What do we do?" she asked.

"I want you to go upstairs," Jon said, slowly. "And stay up there." He moved from her side and went to a cupboard in the kitchen. He pulled out a small box. Inside was a handgun.

"No," she said. Her eyes fixed on the gun. She'd only ever fired one once, when she was much younger. Her father, seeing how much it bothered her, never took her to the range again. "I don't know what you're not telling me, but I'm not going upstairs."

"Please," Jon pleaded.

"Tell me what's going on!"

"I don't know, I don't know," Jon chanted, the gun bobbing up and down in his hand. She wanted to reach over and steady it, but she was afraid. Was it loaded? Did Jon know?

If it does go off, I can only help myself.

They remained in a deadlock until the sound of the rumbling engine faded, followed by the small cab doors opening and shutting. Feet crunching in the snow. Two pairs. Sweat beaded at Jon's brow as he tightened his grip on the gun.

Ana scanned the kitchen, looking for anything to defend herself with. She pulled the largest knife out of the block. Could she actually stab someone with it? She didn't know. She knew only that she was terrified, of something she didn't even yet understand.

Their hearts jumped in unison at the sound of the back door opening. Two voices argued, loudly. Jon opened his mouth, then stopped, and put his finger to his lips as he met Ana's gaze.

"We'll bring the food in later. *Go,*" she heard a very familiar voice say as a man stumbled forward onto the linoleum in the next room. His wet boots squeaked and the sound was piercing in her heightened state.

"Alex," she whispered, quietly enough that only Jon could hear.

He didn't seem surprised at all.

Seconds ticked by painfully. The men's shadows fell over the kitchen before she saw them emerge. A click sounded against her ear as Jon raised the gun.

Finn stepped into the room first, Alex quickly behind him. Ana's eyes fell on the overseer's gun, which was significantly larger than the one Jon held in front of him. Jon, seeming to notice the same thing, shook so violently now that she thought he might fire by accident.

"Jon," Alex greeted. He was almost as nervous and fidgety as Jon. "Ana," he then said as he finally noticed her. There was relief in his voice. "Thank *God.*"

"Alex, what's going on?" She surveyed the situation again. She clutched the knife at her side. Alex perched behind Finn with his gun on him, the melting snow pooling beneath them. Alex was nervous, but he looked far more resolved about what he was doing than Jon.

And Finn. His cheeks were flushed a rosy red. The snow ran down his bruised, bloody face. *My god, what happened to you?*

"I've come to get you out of here," Alex announced. The only sounds were the drip of melting snow and the occasional ragged breath. "To rescue you."

"Rescue me?" She laughed, and the hand holding the knife relaxed. She almost cried with relief. This was all a misunderstanding! Alex and Jon could put down their guns, they could bring in the food and all would be well. "Alex, you have it all wrong. These two saved my life!"

But Alex didn't put the gun down. Nor did Jon. Finn's face remained unchanged. *What do know about this situation that I don't?*

"Stockholm Syndrome," Alex sighed, shaking his head. "I saw a special about it on *Dateline.*" He shoved Finn forward into the kitchen, forcing her out of the way as they both came further into the room.

"Alex, I don't have Stockholm Syndrome. They found me in the snow outside after I fell and hit my head. I'm fine." She lifted her hair back to show the wound, but then remembered it was mostly healed. There was only a light scar where there should have been a nasty wound

"You poor girl," he said. "It's worse than I thought."

Ana wanted to scream. How could he think these two would hurt her?

Neither Finn nor Jon said a word in their own defense. Was Alex insane? Was this normal behavior? He'd always been so kind and helpful to her, but clearly there was more to the man when neither of the brothers were surprised to see him snap.

Ana took a very wary step forward. Jon hissed at her to stay back, but she ignored him. "Alex, please. I appreciate that you were worried for me, but everything's fine. I'm fine." She put up her hand with the butcher knife. "Would they let me have this if they were hurting me?"

Alex flinched and the gun shifted. Finn's face tightened and he squeezed his eyes shut. "Notice they didn't give you the gun?" he remarked, nodding toward Jon.

"I wouldn't even know how to use one," she argued. "This is ridiculous, Alex! I'm telling you, I'm fine!"

"No, my sweet child, you are not. You are not fine at all." His eyes bored holes in her, and she realized there was something else different about him. *He's speaking so succinctly now. His voice is confident. His words are clear.*

Finn spoke up. "Alex, I told you earlier that you should figure out what it is you mean to do with us." His voice sounded far steadier than his face looked. He'd had to weather an entire ride back with this man. *And more,* she thought, eyeing his battered face. "I hope you're ready for what you've just invited."

Jon tensed beside her. Her head spun. *This is it. Finn invited him to kill us. What if he does? What if he's a remorseless killer, disguised as a benign overseer? What if he's not here to save me, but kill us all? What if he kills one of the brothers?*

Will I have to stand there and watch them bleed to death on the floor, unable to do a damn thing to save them?

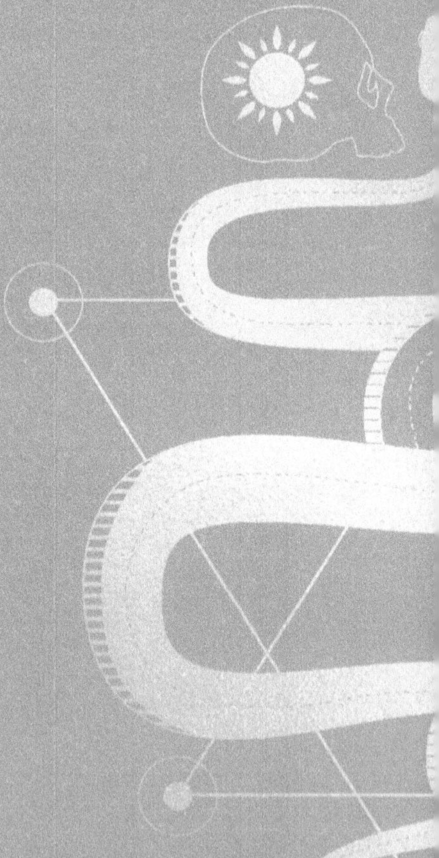

50
ALEX

You had the balls to start this Wexie Wooooo. You better find the balls to finish it.

No, I was doing the right thing! I didn't set out to hurt anyone.

Stupid, idiot, weak boy. When you put a gun to someone's head, someone has to die. You saying you're ready to die?

No. No one has to die. I'll just take Ana and leave.

And go where prissy boy? Laughter. *The second you head out the door, they'll be after you. Did ya forget about all that snow, and the fact that the only vehicle available is something a pansy little shit like you don't even know how to drive?*

What would you have me do? Shoot them both?

Do you see another way out of this, you worthless little shit? She's sympathizing with the two men who've been keeping her hostage. She ain't gonna leave willingly. That sissy vet's got a gun. Finn's a strong kid... would have made a finer son than you. You won't get two steps before one or both of them takes you down, if you try to flee with her. Notice who her knife is pointing at now? That ungrateful little bitch would kill you, too, if she had the chance...

Everything flowed in and out of focus with Alex's heartbeats, each thump causing the room to come alive in stabbing bright light. Ana was breathing heavily, and yes, the knife was now aimed at him, but she was confused. She had to be. Jon and Finn both talked, talked over each other at each other, at him, but Alex wasn't listening. He needed silence to think and they wouldn't *shut up*...

"Alex, put down the gun." Ana this time. In his mind, he heard all the other girls laugh at him. Each of them. All of them. When he'd asked them out. When he'd been trying to do right by them. Save them.

Carla Edgewater. He'd loved her. He'd followed her, everywhere. He wanted to learn her patterns and her likes so he could know more about her, so he could surprise her. He discovered she liked cherry cola from the soda fountain, and that she listened to classical music when no one was watching, dancing to it in her room by moonlight. He knew that once he came to her and told her all he'd learned, she would see what a devoted boyfriend he could be. Did it matter he was almost twenty years her senior? She'd see how much he adored her, and how he'd do anything to please her. How *observant* he was. She would forget all about that cad Lionel Shepherd.

That night, he'd followed her all the way up to the lighthouse. *I'll tell her now. She's alone and the stars are so beautiful tonight.* Then *he* had shown up, and ruined everything. Alex watched as Lionel pushed her clothes aside, and Carla moaned, in pain, lying back against the steel grates with her legs spread as Lionel went to violate her. Alex had come up behind them at just the right moment, shoving Lionel off the edge, between a gap in the railing. Lionel tipped right over, and as he did, his face was a veneer of sheer confusion. That look froze on his face forever as he smashed into the rocks below.

Carla wouldn't stop screaming. She backed away from him

across the deck, her canary yellow sweater unbuttoned, breasts bouncing in the cold air. Her skirt was still hiked up. He could see her lady parts in between the soft white knee socks. Alex could hardly hear her cries above the fierce, whipping wind. He tried to say, *It's okay, I'm here for you!* but that made her scream more and more and more until Alex's head swam with a blinding light.

Minutes later, when his heartbeat slowed once more and the world returned to focus, the ledge was empty. A pain crept into his fists, his first reminder. Peering over the edge, saw what remained of Carla Edgewater's broken, twisted body, next to Lionel's, the corpse bride and groom.

Alex had run then, and kept running. Why did Carla have to go and do that? Didn't she understand how much he loved her? He'd saved her from Lionel's immoral pawing, and she'd taken his side. Alex only wanted to dance with her to classical music by moonlight.

He couldn't save someone who didn't wish to be saved, but he could at least *save her from herself.* Carla was in a better place now, where God could teach her the lessons in kindness and love that she'd been unwilling to learn from Alex.

Just like Alex's mother. He'd set them both free.

Then there'd been the girl in the bar, Sandra Finnerty, and that widow from church, Emily Caldwell. Alex wanted so badly to go to the funerals of these women and tell the family he'd tried. Lord Almighty above, how he'd tried. No one could say Alex Whitman *had not tried.*

As he'd tried when Ana fell into his charge. She was alone, new to the island, and such a nice girl. Unlike the others, he saw himself more as her custodian than lover. But it hadn't taken long at all before he felt that familiar throbbing in his temples, the blinding white, and the feeling—the *insistence*—that this was another one he needed to help. No one else could do it. The system would fail her just like it had failed his mother, and the other women, and that knowledge burned deep within his soul. He'd accepted his calling a long time ago, even if the price was sometimes a cross too heavy to bear.

Ana was still pleading with him to stop, to leave them alone. *Just like Carla. Just like Sandra. Like Emily. Like mother...*

51
OZ

Oz had known from the beginning he'd have to tell Nicolas about the situation with Ana. He'd expected him to be unhappy about it, but he hadn't expected the rage. And he definitely hadn't expected the broken nose. Oz had somehow managed to go his whole life without ever being punched in the face, and he intended to go the rest of his life without it happening again.

He'd never seen Nicolas so angry, but it was that moment of calm, before they left the house, that stuck with Oz. *We're going to suck it up and finish this.*

There were a thousand things Oz wanted to say to Nicolas—a thousand apologies, a thousand explanations—but this wasn't like other arguments they'd had over the years, where Nicolas would pout, or throw a fit and ignore him for a few hours. Nicolas had very calmly pulled himself together and there was no mistaking his disgust. *We owe it to her.* You *really owe it to her.*

This wasn't only about Ana anymore. Nicolas needed Oz,

and he'd never needed him before, not like this. But he'd always been there for Oz when Oz needed him.

When Adrienne went missing, Oz unceremoniously cut Nicolas out of his life. The one person who'd understood and supported him was also the one person he couldn't bear to face, because he reminded Oz so much of Adrienne. Too much. Although they reconnected when Adrienne returned, there was a part of their bond that had never truly repaired. Oz wasn't even sure if it needed to be, or if it was like a ring on a tree trunk, one event in their lives and friendship. Nicolas didn't hold a grudge, but Oz felt the burden of a debt unpaid. He owed something big to Nicolas, some gesture to even the score.

He might hold a grudge this time.

And then there was Adrienne. Nicolas joked that Oz had a "tragic hero complex," but the jab had some truth to it, didn't it? Adrienne was a perpetual damsel in distress. First she'd been a woman trapped in a girl's body, with the mind of a genius and the aspirations of a prodigy. He wanted to remove her from the world she'd grown up in and show her the bigger world she so desired. His goal was always simply to love her as she deserved to be loved. But how much of that was real and how much of it had he created to exonerate himself from being in love with a teenage girl when he was a man grown?

Yet, Nicolas' rage hadn't been for his wronged sister. *You mean Adrienne, right Nic?* Oz had challenged, but he dared say no more. Oz had always wondered about the deeper nature of Nicolas' feelings for his cousin, but he had never, ever spoken about it.

Maybe he isn't even aware of it.

Oz had to fix this for his friend, like Nicolas had helped him fix things. It would be the only way Oz could forgive himself, for both his treatment of Nicolas and of Ana.

He may never forgive me, but I will make this right, somehow.

. . .

THEY STOOD OUTSIDE THE NEIGHBOR'S HOUSE. OZ SAW FIGURES moving through windows in what appeared to be the kitchen.

"Stop," Oz said and put his arm out. "Look."

What they saw left them both speechless: Ana, in the middle of the room, holding a knife out toward a man who held a shotgun to another man's head. Aimed at the man with a shotgun was *another* man holding out a handgun.

"Is this real?" Nicolas asked.

"It's some sort of standoff," Oz murmured, trying to make sense of the scene before them.

Oz heard the questions neither of them voiced. *Do we go in there and try to take them down? Do we try to get ahold of the authorities, despite that it might take them hours, or more, to get here? Do we sneak in? Go in loud? Stand here with our mouths gaping open?*

"At least she's alive," Oz said finally. He started to put his hand on Nicolas' shoulder, then stopped. "I don't know what to do. We aren't armed, and we don't know anything about the situation inside. I think maybe the guy with the shotgun is bad news, since both Ana and another dude have weapons aimed at him. But who are these people?"

"Brothers," Nicolas managed. "Two of them are brothers."

"The one holding a shotgun is one of them?"

"No, I don't think so... hell, I don't know, Ozzy. I don't know any more than you do. Jesus Christ."

"If we barge in there, we might get someone killed. Maybe even Ana."

Nicolas nodded, and reached into his backpack. He pulled out a handgun, and as Oz was formulating the question, Nicolas volunteered the information. "I bought it in town."

"When were you going to tell me this?"

"I'm telling you now."

Oz sighed. He wasn't sure if he felt more, or, less safe with Nicolas packing heat. "Do you even know how to use it?"

Nicolas reached for Oz's gloved hand, opened it, and placed the gun in his palm. "No, but you do."

Oz turned it over in his hand. Years it had been since he fired a gun, and he hoped to hell he wouldn't need to fire one tonight. "We need a plan. If we barge in there, things could get very crazy, very fast," he said warily. He was on pins and needles with Nicolas. Whatever conversation they were having on the surface, there was a larger one brewing beneath.

"We need the element of surprise."

"We can't go in there and subdue them with witty banter. What's more likely to happen is that we go in, chaos ensues, weapons start firing, and someone, or a few someones, get hurt."

"I know, Colin. I get it," Nicolas snapped. *He's doing his best to keep it together, but he'd love to hit me again.* "I actually have an idea that might work."

"I'm all ears."

"We don't barge in. We go in politely."

"*Excuse me*?"

"We get invited in. As a guest."

Oz was still confused.

"Oz, we knock on the damn door."

"At three in the morning?"

"If nothing else, don't you think they'd be curious?

Oz laughed nervously, staking a small sidestep in case Nicolas tried to hit him again. "I don't have a better idea."

"I didn't think so," Nicolas said and walked off toward the house.

52
JONATHAN

Jonathan was mostly indifferent about his existence. He'd never thought about life as a choice, merely something that happened, or didn't.

He found himself thinking about this very thing as he stood in his own home, on the verge of catastrophe, with the only people in his life who mattered. Before, he would've only put Finn on that list, but watching the brave, quiet girl face up against Alex with only a knife clutched in her hand, he realized he cared about her, too. If something happened to her tonight, he'd feel a lot more than indifference.

For all of the things Jon tried *not* to care about, most of them did actually matter to him. His home, his job, and even the other islanders. He may never be at the point where he embraced them, but he couldn't pretend anymore that they didn't *matter*.

Even with a gun in his hand, he felt emasculated. Finn had to feel even worse. He was afraid to use the handgun because Alex's shotgun was still pointed at Finn, and Jon was consumed with the fear that Alex might actually shoot his little brother. If Finn didn't survive this, Jon wouldn't either. It was that simple.

He realized, with increasing panic, that inaction might produce the same result.

Jon couldn't follow what was happening anymore. Ana was trying to reason with Alex, who actually started to *look* crazier by the minute, while Jon attempted to make eye contact with Finn, to try and form some kind of a plan. But neither could process anything except confusion, and their eyes darted between one looming disaster and another.

Then Finn was talking over Ana, and Alex started yelling again, and it was all a mess of words and fear.

During the whole encounter, Alex had looked at no one but Ana. He was *studying* her, and then at times, it was like he saw right through her. He was talking crazy, but his face was perfectly stoic, focused on Ana and Ana alone. Jonathan noted Alex's hands were shaking less.

"Alex, please, this is all a misunderstanding," Ana pleaded. Her words were less useful the more she said them, and Jon wanted to say, *Can't you see it's not working? He's completely insane, just as I always said he was.*

And then, the strangest thing happened.

"Is that the doorbell?" Finn was the first to voice it. Angus drowned out whatever he said next, barking like a madman as he padded into the kitchen to announce the visitor. Alex pointed the gun at the dog for a moment and then quickly put it back on Finn, deciding that the drooling canine wasn't a threat.

"The doorbell," Alex repeated, not quite a question.

"I don't know... at this hour..." Jon left the rest unspoken. They found common ground in their confusion.

The doorbell rang again. Angus barked even louder, and now Mr. Jenkins had chimed in. "Alex, I think we should answer it," Jonathan suggested, asking permission, as he'd read somewhere that if you were ever taken hostage, you should treat your captor like they were in charge.

Alex nodded, clearly glad to be the one making the decision. "Jon, you go. I'll stay here." He nodded at Ana and Finn. "My insurance. So no funny business. Get rid of whoever is foolish enough to be wandering around in the middle of the night."

Jonathan took a deep, calming breath and went to the door. When he answered it, standing before him were two young men completely unfamiliar to him. One of them held a handgun, his face covered in blood, which seemed to come from a crooked nose, and a story that he might be curious about in other circumstances. The other man, the one without the gun, put his finger to his lips. *If they're not from Summer Island, how did they get here?*

Jonathan stared at them, wide-eyed. He couldn't stop looking at the man with the bloody face. Jon wondered if the man even knew his nose was broken. It pointed slightly to the left.

Jesus, Jon, focus.

He'd have to do or say something soon, as Alex wouldn't abide the silence for long. Not that Jonathan would know what to say even if Alex demanded an explanation. He wasn't entirely sure he wasn't imagining the whole thing.

"Where's Ana?" the one without the gun whispered, low enough only the three of them could hear.

"Who the hell are you?" Jon whispered back.

"Here to help. Pretend we're a neighbor."

Jon had to think fast. "Oh, Mrs. Auslander, you shouldn't have come all the way over here. It's not safe," Jonathan said loudly enough for Alex to hear.

"We don't have time," the one with the gun and broken nose asserted. "Is the one with the shotgun dangerous?"

Jonathan nodded, and at the same time realized he trusted them. Wherever they'd come from, they'd come to help, and he didn't need answers now. Not as much as he needed whatever aid might come with their arrival. This might be the moment that would turn the tide in their favor.

"Hurry up!" Alex shouted from the kitchen. "We need to finish our... *card game*."

"Pretend to get rid of your neighbor, and then we'll slip in quietly behind you," the one with the gun and broken nose directed in a voice that, while very low, wasn't lacking in authority.

"You're so kind, Gertrude, we'll make sure to bring back your pie dish as soon as the weather clears. Now get back home and get warm!" Jon scolded the invisible neighbor, good-naturedly. The one with the gun shook his head and sighed, but Jonathan didn't have time to ask him why.

The two men hurried in, and Jonathan closed the door. Jonathan felt a surge of hopeful energy. He had no idea who these men could be or why they were here, but they were there to help.

When he returned, he realized, with a sudden, sinking pit in his stomach, why the man had been shaking his head.

"Where's the pie, Jon?" Alex asked.

That's when the first shot was fired.

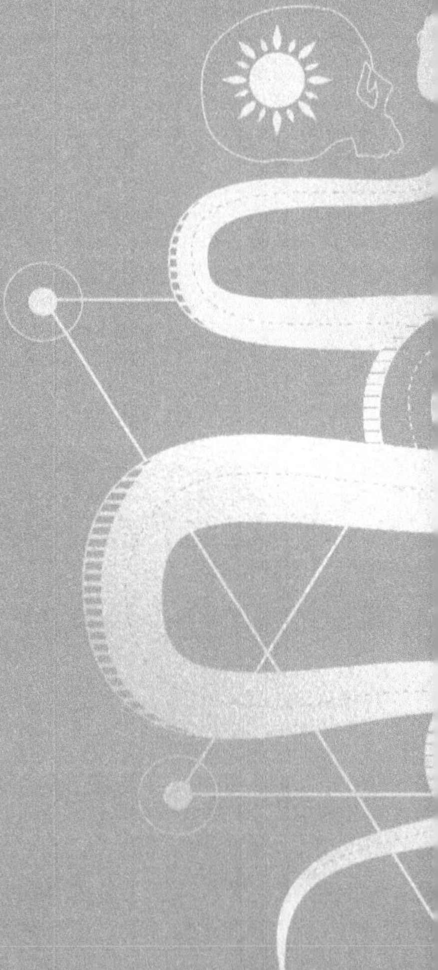

53
NICOLAS

Nicolas stared at Oz in begrudging amazement. When Oz accepted the gun, a change came over him. *He put on his game face*, is what Nicolas would have said if the situation hadn't been so difficult, and his fear for Ana not so tangible.

Oz had taken complete control of the situation. He handled the front door instructions without hesitation. The man at the door was in awe as well, and clearly in need of someone to take over. He trusted Oz right from the start. *Dude, you were totally like The Wolf from Pulp Fiction*, Nicolas would have said to Oz later, if Oz hadn't completely betrayed him.

Nicolas immediately understood the problem with the pie excuse. He didn't blame the nervous guy with the pistol. Everything happened so fast.

"Where's the pie, Jon?" he heard a voice from the kitchen, and everything came together. Alex Whitman. The strange calls, the wild goose chase. *Alex Fucking Whitman*.

That's when Oz fired a shot, into the air. The blast was

deafening, and Nicolas crouched, covering his head as pieces of the ceiling sprinkled down over him.

A commotion started in the kitchen. A dog barked, deep, repetitive woofs adding to the general bedlam. Another dog joined the dysfunctional cacophony.

Oz's face was clear of emotion, but Nicolas saw him trembling and his breathing, while not fast, was deep and heavy.

"Dude," Nicolas whispered, panting.

"Yeah," Oz whispered back, and Nicolas was relieved to feel a piece of the old Oz back, no matter what the circumstances were.

He followed Oz into the kitchen, apprehensive but committed. The wheels were in motion and there was no slowing them now.

The man with the shotgun—who Nicolas now knew to be Alex Whitman—had one hand on the back of the neck of another man on his knees, Alex's other hand still holding the shotgun. Ana screamed, waving the knife in front of her. The man who greeted them at the door waved his gun at Alex, who threatened to kill every last person in the room if they didn't back off.

"Anasofiya," Nicolas calmly interrupted the chaos. When she turned, her face melted into shock. The knife slipped out of her hand and crashed to the floor

"Nicolas?" she whispered. *She loves me. She needs me. I know she does.* His heart felt like jelly. He wanted to rush to her side, but Alex looked ready to snap.

"I'm here, Muffins," he soothed, trying to sound reassuring when all he could feel was uncertainty, fear, and a good measure of confusion. He wasn't thinking about her betrayal, or the secrets she'd kept. He could unravel that later. "I said I'd always be here when you needed me."

Ana gaped at him, lips slightly parted. Nicolas couldn't

imagine what she'd been through. The blonde guy on the floor eyed them both oddly, and a new kind of understanding came over Nicolas. *Another secret? Oh, he is so not your type, Muffins.*

"Nicolas Deschanel," Alex said, looking up from the man he'd been holding at gunpoint. "I told you the island was closed, but this hardly seems the time to quibble over your insolence." Alex's voice was clear and commanding. All of the country dialect was gone. This was a man in control.

"Hardly," Nicolas agreed, the anger bubbling to the top of his jumbled emotions. Uncle Augustus had trusted Alex Whitman first to be their overseer, and then to look out for Ana when she came here alone. "What is it you want, Alex? Money? I have that. Name a figure."

Alex laughed, and the guy on the floor flinched as the gun shifted rhythmically at his neck. "What is it with rich people thinking money solves problems? Is everything about money with you people? I don't want your money. It's probably tainted anyway. There's nothing you could give me that I would want. None of you." He looked around the room.

"Then tell us what it is you do want," Oz said evenly.

Alex took his hand from the guy's neck and pointed at Ana. "I came for her. To rescue her."

Ana shook her head frantically. "Nic, Oz, he's crazy. He wasn't like this before, I don't know what happened, but he has this all wrong. Finn and Jon are my friends," she said and then blushed, as if that were only partly true.

Nicolas looked at the guy on the floor. *I thought you came out here to escape this, Ana?*

"Ana, there's no reasoning with him. He's lost his mind," Jon said.

"Stockholm Syndrome," Alex said airily.

"Well, then that makes everything simple," Oz said,

resuming command. "We're her family, and we're here now, so we've got it covered."

Nicolas could see this wasn't going to work. He wished more than ever he wasn't benign. He'd have given just about anything to blast this man off the face of the earth, but he would've happily settled for something simple like mind control.

He locked his eyes on Ana. She gazed back in childlike desperation. *I want to hate you, but I can't. I want to hate you so badly but the only thing I can think about is taking you in my arms and getting you out of here.*

"Then I'm sorry you wasted your time coming all the way out here. I'm the only one who can help her," Alex said, as if it were obvious.

"Okay, we're done here!" The man on the floor suddenly sprung to life, ending the temporary cease-fire.

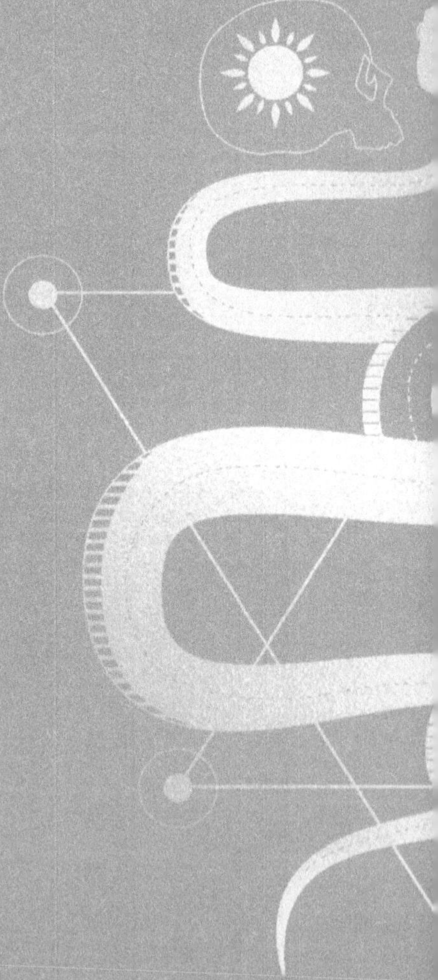

54
ANA

Ana forced herself to ignore Finn's increasing tension because she feared losing her own unsteady focus if she stopped to consider something bad could happen to him.

She was as surprised as Alex when he decided to fight back.

Finn shoved Alex back, and as he fell, the shotgun went off, hitting the large stained glass skylight featured in the coved ceiling of the dining room. The shotgun blast tore into the colorful mosaic, obliterating it into pieces. One huge shard of glass hit Ana on the head, and she fell. Glass rained all around her and her head hit the wood floor with a crack, slivers of colored glass piercing her all over as she landed on top of the remains of the skylight.

She knew she was injured, but the pain didn't register right away.

Before Ana could move, another gun went off, but this one was quieter than the shotgun blast that left her ears ringing. Angus' barking turned to panicked shrieks, another dog going nuts beside him. Finn screamed, then Jonathan.

One more gunshot, then silence.

Jonathan cut through the quiet with a desperate, "Help me!" Ana's head spun, and she turned to see a shuffle of movement as Nicolas and Oz rushed over to his call. Each time she tried to pull herself up, she slipped in the slick blood. *There's so much of it.* Her hands skidded without traction, and she fell back again, panting. She lifted her hand, turning it, to confirm. *My blood.*

The room moved in and out of focus. Her ears were still ringing so she didn't hear Nicolas come to check on her, but when she looked up and saw the horror on his face, panic overtook her and she slipped away into the darkness.

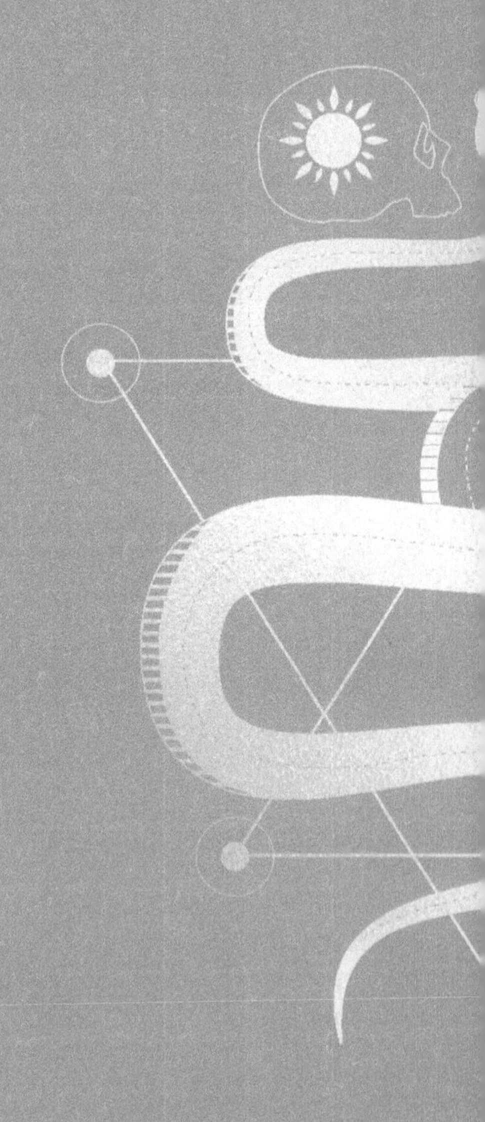

55
FINNEGAN

Finn closed his eyes, but instead of slipping into the darkness, with Ana, he replayed the last, few, chaotic seconds.

He was done. Tired of sitting back and letting the dysfunction unfold around him. Of being effectively neutered by a crazy, sad old man.

Ana was in danger, and he was useless beneath the cold barrel of a maniac's gun, screaming inside. Finn desperately wanted to do as he would normally, taking action, thinking later. He imagined dozens of scenarios to disable Alex and regain the upper hand, but none of them came without risk. He could reconcile himself to his own demise if it saved Jon and Ana, but he wouldn't risk their safety.

Finn watched as Ana tried, and failed, to do his job for him. She tried to reason, then negotiate, with Alex. Finn longed to tell her that she could talk until she was blue in the face, but he knew she needed to try, just as he'd needed his attempt in Jon's office.

Then those other guys had shown up. He didn't know who

the hell they either of them were, but Ana sure did. She went all soft and teary-eyed at the one named Nicolas, and Finn's heart melted to the floor, wondering if this situation could get any worse.

While the others attempted civility, Finn quickly shifted his body weight up and backward, catching Alex off-balance. When the shotgun went off, his ears burned with the pain of the close sound, but then another shot came and a different kind of pain rocked him when a fist of fire punched him in the abdomen.

"I'm hit," he tried to say but what came out was a squeak. He heard Alex go down behind him as another shot fired. He reached to his side and his fingers came back blood-soaked, and he tried desperately to control the rise of panic rolling within him. There was only one other time in his life he'd felt himself in such mortal danger. His father wasn't here to save him this time. *Don't forget Jon. He helped save me too.*

Finn tried to sit up but was overcome with a rush of dizzy weakness. He lay back against the cold, bloody floor, focusing on willing his heart rate to stay steady, to ignore the flood of fear quickly overtaking him. Finn rolled his head to the side and caught a glimpse of Ana lying in a pool of her own blood.

Not again. Please, not again.

Ana, he mouthed.

Finn closed his eyes a second time, and this time, there was nothing.

56

OZ

What was the expression about smoke clearing?

Oz took a moment to take stock of all that had happened, but there wasn't room for emotion. He ran high on adrenaline now, but the moment he stopped to think about the potential losses, he'd completely and totally lose touch. His brief glance at Nicolas confirmed that he still needed to be in control.

The smoke had, literally, cleared. Nicolas knelt next to Ana, crying, while the dark-haired guy was hunched over the blonde one in a panic. Three people were down, one probably dead, and two in no state of mind for clarity.

So, what was his plan? Oz was no doctor, and couldn't assess the severity of either injury. He did know they were on their own. Even if they did reach the Coast Guard, neither Ana nor the blonde guy were likely to survive the time, distance, and cold required for travel. He needed to think fast.

Deciding some action was better than no action, Oz approached Door Man. "Who are you?" Oz inquired calmly. He pointed at the blonde guy on the floor. "And who's that?"

The man responded in a clipped, yet somehow still professional, manner, without looking up from the injured man. "Jonathan. That's my brother. Finn."

Oz nodded. They were brothers, which would make calming Jon harder. "I'm Oz, and that's Nicolas. We came to help Ana, but she's not the only one who needs help now."

Jon grunted something unintelligible, still focused on his brother. Oz took a deep breath.

"Jon. I need to know if there's a doctor anywhere nearby, on this island, or close enough."

Jonathan did not look up from his brother, but said, "I'm kind of a doctor."

"What does that mean?"

"I'm a doctor, but not the kind you mean. I'm a vet. My father, though, he was a doctor. A real one."

Kind of a doctor was certainly better than no doctor at all.

Finn hadn't opened his eyes. Blood bubbled at his lips. Oz didn't know much, but he knew that probably signaled internal trauma. "Jon, I need you to look at me." He waited and when the other man didn't turn, he put his hand on his shoulder. Tears raced down Jon's cheeks. "If you're *kind of* a doctor, then you should have training in how to remain calm in situations like this. I really, really need you to do that for me right now. You're the only chance we might have of saving these two." Oz gestured to Ana, and Jonathan's eyes followed. He seemed to see her for the first time since the chaos. Jon's mouth dropped.

"Do you understand?" Oz asked, forcing Jon to make eye contact. "I need you."

Jonathan looked slowly down at Finn, lips parted in grief. He shifted his gaze to Ana, throat moving up and down as he swallowed hard. *He's in shock, as I probably am, but we need to turn that shock to decisive action.* He turned back to Oz with tortured eyes. "Yes," he said. "I understand."

"Good. Now, I need you to tell me in the plainest of terms what the situation is with these two. I need to know how badly they're injured, if we can save them, and if yes, what needs to happen." Jonathan nodded, but still looked dazed, and so Oz added, "Right now."

Jonathan reached over his brother and said in a shaking voice, "Shot to the abdominal cavity, may have punctured a vital organ, probable massive internal bleeding. I don't know if he can be saved." Jonathan bent his arm to wipe the tears on his sleeve, sobbing with silent shakes.

Oz put his hand out, firm but kind. "Jonathan, *please.*"

Jon lifted his head, nodding again. "I have... some equipment here... I don't know what's there." He looked upward, thoughtfully. "He'll need a blood transfusion..."

So, Finn's situation wasn't good, but at least Oz understood it better. "Now Ana," he directed.

Jonathan hesitated to rise, loathe to leave his brother. "Put your hand here," he instructed Oz, gesturing to where Jon was trying to subdue the abdominal bleeding. "Don't let up pressure, not for a second."

"I won't, I promise."

Jonathan used his bloody hands to lift himself up off the floor and make his way to Ana.

Nicolas held her hand, crying. "Heal," he whispered. "You can do this. You've done it so many times."

"Ana... um..." Jon drew a hard breath, looked up at the ceiling again to collect himself, then looked back down. "Ana has sustained a head injury that will need to be tended to quickly. She's lost a lot of blood as well." He stopped, took his shirt off, and wrapped it around her head, tying a tourniquet.

He looked at Nicolas to ask for his help, then thought better of it. He delicately lifted her arms and legs, and a choked sob escaped from his chest. “She’s sustained cuts over multiple parts of her body. Most are superficial, some are deep. The bleeding is almost uncontrollable.” Jon continued to examine her, tearing off pieces of his shirt to tie up the larger wounds and slow the bleeding. “Deepest cuts are one near her liver, one in her upper right thigh, and one in her shoulder.” He looked at Oz. “She’ll also need a blood transfusion, and I don’t know if I have the tools… I don’t know if I can do this… I’m a vet…”

“Jon,” Oz said, “they’re dying. *Anything* you can do might save their lives.”

Jonathan seemed to respond best when Oz was as direct as possible, and Oz made a mental note of that. “I have two very important questions for you. The first is, if we had the blood available to us, do we have a way to transfer it? Second is, there are two of them and one of you. You’ll need an extra set of hands. Can you give me instructions so that I can help?”

Jonathan thought for a moment about both things, and then replied, “I might still have something in my father’s equipment, but that only helps Finn because I don’t know Ana’s blood type and the wrong one will kill her. As for the instructions, yes, I believe I could, on at least some of it.”

“Nic,” Oz called, and Nicolas cocked his head slightly as he registered the sound of his name. “I need you for one very important thing. To save Ana’s life,” he added.

“Tell me.” Nicolas’ voice was cracked, distant.

“I need to know her blood type. Not a guess, but actually *know* it, as giving her the wrong kind could—”

“A-positive,” Nicolas said confidently, without looking up. “Not a guess.”

“Jon, what are you?”

"B-negative. I can give Finn my blood, but not Ana."

Oz was B-positive. "Nic?"

"I'm a universal donor," he said, and looked at them finally. He gazed at Oz like he was a stranger. "Tell me what I need to do."

Jonathan said moving them could cause more damage, so they'd have to do everything on the floor. He gave Oz a list of things he needed, from sheets, to blankets, to boiling water, and random kitchen utensils. Now that they had a plan, Jon seemed to calm some, and had a sense of purpose about him. Oz quickly retrieved all the items on the list, and by the time he came back, Jon had finished tying up all the open wounds with kitchen cloths. He'd also procured some additional equipment. There were two machines for IVs, bags of saline, gauze, needles, and other things Oz didn't recognize but knew were not found in an ordinary home.

Don't ask, he thought. *There's probably an interesting story here but now isn't the time.*

Jonathan told Oz how to sterilize all the items in the bowl, and Oz did as asked. He watched Jonathan work to set up the transfusions, moving quickly, but deliberately. Finn and Ana were both still unconscious, but he'd slid Ana next to Finn so he could work on them together, with efficiency. Finn and Ana's hands were atop each other.

"Don't tell them about her," Nicolas whispered to Oz. "She wouldn't want them to know." He was looking at Ana and Finn's hands, and Oz realized it had been Nicolas who arranged the contact. *He thinks she can heal him... heal them both.*

Oz nodded. He didn't voice his fear that she may be too injured even to heal herself this time.

Jonathan chased Nicolas off, and assigned him to ripping

apart sheets for more bandages. *Good thinking, Jon. Keeps him busy, and we'll need them later.*

When Oz brought him the bowl of sterilized equipment, Jonathan announced, "I need to remove the bullet." Oz nodded, and came to his side to assist. Jon extracted a thin pair of tongs. "Once we do this, I need you to re-apply the pressure for me. I'm going to start drawing blood from Nicolas. While I'm doing that, you need to keep Finn's bleeding down. Once we have enough blood for Ana and Finn, I'm going to stitch up my brother. I need you to watch carefully because you'll need to do exactly what I do to Finn, to Ana. Okay?"

Oz nodded again. Jonathan was starting to sound rational. He was relieved to not feel so alone. "Okay, go."

It didn't take long for Jon to extract the bullet. He found it quickly, and Finn let out a small gurgling cough but didn't wake. He dropped the misshapen and surprisingly small hunk of twisted metal on the kitchen floor, and it rolled slowly away, under the counter.

"Apply pressure." Oz did.

Jonathan called Nicolas from his sheet ripping and had him sit in a chair nearby. After sliding the needle into Nicolas, the blood moved through the thin tubes and into a large clear pouch. Jon decided all the blood would need to come from Nicolas, as Jon needed to be strong and alert enough to attend the medical needs. Nicolas would be very tired, and weak, but would recover.

Oz tried not to look at Ana. He could still feel the rise and fall of Finn's heartbeat under his palms, but was afraid, if he touched her, he might not feel the same. She'd been alone and unattended long enough for anything to be possible.

. . .

"There's a bottle of water in the fridge, and crackers in the pantry. Take both and go lay on the couch for now," Jonathan advised Nicolas when he was done with him.

Nicolas glanced at Ana, then nodded and went to go do as Jon instructed.

Jonathan came back over to the two patients on the floor. He set the pouch of blood on the sheet and checked both their vitals. "Okay, we need to do this fast," he said. "This isn't nearly enough, but we couldn't take more without hurting your friend. It will have to be enough, for now."

He handed Oz a thin needle and a box of thread. When Oz looked surprised, Jonathan said, "It's not as hard as it looks." He positioned himself on Finn's left side and motioned Oz to sit between the two. "Watch me very carefully. I'm going to start stitching Finn, and I need you to do the same for Ana. Once I finish with his abdomen, I'll move over and help you finish hers. Start with her head, then her abdomen, then her thigh, then shoulder, in that order. Keep it shallow."

"Will she feel this?"

"If she wakes, yes," Jon said. "I didn't dig through boxes for pain medication. They don't have time."

He handed Oz a thick wooden-handled spoon that Oz had sterilized earlier. "Put this between her teeth," Jon said, as he demonstrated with Finn. "So she doesn't hurt herself if she does wake."

Oz fought back a new wave of rising fear. He studied Jon's technique, and was surprised to find that, after the first few stitches, it wasn't so hard. She didn't wake, but moaned in her sleep, and the spoon ended up being useful, after all.

Jon was good as his word, switching to help him with Ana after finishing Finn. He was much quicker than Oz and finished each closure twice as fast. When they were done, Jonathan started hooking up the IV needles to each of them, and the blood quickly flowed through the tubes.

"You said it won't be enough?" Oz asked.

"I don't know," Jonathan admitted. "We're going to have to figure out a way to get them to a real hospital as soon as we can. But I don't know how without working phones."

"So now what?"

"Now we wait," Jonathan said. "And hope."

57
JONATHAN

Jonathan had taken Oz's lead. Although he was the only one qualified to help Finn and Ana, his state of mind made him highly unsuited for the task. Oz had known that, had understood what he needed to say.

His father would've been proud. It wasn't perfect, not by far. Both of their wounds were grievous, and potentially mortal. The equipment he used was old and dusty, and he only hoped Oz had sterilized everything properly because he hadn't had time to check. Even trace amounts of bacteria getting in could cause infections that could kill them in their present state. And they would definitely need a blood transfusion—a better one—soon.

They cleaned up the area and gently slid both patients on top of layers of blankets, spreading even more covers over the top. Both were stabilized, for the moment. They would have to be watched closely. Jon tried not to be overly critical of his work. To not worry that all he did might not be enough, and that one or both could still die. Neither was out of the woods.

Infection was still a high likelihood, even if things had been sterilized correctly.

He glanced at Ana, wondering if her wounds would be healed as miraculously as they were before. He'd seen many things in his career, but never anything like that.

As he'd told Oz, it would be a waiting game. Watch closely, wait for things to pass, and hope that soon they could get out of the house and off the island. The phone lines were still down, and their old radio stopped working years ago. The internet died before the phones.

Jon asked Oz how they'd managed to get to the island to begin with, and all Oz said was, *We can't get back the same way*.

Nicolas rested on the couch. Jon had not been sure what to make of his display at Ana's side. Jon felt protective of Finn when he saw this new man fawning over Ana, but it wasn't the time for questions. Later, as they cleaned up, Oz offered something close to an explanation. Nicolas and Ana were cousins.

"They seem close for cousins."

"They are close," Oz said. "Ana doesn't open up very easily to others. Nicolas is her best friend."

Still odd, Jonathan thought, but didn't say it. He'd been judged long enough to know it was a hurtful and unfair practice. He'd certainly judged Ana quick enough. *And then I slept with her. What a mess.*

Jon prepared to start his vigilant monitoring of the two patients, when Oz reminded him of one huge, glaring, important detail that would have to be dealt with.

"Oh, Christ. Alex," Jon said, hanging his head. He'd been aiming for him when he hit Finn instead. Oz finished it with one of the cleanest head shots Jon had ever seen. Alex likely died immediately. "What should we do?"

Oz's look said, *How should I know*? But then he said, "I'm the one who killed him. I'll take responsibility."

Jonathan shook his head. "No. You wouldn't be in this mess if not for us. If I hadn't been such a terrible aim, it would have been me, not you."

Oz didn't argue. They were both clearly tired. "We can't leave him here in the house. I don't want them waking up to this, not after what they've been through," Oz said. "Is there anywhere we can put him? Until the storm passes?"

"We can try the storehouse. It's worse for wear after the storm, but I imagine it'll be good enough for this."

Oz nodded. "I have to admit, I've never had to give much thought to proper storage methods for a dead body," he said, and then surprised Jonathan by letting out a small chuckle.

Nicolas appeared in the doorway. The color had drained away from his face, but he looked calmer. Clearer. "I want to help."

58
NICOLAS

They didn't want him to help. They said he should be resting, that he was too weak to be up and about. He argued, and they argued back. Finally, as a compromise, he was allowed to help by cleaning the mess left by Alex's body. He didn't mind that so much, because it meant he could still be near Ana, and he didn't like the idea of the only person who knew how to help her leaving, even if it wasn't for long.

Oz and Jonathan put on their snow clothes, and sloppily wrapped Alex in a handful of trash bags. Nicolas could hardly register the fact that there was a dead body in front of him, or that Oz had been the one to kill him. *It should've been me. I should've pulled that trigger, and then kept pulling it.*

He cleaned up as much of the blood as he could, but ruined most of the dishtowels in the kitchen in the process. He hadn't realized until now how much blood was in the human body. And this had only been Alex's. They cleaned up after Finn and Ana earlier.

Nicolas threw the dishtowels away and looked toward the

dining room. Ana and Finn were asleep in a sea of blankets. Above them, Oz had duct-taped garbage bags over the hole where the skylight had been, but the cold wind slipped through anyway.

Nicolas started to take Ana's pulse, but realized he had no clue what normal was. Her chest rose and fell with each soft breath, and she looked peaceful, though he doubted she felt that way, wherever she was. He prayed she'd slipped away to heal herself, the way she'd done every time before this.

When he'd made up his mind about coming to Maine, he wasn't sure what he'd expected to find, but he could say confidently it wasn't *this*. He never made predictions about outcomes. As with everything in his life, Nicolas Deschanel had simply forged ahead, confidently assuming everything would work out.

His decision to come might've been what saved her life. Instead of lying on the floor in critical condition, Ana could be dead. *I probably could've fucking* planned *a bit more, but the fact of the matter is, if we hadn't showed up when we did, this could have been a completely different kind of party.*

Nicolas took Ana's right hand, the one not entwined with Finn's. He couldn't shake from his mind the look on her face when she saw him. Complete vulnerability. Utter loss of control.

"I'm so sorry I wasn't here sooner. I knew something was wrong, and I hesitated," he admitted to her, keeping his voice low. He almost laughed at his attempt at privacy, but who knew how much Finn could understand in his unconscious state? What he had to say wasn't for anyone but Ana.

"I'm kicking myself for not fucking coming *with* you. The truth is, my feelings were hurt that you didn't invite me. I started to wonder if maybe I was smothering you, that... well... that part of why you wanted to get away from New Orleans was *me*." He wanted to stop. The words hurt more said aloud. But he soldiered on. "We always laughed at everyone wondering why we were so close, why neither of us cared about marriage or families, and I always thought that was something we shared together, our own private joke at the world. I felt like I was laughing with you at some of the guys you would date. When you broke up with them, I assumed you didn't care because you never seemed to. But... Oz..." *No, not now. I can't do this now.*

It felt good to get that off his chest. He hadn't let himself think these things before. Action had always come easier than thought. Even when it came to Ana, she needed him, he was there. He didn't need to know why.

"Did I force my own beliefs on you, Ana?" He turned her hand over in his. The scratches were still red but already starting to scab over. *Yes, heal, darling.* He wanted to ask her about what had happened between the last time he talked to her, over a week ago, and the point at which he and Oz joined the insanity in the kitchen. *Did you run away? Did you run away from me? I can understand wanting to be away from New Orleans, and the rest, but me? You knew it would break me, like you knew moving to Oxford would. I know that's selfish, dammit, but you've always stayed before. Why did you leave me this time?*

But that was the paradox of the situation. Instead of staying to protect him, as she once had, she was leaving to protect him. *Or am I just telling myself that, when in fact it has nothing to do with me at all?*

"I guess I don't understand, Ana. I've never turned my back on you, or judged you. I've never made you feel bad about anything you've done. And you could've had anyone in the world, and I'd have supported you, but Oz?"

Their indiscretion brought Ana's behavior, and Nicolas' conflicted, bottled feelings, bubbling to the surface. He pressed his palm to his face to suppress them. Not here. Not yet. Not until she was out of the woods. Not while there was a chance she might not recover.

Her long red hair looked even more beautiful contrasted with her pale, ashen skin. He used to braid her hair, as long as she promised to never, ever tell anyone. He wished he could see her eyes right now. “I don’t know, Ana, have I never married because no woman can measure up to you? Because, truly, I couldn’t love you more than I already do. I’ve never wanted more from you. Being with someone else, I guess for me it meant I couldn’t share this closeness with you the same way, and I’ve never met anyone worth the loss of that.” Nicolas wouldn’t think about how tonight’s bombshell might impact this closeness. *Goddamnit Oz, why did you have to tell me? Why couldn’t you have taken it merrily to your goddamned grave, so Adrienne and I could continue living in blissful ignorance about the people we love?*

He looked over at Finn, in contrast. Finn had rough, ruddy blond hair (*so not her type, she likes dark-haired guys*), a strong jawline (*she always liked the softer types*), and dimples that didn’t require a smile to come out (*too obnoxious*). He had a scar above his lip, and his cheeks had a slight red flush to them (*too roughneck*).

“Apparently he is your type, Muffins. Apparently I don’t know your type. You had your reasons for keeping this from me, just as you kept Oz from me. Did you think my love was conditional on you never changing? Have you been changing this entire time? Did I make you think it wasn’t okay to change?

“I am so sorry,” he whispered, still holding her hand in his. He curled up next to her and closed his eyes, smelling a trace of copper and rubbing alcohol. “I really am.”

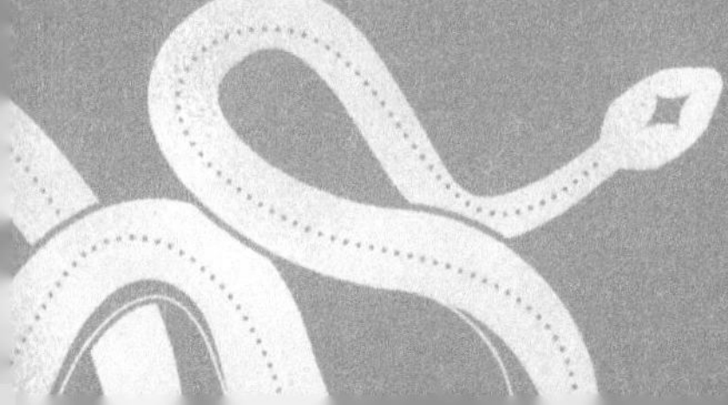

59
JONATHAN

Jon was guilty of murder. It mattered not who pulled the trigger. When he hit Finn, he'd been aiming for Alex, and not a warning shot. He'd never let Oz take responsibility for something that, in his heart and intentions, he was equally guilty of.

They worked quickly, but quietly. He didn't mind Oz, and thought that in better circumstances, they might even get along. He didn't think there'd be a better circumstance for them, though. While bound for life by this experience, this was hardly the activity that created friendships.

"Did you realize your nose is broken?" Jonathan finally asked, as they hauled Alex's body through the snow and out to the shore. It was a slow haul, with the second storm still in full swing around them.

Oz laughed. "Yeah. I'm aware."

"I can set it for you if you want. It might heal properly that way."

"Thanks."

There was no good place to put Alex, so in the end they

placed him closest to where the tanks had spilled. They shoved him under a low bench, wedging him in. The sound of the garbage bags crinkling against the snow made Jon cringe.

"The roof looks unsteady," Oz noted warily.

"The whole thing is unsteady," Jon agreed. "But there isn't anywhere else to put him."

"How long are we going to be stranded here?" Oz asked, with a glance back up at the house.

Jon hesitated before speaking. "I'm going to try to figure out the snowcat, and drive it down to the ferry station to radio for help."

"I'll come with you," Oz offered.

Jon shook his head. "You're the only one who knows what I did to keep them stable. Her cousin isn't in any shape to take care of them alone."

Oz nodded, but it was clear he didn't like the idea of splitting up in the storm.

"One thing we'll need to figure out," Jon broached, "is what we are going to tell the police."

Oz stopped, hand on the back door. He couldn't be much older than Finn, but in that moment he seemed a hundred years old. "The truth, I suppose. I mean, it's not like a lie could be any weirder."

Jon laughed, his first laugh in a long while, and the sound was foreign and coarse to his ears. "You're most likely right."

"What will people here think?" Oz pressed. "About what happened to Alex? Will they miss him? Martyr him? Think it's all a misunderstanding?"

Jonathan frowned. "A mixed bag, I suppose. Most residents thought him harmless."

"Not you, though."

"I suspected he had a hand in his parents' deaths all those years ago, and the sheriff thinks so, too."

"Well, he certainly had murder on the brain tonight," Oz concluded. He turned to look at Jon. "When Ana wakes, let's spare her the details."

Jon started at him, not understanding.

"She's probably going to blame herself already for what happened tonight, but I don't want her to blame herself for Alex. I did it. That was my choice, and I'd do it again."

"So we tell her..."

"That we took care of it. And leave it at that."

Jon had so many questions, as he was sure Oz did, but he couldn't bring himself to ask any of them. The situation was still so tenuous, and they were a long way from small talk.

The image of Ana on the floor hadn't left him. His stomach was in knots, a feeling quite unfamiliar to him, and he'd felt it earlier. He felt it the moment she brought that stray animal to him, and again in the shower. It wasn't until he rushed to save her life a second time that he connected those feelings into something cogent.

No. It doesn't matter if you have these feelings. She could be your soul mate, and it wouldn't matter, because your brother has finally found something other than his own stubbornness and the sea that makes him happy. You know you're the reason he's stayed on this island. He won't admit it, but you know. You will not take this from him.

They found Nicolas curled up next to Ana. Jonathan's heart stopped for a moment until he could see both Finn, and Ana, were breathing, and only then he was able to step fully into the room.

"I tried to check their pulses, but I don't know what's normal and what isn't. They didn't stop breathing though, so that must be a good sign," Nicolas said lightly.

"Thanks," Jon acknowledged and dismissed Nicolas with a hand. Kneeling by Ana's side, and then Finn's, he took both their vitals, finding nothing out of the ordinary. After a deeper search of his father's office before they'd ventured outside, he'd found some morphine, and it was the only relief he'd been able to give them for the pain.

"We really need to find a way off the island," Jonathan pressed, as he faced the other two men, strangers before tonight but now bonded to him in a way even he didn't understand yet. "They both need proper medical attention. I've done all I can for them."

"There's no hospital here, right?" Oz asked.

"No," he said. "Only the stuff I have from my father's old clinic. We need to get to the mainland to get them the right help."

"Does your phone work?" Nicolas wondered. "Or was that more lies from Alex?" He seemed to have a bit of his spark back.

"It did for a few days, but the lines have been down for nearly a week. Internet is down, too, and the nearest radio is at the ferry station a mile west."

"What about that big thing outside?" Nicolas asked, pointing toward the snowcat.

"I'm going to try and get it to the ferry station, and see if their radios are up," Jon replied.

"No, man. I mean, doesn't that thing *have* a radio?"

Jon's hopes soared. Why didn't this occur to him sooner? There *should* be a working radio, and perhaps they could reach the Coast Guard. If not, he could still take the snowcat down to the ferry terminal and try the radios there. But if this worked, it would be much quicker.

Before Jon could say anything, Oz asked Nicolas to join him in checking the radio.

As the door clapped behind them, Jon realized he was alone for the first time since the world had come crashing down around their heads.

What would he do if Finn died? Finn was more than his brother. He was his anchor. Jon had long believed he needed no one, but was allowed the luxury of such nonsensical thoughts *because* Finn was at his side. Finn protected Jon. He brought him closer to humanity.

Jon didn't understand the nature of Finn and Ana's relationship. How could they have such a bond already? He hadn't ever seen them together, and Finn had hardly mentioned her until the night she ended up half-dead on their beachfront. How could that kind of love have grown while Ana was sleeping? He thought of Finn spending every waking moment by her side, talking to her, reading to her. Could she have known? Was what they had love?

He wished he knew, because that feeling was back as he watched her, and he realized with both guilt—for Finn—and resentment—for himself—that he shouldn't have pushed her out that night she came to his office with Cocoa. If he'd opened his eyes. he might have seen her, really seen her for who she was. Someone who might understand him, and not try to change him, as Shannon had. Had he been open to her, he might have finally found something to give his life the meaning he pretended to not crave.

60
AUGUSTUS

Augustus was displeased with the hospital staff. They were properly courteous and attentive, but he didn't feel they were nearly experienced enough. She'd been in the hospital for five days, and they still weren't ready to release her. And now they were annoyed with *him*. He'd thought they'd be pleased he was willing to send for doctors from New Orleans to take over.

He resisted the urge to tell them her sleeping was *normal*, that she was healing herself. He was the only person who knew how to care for her in such a state.

Your daughter and her friend should both be dead, the doctor said. *It's a miracle. Unlike anything I've ever seen.*

Yes, thought Augustus, *I've seen a miracle or two in my time.*

When Nicolas had called him from the hospital, Augustus was already making arrangements. He'd traveled north with the family doctor, and their lawyer, Rory Sullivan, was also staying nearby. His niece, Adrienne, was a complete mess, so his first order of business upon arrival had been to send Oz promptly back home. The police had more questions for Oz, but Augustus convinced them, in the way only he could, that the investigation was officially closed.

Now it was only Augustus and Nicolas standing vigil in her room... and occasionally that tall, quiet fellow, Jonathan. The nurse said he had medical experience, but wasn't a doctor.

"Tell me, what kind of person has medical experience but isn't a doctor?" Augustus had demanded.

"The kind as unique and different as Jonathan St. Andrews," she simply said. "But he saved your daughter's life, so I'd say his 'medical experience' came in handy."

This was true. If not for this man, Ana might not have survived long enough to heal herself.

Although, if not for him, she wouldn't be in this situation to begin with.

Oz had laid the entire story out, Nicolas and Jon backing him up. Even with their matching accounts, the Portland police had been skeptical that the middle-aged overseer was capable. Then the sheriff of Summer Island had stepped in, insisting Alex Whitman had long been on his radar for several heinous crimes, and was not the *least* bit surprised. Following this was Sheriff Horn's ceremonious visit to Alex's house, where they discovered a room filled with peculiar artifacts and articles about a number of women who'd died mysteriously. *Ayuh, I knew it all along,* the portly sheriff had insisted.

"In that case, I'll look for you to assume culpability for the avoidable injuries inflicted upon my daughter," Augustus snapped, promptly shutting down the sheriff's prideful boasting.

One evening, Jonathan walked in. Augustus distrusted the man, but whatever had actually transpired that night, he'd saved Ana, and for that reason alone, Augustus didn't ban him from visiting. The man's brother, Finn, hadn't regained consciousness. Neither had Ana, but Augustus wasn't worried about her, anymore. She was out of the woods, and her body was doing what it did best now.

"We should really consider moving them into the same room," Jon tentatively suggested.

Augustus rejected the idea. The boy had gotten her into this mess.

When Augustus didn't respond, Jon added, "They say she'll be able to go home soon."

"They say a lot of things," Augustus said, venting a small measure of his ire, "but I have little confidence in the care she's received in this facility."

"It was the best we could do under the circumstances," Jon apologized. He shoved his hands in his pockets, looking uncomfortable and out of place in the room. Augustus watched Jon gaze at Ana, and a disturbing realization came over him.

"Your brother is coming along, I assume."

"Not as well as we'd like," Jonathan admitted. Augustus realized he hadn't followed the other boy's progress, but had naturally assumed he'd be doing well enough. "The infection has spread and they may need to operate again."

"I'll pray for his recovery."

"Thank you." Jon sat on the other side of Ana's bed. He pretended to look out the window, but Augustus was old, not blind. There was pain in Jon's face as he watched her. "If you wanted to go stretch your legs or get a bite to eat, I could stay here for a bit," Jon added.

And leave you alone with her? I think not. "Thank you, but Nicolas is tending to my dinner and I got a walk in earlier."

Jonathan nodded as if to say, very well. He stood to leave, but Augustus didn't miss him graze Ana's arm with his hand and the small, sad smile on his face. Augustus never missed much. "Please, reconsider the request to move them together. They might both heal faster," Jon speculated. The look he gave him made Augustus wonder how much Jon St. Andrews knew about the Deschanels.

"Tell me why, exactly, you're so insistent on moving your brother next to Ana when you are clearly in love with my daughter yourself?"

The boy first blushed, then balked. "With all due respect, I like Ana a lot. But I'm not in love with her."

"I'm not a fool."

Augustus had a lot of experience reading people, and he read a tremendous amount of conflict in the boy. Jonathan spoke slowly, carefully selecting his words. "She's not mine to love."

"My daughter belongs to no one," Augustus said evenly. "Not you, not your brother." *Not even me.*

"I understand, but she's made her choice. I respect that."

Augustus couldn't help feeling a twinge of pitiful admiration for the boy. His concern for Ana had been apparent since the day Augustus arrived, and yet he cared enough for her that he'd set that aside. "Very well, then. I'll have them moved together, if the doctors will allow it."

"Thank you," Jonathan said quietly, and left.

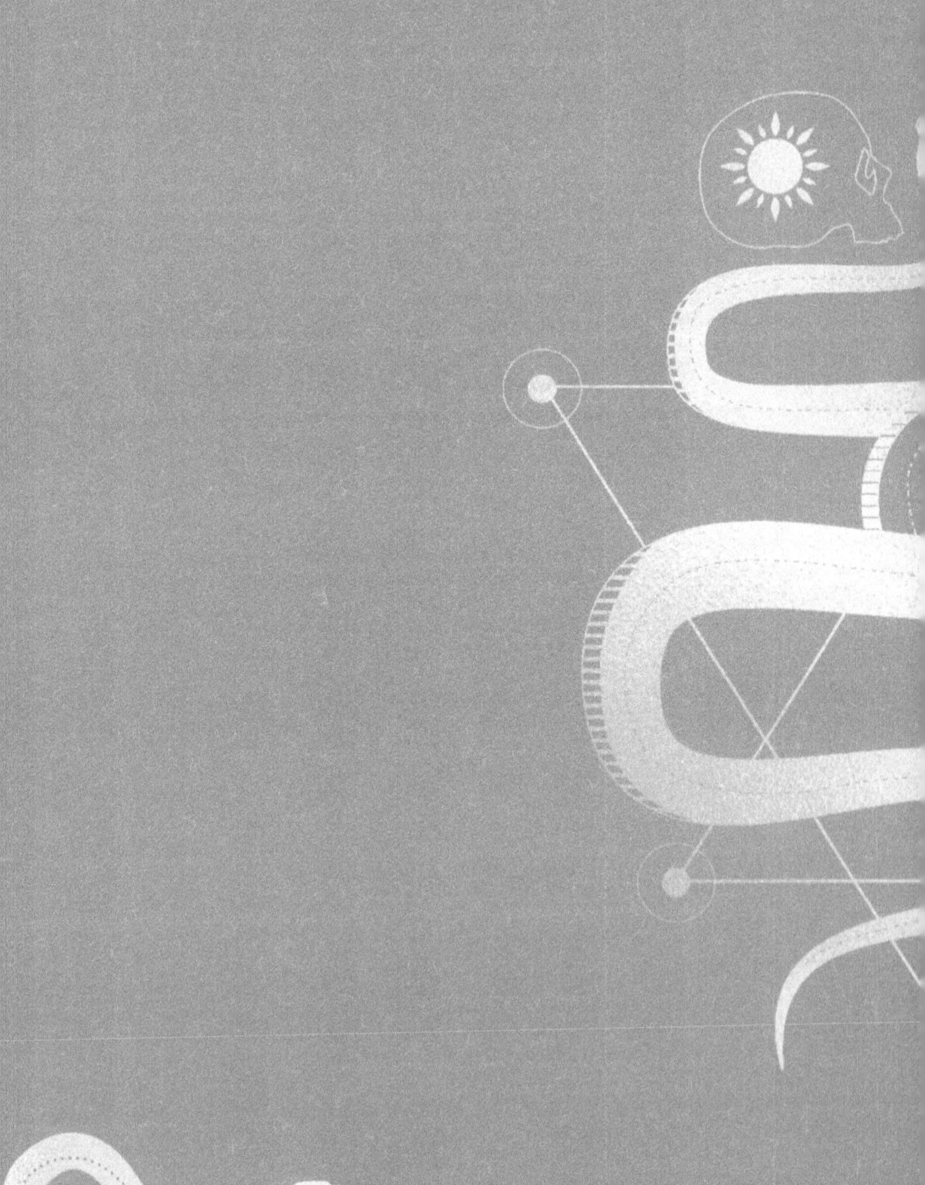

61

ANA

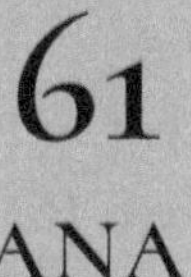

Ana had been released a week ago, but she hadn't left the hospital. Her father was frustrated. He didn't understand why she wouldn't return home to New Orleans. He'd cautioned her that Finn may have a lengthy recovery, and now he'd slipped into a coma. She was angry that no one had moved Finn into her room sooner, but how could she tell people she might have healed him?

"He matters to me," is all she'd say. Her father shook his head so much over the matter she thought it might fall clean off his shoulders.

"He might never come out of that bed. You have a life to lead, Anasofiya. A future to think of. You hardly know that boy," he said, over and over, until they were both tired of the words. "Besides, we both know your abilities are rather one-sided."

"I healed him once before," she declared boldly.

"He's not your responsibility. Or your future."

"My future *is* here. At least for now," Ana insisted. *I know you don't understand. I don't expect you to. I've done a lot of things... terrible things... because I didn't understand myself. Now I have a chance to put that all behind me. I can save him. I have saved him. And that means something.*

But she'd never say all that to her father. He'd given up on love when Ana's mother died. His second marriage was of a more dutiful, practical nature, and he seemed perfectly content with that.

"Your choices are entirely illogical," her father capitulated. "I won't pretend I think you're doing the right thing. But you're a grown woman, and I'm under no illusion I have any authority in the matter."

And so he'd left. Not necessarily on bad terms, but there would need to be some healing there, for both of them. Ana loved her father very much. If he'd raised her with more warmth, she might have thrown herself into his arms and told him as much. Instead, she'd taken his hands in hers, squeezed, then let him go.

She still had trouble wrapping her head around the events of that night, especially Alex's transformation. The whole thing had a dreamy, surreal haze to it, and she couldn't stop replaying every conversation she'd ever had with the man, searching for signs she'd missed.

At least her father had agreed to fund the lighthouse restoration. Her request hadn't been fueled by her care for Alex, as she once envisioned, but her desire to give the island community some needed closure.

Nicolas and Oz appearing at the house in their moment of need had been strangest of all. She should've known Nicolas wouldn't sit back idly without hearing from her, but seeing him was no less shocking. And Oz, why had he come? Guilt?

He stopped by her room before he left for New Orleans.

"How are you feeling?" He took a seat near her bed. Casually, as if there was no sordid, uncomfortable history between them.

"Good as new."

"I'm glad to hear it." Though sitting right next to her, Oz seemed far away.

"Thank you for coming out," she offered. "I appreciate what you did. You didn't have to."

"I did have to," he asserted. He looked at her, his green eyes large, and sad. "I'm sorry, Ana, for everything. I didn't mean for things to end up like this."

"We never do, Oz. But all we can do is try to move forward. There's nothing to be gained from dwelling on mistakes, if nothing changes."

He nodded, but there was more behind his eyes. "I love you, Ana. I always have. You're one of my oldest friends in the world, and you've always been there for me. I'm sorry for making you feel like you weren't good enough, that there's something wrong with you. There isn't."

"Why are you telling me this?"

"I don't know," he said. Oz got up from the chair and leaned over her, brushing his lips against her forehead. He moved toward the door. "Maybe I needed to say it. Maybe you needed to hear it."

Pausing with a sigh, he looked at her one last time. "Nicolas knows about us. I couldn't keep it to myself anymore. If it helps, I think he blames me."

Then, Oz bowed his head and left, leaving her staring at the door in stunned silence.

For a week, Ana stayed by Finn's bedside. She'd read to him, talked to him, told him all the stories of *her* childhood, all the things he'd so selflessly done for her when she was convalescing.

She didn't do them alone.

When it was time to eat, Jon and Ana rotated food duty. The hospital brought in a couple of fold-out beds for them to sleep in, and there was a little more room once Finn was moved into a larger, more private space.

And still, Nicolas didn't visit. *Nicolas knows about us.* The words haunted her, hung heavy over her heart. *He should've been my first visitor. He should've been here the moment I was awake.*

Jon told her Nicolas hadn't left for New Orleans yet. That he was harassing the doctors on a regular basis, and generally being obnoxious.

But, still, he didn't come.

Ana should feel better with that heavy lie no longer between them, but instead she felt as if she had lost the only thing that ever mattered to her. Whatever else had come at her in life, there was always Nicolas, holding her hand, believing in her, understanding her, encouraging her. Loving her.

His silence spoke volumes.

EPILOGUE

"*It is a far, far better thing that I do now, than I have ever done. It is a far greater rest I go to now, than I have ever known,*" Ana whispered, closing *A Tale of Two Cities*. "I'm determined that you'll get all the classics until they kick me out," she joked.

"Finn always did like to read," Jonathan said, looking up from the movie he'd been watching.

"That pile of books is his, isn't it?"

Jon nodded.

Finn still wore the two crosses around his neck. The nurse wanted to remove them, but Ana insisted they stay. They weren't hurting anything and she thought maybe they even helped him.

"I know you said he probably doesn't know I'm doing this, but I knew, when he did it," Ana explained.

"He's very lucky," Jon affirmed, but there was something in his voice she couldn't quite detect.

"I'm doing no more than what he's already done for me," Ana insisted.

"You love him," Jon stated. It wasn't a question, but he watched her closely, as if hoping to be surprised by her answer.

"I don't know what it feels like to be in love," she admitted.

"I don't believe that."

"Don't you?" She met his gaze squarely. "I'm not the only one."

Jon held her stare for a moment, and then dropped his eyes. "People like us, maybe we aren't meant for that."

"What a lovely sentiment." She laughed it off, but the comment hit close. Had that not always been in the back of her mind? She was afraid of sharing herself. Afraid the other person would expect more from her than she could give.

Finn was so understanding, but their connection had been born from unfortunate circumstances. Ana knew he cared for her, but why? Did he see the darkness inside her? Did he understand her craving to be alone more than with others? Maybe he did; he did live with Jon, after all. But was that what he wanted from life? To escape one for another?

Am I trying to sabotage this, before it even gets off the ground? To convince myself this will end up the same as the others, so I can walk away without remorse? What am I doing here? Why did I stay?

Jonathan reached out and took her hand in his, a gesture that both surprised her and brought more comfort than she would've guessed. He didn't say anything, and neither did she, both enjoying quiet understanding.

Then, suddenly, his hand felt like poison. Ana exhaled.

Jon is my darkness. To accept him is to accept that part of myself, and if I do that, I'll never be rid of it. He'd accept the things about me I desperately want to change. I'd slip deeper and deeper into the dark recesses of my own mind, and so would Jon.

But Finn could accept her darkness without allowing it to grow further out of control. He could live with who she was, because he'd lived with someone like her, his whole life. He knew what to expect and would help her find a way to come to terms with it, and, maybe temper the parts that caused harm to herself and others.

With Finn, she could be herself, but she could also be free.

FINN WAS FINALLY READY TO COME HOME. HE'D NEED SOME additional care, but Jon and Ana were more than capable.

"I've never been so happy to see a face in my entire life," Finn had said when he awoke to find Ana at his side.

"I know the feeling." Ana kissed his hand. She wanted to do more, but Jon was nearby and she felt him wince at even the small amount of shared affection. This would be a complicated arrangement, but they'd figure it out, somehow.

Ana packed Finn's things while Jon completed the necessary discharge paperwork. As she shoved Finn's clothes into the white plastic bag, she felt a presence behind her. She turned to find Nicolas.

Her heart caught. She tentatively stepped forward and wrapped him in her arms. "You're here," she whispered. "I've missed you so much."

Nicolas didn't embrace her back. He went rigid, arms held stiffly at his sides.

Ana peeled herself away with reluctance. The expression on his face pierced her heart.

"I came to say goodbye," Nicolas said. His voice was flat, and his eyes, cold and distant, looked toward her but not at her. He took another step back, putting more space between them. "I waited, until you were awake."

"I guess my father told you I'm staying then," she said. Her heart skipped. She knew this wasn't what he meant with his goodbye, but she couldn't bear to hear what she knew was coming next.

"I don't give a fuck what you do anymore, to be honest, Ana."

The tears welled in her eyes, threatening to spill. This was happening. This was her punishment. Not what she'd expected, but it was no less deserved.

Ana felt her sacred control slipping away. "Nic, I didn't do it to hurt you—"

"Fuck you. You might not have done it to hurt me, but you knew it would and did it anyway." He ran his hands through his dark hair . "I've always bent over backwards to accommodate your feelings and I've never asked you to do anything for me. *Ever*. But if I expected loyalty from anyone, it was *you*."

"This had nothing to do with you!" She moved toward him again but he recoiled, flinching.

"It had *everything* to do with me!" Nicolas thundered.

His words hung heavy between them, as well as all the other ones left unspoken. The beeping from the monitor in the next room broke through the silence.

"Have you asked yourself why you're so hurt by this?" she asked quietly. She didn't want his answer, but if he was determined to go there, then they'd do exactly that. "I've wronged your sister, and I've wronged myself. But you? This isn't about you. You know it isn't, and yet here you are, accusing me of betraying the one person this had absolutely nothing to do with."

Nicolas took a deep breath. "You could've fucked anyone in the world, Ana. Anyone. I knew none of those assholes meant anything to you. But you had *feelings* for Oz, once upon a time. Hell, maybe you still love him, after all these years? Please, don't answer that. Were you pushing me, to see what it would take to break me?"

"That's so unfair, and you know it." The tears flowed unabated now, streaming down her cheeks. She didn't have the energy to fight. "I've made my share of messed-up decisions, but it's not you I owe penance to."

He laughed, a cruel, cold sound that pierced her heart. "We're all messed up. That's such a bullshit excuse. Both of you seem to think you can do whatever the fuck you want, because you're both *so messed up,* and that makes any bad decision okay."

"I didn't say it was okay," she cried. "I came here, to give Oz some space, because of how not okay it was! But I'll ask you again, Nicolas. *What does this have to do with you?*"

"You are not gonna play dumb with me," Nicolas said, through gritted teeth. "Damn you, Ana, we've been close for too long for you to pretend you *don't fucking know*."

Ana wished, then, that she hadn't forced him down that path. The path that led them both away from their ignorance, and toward a truth that would destroy them, and what they had, forever. She longed for his comforting arms around her, for everything to be okay again. In her mind's eye, she saw him in that pink shirt he wore to her graduation; his goofy, warm smile. *I'll always be here for you, Muffins.*

Ana reached forward and tugged at his hands. "Nicolas. Please."

Nicolas pushed her, and she stumbled back. "It took me years to realize this, but you don't give a shit about me. You ruined my only friendship that ever mattered, and you..." His voice trailed off. He drew a deep, stabilizing breath. "I deserve so much better."

Ana stepped further back. Her tears froze against her face, in suspended animation, her emotion locked on something she couldn't yet define. "That isn't true. You know it's not true. I'd do anything for you. Our whole lives—"

Nicolas turned to the side, disgusted. "I can't even look at you."

Ana searched his face for any signs of warmth, of the old Nicolas. She found none.

"I want you and Oz to leave me alone, both of you. Don't call me. Don't drop by. Don't invite me to things." Nicolas moved closer then, and she cringed. He laughed. "Really? Would I really hit you? Fuck's sake, Ana."

"I didn't think—" she started to say, then stopped herself. This was her last chance to say the things she wanted to say. If she wasted it, she'd regret it, always. "Your feelings, your hatred, they're off the mark, Nicolas. I've always needed you. I've always loved you." She reached her hand out and touched his arm. He looked at her hand the way he might look at a mosquito that had the audacity to land on him. "I'd never intentionally hurt you. Not you."

"That's irrelevant," he snapped. She dropped her hand. "It's my own fault for loving you so fucking much. It's not natural."

"Please don't go. Not like this," she croaked, but the plea was weak. There was nothing she could say, after that admission. *I love you, but not like that. I need you, but not the way you need me.*

For a moment his eyes filled with familiar warmth. But as quickly, the tenderness was gone. "I *can't* anymore, Ana. And I won't."

Nicolas turned and left without another word.

Ana dropped to the hospital bed with a heavy exhale. The tears came with short, desperate sobs, ones that started somewhere deep within her. She gripped the bed frame, struggling for breath.

You're not going to play dumb with me. Those words had driven a wedge between them bigger than any imagined betrayal. *It's my own fault for loving you so fucking much. It's not natural.*

Ana couldn't dwell on his words. She could spend years dissecting their meaning, but the truth would leave her emptier than she felt watching him walk out of her life. If she was honest with herself, she'd always known the truth, but hoped they could go their whole lives without the ugliness of it rolling, unabated, to the surface.

How much of her life had she given up, in order to live in the comfort of his unconditional love? How many experiences? How many relationships? *It's not your fault, Nic. It's mine. I chose this path because it was easier to be loved by the wrong person than to be hurt by the right one.*

A ray of sunlight passed through the dark storm clouds, penetrating the grimy window and lighting the floor near her feet. The warm colors danced and sparkled on the cold linoleum as the clouds moved across the sky.

She stared at the dancing patterns for a while. Her tongue found the roof of her mouth, and her toes curled tightly in her tennis shoes. *Breathe.*

Ana had never realized how much she relied on Nicolas to keep her stable, and secure. How she'd taken for granted not only his loyalty, but his unwavering persistence.

I never want to rely on another person that much ever again.

As the clouds left the sky, so her thoughts cleared as well.

I am my father's daughter.

Slowly, her control trickled back. Her breathing calmed, her heart rate returned to normal. The heat in her cheeks subsided.

Jon popped his head in the door. He turned around and wheeled Finn into the room. They both smiled at her. She smiled back, but turned her focus to the younger brother.

Finn's eyes were filled with love, but also, understanding and acceptance.

"You ready?" Jon asked.

I'm ready to leave the past behind.

In letting me go, Nicolas may have given me the greatest gift of all.

Ana inhaled, standing straighter, Finn's bag of clothes tucked under one arm.

Yes, she was ready.

Jon's embrace of darkness soon turns to dangerous cruelty. What happens when Ana can't stay on Summer Island anymore?

Don't miss a minute. Download *Shattered* today.

Here's what readers are saying about Shattered:

"I love, love, love Sarah Cradit's amazing series! I have read all of her books and can't wait for more. She has a way of writing that just sucks you in and doesn't let go. I would recommend Shattered to everyone."

"This is one of those books that you will stay up all night reading, so get cozy!"

"Whoa. Just, whoa. I just finished reading Shattered and I just. . .whoa."

"Raw and edgy, leaving the reader holding their breath in anticipation."

"Packs quite a punch with twists and turns that I definitely didn't see coming."

Pick up your copy of *Shattered* now, and have it ready to curl up at your next reading session!

CAN'T WAIT? READ FURTHER FOR AN EXCERPT.

SHATTERED EXCERPT

Anasofiya Deschanel sat before the antique glass vanity, gazing mournfully at the contents of her cosmetic case. The notion of being on display all night was horrifying, and rather than preparing, as she should have, she pushed it out of her mind until the moment was upon her. Now, her heart and stomach were both a fluttery mess.

Ana successfully avoided the spotlight most of her life. Growing up in one of the most prominent families in New Orleans, her father Augustus graciously protected his only child, accepting her innate discomfort with society life. He wasn't so different himself. He'd taken a backseat for years, letting his sister, Colleen, run the family when their older brother, Charles, died.

When she did need to put on a brave face, Nicolas was a comforting distraction from her unease. But this was not New Orleans. Nicolas and her father were not here.

When Ana proposed the restoration of the Casco Bay Lighthouse, she assumed it would be a simple matter, her father giving the nod to his accountant. She hadn't foreseen the outpouring of appreciation and warm wishes from Summer Island, Maine's two hundred residents—people who had recently been so cold and unwelcoming—nor that Mayor Cairne would join forces with the city of Portland to host a celebration aboard the Grand Atlantic.

It won't be nearly as unpleasant as you're expecting, her father promised, when the invitations went out. *In any case, your attendance is perfunctory this time, as my schedule isn't flexible, sweetheart.*

Ana suspected he could've moved things around, had he truly wanted to. He was punishing her, for her decision to stay in Maine with Finn. Her father had somehow resisted being overly critical of her decision not to join the family business, but apparently drew the line at his daughter dating a lobsterman. It didn't seem to matter that Finn had turned a hobby into a successful business venture, just like Augustus had, once upon a time.

In light of her father's displeasure, Ana had expected him to bargain with her when she proposed the restoration; to request she come home, in exchange. But when she spoke to him on the phone about it, he hesitated for only the briefest of moments before agreeing.

If this puts the Alex Whitman issue to bed, consider it done, he'd said.

Ana didn't think anything could do that. Alex hadn't only terrorized her, Finn, and Jon, but his sadistic behavior had left a lingering mark on every resident on the island. No one would've guessed quiet, unassuming Alex Whitman was responsible for the four unsolved murders that ravaged the small community over the years. Ana wouldn't have suspected it either, had he not come after her with the same single-minded determination. She was incredibly fortunate to be alive. Finn too.

Alex was gone now, a single shot to the head ending his reign of terror on Summer Island. Following the showdown at the St. Andrews house, Ana and Finn spent several weeks in the hospital convalescing. Ana recovered first. She was a healer, after all, even if this unique ability usually only worked on herself. Most Deschanels were born with unusual talents, or "gifts" as they called them, and she'd never been more grateful for hers. Finn's recovery took longer, his wounds being more grievous. *Yes, but he's alive, at least in part because of you,* she reminded herself. *He's the first person you've ever been able to heal other than yourself. That means something.*

Perhaps it did, but Finn wouldn't have been shot to begin with if she'd never come to Maine, running from her personal demons.

The mirror filled with Finn's kind face, smiling back at her. Ana nearly jumped. Lost in her reverie, she hadn't heard him come in. "We have to leave in ten," he said, kissing the top of her head. "Everything okay?"

Ana nodded, smiling to push away the dark memories.

"You look..." Finn cocked his head, parting his lips in contemplation. "Beautiful? No, that's not quite right."

"Horrified?" Her strained face stared back from the mirror.

"I'm not a fan of crowds either," Finn commiserated. Mindlessly, he pulled her red hair back from her face, twisting it in his hands, before letting it fall softly across her bare shoulders. "But you're a local hero now, Ana. Hell, I bet you don't even pay for your own drinks tonight!"

Ana laughed at the scandalized expression he made in the mirror. "That's clearly the watermark for the big time," she agreed. Setting her misery aside for a moment, she allowed herself to really look at him, something normally reserved for when he slept peacefully beside her.

Finn was beautiful. He was tall, built strong and sturdy, for the sea. His blonde hair grew darker as the winter wore on, but his blue eyes were as bright as his beloved Atlantic. Behind them, a sea of imagination, and thoughts unspoken. For all his skill with his hands, Finn had an equally gifted mind, possessing endless curiosity about the world around him.

Though, none of those qualities were what Ana loved most. With Finn, she was accepted, safe, and loved unconditionally. With Finn, she could be herself.

Seeing him in the black tux that once belonged to his father, Ana thought he looked like the perfect gentleman. *There are many, many sides to Finnegan St. Andrews.*

Ana was so unprepared for the event, shopping for a dress hadn't occurred to her until that morning. The mainland was an hour on the ferry, so she rummaged through her mother's closet, hoping to find something suitable. What she found was mostly cable knit and corduroy, but she eventually discovered an old, strapless blue evening gown, wrapped in dusty plastic, hiding in the back.

This could work. The only problem was the size of the tailored gown. Ana's mother had been more petite than her daughter, with the spindly limbs of a ballet dancer. Ana was lean, but developed in areas her mother hadn't been. She feared one wrong move might leave either her top, or bottom exposed, for all of Summer Island's fine citizens.

"Like a Celtic princess," Finn concluded, as he watched her thoughtfully in the mirror, his blue eyes widening. "Yes, that's it."

"Stop," she demurred, the blush rising to her cheeks genuine. "I need to finish getting ready."

"Of course. Can you check my tie real quick?" he asked, leaning over her.

She eyed him suspiciously. "It looks fine, but you knew that."

Finn produced a single strand of freshwater pearls, slipping them from his front pocket. As he reached behind her neck to secure them, his youthful smile widened. "Guilty. But it was more fun than just handing these to you. They were my mother's."

Ana admired the heirloom in the mirror, smiling despite her ill humor. She knew what Finn's mother had meant to him, what these must also represent. Her voice caught in her throat as she whispered, "Thank you."

Finn's face erupted into a spirited, sly grin, as he added, "*Aaand*, it was a great way to snag a glimpse down that slightly ill-fitting dress of yours."

Ana playfully swatted him away, but he snuck in a cheek kiss. "I'll ask Jon to warm up the car," Finn said. As he reached the door, he winked at her reflection and mimicked dropping his trousers. When he saw her eyebrows raise in the mirror, he laughed and left. He always knew how to bring a smile to her face, no matter the darkness in her heart.

After he was gone, her smile faded.

Jonathan.

She'd forgotten him for a few, peaceful moments. On top of everything else, he'd be a constant presence tonight, when what she most needed was peace.

ALSO BY SARAH M. CRADIT

KINGDOM OF THE WHITE SEA

<u>Kingdom of the White Sea Trilogy</u>

The Kingless Crown

The Broken Realm

The Hidden Kingdom

<u>The Book of All Things</u>

The Raven and the Rush

The Sylvan and the Sand

The Altruist and the Assassin

The Melody and the Master

The Claw and the Crowned

THE SAGA OF CRIMSON & CLOVER

<u>The House of Crimson and Clover Series</u>

The Storm and the Darkness

Shattered

The Illusions of Eventide

Bound

Midnight Dynasty

Asunder

Empire of Shadows

Myths of Midwinter

The Hinterland Veil

The Secrets Amongst the Cypress

Within the Garden of Twilight

House of Dusk, House of Dawn

Midnight Dynasty Series

A Tempest of Discovery

A Storm of Revelations

A Torrent of Deceit

The Seven Series

1970

1972

1973

1974

1975

1976

1980

Vampires of the Merovingi Series

The Island

and more

The Dusk Trilogy

St. Charles at Dusk: The Story of Oz and Adrienne

Flourish: The Story of Anne Fontaine

Banshee: The Story of Giselle Deschanel

Crimson & Clover Stories

Surrender: The Story of Oz and Ana

Shame: The Story of Jonathan St. Andrews

Fire & Ice: The Story of Remy & Fleur

Dark Blessing: The Landry Triplets

Pandora's Box: The Story of Jasper & Pandora

The Menagerie: Oriana's Den of Iniquities

A Band of Heather: The Story of Colleen and Noah

The Ephemeral: The Story of Autumn & Gabriel

Bayou's Edge: The Landry Triplets

For more information, and exciting bonus material, visit www.sarahmcradit.com

ABOUT THE AUTHOR

Sarah is the USA Today and International Bestselling Author of over forty contemporary and epic fantasy stories, and the creator of the Kingdom of the White Sea and Saga of Crimson & Clover universes.

Born a geek, Sarah spends her time crafting rich and multi-layered worlds, obsessing over history, playing her retribution paladin (and sometimes destruction warlock), and settling provocative Tolkien debates, such as why the Great Eagles are not Gandalf's personal taxi service. Passionate about travel, she's been to over twenty countries collecting sparks of inspiration, and is always planning her next adventure.

Sarah and her husband live in a beautiful corner of SE Pennsylvania with their three tiny benevolent pug dictators.

www.sarahmcradit.com

www.ingramcontent.com/pod-product-compliance
Lightning Source LLC
Chambersburg PA
CBHW020341310726
48979CB00015B/2463/J
* 9 7 8 1 9 5 8 7 4 4 0 0 0 *

www.ingramcontent.com/pod-product-compliance
Lightning Source LLC
Chambersburg PA
CBHW020342310726
48979CB00015B/2465/J

* 9 7 8 1 9 6 0 3 4 3 1 7 8 *